STINGS AND Stones

An Elemental Assassin Short Story Collection

JENNIFER ESTEP

Stings and Stones
Copyright © 2023 by Jennifer Estep

Haints and Hobwebs
Copyright © 2012 by Jennifer Estep

Parlor Tricks
Copyright © 2013 by Jennifer Estep

Spider and Frost
Copyright © 2023 by Jennifer Estep

ISBN: 978-1-950076-21-5

Cover Art © 2023 by Tony Mauro

Published in the United States of America

*To all the fans of the Elemental Assassin series
who wanted more stories, this one is for you.*

To my mom—for everything.

Author's Note

Stings and Stones is a collection of **Elemental Assassin** short stories. Some of the stories previously appeared on Jennifer Estep's website, while others have been featured in anthologies. The stories are told from the points of view of Gin Blanco and the secondary characters and take place during different time periods.

Haints and Hobwebs was first published in ***The Mammoth Book of Ghost Romance*** in 2012.

Parlor Tricks was first published in the ***Carniepunk*** anthology in 2013.

Spider and Frost was first released as an ebook in 2023.

Spider's Bargain

This story takes place before *Spider's Bite*, book 1.

Gin Blanco

The cop was going to die tonight.

He just didn't know it yet.

For Detective Cliff Ingles, this was just another Saturday night in the Southern metropolis of Ashland, and he was spending it the way he did all his other Saturday nights: slugging down drinks and ogling the waitresses at Northern Aggression, the city's most popular nightclub.

Just before midnight, people were packed into the club, all looking for their particular brand of poison. Blood, booze, drugs, sex, smokes. Northern Aggression offered all that and more, as long as you had the cash or the plastic to pay for your favorite vice.

The nightclub had a decadent style, with red crushed-velvet drapes covering the walls and a soft, springy bamboo floor. But the most striking feature was the bar that ran down one wall—a long, thick, solid rectangle made entirely of elemental

Ice. Runes had been carved into the slick surface of the Ice, mostly suns and stars, symbolizing life and joy. The symbols were rather appropriate, given all the people getting hot 'n' heavy in the booths in the back of the club.

I'd spent the last hour sitting at the Ice bar—along with Cliff Ingles.

The detective threw back his third whiskey of the evening, then leaned forward and murmured something in the ear of the vampire waitress who'd brought over his drink. The two of them were near the center of the enormous Ice bar, about thirty feet away from my position around the curve and up against one of the walls.

Ingles never had a clue that I was watching him. No real reason he would. If the detective had bothered to look in my direction, all he would have seen was another woman drinking her way through a night out on the town.

Even if he had noticed me, even if he'd come over and talked to me, I would have told him exactly who I was. Gin Blanco. A part-time cook and waitress at the Pork Pit barbecue restaurant in downtown Ashland. And the assassin known as the Spider.

I would have even told the detective about my current mission—to make sure he quit breathing before the end of the evening.

But there was no danger of Ingles noticing me. I wasn't his type; the bastard preferred to assault young girls. Given the five silverstone knives hidden on my body, I was anything *but* helpless.

I took another sip of my gin and tonic and studied my target, comparing the man in front of me to the photo that had been in the file of information that my handler, Fletcher Lane, had given me when he'd told me about the job.

Detective Cliff Ingles was six feet tall, which was a good foot shorter than the giant bouncers who patrolled the club and kept everyone in line. Still, at more than two hundred fifty pounds, Ingles wasn't a small guy, although his once trim, hard-muscled body was slowly giving way to flabby fat underneath his expensive navy suit.

With his thick honey-blond hair, wide smile, and square chin, Ingles was an attractive man, but his ruddy skin got a little more flushed and his brown eyes got a little meaner with every drink he downed. Now he reminded me of a copperhead, all coiled up and ready to lash out and sink his venomous fangs into whoever crossed his path.

Ingles wore his gold detective's badge openly on the brown leather belt around his waist, along with his gun, almost like being a member of the police force was something to be proud of.

I snorted into my drink. Everyone knew that the majority of the Ashland cops were dirtier than the graffiti that covered so many of the city's buildings. Ingles was no exception. Fletcher had dug up all sorts of nasty business that the detective was involved in. Extortion, blackmail, stealing drugs and money from crime scenes. Ingles was a real classy guy all the way around.

But he wasn't going to die for those sins. No, Cliff Ingles was getting my particular brand of attention because he'd tried to lure a thirteen-year-old girl named Rebecca into his car. When Rebecca had resisted, Ingles had badly beaten her, among other horrible things. Ashland was a violent city, full of bad people doing lots of bad things, but Cliff Ingles was the lowest sort of scum.

And I was here tonight to make sure that he never hurt any-one else—pro bono.

Normally, I didn't work for free. Mine was a highly specialized skill set, and I liked getting paid for it. I *earned* it, if only for all the blood I had to wash out of my clothes and hair after the fact.

As the Spider, I got paid—a lot—to kill people. I'd been in the assassin business since I was thirteen. Now, creeping up on thirty, I had more money tucked away than I could spend in two lifetimes. Which was one of the reasons why Fletcher, who was also my foster father, kept nagging me to retire. The old man wanted me to live long enough to actually spend and enjoy my ill-gotten gains.

So far, I'd only listened to Fletcher with half an ear. Killing people and cooking barbecue were all I knew how to do. What would I do if I retired? Take up knitting? Adopt stray puppies? Move to the suburbs and try to put my bloody past behind me?

None of those things particularly appealed to me. Well, except adopting the puppies. I'd always been a dog person, especially when it came to corgis.

But the simple fact was that I liked my job. Sure, it was dark, dirty, dangerous work, but the blood and the screams didn't bother me, and I'd long ago accepted that I was one of the villains. Besides, every once in a while, I got to take care of somebody like Cliff Ingles. Got to make the city just a bit safer in my own twisted way.

It was the little things in life that made me happy.

Cool magic surged through the air, interrupting my musings. I glanced over at the bartender, whose eyes glowed a bright blue-white in the semidarkness of the nightclub. The Ice elemental responsible for keeping the bar in one piece for the night was feeding some more of his power into the cold, solid structure.

My own sluggish Ice magic responded to the familiar influx of power trickling into the bar. I was an elemental too, with the rare ability to use two of the four elements, Ice and Stone, although my Ice magic was far weaker than my Stone power. But as the Spider, I didn't usually use my elemental powers to take down targets.

That's what my knives were for.

I uncurled my hand from around my drink and stared down at the scar embedded in my palm. A small circle surrounded by eight thin rays—a spider rune, the symbol for patience. My namesake, in more ways than one. A matching scar adorned my other palm.

The spider rune had once been a pretty pendant that I'd worn around my neck as a child, until a Fire elemental had superheated the metal and burned the symbol into my palms, marking me forever the night she'd murdered my family—

"Disgusting pig!"

The waitress that Ingles had been propositioning spat out the words, then drew back her hand and slapped him across the face. Despite the thumping music, I still heard the sharp, stinging *crack* of the blow at my end of the bar. There weren't many things you couldn't do at Northern Aggression, which made me wonder exactly what revolting thing Ingles had just suggested.

"Bitch!" the detective snarled. He surged to his feet, and his hand dropped to the gun on his belt, like he wanted to grab it and hit her with the weapon.

The waitress's dark eyes widened, and she backed up a couple of steps and made a small, discreet hand signal. One of the giant bouncers immediately cut through the crowd and took up a defensive position in front of the waitress, using his roughly seven-foot frame to shield her from Ingles. The giant's shaved head gleamed like polished ebony under the club's dim lights.

"Is there a problem?" the giant rumbled, his deep baritone voice cutting through the pulsing beat of the music.

I'd seen this particular giant around the club before. Hard to miss almost seven feet of solid muscle. Xavier was his name.

Ingles's dark, angry gaze cut to the waitress before flicking back to Xavier. The waitress's handprint marked the detective's cheek like a scarlet letter, but he made a visible effort to get himself under control. He might be a member of the po-po, but Ingles knew he'd get his ass kicked if he kept pushing things. Even cops couldn't get away with assaulting people—at least not in such a public place like Northern Aggression where everyone had their phone in one hand and a drink in the other.

"No problem." Ingles spat out the words. "The bitch isn't worth it. I was just leaving."

Xavier nodded. "You do that."

Ingles's eyes narrowed to slits, but he reached into his pocket, drew out a couple of bills, and tossed them onto the bar. Then he shoved his way through the crowd, heading for the exit.

Instead of immediately following him, I skimmed the scene, my gaze moving from the people clustered three deep around the bar to those grooving out on the dance floor. Looking for trouble, searching for anything out of place, anyone who was taking an interest in my target—or, worse, in me. I'd been an assassin for almost twenty years, and I hadn't survived this long by being reckless and sloppy.

Once he'd made sure Ingles was really leaving, Xavier turned back to the waitress, and the two of them started talking. To them, the detective was just another creepy customer they'd kicked to the curb. It happened, even here at Northern Aggression, where very little was off-limits. But no one else showed any interest in the detective or, more important, in me.

Time to make my move.

I swallowed the rest of my gin and tonic, enjoying the sensation of the cold liquor sliding down my throat before starting its slow, sweet burn in the pit of my stomach. Then I paid my own tab, stepped away from the Ice bar, and sauntered out of the club, moving toward my prey.

The Spider was finally ready to spin her deadly web for the evening.

✲

It was late July, and the night air was sticky and soupy with humidity. Ashland was situated in the hilly corner where Tennessee, Virginia, and North Carolina met in the heart of the Appalachian Mountains, so muggy summer nights were part of the region's many charms. Dozens of fireflies winked on and off in the darkness, their quick little flashes matching the smoldering red glows from the folks smoking cigarettes.

Even though it was almost midnight, a long line of people still stood outside the club waiting to get in past the giant guarding the red velvet rope by the front entrance. Above the giant's head, a neon sign shaped like a heart with an arrow through it flashed red, then yellow, then orange. The rune for Northern Aggression, the symbol Roslyn Phillips used to promote and identify her business.

I walked away from the entrance, scanning the rows of parked cars, looking for Ingles. Ten . . . twenty . . . it didn't even take me thirty seconds to spot him.

Ingles had moved off into the parking lot and was now stalking back and forth underneath the gently swaying tendrils of a weeping willow. The detective's black, city-issued sedan sat on the pavement next to the large tree. The car's license plate and description had been in the file of information Fletcher had given me. The old man was nothing if not thorough.

I looked at everything, from the people still standing in line in the distance, to Ingles, to the few folks staggering out to their cars in the side lots that flanked the club. Nobody gave me a second glance, and nobody was sober or close enough to notice anything happening over here in the shadows. Perfect.

I smoothed down my knee-length black leather skirt and put a little extra swing in my hips as I approached the detective. If I'd just come to the club to enjoy myself, I would have worn my usual outfit of jeans, boots, and a long-sleeved T-shirt. But tonight, since I was out on the town as the Spider, I'd dressed up a bit, just in case I had to use my feminine wiles to lure

Ingles to my side long enough to stab him to death.

In addition to the leather skirt, I was also sporting a long-sleeved red silk shirt and a pair of black stiletto-heeled boots that stretched all the way up to my knees. I'd even teased out my bleached-blond hair to epic proportions. In short, I looked like someone out to have an evening to remember.

Cliff Ingles certainly wouldn't forget meeting me.

I didn't bother to walk quietly, and the sharp *crack-crack-crack-crack* of my heels on the pavement quickly caught Ingles's attention. He glared in my direction, but the hot anger simmering in his brown eyes soon turned to something darker and uglier as he focused in on me.

I tossed my hair back over my shoulder and took another glance around, but nobody was looking in our direction. Excellent.

I finally stopped when I was within arm's reach of Ingles. I put one hand on my hip and struck a pose, letting him get a good, long look at me.

"Hey there, sugar," I cooed in my best slow, sweet, Southern drawl. "Got a light?"

Ingles's gaze flicked down my body and back up again, and a cruel smile lifted his lips. He must have liked what he saw.

"For you, darling? Of course," Ingles murmured.

He started patting the pockets of his suit jacket, looking for his lighter. While he was distracted, I slid my right arm behind my back and palmed a silverstone knife. A second knife was tucked up my other sleeve, while a third rested in the small of my back. Two more were hidden in the tops of my boots. My usual five-point arsenal. Never left home without 'em.

While Ingles searched for his lighter, I scanned the area around us one more time. But the closest person was more than a hundred feet away, and the music drifting out of the club would cover any sound the detective might make.

My hand tightened around my knife, the hilt cold, hard,

and solid against my skin. The sturdy weight and heft of the weapon comforted me the way it always did.

Ingles finally fished his lighter out of his pocket, flicked it on, and held it up to me. The flame wavered in the darkness between us, a tiny beacon of sputtering red, yellow, and orange light that mirrored the club's neon sign still flashing in the distance.

He frowned when I didn't immediately produce a cigarette, lean forward, and let him get a better look at my chest.

"Hey," he snapped. "Don't you have a smoke on you? Because I'm not giving you one of mine. Damn things are too expensive for that these days."

He paused, his eyes narrowing and his smile getting that much crueler. "Unless you want to trade me something for it."

Oh, yeah, Cliff Ingles was a real class act.

I'd rather have stabbed myself than let him touch me, but I eased a little closer and gave him my most winsome smile, keeping up the charade. "Nah. I don't have a smoke on me. I've got something better. This."

I brought my hand around from behind my back and showed him the knife. The silverstone glinted dully in the semidarkness.

Ingles's eyes widened in surprise, but before he could open his mouth to scream, my arm punched forward, and I buried the blade in his stomach.

Ingles sucked in another breath, but before he could scream it out, I surged forward and clamped my free hand over his mouth, my fingers digging into his skin.

Since he couldn't yell for help, Ingles dropped his lighter and lashed out with his fists, raining hard blows down on my chest and stomach. The solid impacts made me grunt with pain, but I'd been an assassin a long time, and I'd taken my share of punches from giants, dwarves, and vampires over the years—all of whom were a lot tougher and stronger than the human in front of me. Ingles's blows hurt, but not enough to make me release him or drop my knife.

We seesawed back and forth in the darkness underneath the weeping willow for the better part of a minute, before Ingles's body began to shut down from the massive trauma it had just received. When I felt the fight in him start to ebb, I pushed him deeper into the shadows, until his back was against the tree's rough bark.

At this point, tears of pain, fear, and panic dripped down Ingles's face and spattered onto my red silk shirt—along with his blood.

"You know," I said in a conversational tone, twisting the knife in a little deeper, "it's bad enough that you swipe drugs and cash from crime scenes while you're on duty, supposedly protecting and serving the good people of Ashland. But to brutally assault a thirteen-year-old girl like you did? That was just sick. Evil. And now it's going to be the death of you, Cliff."

Usually, I wasn't this chatty when I was killing someone. But the soft murmur of my words helped to cover up the detective's muffled gasps and the scrape of his limbs flailing against the tree trunk. Still, if anyone had been curious enough to look this way, they would have probably thought the detective and I were having a grand old time making out.

But only one of us was getting fucked over tonight, and it wasn't me.

I yanked the knife out of Ingles's stomach, and more of his blood splattered onto my clothes. The warm, sticky fluid also coated my hand, but I barely noticed it. I'd wash it off later, the way I always did.

By this point, the fight and the life were all but gone from Ingles. I finally released him, and the detective slid to the soft ground beneath the tree. His breaths came in shallow, raspy gulps now, indicating that he'd be dead in another minute, two, tops.

Still, I crouched down next to him, bloody knife in my hand, just in case he made a last-ditch effort to do something stupid—like try to scream for help or grab the gun on his belt and shoot me.

"Who . . . are . . . you?" He wheezed out the words.

"Some folks call me the Spider. Perhaps you've heard of me."

Ingles's mouth twisted with anger and disgust. "Fucking . . . assassin . . . bitch . . ."

"Yeah," I drawled. "That's me to a T."

Those were the last words the detective ever said. Ten seconds later, Ingles rasped out his last breath, his head lolled to the side, and his eyes stared at nothing. But my job wasn't through just yet. Rebecca's mother had made a specific request about what she wanted done to Ingles's body, so I made a few more cuts with my blade.

When that was done, I wiped my knife off in the grass and tucked it back up my sleeve. Then I stood up and looked around, once again peering into the darkness, but everything was the same as before. People waiting in line to get into the nightclub or smoking or drunkenly stumbling over to their vehicles. No one had noticed me killing Ingles.

I should have been moving through the parking lot before someone spotted the detective's body and raised the inevitable alarm. But instead, I found myself staring down at Cliff Ingles.

The detective's eyes were now just as empty and soulless as those of the girl he'd beaten. Fletcher had shown me a photo of Rebecca when he'd asked me to kill Ingles. I'd immediately recognized the look in her eyes—a shattered, broken expression of innocence lost.

Of everything lost.

I'd had that same look for months after my family had been murdered. Even now, all these years later, I still sometimes caught a glimpse of it whenever I stared into the mirror just a little too long.

Maybe it was because I'd been thirteen—the same age as Rebecca—the night my family had been murdered. Maybe it was because in Ashland, there were some people who just deserved death. Maybe it was because Fletcher hadn't sent me out on a job in more than a month and I was bored.

But I'd looked at the girl's photo, and I'd told Fletcher I'd do the job for free.

Ingles had deeply wounded the girl with his horrid actions, and I'd made him pay for it tonight. Maybe knowing that he was dead would bring Rebecca some peace.

Maybe not.

Either way, I'd held up my end of our deadly bargain, and the Spider had done her work for the evening. I'd helped in the only way I knew how, and now it was time to go home and wash the blood out of my clothes once again.

So I stepped over Ingles's body and headed toward the back of the parking lot, away from the lights, noise, and people around the front of the club.

As I walked under the weeping willow, a cool mountain breeze rustled the tree's branches, and the soft, trailing tendrils kissed my face the gentle way a mother might show affection for her child. For some reason, I stopped and waited until the breeze and the tendrils died down before moving on.

The summer fireflies lit the way as I stepped into the waiting darkness.

Web of Death

Gin Blanco

So far, my retirement was turning out to be a gigantic bore. I should have expected it to go this way. Mainly because my day job, well, my night job, had always been far more interesting than the professions of most folks. No pushing papers around a desk for me. Instead, I'd moonlighted as the assassin the Spider for the last seventeen years.

That's right. An assassin. Someone who killed people for money. And I'd been exceptionally good at my job. Why, some folks might even say I'd been the best. Which is probably why making the adjustment to just being myself, Gin Blanco, had been a little more difficult than I'd expected it to be.

But there was one thing that was slightly more boring than my retirement: moving.

I stood outside on a chilly October evening, peering into my car's trunk at the cardboard boxes that held all my worldly possessions. Books, mostly, along with some high-end cookware and knives—*lots* of knives. Most of which were used for slicing and dicing much more than just fruits and vegetables.

As the Spider, I'd never gone anywhere without my silverstone knives, and I saw no reason to change that habit just because I was plain ole Gin Blanco now, a supposedly respectable, ordinary citizen. Even tonight, alone in the twilight, I was still equipped with five knives—one tucked up either sleeve, one nestled in the small of my back, and two more hidden in the sides of my boots.

Carrying my knives comforted me the way it always did, but I still sighed, my breath frosting away in a faint cloud.

A few weeks ago, my mentor, Fletcher Lane, had been horribly tortured and murdered in the Pork Pit, the barbecue restaurant he'd founded in downtown Ashland. I'd killed Alexis James, the Air elemental responsible for his death, but that didn't keep me from missing the old man, who'd taken me in off the streets when I was thirteen. That was one of the many reasons I'd decided to move into Fletcher's house, which he'd left me in his will, along with the Pork Pit. I supposed it was my way of staying close to the old man, even though he was cold and buried in his grave now.

The three-story clapboard structure stood behind me, looming like a hulking ghost in the approaching darkness. The building had been standing for decades, and lots of sections had been added onto it over the years, all in a variety of different clashing styles, including brown brick, gray stone, and red clay. The various materials made the house look like a patchwork quilt, stitched together with a tin roof, blue eaves, and black shutters. Still, it had been Fletcher's home, and now it was mine for the second time, since I'd also lived here while I was growing up.

I sighed again, this time with longing. I wished the old man were here, that I'd gotten to him in time that awful night. That

I'd been able to save him the way he had saved me all those years ago—

A scream ripped through the air.

I whirled toward the sound, a knife sliding into my right hand. Another scream ripped through the air, a little louder and closer than before. A woman, judging by the high-pitched voice. I peered around the open car trunk and scanned the trees that flanked the house, wondering who was out here and why she was making enough noise to wake the dead.

A wayward hiker, perhaps? Someone who'd stumbled across a black bear in the woods? The creatures were quite common in this corner of the Appalachian Mountains. High ridges and dense stands of woods covered the region like a gray and green carpet, especially here at Fletcher's house, which was perched on top of a particularly remote, rocky mountainside.

Bears didn't frighten me, though. Not much did. In addition to being the assassin the Spider, I was also an elemental, someone who could create, control, and manipulate one of the four elements. Well, actually, two in my case, Ice and Stone. My Ice magic was fairly weak, and all I could really do with it was make small shapes, like cubes, balls, and whatnot. But my Stone magic was strong, so strong that it would let me harden my skin into an impenetrable shell, one that even a bear's claws wouldn't be able to tear through.

A third scream zipped through the air before abruptly cutting off. Whatever—or whoever—had been threatening the woman had just caught up with her.

Two choices now. Go investigate what the fuss was all about and amuse myself for maybe an hour, or stay here and haul boxes of books into Fletcher's ramshackle house. Along with teaching me everything he knew about being an assassin, the old man had also instilled a healthy dose of curiosity in me. Something that always seemed to get the best of me, no matter how hard I tried.

So I palmed a second knife, left the open trunk and boxes of books behind, and headed toward the woods.

Despite the growing twilight that painted the landscape in increasingly dark shades of gloomy gray, it was easy enough to make my way through the thick woods—I just followed the sounds of the screams.

Only they weren't so much screams now as choked sobs, moans, and whimpers that indicated the woman making them was in serious trouble.

Thwack-thwack-thwack.

Some new sounds echoed through the dense evergreen trees, followed by yet another low, choked sob. My eyes narrowed. I recognized what that sound was too: someone getting severely beaten. Well, well, well. Looked like there was a different kind of bear in the woods tonight.

I moved more carefully now, more quietly, making sure that my boots didn't scuff, smash, and crackle through the ruby- and citrine-colored autumn leaves that covered the ground like piles of jewels slowly losing their sparkle. The half-swallowed sobs and *thwacks* of fists hitting flesh grew louder and sharper, and a low hiss of laughter curled through the air like a rattlesnake getting ready to strike. Someone was enjoying the show.

I stopped behind the knotty trunk of a gnarled pine whose sharp, tangy scent tickled my nose. Then I slowly eased to the side, my face hidden in the shadows from the overhanging branches, and studied the landscape before me.

This pine was one of several that ringed a small clearing in the woods about a mile from Fletcher's house. A few boulders bubbled up like gray blisters here and there on the forest floor, but for the most part, the ground was smooth and clear, with the rich black earth peeping up through the shallow scattering of pine needles and disintegrating autumn leaves.

In the middle of the clearing, a seven-foot-tall giant with short blond hair, brown eyes, and pale skin was looming over a woman. One of the giant's large hands was twisted in the woman's long, curly red hair, holding her still, while he used his other hand to slap her.

Thwack-thwack-thwack.

He hit her three times in rapid succession before a second, much shorter man with black hair and eyes and tan skin stepped forward and put a restraining hand on the giant's bulging bicep. The woman choked back another moan of pain.

"Geez, Willie," the second man said. "Don't kill her. We haven't had nearly enough fun with her yet."

His lips drew back into an evil grin, revealing a set of white fangs that marked him as a vampire.

A giant and a vampire walking into the woods sounded like the start of a really bad joke that Finnegan Lane, my foster brother, would tell, but wariness filled me. In addition to their enormous strength, giants' thick musculature made them tough to bring down, and vamps were no pushovers either. They weren't nearly as strong as giants, but their sharp canines could rip through a person's throat in a heartbeat.

Both men were dressed in outdoor clothes—black hiking boots, matching jeans, and red plaid flannel shirts partially covered up by black fleece jackets. The vampire also had a small black backpack slung over his shoulder. Their clothes and gear indicated that they'd planned to be out here in the middle of nowhere this evening—probably so no one would hear the woman scream.

"You're right, Ted," Willie, the giant, rumbled. "Hitting people isn't nearly as much fun after they're dead."

Ted nodded, as though Willie had just revealed one of the universe's greatest secrets. "And we need to teach this bitch a lesson, remember? One that she and my other workers won't ever forget."

Willie kept his grip on the woman's hair, while Ted circled around her. The woman's split, bloody lips drew back in a pain-filled grimace, and I spotted a set of fangs in her mouth as well, marking her as another vampire.

With her red hair, hazel eyes, and pale, freckled skin, she would have been quite pretty if not for the thin crimson scratches and puffy violet bruises that covered her face, arms, and legs. Ted and Willie must have brought her out here, turned her loose, and then chased her down, like a sick version of hide-and-seek.

Unlike the two men, the woman was not dressed for the rugged terrain. Instead of jeans and boots, she wore a short-sleeved white shirt with a black bow tie and a short black skirt that looked like the uniform for a cocktail waitress. The silver sequins on her black bow tie and skirt caught the dwindling twilight and flashed it back, like dozens of fireflies winking on and off. The woman was also wearing a pair of black stilettos, although the heels had broken off during her mad dash through the woods.

"I never thought you were all that smart, Jordan," Ted, the vampire, said. "But you got real stupid, thinking you could leave me. Thinking you could quit working at my club just because you got a better offer from Roslyn Phillips."

My eyebrows shot up in surprise. Oh, yes, things got more interesting by the second. Roslyn Phillips was the vampire who ran Northern Aggression, Ashland's most decadent nightclub.

Ted's one-sided conversation with Jordan indicated that he was most likely the owner of a rival nightclub and that Jordan was one of his workers. Not unusual. All vampires needed blood to live, just like humans needed food and vitamins, but lots of vamps also got the same kind of healthy high from sex, which was why so many of them worked in Ashland's various clubs. For the vamps, it was win-win. Money and a power boost, all at the same time.

"Stupid bitch," Ted muttered.

He stopped his circling and lashed out, kicking Jordan in the face with his hiking boot. Her head snapped back, and she would have pitched backward onto the ground if Willie hadn't still been clutching her hair. The two men laughed, but Jordan didn't hear them. Her limp body dangled from the giant's hand, and she was clearly unconscious.

"Keep an eye on her," Ted said, "while I get things set up."

He crouched down, slung the backpack off his shoulder, and started rooting around inside it. A few seconds later, he pulled out a hammer and four metal spikes with tan leather loops on the ends. Then he started pounding the stakes into the soft soil with his hammer. All four of them, marking the shape of a woman-sized rectangle.

I stared at the dried, rusty splotches that covered the tan loops. It didn't take a genius to figure out that those were bloodstains and that Ted and Willie had done this before. Bringing Jordan out here into the woods and chasing and beating her weren't enough. No, now they were going to tie her down and hurt her even worse before they finally killed her. Sick bastards.

Of course, some folks would have thought that I was sick too, for eliminating so many people for money over the years. But I had a code that I followed, rules that I lived by. No hurting kids or pets. No framing someone for my crimes. And most especially, no torture. I might have killed people as the Spider, but I did it quickly and efficiently with my knives. I'd certainly never tied anyone down to the ground just so I could take my time hurting them.

But now I had a decision to make. Ted and Willie hadn't seen me hiding in the shadows. Nobody ever did, until it was too late. So I could easily slip away, leave Jordan to her gruesome fate, and walk back to Fletcher's house without anyone being the wiser—except me.

But I'd recently learned that Fletcher had had quite a large altruistic streak. That back when he was the assassin the Tin Man, Fletcher had helped people who couldn't help themselves. Pro bono, as it were. And Jordan certainly needed help right now.

Maybe it was my soft sentiment for the old man, or how much my heart still ached from his loss, but I found myself actually wanting to rescue the other woman. Actually wanting to use my knives and deadly skills for something far more worthwhile than money.

Besides, I thought, smiling a little, it sure beat unpacking boxes.

So I tightened my grip on my knives, stepped out from the shadows, and strode forward into the clearing, softly whistling all the while. Both men's heads snapped around at the light, cheery, unexpected sound.

I stopped about ten feet away from the two men, my knives tucked up against my forearms. The hilts of the weapons rested on the scars embedded in my palms. A small circle surrounded by eight thin rays—a spider rune, the symbol for patience. My assassin moniker and so much more.

"I hope you boys brought some shovels with you," I drawled in a pleasant voice.

Ted and Willie glanced at each other, then looked back at me.

"Why is that?" Ted asked in a guarded tone, clearly wondering who I was and what I was doing in the woods.

I grinned. "Because otherwise, I'll just have to leave your bodies out here for the animals to gnaw on instead of burying you all proper-like. Wait. You know what? Actually, now that I think about it, forget the shovels. The animals have to eat too. If they could even stomach the likes of you two cruel bastards."

"Willie," Ted growled, "I think we need to teach this bitch the same lesson that Jordan just learned."

The giant nodded and released his grip on Jordan's hair. She crumpled to the ground, still unconscious. Good. She'd already been through enough this evening, and I didn't need an audience for this.

Willie let out a loud bellow and charged in my direction, his hands reaching out to pull me into a bone-crushing bear hug. He never even noticed my palmed knives.

Thud-thud-thud-thud.

This time, instead of the sound of fists hitting flesh, the solid smacks of my knives punching into Willie's chest filled the air. The giant screamed, much like Jordan had done earlier, and stumbled back. His sharp movement jerked my knives out of my hands, but that was okay, because they were still stuck in his body—one in his stomach and the other in his heart, which was more than enough damage to kill him.

Sure enough, Willie stumbled around the clearing for about ten seconds before his legs gave out and he thumped to the ground, well on his way to being dead—

I spotted a flash of movement out of the corner of my eye. I ducked, and Ted's hammer whistled by my head. The vamp was quicker than I'd thought, because even as his first blow missed, he was already pivoting and bringing the hammer back up for a second strike.

Instead of ducking again, I stepped into his body and grabbed his arm. Then I spun around and used the vampire's own momentum to flip him up and over my shoulder.

Ted hit the ground hard, groaning with pain, and the hammer slipped from his fingers. Before he could recover, I leaned down, grabbed the hammer, brought it up, and slammed the tool into his windpipe several times, crushing it.

Ted's dark eyes bulged so wide I thought they might pop right out of his head. He made a series of choked gurgles, not unlike the ones Jordan had made earlier when Willie was hitting her.

"You really should have found somewhere else to play your little hunting game," I murmured, crouching down beside him. "Because this land belonged to Fletcher Lane and now belongs to me. And believe me when I tell you that I'm the only predator allowed around here, sugar."

All Ted could do was gape at me and gasp for air as his body quickly shut down from the trauma it had received. I stayed where I was and watched him die. It didn't take long. It never did.

When Ted was gone, I went over to Jordan, who was still unconscious. Her face was a mess, and she probably had some broken ribs and internal bleeding from where Willie had hit her. But she'd be okay until help arrived, and I knew just whom to call about that.

I gently rearranged Jordan's arms and legs, easing her into a more comfortable position on the ground. Then I went back over to Ted and rifled through the dead vampire's pockets until I found his phone. I dialed a number I had memorized a few weeks ago. Four rings later, she picked up.

"Roslyn Phillips." Her sultry voice filled my ear.

"Hello, Roslyn," I said. "Your friend Jordan is out here in the woods. She and the two guys with her had a nasty run-in with a black bear. At least, that's what you can tell the cops."

I told her what had happened and where to find Jordan.

"Who is this?" Roslyn asked when I finished.

"You know *exactly* who this is. And you owe me, remember? So quit asking questions, and get out here."

"Gin?"

I hung up without answering.

Roslyn knew exactly what I'd done before I'd retired, especially since I'd killed her brother-in-law, who'd been abusing her sister and her young niece. Roslyn talking about such things to the wrong people was partly the reason Fletcher had been murdered—because the wrong person had learned about the old man and the fact that he was my handler.

I'd confronted Roslyn about her mistakes at Fletcher's funeral a few weeks ago. I'd told the vampire in no uncertain terms that she would do whatever I wanted until she'd worked off her debt to me—or else. And as much as I'd loved the old man, that would be a bloody long while indeed.

I pushed Roslyn out of my mind and went about erasing any trace that I'd been here, including retrieving my knives from Willie's body. I might officially be retired from being an assassin, but I wasn't going to be stupid or sloppy enough to leave any evidence behind.

As I worked, every once in a while, I looked over to check on Jordan.

"Don't worry, sweetheart," I murmured, even though she couldn't hear me. "The cavalry's on the way."

Sure enough, about thirty minutes later, I heard the sharp crackle of heavy footsteps on the fallen leaves. From my hiding spot on the far edge of the clearing, I saw flashlights bobbing through the trees.

"Over here!" a man rumbled. "I see her!"

"Where?" Roslyn's concerned voice drifted over to me. "Jordan! Jordan, are you okay?"

After that, things went pretty much as I'd expected them to.

Roslyn and Xavier, a giant who worked as a bouncer at her nightclub, rushed into the clearing. Roslyn hovered over Jordan, while Xavier called the police. Several cops arrived on the scene to try to figure out what had happened, although they probably wouldn't work too hard at that, since the majority of the members of the police department were known for their rampant laziness, avarice, and love of bribes.

Still, a few good, honest, devoted cops roamed through the clearing, collecting evidence. Jordan was packed up and carted off to the closest hospital to get treatment, while the coroner was called to come out and collect Ted and Willie. And so on and so forth.

Once Jordan had been stabilized and taken away, I saw no reason to hang around any longer. I just killed people. I didn't patch them up after the fact. Besides, I'd already done my part by keeping Jordan from getting dead in the first place.

So, softly whistling once again, I hiked back through the woods to Fletcher's house to start unpacking my boxes, feeling lighter and more cheerful than I had in weeks.

It had been a good night's work for the Spider.

Web of Deceit

This story takes place several years before *Spider's Bite*, book 1.

Fletcher Lane

The girl was a natural-born assassin.

Cold, calm, centered. Confident in herself and her abilities. As she bloody well should be. I hadn't spent the last three years training her to be a shrinking violet.

As an assassin myself, as the Tin Man, I'd killed my fair share of evil folks—for money or revenge, mostly. Sometimes because they'd simply needed killing. But the years and the injuries and the blood had started to wear on me, more so since a job of mine a few years back had gone so badly for everyone involved, and innocent folks had died as a result.

Eventually, every assassin needed an apprentice—a fresh face, a young, strong body, and a clean, steady set of hands to take over and do what needed to be done—and Gin Blanco was mine.

I'd dubbed her the Spider, partly because that's what she'd reminded me of the first time I'd seen her cowering in a small crack in the alley wall that ran behind the Pork Pit, my barbecue restaurant. Thin arms, spindly legs, gaunt face. To me, Gin was a black widow come to life, full of venom but not strong enough to bite back at those who'd done her wrong—not yet.

Mostly, though, I'd named Gin the Spider because of the scars that adorned her palms. A particularly vicious Fire elemental had tortured the girl by melting a silverstone pendant shaped like a spider rune into her hands, but Gin had lived to tell the tale, one of many ways in which she was a survivor as well as an assassin.

I stood in the coal-black shadows across the street from a three-story house in Southtown, the part of Ashland that was home to the downtrodden, down-on-their-luck, and just plain dangerous. With its peeling gray paint, plywood-covered front door, and barred windows, the ramshackle house had a forlorn, abandoned air. Everything about it suggested that no one lived there anymore, and the steps leading up to the front porch sagged like the skin under an old man's neck. The outside was a disguise, though, a misleading façade to hide the true danger lurking within.

Inside, the house boasted the finest things money could buy. Expensive furniture. Gilded mirrors. Beds made up with silk sheets. Even mints placed on the pillows just so. The fancy furnishings made it easier for a scumbag like Arlo Fazzone to lure the rich folks who lived in the elegant confines of Northtown down here to his illegal casino.

Arlo Fazzone was something of an Ashland success story— a poor giant gangster who'd scraped together enough cash to fix up a place, increase the quality of the drugs he sold, and market his services to a richer clientele. Which, in turn, upped his profits even more.

His game was simple. He lured runaway teenagers into his casino, got them hooked on drugs, and then made them do all sorts of unsavory things to get their next fix—or just enough food to eat. And when he ran low on workers, Arlo snatched unwilling kids off the street to be the grist in his ever-grinding mill.

The giant's most recent victim had been Vana Wickersly, a sixteen-year-old girl who had gone to a party with some of her friends and never returned home. A week later, Vana had been found dumped in a Southtown alley, more dead than alive from a vicious beating.

Three days later, while Vana was still in the hospital, Vernon, her father, had reached out through my various back channels and asked me to find out who was responsible for his daughter's kidnapping and beating and do something about them—permanently. To most folks, I might be Fletcher Lane, restaurant owner, but as the assassin the Tin Man, I had a reputation for tracking down people who did bad things and making them pay with their lives.

People had talked, the way they always did, and the rumors had quickly led me to Arlo and his illegal casino. Apparently, Vana had tried to escape, tried to get back home to her father, and Arlo had beaten her to teach the other teens under his control a lesson. But whoever had dumped her in that alley hadn't made sure she was dead, and Vana had managed to survive.

I'd spent a week doing recon, then another prepping Gin for this, her first solo job as an assassin, as the Spider. Now all that was left was to wait for my apprentice to arrive and see how well she'd learned all the deadly skills I'd taught her.

"Are you sure she's ready for this, Fletcher?" a light, sweet voice whispered in the darkness beside me.

I looked over at Jolene "Jo-Jo" Deveraux, one of my oldest and dearest friends. Even though we were haunting this dangerous neighborhood just before midnight, the five-foot dwarf wore a pink flowered dress trimmed with white lace and a pair of matching pink sandals. A set of pearls topped off Jo-Jo's dress, and the moonlight made the milky stones gleam like round teeth strung together. Her getup would have fit in perfectly at one of those swanky Northtown garden parties that she was always attending.

Maybe I should have brought Jo-Jo's sister, Sophia, along tonight instead of my middle-aged dwarven friend. With her usual dark clothes, the younger dwarf would have blended perfectly into the shadows with me, but Sophia didn't have the healing Air elemental magic that Jo-Jo did—magic that Gin might need before the night was through. This might be the Spider's first solo job, but the Tin Man was going to look after his apprentice.

Especially since I hadn't managed to do that before, a few years ago, when Gin had really needed me. I had vowed to never fail her again.

"She's ready," I replied. "She's been helping me on my missions for more than a year now, and she practically did the last two herself. That girl can wield a knife like no one I've ever seen before. And the blood doesn't bother her at all. That's important, you know."

"Maybe," Jo-Jo murmured. "But you know as well as I do, Fletcher, that deep down, Gin is still just a girl who's missing her family, even though it's been three years since they were murdered."

The dwarf stared at me, her pupils looking like dots of black ink in her clear, almost colorless eyes. No judgment filled her gaze, no accusation for what I'd failed to do, and I knew it never would. Still, I shifted in the shadows, although the movement didn't do anything to lighten my guilt. Gin was one of the many heavy weights that circled my heart like the slow arc of a clock hand. Turning, turning, turning, and never stopping, not even for a second's respite.

A black SUV coasted down the street, stopping in front of the house, and a boy of about eighteen hopped out of the driver's seat. His tall, thick, six-foot-six frame marked him as a giant, although he wasn't fully grown yet. With his blond hair, blue eyes, and tan skin, he looked like a star quarterback, right down to the blue letterman's jacket that he wore over his white T-shirt, blue jeans, and expensive sneakers. Hadley Fazzone, Arlo's younger brother, who was responsible for trolling local high-school football games, dances, and parties in search of fresh young workers for the older giant's operation.

Hadley hurried around the vehicle to open the passenger-side door. He held out his hand and helped the girl inside step out onto the sidewalk—Gin Blanco.

At sixteen, Gin was still lean and thin, with a body that hadn't quite filled out yet. She wore a dark blue T-shirt, jeans, and sneakers, although she'd topped off her outfit with a navy fleece jacket. All the better to hide the silverstone knives she had tucked up her sleeves.

Gin had pulled her dark brown hair back into a high ponytail, which made her look younger, softer, innocent even. But I knew that her innocence had been burned away the night her mother and older sister had been murdered by a Fire elemental.

Hadley said something, then laughed at his own joke. Gin laughed as well, although her smile didn't thaw the coldness in her wintry gray eyes. Hadley didn't notice, though. Targets never did, until it was too late.

Hadley opened the back door of the car and reached inside for something, so Gin started scanning the house. We'd gone over the photos and blueprints a dozen times, and Gin was probably comparing the physical house with the images I'd shown her, as well as marking all the entrances and exits, just in case things took a bad turn.

Our plan was simple. Gin would attract Hadley's interest when he made his usual round of weekend parties, tell him she was a runaway, and get him to take her back to his older brother Arlo's casino. Once inside, Gin would kill Arlo and whoever else got in her way, leave the house, and walk the several blocks over to the Pork Pit, where I'd be waiting.

I hadn't told my apprentice that I'd be watching from the shadows to make sure everything went smoothly. No reason to hurt Gin's pride just because I worried about her as if I were her real father. Just because I didn't want to admit that she was growing up and coming into her own as an assassin, as the Spider. She was already much better than I'd been at her age. Colder. Calmer. More focused. One day soon, she'd be better than I had ever dreamed of being.

I just hoped my training would be enough to make up for how I'd failed her so miserably before. For my part in her mother's and older sister's deaths. For how I'd failed to protect Gin and the rest of her family from the fiery wrath of Mab Monroe.

Perhaps it was my dark thoughts or the intense focus of my gaze, but Gin turned away from the house and scanned the rest of the block. Maybe the cracked pavement under my boots had given me away. As a Stone elemental, Gin could sense emotional vibrations in whatever form the element took around her, from a brick house to a concrete sidewalk to a weathered granite tombstone. Over time, people's feelings sank into the stone around them, and Gin could listen to and interpret those impressions. Perhaps she could sense my worry and pride even now, rippling through the pavement toward her.

Hadley took Gin's arm, escorted her up the sagging steps, and opened the front door. Golden light from inside the house slanted across Gin's face, emphasizing the hard set of her features. Whatever she might be feeling, no emotions flickered in her eyes. No doubt about what she was here to do, and certainly no fear. My heart swelled with even more pride.

"I can't wait to introduce you to my brother." Hadley's voice drifted across the street to where Jo-Jo and I stood in the shadows. "He's going to love you."

"Of course he will," Gin drawled. "He's going to love me to death."

With those ominous words, my apprentice entered the house.

The door had barely closed behind Gin when Jo-Jo poked me in the shoulder.

"Well? What are you waiting for?" the dwarf demanded. "Go around to the back of the house and keep an eye out in case Gin needs any help."

I saluted her with my hand. "Yes, ma'am."

Jo-Jo's pale eyes narrowed at my light tone, but her lips curved up into a smile, deepening the laugh lines on her face. "Don't you tease me, Fletcher Lane. I'm almost two hundred years older than you are. Didn't your mama ever teach you to respect your elders?"

"Yes, ma'am," I repeated, and ducked out of the way before Jo-Jo could poke me again.

I left the dwarf behind, crossed the street, and slipped into the alley that ran beside the house. Garbage carpeted the ground, and the steady, cool October breeze sent more than one empty can skittering along the cracked asphalt. The area reeked of rancid beer, stale cigarettes, and sour sweat, and a sense of desperation hung in the air like an invisible cloud about to rain down on me.

I wondered if Gin could sense that desperation with her Stone magic. She probably could. Sometimes I thought it was better to be a simple human and largely ignorant of such things.

It took me less than two minutes to work my way around to the back of the house and crawl up onto the top of a large, sturdy trash bin. From there, I was able to grab hold of the metal fire escape and scale the rickety ladder up to the third story, something I did with ease, despite my sixty-some years. Gin always called me an old man, although it was a term of endearment on her part. Maybe I was an old man, with my wispy, whitening hair and tan, wrinkled skin, but I was still as spry as ever.

My position in the shadows on the fire escape gave me a clear view through a window into Arlo Fazzone's office. If there was one thing I'd learned from all my years of being an assassin, it was that nobody ever bothered to close their curtains above the first floor. Arlo was no exception, which was why I was able to spot him sitting at a chrome-and-glass desk.

Arlo Fazzone was a thirty-something, seven-foot-tall giant with a strong, thick, muscled body. He had blond hair, blue eyes, and tan skin just like his kid brother, Hadley, but the sheer meanness in his gaze twisted his good looks into something dark, hard, and ugly. He sported a slick black suit, as though he were a real businessman instead of a greedy bastard who made his money by swindling gamblers and forcing desperate kids to work for him.

Arlo shuffled a few papers around on his desk. I reached into my coat pocket, drew out my phone, and hit some buttons so that I could listen in on the office through the devices I'd planted there a few days ago.

A knock sounded on the door, and Gin stepped into the office, followed by Hadley. The younger giant closed the door behind the two of them, then discreetly locked it.

Gin's eyes cut to the side, and I knew she'd heard the lock *click* home. Her right hand twitched, like she wanted to palm the knife hidden up her sleeve, but she restrained herself. Good. If she moved too early, she ran the risk of missing Arlo. Gin knew as well as I did that the giant would try to pummel her to death with his fists if he thought she was any kind of threat. That's how Arlo had gotten to where he was in the first place, by beating down any opposition and competition that came his way.

Since it was Monday, the casino was closed, which meant that no strangers were coming and going, and there was less risk of anyone seeing Gin and identifying her later. Arlo did have a couple of giants stationed throughout the lower two floors of the house, making sure things ran smoothly and none of the teens tried to bolt. The bars on the windows helped with that too.

But I wasn't worried about Arlo screaming for help, since his office was soundproofed to keep other folks from hearing all the horrible things that happened inside. Arlo just hadn't realized that one day, something horrible might happen to him in there too.

"Arlo, this is Gin," Hadley said, his voice streaming out of my phone as he led her forward. "Gin, this is Arlo, my big brother."

Arlo got to his feet, buttoned his suit jacket, and extended a hand. "Gin, it's nice to meet you. Hadley's told me so much about you."

Gin shook the giant's hand, although she let out a little snort of disbelief. "Really? I find that hard to believe, since I only met him, like, an hour ago."

Arlo's blue eyes narrowed at her mocking tone, and he gave Hadley a dark look. Arlo wasn't stupid. Like most predators, he could sense when others were near, and his radar was already pinging when it came to Gin. He dropped her hand and stared at her with suspicion, but she just gave him a winsome smile and started exploring the room the way any curious teenager might.

"Gin's a runaway," Hadley explained, trying to smooth things over.

"Is that true?" Arlo asked.

Gin shrugged and picked up a crystal vase. "Not really.

But my family's all dead and burned to ash, so what does it matter?"

He frowned, but Gin put the vase down and moved over to a landscape painting hanging on the far wall. To a casual observer, she was just wandering aimlessly around the room, but she was doing exactly what I'd trained her to do: scanning the area for weapons, panic buttons, or anything else that might be a threat to her.

Arlo watched Gin, but when she didn't do or say anything else suspicious or threatening, his unease faded away, and he looked her up and down. I could almost see the dollar signs flashing in his eyes as he calculated how much money he could make off her suffering.

Arlo stepped out from behind his desk, moved over, and sat down on a wide white couch that took up the better part of one wall. He patted the thick cushion beside him. "Why don't you come over here? I'd like to get to know you better. Hadley's told you what we do here, right? How we run a sort of . . . halfway house for kids who don't fit in anywhere else?"

Hadley fed that bullshit line to teens to get them into the house. After that, Arlo, his goons, and his drugs made sure they didn't leave until they were all used up—or dead.

"Sure," Gin chirped in a bright voice, but once again, her smile didn't thaw the ice in her eyes. "Sounds great."

She moved over and plopped down onto the couch next to Arlo, while Hadley sat in a chair across from them. Neither giant noticed Gin's right arm drop down to her side—or the bit of metal that glinted in her right hand.

"So," Gin chirped again. "Is this where you assault all the kids you bring to your casino? Or do you drug them first so they don't fight back? Is this where you beat Vana Wickersly for trying to escape?"

For a moment, Arlo's mouth gaped, and Hadley wore a similarly stunned expression. Big brother was a little quicker on the draw, though; his mouth snapped shut, and his eyes narrowed.

"How do you know that name?" Arlo growled, suspicion filling his face.

Gin smiled at him, but it was a cold, sharp expression. "Because I visited Vana in the hospital a few weeks ago, and her father wanted me to come here tonight and say hello for him."

"What the—" Hadley sputtered.

Gin ignored him, surged forward, snapped up her hand, and drove her knife into Arlo's chest. The giant's eyes bulged in pain and surprise, and he opened his mouth to scream for help, even though it wouldn't do him any good in the soundproofed office. But Gin didn't give him the chance to yell. She leaped on top of the giant, even as she yanked the knife out of his chest.

And then she cut his throat with the blade.

She turned her head, and blood spattered onto the side of her face, speckling her pretty features like thick drops of red, sticky paint. Gin's lips tightened at the sensation, but she kept her eyes open and focused on Hadley, already thinking about how to take out her next target, since Arlo was already more dead than alive.

"You bitch!" Hadley screamed, scrambling to his feet. "This was a setup!"

Gin pushed herself up off the couch and leaped at Hadley, but he lurched backward, knocking over the chair he'd been sitting in. She landed at his feet, and he drew back his foot and kicked her in the ribs. Gin grunted at the brutal contact and rolled away from the enraged giant. She popped back up onto her feet, her knife still clutched in her hand.

Hadley stared at his big brother, still sprawled across the couch, his blood soaking into the white cushions. "You killed him! You killed Arlo!"

With a roar, he charged at Gin and slapped her knife away. Hadley grabbed Gin's jacket, yanked her forward, and punched her repeatedly in the stomach.

I didn't remember reaching for the gun I had tucked into the small of my back earlier tonight, but suddenly, I was clutching the weapon. Worry burned through my veins like a wildfire roaring out of control. Gin's pride be damned. I wasn't going to let her die, not like I'd let her mother and older sister—

Gin groaned, but she reached up and clawed at Hadley's eyes. He jerked back in surprise, and Gin managed to spin around and all the way out of her jacket. She stumbled across the room and fell on top of the desk, gasping for air. Her eyes landed on something resting on the smooth glass, and her hand snaked forward.

Hadley cracked the knuckles on both his hands. "Time to die, little girl."

He grabbed Gin's shoulder, yanked her away from the desk, and turned her around toward him. Hadley drew back his fist to punch her, and I took a little better aim with my gun—

Gin surged forward, snapped up her hand again, and stabbed him in the throat.

Somehow she had palmed a long, slender letter opener with a shiny pearl handle off the desk. It wasn't as sharp as one of her knives, but it did the job, especially since she buried it up to the hilt in Hadley's throat.

Hadley tried to scream, but all that came out was a series of strangled gasps and gurgles. Gin pulled the makeshift weapon out of his neck and shoved him away. The giant stumbled over his fallen chair and went down onto the floor on his back. Gin didn't hesitate. She raised the letter opener again and used the weight of her entire body to drive it deep into his chest.

Hadley didn't get up after that.

When it was over and Hadley was as dead as his older brother, Gin slowly pushed herself up and onto her feet. She stood in the middle of the office, swaying back and forth, eyes wide, with fear, panic, and more than a little disgust filling her face at what had just happened, at what she'd just done.

"Come on, Gin," I whispered. "Pull yourself together. You can do it. This is what you were born to do, what I've been training you for."

Gin closed her eyes and shuddered out a breath. When she opened them again, her gray gaze was sharp and bright as silverstone once more. Now she was the Gin I knew—the girl with an iron will and a heart of stone that had let her survive so many terrible things. The death of her mother and her older sister, being tortured by Mab Monroe, living on the streets, being trained by an assassin like me.

Gin sucked in a breath and stared at the two bodies. For a moment, I wondered if she'd be able to go through with the final part of the assignment. But her face hardened, and her lips flattened out into a thin line. Gin tiptoed over to Hadley, leaned down, and checked the pulse—or lack thereof—in his neck. Just because someone looked dead didn't mean they actually were. You always had to check and make sure. She quickly moved over and repeated the process on Arlo.

I nodded in satisfaction. Good. She'd done everything I'd told her to—and then some—and she'd made me prouder than I'd thought possible.

I'd been right when I'd told Jo-Jo that Gin was ready for this. She was more than capable of doing jobs on her own. And soon, in a few more years, she'd be the equal of any assassin working today. And someday, maybe sooner than I realized, she'd be ready for what I was ultimately training her for: to kill Mab Monroe.

When Gin was satisfied that the two giants were dead, she shoved the bloody letter opener into her jacket pocket, then grabbed her knife from where it had landed on the floor and tucked it back up her sleeve. Then she went over, unlocked the door, and left Arlo Fazzone and his younger brother Hadley behind in the office.

She didn't look back.

An hour later, Gin pulled open the front door of the Pork Pit, making the silver bell chime. She stepped inside, and her gaze skimmed over the blue and pink vinyl booths, the matching pig tracks on the floor, and finally back to the counter, where I sat reading an old, battered copy of *To Kill a Mockingbird*.

"Is the job done?" I asked, using one of the day's credit-card receipts to mark my place in the book.

"You shouldn't ask me that," she said, a slightly hurt tone in her voice. "I wouldn't have come back unless it was done."

I nodded. "You're right. Forgive me."

Gin nodded back, then walked over and hopped up onto one of the stools in front of the counter. I looked her over, but her navy jacket did a good job of hiding the blood she'd gotten on her while killing the Fazzone brothers. She'd taken the extra step of zipping up her jacket to cover whatever stains might be on her T-shirt, and somewhere along the way, she'd scrubbed the blood off her face and hands. Overall, she'd covered her tracks well.

"Are you hurt?" I asked, thinking of the punches she'd taken in the office. "Do we need to get Jo-Jo to heal you?"

I'd sent the dwarf home after Gin had walked out of Arlo's office, but I'd told Jo-Jo that we might come over to her beauty salon later, depending on how Gin felt.

She shrugged. "I have some bruised ribs, but that's all. Nothing that can't wait until morning. What I'd really like is some food. I'm starving, Fletcher."

I grinned. "I'm one step ahead of you there."

I turned around and retrieved the plate of food that I'd

prepared for her. A thick, juicy cheeseburger with all the fixings, crispy fries, crunchy coleslaw, and baked beans smothered in the Pork Pit's famous barbecue sauce. All of Gin's favorites.

I pushed the food across the counter, along with a chocolate milkshake, and she immediately dug in. I knew she was hungry. I hadn't let her eat supper before she'd gone to meet Hadley, for fear that she might throw up before or even during the job. It was always better to do a job on an empty stomach—especially the first time you went solo.

I let her get halfway through her food before I asked the inevitable question. "So how was it?"

I watched her carefully, looking for any sign of fear, regret, anger, or disgust. By now, she had had time to really think about what she'd done, and I didn't want her emotions to start gnawing at her. But no guilt flashed in her eyes, and no self-loathing twisted her features. Instead, she sat at the counter, chewed her food, and thought about my question.

"It went okay," Gin finally said. "I didn't do a very good job convincing the Fazzone brothers that I was a runaway. I was too angry about what they were doing to really play the part like you told me to."

Her self-analysis was spot-on. Her acting could have definitely used some work, but she'd gotten the job done. And next time, I knew she'd correct her mistake. I only had to tell Gin something once, and she did it, without hesitating and without asking why.

"Well, it doesn't much matter now, does it?" I asked. "The Fazzone brothers are dead, and you're not. I'd say that makes the evening a grand success."

I hesitated, not quite sure how to say what I really wanted to—or how it might sound to a sixteen-year-old girl who'd just killed two men. In the end, I decided on the direct approach. I'd never been one for smooth words, not like my son, Finnegan. That boy could charm the wings off a butterfly.

"I'm proud of you, Gin."

"Really?" she asked in a soft, shy voice. "Really and truly, Fletcher? I did good?"

I nodded. "You did good, really and truly. The Fazzone brothers won't be hurting any more kids, and you got justice for Vana Wickersly. Maybe what you did will bring her and her father a little bit of peace."

She smiled then, and it was as if the moon had suddenly burst into the Pork Pit, bathing everything in its soft, silvery light. Still smiling, Gin turned her attention back to her food.

I picked up my book again, but I couldn't quite focus on the words—or hide the proud grin that quirked my lips.

Oh, yes. The girl was a natural-born assassin.

And I was going to make her the very best there was. So she could do what needed to be done—for herself and for her younger sister, Bria.

One day, Gin Blanco was going to grow up, get her own justice, and kill Mab Monroe. And I, Fletcher Lane, the Tin Man, was going to help her every step of the way.

Poison

This story takes place several years before **Spider's Bite**, book 1.

Finnegan Lane

I *hated* the girl.

I hated everything about her, from her painfully thin body, to her big, wounded eyes, to her absolute eagerness to do whatever my father, Fletcher Lane, told her to.

But I especially hated the fact that Dad had decided to train *her* to be an assassin instead of *me*.

The girl set a triple chocolate milkshake down on the counter in front of me. "Here you go, Finn."

Her voice was soft, just like everything else about her. Soft brown hair, soft gray eyes, soft small body. Even her clothes were soft and baggy and utterly forgettable. She never raised her voice, she never interrupted a conversation, she never did anything the least bit dangerous or naughty or risky. It was as if she was determined to draw as little attention to herself as possible and blend into the background, no matter what.

She was *so* annoying.

I didn't even say thanks as I stuck a straw into the frothy concoction and started sucking down the milkshake.

"Do you like it?" the girl asked, a bit of hope creeping into her voice. "I followed Fletcher's recipe, but then I decided to add in even more chocolate to make it really rich and creamy."

The milkshake was wonderful, absolutely wonderful, and even better than the ones that Dad made for me here at the Pork Pit. But I wasn't about to tell *her* that. Most days, I didn't even bother to speak to her.

I grunted. "It'll do, I suppose."

Behind the counter, Sophia Deveraux gave me a sharp look. Most people would have been intimidated by her glower, since the dwarf was as hard and muscled as the girl was soft and thin. Sophia wore solid black, from her heavy boots to her jeans to her T-shirt to the leather collar that wrapped around her neck. Even her hair was black, and she'd painted her lips the same color. The Goth dwarf was the real deal, a true badass, and she made the wannabes at my high school look like kids playing dress-up, which, of course, they were.

But Sophia's pointed glare didn't faze me. Sophia and her older sister, Jo-Jo, had helped Dad raise me, and I knew that the two dwarves thought of me as their own son. For some inexplicable reason, though, both Sophia and Jo-Jo had taken an immediate liking to the girl, fussing over her just as much as they did over me. I didn't know why. I didn't think there was anything to like about Gin.

Gin—that's what the girl called herself. Heh. We all knew that wasn't her *real* name, but Dad had accepted it anyway. He'd even given her a last name too: Blanco. Gin Blanco. As if that wasn't the cheesiest thing anyone had ever heard.

But Dad hadn't stopped there. He had created a whole new identity for the girl, claiming that she was some distant cousin he'd taken in after her family had died in a car accident. She'd been with us several weeks now, and Dad had bought her clothes and fed her and even enrolled her in school. Since she was thirteen and I was fifteen, she wasn't in my class, though. One small thing to be happy about.

Since I was tired of looking at Gin, I swiveled around on my stool, still sucking on my milkshake. It was Monday afternoon, and business was a little slow at the Pork Pit, Dad's barbecue restaurant. Only a few customers sat in the blue and pink vinyl booths by the storefront windows, although they were all eating their barbecue sandwiches, baked beans, coleslaw, onion rings, and thick steak-cut fries with obvious enthusiasm.

A girl about my age put down her iced tea, slid out of a booth, and followed the faded, peeling pink pig tracks on the floor over to the women's restroom. I grinned at her, and the girl stopped to look at me. With my walnut-colored hair, green eyes, and tan skin, I was the spitting image of my dad and just as handsome as he was. I winked at the girl, who giggled, ducked her head, and hurried on by.

Normally, Fletcher would have been here, sitting on a stool behind the cash register and reading a book in between helping Sophia and Gin dish up barbecue. But Dad was off on one of his jobs this evening, righting wrongs and eliminating bad people. Something he excelled at, as the assassin the Tin Man.

And now he was determined to teach Gin everything he knew about being an assassin.

He'd told me about his plan last night, even though I'd seen it coming way before then. A few weeks ago, a giant named Douglas, one of Dad's disgruntled clients, had stormed into the restaurant. Douglas would have killed Dad—and me too—if Gin hadn't stabbed him to death with the knife she was using to chop onions at the time.

For some reason, Dad thought that stroke of blind luck made Gin a prime candidate to become an assassin, just like him. He'd already given her a moniker: the Spider. Another fake, cheesy name to go along with her other one.

He should have been training *me*. After all, *I* was his son, his flesh and blood. My mother had died when I was a baby, and it had always been just the two of us, along with Sophia and Jo-Jo. I didn't understand what Dad saw in Gin that he didn't see in me. What he thought *she* had that *I* didn't.

I was older than her, smarter, stronger, tougher. I was already as good a shot as Dad was with his rifle. I wanted to learn the rest of the business too, but Dad didn't see it that way. He claimed that Gin would make the better assassin, that she had the patience for it and I didn't.

That had hurt worse than anything else he'd ever said to me.

The milkshake soured in my stomach, as though I'd been drinking pure poison instead of melted chocolate. Maybe I had been. I'd seen what Gin had done to Douglas with that knife. She'd stabbed the giant over and over like he was a piñata that she was cutting all the candy out of. I wouldn't put anything past her, not even poisoning me so she could have my dad all to herself.

I swiveled back around to the counter, slammed my empty glass down, and shoved it away.

"You must have liked it," Gin said, giving me a small, tentative smile. "You drank all of it."

Instead of responding, I got to my feet, grabbed my jacket off the stool next to me, and put it on. It was the second jacket I'd bought in as many weeks. Gin had given my first one away to some homeless kid, just plucked it off the coat rack in the restaurant like it was *hers* instead of *mine*. Something else that had pissed me off. That poisonous feeling expanded in my stomach, burning like acid.

"Whatever," I growled. "I'm out of here."

"Where?" Sophia rasped in her harsh, broken voice.

I shrugged. "A party with some friends."

Gin frowned. "The party that Fletcher said you couldn't go to?"

I didn't respond.

"Fletcher's not going to like that," Gin said in that soft voice again, the one that made me grind my teeth. "Especially since it's over in Southtown. That's why he said you couldn't go in the first place. Because it's dangerous over there."

Next to Gin, Sophia grunted her agreement.

"I don't care what Fletcher does or doesn't like," I growled. "Because he certainly doesn't give a damn about what *I* do or don't like. For example, I didn't like it when he took you in. I still don't. Not one little bit. But yet here you are anyway."

Gin didn't flinch at my words, but hurt and sadness sparked in her gray eyes. For some reason, it made me feel awful, like I'd done something wrong. But she was the trespasser here, not me.

"Finn," Sophia snapped, clearly wanting me to apologize.

For a moment, I opened my mouth, intending to do just that—to force out a gruff *sorry*. I knew that Gin had been through something horrible, something that had forced her to live on the streets, and I'd seen the spider runes that had been brutally branded into her palms. But I just didn't understand how or when or especially *why* her problems had become Dad's problems—and now mine too.

"It's okay, Sophia," Gin said in that same soft, resigned voice. "Let him go."

Then she turned away, grabbed a serrated knife, and started slicing a tomato. She didn't yell or scream or curse at me, and she didn't give me another wounded look. She just went about her business like I wasn't even there, like I didn't even *matter* to her or anyone else.

She had no right to do that—no right at all. This was my dad's restaurant, not hers. He was *my* dad, not *hers*. But here she was, slowly taking over, taking away everything that was *mine*.

That poisonous acid flooded my veins again, burning even

hotter than before. I wasn't going to apologize to her. Not now, not ever.

So I stalked across the floor, flung the door open, and stormed out of the restaurant.

I'd had too much to drink. Or maybe just enough. It was hard to tell. Everything seemed soft and hazy in the dark.

The party had been held in an abandoned building over in Southtown. There had been lots of loud music, lots of people, and lots of booze. Everything else was a bit of a blur.

Now I was trudging back to the Pork Pit, planning to use my key to let myself into the restaurant so I could sleep in one of the booths for the rest of the night. Dad would severely punish me in the morning for disobeying him, but going to the party had been worth it.

Getting away from Gin for the night had been worth it.

A group of us had left the abandoned building together, but one by one, my friends had peeled off, going their respective ways, until now it was just me, walking alone. I wasn't too worried, though. I was only about seven blocks from the Pork Pit now. Surely, I could make it seven more blocks without something bad happening . . .

One minute, I was stumbling down the street, trying not to trip over the cracks in the uneven sidewalk. The next, I was pinned up against the side of a building by two guys, with a third guy standing in front of me, holding a knife. I still wasn't too worried, though. Muggings were as common as sunsets in Ashland, especially in Southtown.

"Hey, hey," I said, giving them a crooked smile. "There's no need to be rough about things. Take my wallet if you want, although I've got to warn you, there's not much in there."

"Don't worry, dude," the guy with the knife said. "We will.

And we'll take your blood too. Every last drop of it."

He smiled, revealing two yellowish fangs in his mouth. They were vampires. Hungry ones too, from the way they were eyeing me.

Suddenly, I was extremely worried.

If I'd been sober, I probably could have fought back, broken free from the two vampires who were holding me, and run away as fast as I could. But I wasn't sober, and the third guy had a knife. Not good odds. Still, I struggled anyway, but my limbs felt slow and heavy, like I was trying to fight through water. The two vampires just laughed and tightened their grips. If I got out of this in one piece, I was never drinking again. Well, not until the next party, at the very least.

"Hold him still," the guy with the knife said.

One of the other vampires forced my head back against the cold brick, exposing my neck. The vampire with the knife licked his lips and leaned forward. I winced, waiting for the pain from his vicious bite—

"Uh."

Instead of tearing into my neck, the vampire let out a low grunt and slumped forward, his body pressing up against mine.

"Brent?" one of the other vampires said, looking at his buddy. "What are you doing? Quit messing around. The rest of us want a taste too."

He reached out and shook Brent, who pitched to the side and crumpled into a heap on the sidewalk.

The other two guys cursed and jumped back, but I wasn't paying attention to them anymore. Instead, I was looking at the slender figure in front of me.

Gin Blanco.

She looked rather ridiculous, standing there in her baggy jeans and fleece jacket, her hair pulled back into a ponytail, a bloody knife clutched in her right hand. I recognized the silverstone blade. Dad had given her the weapon to start practicing with—and she'd just used it to save my life.

"Leave him alone," Gin growled in a voice that was as cold and hard as the brick building behind me.

And suddenly, I saw what Dad saw in her: the fierce determination, the iron will, the unwavering loyalty. Even though I'd treated her awfully tonight, and every night since Dad had taken her in, Gin had still cared enough to follow me from the party just to make sure that I got back to the Pork Pit okay.

I knew it as instinctively as I knew that I would never resent her again—*never*.

The two vampires looked at each other, then at their fallen buddy, and then back at Gin. They launched themselves at her, but she stood her ground.

Gin stabbed the first guy in the chest, driving the blade into his heart before yanking it out. He dropped without another sound, but the other guy was quicker. He leaped forward and managed to drive Gin down to the sidewalk and started grappling with her, trying to knock the knife out of her hand. But she fought him back just as hard, trying to stab him to death.

I stumbled forward, dug my hands into the vampire's jacket, and yanked him off her. Then I forced the guy up and back and rammed his head into the brick wall. He moaned and flailed at me with his arms, so I heaved him forward and then shoved him back again—and again and again, until his head was a bloody, pulpy mass.

Finally, I released the vampire, who toppled to the pavement. More blood gushed out of his head and filled in some of the jagged cracks in the sidewalk, looking like a glistening crimson spiderweb.

Gin got to her feet, and the two of us stood there, breathing hard, the bodies of the three vampires at our feet.

I looked up and down the street and listened, but I didn't see or hear anyone. Good. The area being deserted had gotten me into this mess in the first place, and now it was going to get me and Gin out of it. Deaths were almost as common as muggings in Southtown, and since most of the cops were as crooked as the day was long, they probably wouldn't search too hard for the vampires' killers.

I looked over at Gin. "You've been following me this whole time?"

She nodded. "I trailed you over to the party and hid outside until you came out of the building."

It was close to midnight now, and I'd been at the party for several hours. I couldn't believe she'd spent all that time just waiting for me to stagger outside. I certainly wouldn't have had the patience for that sort of thing—or have been smart or concerned or thoughtful enough to attempt it in the first place.

Maybe Dad was right about Gin. Maybe he was right about a lot of things.

"Why?" I asked. "Why would you do that?"

She frowned, like the answer should be obvious. "Fletcher wouldn't like it if anything bad happened to you. And I wouldn't either." Gin paused, and when she spoke again, her voice was a low, raspy whisper. "Enough bad things have already happened to the people I care about."

And just like that, all my poisonous jealousy vanished. She was trying so hard—to please Dad, to please *me*. The least I could do was meet her halfway, especially since she'd just saved my life.

I wasn't an Air elemental, so I couldn't see the future like Jo-Jo could, but I had a funny feeling this wouldn't be the last time Gin got me out of a tough spot. I only hoped that I could do the same for her someday.

"Come on, Gin," I said, holding out my hand to her. "Let's go home."

She wiped off her bloody knife on the closest vampire's

shirt and slid it back up her jacket sleeve. She also scrubbed her skin clean before slipping her right hand into mine. Her fingers felt strong and warm in my own.

Then we stepped over the vampires' bodies and headed for the Pork Pit—together.

Wasted

This story takes place after *Web of Lies*, book 2.

Finnegan Lane

She was one of the most beautiful women I had ever seen.

Everything about her was perfect and exquisite and whispered of money, from the artful tousle of her blond curls, to the diamond brooch set into her mint-green suit jacket, to the subtle shine of her French manicure. This was a woman who took excellent care of herself, probably with an organic diet, a vigorous exercise regimen, and Air elemental facials. Why, she might even be one of Jo-Jo Deveraux's clients over at the dwarf's popular beauty salon. I made a mental note to ask Jo-Jo the next time I saw her.

The woman stood in the lobby of my bank, First Trust of Ashland, and stared out over the gray marble floor, antique wooden desks and chairs, and crystal lamps. The woman scanned the long counter that ran along the back wall before glancing over at the steel door in the left corner. Beyond that door, a staircase went down to the basement where my office was located, along with several others. The bank's most secure vault, which I had jokingly dubbed Big Bertha, was also on the basement level.

I was on the opposite side of the lobby, perching on the edge of a desk, and talking to Pete, one of our stock analysts, about the shopping trip he'd recently taken with his husband to Bigtime, New York, and all the divine Fiona Fine menswear they'd bought.

"Duty calls," I said, getting to my feet.

Pete followed my gaze and snorted. "It always does every time a pretty woman walks through the door, Finn."

"You're just jealous that she's not a handsome dude."

"Hardly. David and I are very happy."

I grinned. "But it never hurts to look, does it?"

Pete just laughed and concentrated on his computer monitor again.

I smoothed down my green tie, the one that brought out the matching color of my eyes, and headed over to the woman. My wing tips clacked on the floor, drawing her attention. She glanced up at my approach, and I hit her with a wide smile, which she naturally returned. I was Finnegan Lane, after all. Charming, handsome, confident. A hard combination for anyone to resist.

I stopped a few feet away. Up close, she was even more stunning, with bright hazel eyes and sun-kissed skin. A small set of gleaming white fangs marked her as a vampire, but that didn't matter to me in the slightest. Giant, dwarf, vampire, elemental, a regular old human like me. A beautiful person was a beautiful person, no matter what kind of strength or magic they did or didn't have.

"Are you the manager?" she asked in a light voice.

I breathed in. Her perfume smelled of honeysuckle, light, sweet, and subtle. "Nope, I'm not the manager, but I'm sure I can help you. The name's Lane, Finnegan Lane. My friends call me Finn."

The woman's smile abruptly vanished, and her mouth flattened out. "Oh. Well, where is the manager?"

"I'm sure that I can help you," I repeated, giving her my most charming smile. "I'm one of the senior investment bankers."

If anything, my polite offer repelled her even more.

"No," she said, tightening her grip on the designer bag hanging off her slender shoulder. "I need to see the manager. I don't want anyone else."

I frowned. "But—"

"What seems to be the problem here, Lane?" A man's voice cut in.

Tripp Hartford, the bank manager, stepped up to us. Tripp was a tall, trim, attractive fellow with blond hair, brown eyes, and ruddy skin. He could also be just as charming as me, something it pained me to admit.

"Are you the manager?" the woman asked.

Tripp nodded. "I am. How can I help you . . ."

"Clarissa," she replied, holding out her hand. "Clarissa Drystan."

Tripp dropped his head, doing a smooth little bow over her hand before releasing it. "Well, Ms. Drystan, it's a pleasure to meet you. How can I assist you?"

Clarissa gestured at her shoulder bag. "I have some family jewels that need to be put in a safe location. Some items that my soon-to-be-ex-husband doesn't need to know about. I was told that you could help me with that sort of thing."

Tripp nodded. "Of course. If you'll just come with me, Ms. Drystan, I'm sure we can find a solution to your problem."

Clarissa smiled at him, a big, bright, dazzling smile that only enhanced her beauty.

Tripp gave me a triumphant grin. Then he escorted Clarissa across the lobby and through the door at the far end of the counter to take her to his downstairs office. Of course, he could have asked one of the tellers here in the lobby to set her up with a safety-deposit box, but I knew that Tripp wanted to give Clarissa some extra attention in hopes of earning even more of her business—and potentially scoring her phone number so he could ask her out later.

I would have done the same thing if I'd been in his wing tips.

Clarissa came into the bank several times after that.

On her second visit, Tripp walked up to the lobby to meet her. On her third visit, she came in just at closing, and the two of them left together. On her fourth visit, the very next day, she walked over to the door by the counter, and Tripp buzzed her down to his office. After that, Clarissa came and went as she pleased, so often that the giant guards stationed in the lobby automatically opened the downstairs door for her.

If I'd been dating someone as beautiful as Clarissa, I would have bragged about it to everyone, from the folks at the bank, to my friend Jo-Jo and her sister Sophia Deveraux, to my foster sister, Gin Blanco. Tripp was much more restrained, and he merely smirked at me every time Clarissa strolled into the bank.

It still made me want to punch him, though.

One day, about six weeks after Clarissa's initial visit, I was in my office trying to find a new mutual fund for Mallory Parker, one of my dwarven clients, to put some more of her considerable fortune into when the phone on my desk rang.

"Yes?"

"You have a visitor, Finn." The voice of Cecily, one of the tellers, filled my ear. "A giant. Says his name is Xavier."

"Bring him on down."

"Roger that."

I wasn't sure why Xavier wanted to see me, since, to my

knowledge, the giant didn't have any money that needed hiding from anyone, but maybe he'd surprise me. I'd be happy to help him move some cash around—for a small fee, of course.

A few minutes later, Cecily knocked on my open door and gestured for Xavier to step inside. He maneuvered around her and walked over to my desk.

Like most giants, Xavier topped out at around seven feet tall, with a thick, muscular body that was incredibly strong. We shook hands, and I could tell that he was taking care to keep his grip light, something my much more fragile human bones appreciated.

His shaved head, dark eyes, and ebony skin gleamed under the lights, and a navy suit jacket paired with a white shirt stretched across his broad shoulders. Nice cut, quality fabric, perfectly draped. I always appreciated a well-made suit, and Xavier was totally rocking this one.

I sat back down in my chair and gestured for Xavier to take the seat opposite mine.

The giant settled himself, then looked around the office and let out a low whistle. "I should have been a banker like you, Finn."

I'd been at First Trust for several years now, ever since I'd graduated from business school, and as a result, my office was one of the biggest ones on this basement level. Tripp's office was located here too, farther down the hall and closer to Big Bertha, the main vault.

I'd decorated my office in a style that was unapologetic, in-your-face, ostentatious comfort. I had the best of everything, from the thick rugs that covered the floor, to the first-edition volumes on the bookshelves, to the Brighton's Best whiskey that gleamed in its bottle inside the liquor cabinet in the corner.

My wide, antique mahogany desk was beautiful and sturdy and studded with almost as many secret compartments as the vault had safety-deposit boxes. All those little hidey-holes and false bottoms were perfect for storing certain supplies. Passports, a small bag of diamonds, a few bricks of cash, my guns, and the ammunition for them. When you swam with the sharks like I did, you never knew when you might need to get out of town in a hurry. My father, Fletcher Lane, had prepared me for that dangerous scenario, along with many, many others.

My only real concession to modern functionality was the TV mounted on a stand to my right. Currently, it was tuned to a live feed of the bank lobby, which showed customers coming and going, tellers cashing checks, and more. In addition to working with clients, I also had a hand in security, thanks to the various favors that Stuart Mosley, the bank president, owed to my dad. Besides, I liked to keep a vigilant eye on all things money-related.

"Investment banker," I said, correcting Xavier's earlier statement. "And yes, it pays very, very well. Especially in a place like Ashland, where so many folks have so much money to hide—and so many bodies too."

Xavier nodded, but he didn't smile at my dark humor. Normally, cracking a joke about Ashland being such a corrupt, violent city would earn me a small chuckle from even the most jaded resident. No, the giant was all business today. Pity.

"What I can do for you, Xavier?" I asked. "Because as much as I like you, I know that you didn't just come here to shoot the breeze with me."

The giant hesitated, staring down at his shoes. Then he raised his dark gaze to mine. "I have a problem."

Not what I'd expected him to say. With his size and strength, there weren't too many problems that Xavier couldn't handle all by himself, especially given the fact that he was a cop for the Ashland Police Department.

"What kind of problem? What do you need my help with?"

"It's not that I need *your* help, Finn," Xavier said in a careful voice. "What I really need is *Gin's* help."

My eyebrows shot up in surprise. In addition to being my foster sister, Gin Blanco was also the assassin known as the Spider.

Gin wasn't just any assassin, though. She was one of the best in the business. At least, she had been. She'd retired a few months ago after my father and her mentor, Fletcher Lane, had been murdered. Now Gin spent her time running the Pork Pit, Dad's barbecue restaurant, but she hadn't forgotten any of her training, and she would whip out her silverstone knives without hesitation if she thought there was a call for them.

"What do you need Gin's help with?" I asked, my voice calm, my face giving nothing away. I wanted to see exactly what Xavier knew about what Gin did—and how much of a threat he might be to us.

"Well, first, I guess you should know that Roslyn and I are sort of . . . involved," Xavier said.

My eyebrows climbed a little higher on my face. This just kept getting more and more interesting. Roslyn Phillips was the vampire who ran Northern Aggression, the city's most decadent nightclub. Xavier moonlighted as the club's head bouncer, the guy responsible for making sure that everyone stayed more or less in line.

"*Involved?*" I asked. "As in you and Roslyn are together now?"

"Sort of. I mean . . . it's just . . . complicated." He winced. "I hope you don't mind me talking to you about this. I know that you and Roslyn used to be . . . friends."

That was a polite way of saying that Roslyn and I had occasionally been friends with benefits.

"Sure," I replied in an easy tone. "Roslyn and I are friends—*just* friends, now. But if you're with her, then congrats to you. Because she is smart, tough, strong, and beautiful, inside and out."

Xavier smiled, but it wasn't just any old smile. No, he

practically *beamed* with the look of a man completely in love.

I sighed. I might be a greedy, coldhearted bastard most of the time, but I had a soft spot for Roslyn. I'd really hate to threaten someone who cared that much about her, but I'd do it just the same—just like Gin would—in order to protect our secrets.

Xavier cleared his throat. "Anyway, there's been a . . . problem at the club lately. And from some things Roslyn has said, I thought Gin might be able to help."

His careful words and tone told me exactly what he'd picked up from Roslyn: that Gin was an assassin. Roslyn knew all about what Gin did, since Gin had killed the vampire's abusive brother-in-law not too long ago.

Roslyn had first come to me about finding someone to kill her brother-in-law. I had denied all knowledge of such things, but not too long after that, the brother-in-law had met with an untimely demise. Roslyn was smart, and she'd put it all together—me, Gin, Dad, and what we did. In fact, Roslyn talking to the wrong person about Gin being an assassin had eventually led to my dad's death.

Gin didn't think I knew about that, though. Gin didn't think I knew about a lot of things. Killing was her specialty, but ferreting out information was mine.

"Finn?" Xavier asked, wondering at my silence.

I sighed again. "No more word games. Just lay it out for me, Xavier."

To my surprise, he did. For the next five minutes, Xavier sat there and told me what was going on. Every word he said made my stomach twist a little more with disgust and worry. Gin was not going to like this—not one little bit. I didn't like it either, but Gin was going to take it *personally*. She was going to blame herself for what was happening at Northern Aggression.

"So do you think Gin will help?" Xavier asked in a low voice after he finished his story.

"Help?" I barked out a harsh laugh. "Of course she'll help. She's going to feel responsible for the whole horrible situation."

Xavier shook his head. "It's not her fault."

"Gin won't see it that way. She may be as cold as ice, but if you mess with somebody she cares about—even a friend of a friend—then you'd better watch out. Because she will bury you six feet under and not think twice about it."

I started brooding then. About Roslyn and Xavier, about Gin, about the whole messy situation. I don't know how long I might have sat there lost in my own thoughts if Xavier hadn't cleared his throat and pointed at the TV screen.

"Uh, Finn, who is that? And why are all those men with her?"

On the screen, Clarissa strode into the lobby. The vampire looked as gorgeous as ever, but for once, she wasn't alone. Six giants wearing dark suits and carrying briefcases flanked her.

"Oh, those guys?" I replied. "They're here to rob the bank."

Xavier frowned. "Here to *rob the bank*? How do you know that?"

"Because I'm Finnegan Lane, and I know things."

Xavier kept staring at me so I told him the story about my very first meeting with Clarissa and all the times she'd returned to the bank since then.

"I was immediately suspicious when Clarissa went for Tripp instead of me," I said, straightening my tie the tiniest bit. "Since I'm obviously the much better catch."

Xavier let out a derisive snort. "Obviously."

"Hey, now, keep the sarcasm to a minimum."

A grin crooked up the corner of the giant's lips.

I rolled my eyes. "Okay, so what really made me suspicious was how Clarissa insisted on seeing the manager, even though I repeatedly said that I could help her."

Xavier frowned again. "Isn't asking to see the manager a pretty common thing?"

"Yeah, but it was the *way* she asked and especially how she lost all interest when I told her I wasn't the manager." I shook my head. "Something about it just didn't seem right, so I did some digging. There is no Clarissa Drystan in Ashland or anywhere else that I could find. However, there *is* a Clarissa Dagon, who has quite the reputation among the underworld. Guess what her specialty is?"

"Robbing banks?"

I shot my thumb and forefinger at him. "Bingo. First, Clarissa visits the bank, rents a safety-deposit box, and charms the manager. When the poor fool is head over heels, Clarissa goes to the bank with her crew. They rob the place and pretend to take her hostage. Since the manager doesn't want his lady love to get hurt, he's more than happy to give the thieves access to whatever they want, including the vault. Once the vault is empty, the thieves take Clarissa with them, supposedly using her as a human shield. Of course, it's all just part of her getaway plan."

Xavier nodded. "Smart. So what happens after Clarissa and her crew leave the bank? Do they just disappear until they pull another heist?"

I shook my head. "Not exactly. A couple of days after the robbery, the cops will get a tip about an unidentifiable body dressed in whatever Clarissa was wearing while she was in the bank, and everyone will assume that the robbers killed her. Then, a few weeks later, the police will find the robbers' bodies somewhere. Clarissa doesn't like to share her loot, so she offs her own crew after the job is finished. With no one to chase after, the cops eventually lose interest, the case is closed, and Clarissa is off to build a new crew of suckers and find a new bank to rob."

Xavier whistled. "That's pretty slick."

I nodded. "Yeah, it is. Just watch the monitor, and you'll see."

Sure enough, it happened just like I said it would. One of the guys with Clarissa pulled a gun out of his briefcase, grabbed her, and pressed the weapon to her temple. After that, there was lots of screaming, so much that I had to mute the sound on the TV.

The bank guards surrendered, and the tellers emptied out all the cash drawers. Then the thieves started threatening to kill Clarissa unless the manager stepped forward. A few seconds later, Tripp shuffled out from behind the counter, where he'd been standing when the thieves had first entered the bank. The thieves waved their guns around some more, and Tripp quickly caved. He headed toward the door that led to the basement—including the vault.

"All right," I said, getting to my feet. "I'll get Gin to help you and Roslyn with this problem you all are having at Northern Aggression."

Xavier blinked. "Just like that?"

I nodded. "Just like that. I owe Roslyn that much. But right now, I'd like you to help me. After what you just told me about Roslyn, I really want to punch somebody. Want to help me stop a robbery? Stuart Mosley will be very grateful. Why, the police department might even give you a commendation for it."

Xavier cracked his knuckles. His grin matched my own.

I hit some buttons on my desk. A couple of panels silently slid open, and I grabbed the guns hidden inside, along with a couple of other useful items. Gin might be the assassin in the family, but Dad had taught us both how to defend ourselves. Despite Gin's skill with knives and her Ice and Stone elemental magic, even she admitted that I was much better with a gun than she was.

I offered a weapon to Xavier, but he declined. Then again, he didn't really need a gun. As a giant, he was strong enough to beat someone to death with his bare hands.

We turned off the lights in my office. Since it was late Friday afternoon, everyone else had already gone home for the weekend, and I was the only one still working down here on the basement level. Good. I didn't want any innocent folks getting hurt.

We didn't have to wait long. We left the office door cracked open, and less than two minutes later, footsteps clacked on the marble floor and echoed down the hallway.

"Secure the basement, and make sure all the offices are empty," one of the thieves said. "I don't want anyone coming up behind us trying to play hero. The rest of us are going to the vault. That's where the real money will be."

"Got it," another man replied.

Most of the footsteps moved on and then faded away, as the thieves, with Tripp and Clarissa in tow, headed toward the vault. But some of the footsteps grew louder and closer, clearly heading in this direction—two men, one to run point and the other for backup.

Thanks to the TV screen, I could see that two of the thieves had stayed in the lobby to keep the guards, tellers, and customers under control. Since two were now headed this way, that meant Clarissa had taken two more to the vault with her, along with Tripp.

The guys were thorough, I'd give them that. One by one, they peered into all the offices, turning on the lights and making sure they were empty before closing and locking the doors behind them. Clarissa had put together a decent crew—it was just her bad luck that she'd picked *my* bank to rob.

I might hide money for my clients like a squirrel storing nuts for the winter, but I always protected what was mine—and this bank was *mine*. I was rather like Gin that way.

Finally, the thieves reached my office. The first guy stepped inside and flipped on the light switch.

"Clear—"

Xavier stepped forward and slammed his fist into the other man's face, and the guy dropped like a stone. I couldn't tell if Xavier had broken his neck or just knocked him out.

But the guy's buddy must have heard the *crack* of Xavier's fist connecting, because he rushed into the office and aimed his gun at the giant. "Who the fuck are you—"

I slid out from behind the door and jammed my gun into his side. The thief froze.

"I was just going to ask you the same thing," I drawled. "But I don't really care who you are. I'm more interested in your boss, Clarissa. Xavier, if you would do the honors, please."

Xavier pulled the roll of duct tape that I'd given him out of his pants pocket and went to work on the thieves. A minute later, he had them both trussed up like Thanksgiving turkeys. We left them in my office and headed toward the vault.

Clarissa had left one guy behind in the corridor, but he was more interested in glancing at the vault than in keeping watch like he was supposed to. One quiet, well-placed blow from Xavier, and he was down for the count. That left one more guy to take care of, along with Clarissa herself.

Xavier dragged the unconscious thief back into my office, while I peered into the vault. The door was standing wide open, revealing row after row of safety-deposit boxes, and the keyholes glimmered like hundreds of silent eyes, all staring at me. I slipped back into my office just as Xavier finished trussing up the thief.

"Think you can handle the two guys still up in the lobby?" I asked.

Xavier cracked his knuckles again. "Happily."

"All right. I'll take care of the other guy down here, along with Clarissa."

Xavier nodded back, left my office, and headed upstairs. I slipped off my wing tips so they wouldn't clack on the floor and crept down the corridor toward the vault.

The clangs, bangs, and curses grew louder as I neared the open vault door. Sounded like someone was using a crowbar to pry the safety-deposit boxes out of the walls. Crude but effective, especially since the contents of just one box would make this whole operation worthwhile.

I reached the open door, but instead of going inside, I crouched down. I pulled a compact mirror out of my pocket—one of the other items I'd had stashed in my desk—and angled it so I could see inside the vault.

The last thief stood in front of one of the rows of safety-deposit boxes, shoving a crowbar in between the creases in the metal and popping them out like they were peanuts he was shelling. Easy enough for a giant like him.

Meanwhile, Tripp and Clarissa stood off to the side of the vault. Tripp looked dumbstruck. Every once in a while, a few tears would trickle down Clarissa's face. The vamp was still playing her part to the very end of the game. I admired her professionalism and dedication to her craft.

I put the mirror away, straightened up, and stepped into the vault, my gun still clutched in my hand. "Don't y'all know that it's not nice to steal from other people?"

Startled, the giant whipped around. He snarled and charged at me, so I raised my gun and shot him twice in the chest. His crowbar hit the floor a second before his body toppled on top of Tripp, driving the bank manager to the ground.

Tripp started yelling and blubbering about all the blood and guts dripping all over him, but the giant was so big and heavy that Tripp couldn't wriggle out from underneath his body. I grinned. Maybe it was wrong, but I got quite a bit of satisfaction out of hearing Tripp squeal.

Clarissa immediately crossed the vault and threw herself into my arms. "Thank you! Thank you for saving us!"

She hugged me tight once, twice, three times. Most folks probably would have thought she was clinging to me for comfort, but I knew better.

Amused, I let her hang on to me for a few more seconds, then drew back and gently put my gun up against her heart.

Clarissa froze, one of her hands still curled around my neck. "What—what are you doing?"

"Oh, please," I said. "Cut the act. How much longer were you going to keep hugging me before you stabbed me with that knife? Hmm? Where was it, by the way? I'm guessing tucked into the small of your back underneath your suit jacket. That's where my sister keeps one of her knives."

Clarissa stepped back, a knife clenched in her right hand that looked eerily similar to the blades that Gin used. The only difference was that hers would have been buried in my back in a few more seconds.

"How did you know?" she demanded.

"Your insistence on seeing the manager, for starters. Plus, you made far too many trips to the bank over the past few weeks simply to be squirreling jewelry away in a safety-deposit box. Even Mallory Parker doesn't have that many diamonds."

"Aren't you the detective," Clarissa muttered.

I grinned. "I do try."

"Mmm." Clarissa studied me, and a sly smile slowly spread across her face. "Well, I'm sure that we can come to some kind of arrangement . . ."

"Finn." I cheerfully supplied my name when it became apparent that she didn't remember it. "But I'm afraid it's too late for that. You underestimated me. Even worse, you bruised my ego, and there's just not enough money in the world to soothe Finnegan Lane's ego when it gets bruised. Especially not money stolen from my own bank. Sorry, Clarissa. Your impressive charm might have worked on Tripp, but I'm a tad bit smarter than he is."

Clarissa's eyes narrowed to slits. "And you should know exactly how good I am with this knife," she growled, flashing the blade at me. "I've killed more than one person with it over the years. I'll kill you with it too."

"I doubt that, since I'm the one holding the gun."

She eyed the weapon, which I'd lowered to my side once she'd backed away from me. "You really think you can get a shot off before I slit your throat? You're just a human, after all. Slow, weak, and plodding. I'm a vamp, so my reflexes are much better and faster than yours."

I shrugged. "Try me and find out."

We stared at each other. I might not have had enhanced senses like the vampire did, but I could still see her hand tightening around the knife, along with her weight shifting forward as she got ready to attack me.

Clarissa had just made the wrong choice—the very last choice of her life.

"Don't do it," I warned. "Crooked as you are, I'd still hate to kill you."

Clarissa smiled and crouched down like she was going to put the knife on the floor. But there was no warmth in her eyes, no give, no surrender. Her hand tightened a little more around the hilt, and she launched herself at me, the blade slashing through the air—

I snapped up my gun and shot her three times in the chest.

Clarissa staggered back, and the force of the bullets slammed her body up against one of the vault walls. She hung there a moment, suspended in midair, before her limbs crumpled, and she slowly slid to the floor.

I waited a few seconds to make sure Clarissa was dead, then walked over and crouched down next to her. Despite the blood splattered all over her, I could still smell her perfume—that light, sweet honeysuckle scent, now horribly, irrevocably tinged with copper.

Even in death, she was still one of the most beautiful women I had ever seen.

"What a waste," I murmured. "What a waste of your life."

Then I stepped over Clarissa's body and headed out of the vault to deal with the rest of the mess she had left behind.

Tangled Dreams

This story takes place after *Venom*, book 3.

Part One ~ Jo-Jo Deveraux

The knock on my front door came just before midnight.

Most folks would have already been tucked in their beds fast asleep, but I'd had a dream that she'd run into trouble tonight, so I'd waited up for her. I glanced at the cloud-shaped clock on the wall. Gin was late—an hour later than I'd expected her to arrive.

Then again, no psychic was perfect, especially not me.

The knock sounded again, a little harder and louder this time. Gin was the most patient person I'd ever met, but she hadn't even given me time to get up out of my chair, much less get to the door. She must be hurt badly.

I put down the beauty magazine I was reading and left the kitchen. It was a cold, snowy night, and my old house creaked, cracked, and moaned as the December wind howled around it like a pack of wolves. The sounds matched the *snap, crackle,* and *pop-pop-pop* of my bones as I shuffled toward the front of the house. Two hundred fifty-seven years of living would take its toll on anybody, even an Air elemental dwarf like me.

I opened the front door without bothering to peer through the peephole. I knew exactly who was out there and what she wanted—what she always *needed*, whenever she came calling in the blackest hours of the night.

Sure enough, Gin Blanco slumped against the side of the house, blood slipping off the fingers of her left hand. *Drip-drip-drip*.

A small scarlet puddle had already formed on the white boards next to her black boots. Sometimes it seemed like I spent more time painting over the blood that Gin left on the front porch than I did doing people's nails in my beauty salon in the back of the house. But I didn't mind the extra work. I loved the girl like she was my own.

In a way, Gin was the daughter I'd never had—the dark, dangerous daughter of my dreams. The one who was always surrounded by so much blood and so many bodies as the assassin the Spider.

I'd left the porch light on, and I stepped outside so I could get a better look at her. Despite the vision I'd had of Gin being injured, she was in worse shape than I'd expected. Blood and bruises coated her face like makeup, and one of her eyes had already blackened and puffed up like a proud purple peacock.

I couldn't see what other injuries she had beneath her fleece jacket, but I was willing to bet she had a few bruised ribs, given the fact that she had her right arm wrapped around her waist. Maybe a knife wound too, with all that copper-scented blood still dripping off her left fingers. Either way, I needed to start healing her—now.

Some of my concern must have flashed in my eyes, because Gin smiled. Even her teeth were crimson-coated, showing me just how bad a beating she'd taken.

"Aw, don't look so worried, Jo-Jo," Gin drawled. "This is

nothing. You should see the other guys."

With those light, cheerful words, Gin's gray eyes rolled up into the back of her head, and she passed out.

I jerked forward and caught Gin before her head slammed into the porch. She didn't need a concussion on top of everything else. I put my arm under her shoulders, hefted her upright, and pulled her into the house. To most folks, she would have felt like deadweight, but my dwarven strength made it easy for me to maneuver her around like she was as light as a rag doll.

Another gust of wind and snow zipped in through the front door before I was able to shut it, and the cold snapped Gin awake. She opened her eyes and sighed.

"Sorry about the blood on the porch," she murmured. "I know you just repainted it—again."

I'd repainted it twice, actually. The first time after Gin came in one night after Elliot Slater had almost beaten her to death at Ashland Community College and the second when she'd returned a few days later after killing some of Slater's men and taking several hard licks herself in the process.

"That's all right, darling," I replied. "Let's get you into the salon so I can take a better look at you."

I hauled Gin down a long hallway that opened up into a room that took up the back half of the house. As Jolene "Jo-Jo" Deveraux, I ran an old-fashioned beauty salon that catered to clients in Ashland and beyond. Air elemental magic like mine was great for smoothing out wrinkles and fighting the ravages of sun, time, genetics, and everything else that took its toll on a person's appearance.

Padded cherry-red swivel chairs filled my salon, along with a variety of hair dryers, combs, scissors, and curling irons. Stacks of beauty magazines littered the tables, along with tubs of makeup and bottles of nail polish, most of which were some shade of pink, my favorite color. The harsh aroma of perms, hair dyes, and other chemicals filled the air, softened a bit by the vanilla-scented lotions, ointments, and other items I saturated with my Air magic and then used in various skin, hair, and nail treatments.

I eased Gin down onto one of the salon chairs and helped her lean back and make herself comfortable. Then I went over to the sink along the wall and washed my hands. Of course, I wouldn't be touching Gin to heal her—not exactly—but I still soaped up my fingers as thoroughly as a surgeon would. It was a quirk my mama had instilled in me when I was a girl—a lady always has clean hands.

Rosco, my beloved basset hound, cracked his brown eyes open from his basket in the corner of the room. When he realized that I didn't have any treats, he shut his eyes and went back to his dream of chasing rabbits.

Most folks thought Rosco was just plain lazy, but really, the dog knew what the important things in life were: food, sleep, and getting his tummy rubbed. If there wasn't a good chance of one of those things happening, then Rosco usually decided to conserve his energy until a better opportunity presented itself. Smartest dog I'd ever had.

I turned off the water and dried my hands. Then I dragged a freestanding light over to Gin, turned it on, and sat down on a low stool next to her.

"Did you run into some more of Mab Monroe's men?" I asked, peering at her battered face.

Mab was the cruel, vicious Fire elemental who'd murdered Gin's family, and Gin had vowed to kill Mab—or die trying. Of course, Gin didn't think I knew about the *die trying* part. Then again, she didn't think I knew about a lot of things.

She shrugged and then winced as a new wave of pain flooded her body at the motion. "No, I didn't run into Mab's men. It was a fluke, really. I was taking out the last bag of trash for the day and stepped out into the alley behind the Pork Pit. I heard screams, so naturally, I went to investigate."

"Naturally," I drawled.

Gin was just as curious as Fletcher Lane, her assassin mentor and my old friend, had been before his murder a few months ago. Fletcher had been an assassin himself—the Tin Man—and he'd taught Gin everything she knew about killing people, which was why she was still breathing tonight. More than anything else, Fletcher had taught Gin how to be a survivor, something she needed in the wild and wicked ole world of Ashland.

"Anyway," Gin continued, "I followed the sounds of the screams around the corner, and I saw six guys carjacking a mom and her little girl on one of the side streets. They knocked the mom unconscious, and the girl couldn't have been more than two, three tops. So I decided to do the cops a favor and take them out, just like the restaurant's trash."

"Then what happened?" I asked, gesturing for Gin to sit up so I could peel off her bloody jacket.

When I finished, she fell back against the chair, panting from the movement. It took her a few seconds to get her breath back.

"Then I jumped them," Gin replied. "Only they were a mix of dwarves and vampires, and a little tougher and stronger than I'd expected. Still, I was holding my own, until one of them got in a lucky shot on my face with a tire iron. I went down, and they piled on, punching and kicking me. One of them even sliced my arm with a switchblade, but he got too close, and I was able to take him out with one of my knives. After that, the rest were easy pickings. Well, except for the last guy. He clocked me with the tire iron again, then ran away before I could finish him off with the rest of his buddies."

"Oh, I wouldn't worry about the one who got away." I had a good idea where the sixth man was going to be in a few minutes. I'd seen that in my dream too.

Gin looked at me, suspicion flaring in her eyes. "Why do

you say it like that? Did you have one of your visions?"

Gin knew that I was something of a psychic, with a bit of precognition. In addition to tapping into and controlling all the natural gases in the atmosphere, Air elementals could also hear all the whispers of what might be in the wind around us. What Gin didn't know was that I had dreams too—vivid, vivid dreams. About her, about Mab Monroe, about their final, inevitable confrontation. Among other things.

I'd never told Gin about the true depth and clarity of my visions, though. She was better off not knowing some things. Besides, she had enough to worry about right now, since she'd used her alter ego the Spider to declare war on Mab. Also on Gin's mind was her younger sister, Bria, who was finally back in town and a detective on the police force to boot—one who wanted to bring both Mab *and* the Spider to justice.

"Jo-Jo?" Gin asked, interrupting my thoughts. "Did you see something about the guy who escaped?"

"Not really," I fibbed. "I just had a feeling, that's all. Don't worry. I don't think your missing carjacker will get far."

"Well, he shouldn't," Gin said. "Finn was eating a late dinner at the Pork Pit and came out into the alley to see what was taking me so long. He called Xavier and got the giant to come over and take the mom and the little girl to the hospital. Finn wanted to drive me over here to the salon, but I said I could make it myself and sent him out to look for the last carjacker. And of course, Sophia was working her usual shift at the restaurant. She was cleaning up the blood when I left."

Finnegan Lane was Fletcher's son and Gin's foster brother, while Xavier was one of Gin's friends who worked as both a cop and a bouncer. Sophia Deveraux was my younger sister, who disposed of many of the bodies Gin left behind as the Spider.

We might not all be related by blood, but we were a family, and we always looked out for and took care of each other.

Which is what I needed to do for Gin right now.

I raised my right hand and reached for my Air magic. I didn't know what other elementals' power felt like to them, but mine was as cool and refreshing as an autumn breeze kissing my face. My palm began to glow an opaque buttermilk white, and I didn't have to look into the salon mirrors to know that the same magical light filled my eyes.

"Now, hold still, darling," I warned. "Because this is going to hurt before it gets better."

I leaned toward Gin and held my glowing palm over her battered face. Back and forth, I moved my hand over her features, grabbing hold of the natural oxygen in the air and forcing it into her body, making the healing gas circulate through her wounds, clean out the cuts, and draw the ragged edges of her skin back together again. Once the bruises and swelling had faded and her face looked the way it was supposed to look again, I moved on to her cracked ribs, the knife wound on her arm, and the rest of her injuries.

Gin hissed the whole time I used my magic. She usually did. Low and steady, like a teakettle that was almost ready to let out a final high, piercing whistle. My Air magic was the opposite of her own Ice and Stone power, and Gin had said more than once that it always felt like I was stabbing her with red-hot needles whenever I healed her.

I'd never told her that I could feel her magic too.

To me, Gin's Ice and Stone magic was a cold, concrete shell that coated her from the inside out. More than once over the years, I'd reached out with my own Air power, testing it against hers and trying to break through that protective shell.

I had failed every single time.

Gin simply had no idea how strong she was as an elemental— or how much stronger she was going to become as she aged and her magic kept growing and growing. If I told her, it might scare, worry, or upset her.

Mab Monroe had used her Fire magic to murder Gin's mother, Eira Snow, despite the fact that Eira had been a powerful Ice elemental. As a result, Gin simply didn't trust her own Ice and Stone magic, didn't think it would be strong enough to help her defeat Mab. But she was going to find out soon enough on her own. About that and a lot of other things—all the things I'd dreamed about over the years.

"There," I said, dropping my hand and releasing my magic when I'd healed the last of her wounds. "All better."

Gin let out a long, shuddering sigh, unclenched her blood-stained fingers from the arms of the salon chair, and closed her eyes. All the tension went out of her then, like water swirling down a drain. I knew it was because I'd quit using my magic, and she didn't have to feel it anymore, instead of the pain of her injuries finally being gone.

"Sleep now, darling," I murmured, smoothing a strand of her dark brown hair back from her sweaty face.

Being healed by an Air elemental always drained a person, as the brain struggled to catch up and realize that the body wasn't on the brink of death anymore. Given the severity of her injuries and the amount of magic I'd used to heal them, Gin would sleep for several hours, maybe more—as long as nothing else happened tonight to disturb her.

"Okay," she said in a tired voice, finally giving in to the inevitable. "I'll do that."

She was asleep before I got up from my stool.

I covered Gin with a soft fleece blanket, then went back over to the sink and washed my hands again. I dried my hands off and stared at my reflection in the mirror. My skin was pale, and my eyes were clear, almost colorless, really, except for the tiny pinprick of black in the center of my irises. My white-blond hair was rolled up in pink sponge curlers for the night, and I wore one of my many pink housecoats, topped off by a string of pearls that hung from my neck.

I reached up and stroked the large white beads. My mama, Jodie, had never had a string of pearls, though she'd often wished for them. But we'd been far too poor for that. Even things like shoes and socks had been luxuries at times, and I'd gone barefoot through more than one winter. I looked down at my bare toes. Something I continued to do to this day, though by choice, since I'd long ago amassed more money than I could ever spend, thanks to my salon's success.

I'd just never cared much for socks. They always seemed to fall down around my ankles, and I got tired of constantly yanking them back up. So these days, I just went without them more often than not. Besides, I was a tough old dwarf. Cold feet didn't bother me.

While Gin slept in the salon, I headed into the kitchen to put on a pot of chicory coffee for Finn. He'd be here sooner or later to check on Gin. So would Sophia, after she cleaned up the carjackers' blood and bodies.

I got out the fancy coffee maker Finn had bought me for Christmas last year, then pulled a heavy cast-iron skillet out of a cabinet. Even though it was late, I felt like making some corn bread. I had a jar of sourwood honey I'd gotten from Warren T. Fox, one of Fletcher's friends, which would add the perfect touch of sweetness to the bread when it came out of the oven. Gin might be the best cook in the family, but I could hold my own—at least when it came to corn bread.

I'd just reached back into the cabinet for the cornmeal when the front door screeched open. A few seconds later, footsteps scuffed on the floor, and a menacing shadow appeared in the doorway. I turned to look at the intruder in my house and smiled.

"Why, hello there," I drawled. "I've been expecting you."

The shadow stepped forward, congealing into the shape of a man. A tire iron dangled from his right hand, which was no doubt what he'd used to pry open the front door and barge into my house. He was short, right at five feet tall, and a dwarf with thick, powerful muscles, just like me.

I eyed his biceps, which looked like they were about to pop out of his black leather jacket. No wonder Gin had had problems taking him down. Dwarves were always hard to kill, even for a skilled assassin. Our heavy musculature often made it tough to do much damage with traditional weapons like guns and knives. Most dwarves could even take a couple of blasts of elemental magic to the chest and keep on going.

"Let me guess," I said. "You're here for the woman, right? The one who killed all your friends?"

In my dream, I'd not only seen Gin bruised and bloody, but I'd also seen the dwarf breaking into my house, hoping to finish what he'd started and beat her to death. But I wasn't about to let that happen, so I closed the cabinet door and put my hand down on the counter, right next to my corn bread skillet.

"You got it, lady," the dwarf snarled. "I followed her all the way from that stupid barbecue restaurant downtown. Tell me where she is, and I might let you live."

Despite his threats, I felt vaguely sorry for him. Poor fellow. He had no idea who he was dealing with. I might not be as deadly as Gin Blanco was as the Spider, but Jo-Jo Deveraux could take care of herself. I'd lived through the Great Depression and a host of other bad things over the years. An armed intruder in my house was nothing compared to all that.

"I don't think so," I replied in a mild voice. "You have two choices. You can turn around, skedaddle out of my house, and leave Ashland forever right now. If you do that, well, I can't promise that you'll have a long and happy life, but you'll at least have a few more years left to terrorize folks."

His dark eyes narrowed. "And what's my second choice?"

I fixed him with a hard stare. "Or you can die right here and now in my kitchen."

The dwarf stared at me for a moment. Then he smiled, show-ing off his crooked teeth. He sauntered toward me, casually swinging the tire iron back and forth. When he was right in front of me, he stopped and sneered at me again.

"You know what? I think I'll have some fun with you first before I find that other bitch."

I nodded. "Have it your way, then."

"Oh," he practically purred, "don't worry. I will."

He reached for the front of my housecoat, and I snatched up my cast-iron skillet and slammed it into his face.

The blow surprised the dwarf, who staggered back. But it didn't put him down. Not even close. He was a tough old dwarf, just like I was.

"Bitch!" he hissed, rubbing the red welt that had risen on his left cheek. "You're going to pay for that!"

He growled and lashed out at me with the tire iron. His weapon *clanged* against my skillet, shooting sparks every-where. I ignored the flickers of light, grabbed the pot from Finn's fancy coffee maker off the counter with my free hand, and smashed it into the dwarf's head. Glass rained down on both of us and tinkled across the floor like we were stepping on piano keys.

The dwarf finally realized that I wasn't just going to lie down and die, and he got serious about attacking me. Back and forth, we moved through the kitchen, him trying to hit me with his tire iron and me blocking his attacks with my skillet. I got in a couple more good whacks before the dwarf managed to knock the skillet out of my hands.

A triumphant smile curved his lips. "Now what are you gonna do?"

"Nothing much," I drawled back. "Just this."

I lifted my right hand and aimed it at his mouth. Then I reached for my Air magic and sucked all the oxygen out of his lungs.

I hadn't used my magic to start with for fear of the sudden influx of power waking Gin. The noise of my fight with the dwarf probably wouldn't penetrate her deep, dark sleep, but the feel of my magic surging through the house was one of the few things that might snap her wide awake.

Gin needed her rest, but if she heard me and the dwarf struggling, then she would charge in here trying to help me and probably get hurt all over again. I didn't want that to happen, but I couldn't beat the dwarf any other way now.

The dwarf's eyes bulged in confusion, and it took him a few seconds to realize what was happening. He coughed and clawed at his throat, as if that would somehow put all that precious oxygen back into his lungs. When that didn't work, he raised his tire iron and staggered forward, trying to hit me and get me to release my magic.

Too little, too late.

He fell to the floor at my feet—unconscious—and the tire iron tumbled end over end across the kitchen floor. As tough as we were, as much of a physical beating as we could take, even dwarves needed oxygen. Take that away, and we weren't nearly as strong—or as difficult to kill.

But the job wasn't quite finished, as Gin would say. Oh, I could have held on to my Air magic until the dwarf was completely suffocated, but every second I used my power increased the risk that Gin would feel my magic, wake up, and stumble into the kitchen to investigate. So I released my power, got down on my knees beside the dwarf, grabbed my skillet, and went to work.

It took me several solid whacks, but his skull finally cracked open. I only stopped hitting him when there was more blood on the floor than there was left in his head.

When I was sure he was dead, I set the skillet aside and pushed myself up to my feet, my bones once again snapping, cracking, and popping. I stood there over the dwarf's body, breathing a little harder than I would have liked. No doubt about it, I was getting older, but I was still strong and tough enough to take care of my family, and that was all that really mattered.

"Jo-Jo?" Gin's soft, sleep-filled voice drifted out of the salon. "Is everything okay? I thought I heard a noise."

"Everything's fine, darling," I called back in a light, cheery tone. "I just dropped a skillet on the floor. You go back to sleep, now, you hear?"

"Okay, if you're sure . . ." Gin's voice trailed off, indicating that she was sinking back down into the restful darkness. Good.

I looked around at the mess in the kitchen. During our struggle, the dwarf and I had knocked over everything from the supper dishes that had been on the table to the oven mitts that had been beside the stove to the towels embroidered with my personal cloud rune that had been piled next to the sink.

I shifted my weight, and something crunched under my bare feet—glass from Finn's fancy coffeepot. The shining shards littered the floor like splintered flakes of snow. He would be more upset that I'd broken his expensive gadget than about anything else, including the blood that had spattered everywhere. Finn would be here soon, though, and so would Sophia. They'd help me clean up the mess before Gin woke up again and realized what had happened.

There was nothing to do but wait for them, so I went over to the sink and washed the dwarf's blood off my hands, making sure that I scrubbed every single speck of it away. I dried off my hands with a clean dish towel and righted one of the overturned chairs. Then, I picked up my beauty magazine from where it had fallen to the floor, settled myself at the table, and started reading again.

A lady always has clean hands, even when there's a dead body cooling on her kitchen floor.

Tangled Dreams

Part Two ~ Sophia Deveraux

"I'm sorry I made such a mess," Jo-Jo said in a sweet, apologetic tone. "I tried to reason with him, but of course, he wouldn't listen, so it had to be done."

"I think *mess* is a bit of an understatement, don't you, Sophia?" Finn looked at me with his bright green eyes.

"Big mess," I agreed in my low, raspy voice.

And it was. Jo-Jo had pretty much demolished the kitchen in her struggle with the dwarf who'd broken into our house and come looking for Gin.

Trampled magazines, smashed dishes, and tattered dish towels littered the floor, while Jo-Jo's favorite cast-iron skillet rested in the pool of blood that had oozed out from underneath the dwarf's head. I sighed. No fresh, hot corn bread for us tonight.

"I can't believe you broke my espresso machine," Finn said in a sad, woeful tone, bending over and picking up something from the mess on the floor. Jagged glass jutted out from the curved black handle in his hand. "How am I supposed to make my chicory coffee now?"

"You'll live, darling," Jo-Jo replied. "First thing in the morning, we'll go and get you a brand-new coffeepot."

Finn sniffed. "It's not a *mere* coffeepot. It's a state-of-the-art, top-of-the-line espresso machine that makes every coffee drink you could imagine. It's part of Bella Bulluci's new housewares line."

Jo-Jo shook her head and looked at me, but I just grinned in return. We all knew that Finn couldn't function without his coffee, and he'd pout about the broken espresso machine the rest of the night.

"Well, we'd better start cleaning up before Gin wakes up and wonders what happened," Jo-Jo said. "Sophia, do you mind? I know you've had a long night already, taking care of the bodies of those other carjackers."

Air elemental magic ran in the Deveraux family, but Jo-Jo and I each wielded our power in very different ways. My sister used her magic to heal, to sew ripped skin and knit broken bones back together again.

I used my magic to tear things apart, to grind them into dust and scatter the pieces on the wind. Blood, skin, tendons, bone. Air magic could disintegrate all those things and more just as easily as it could glue them back together again.

And our magic wasn't the only way in which we were polar opposites. Jo-Jo was more than a century older than my one hundred thirteen years and had already slipped into middle age, at least for a dwarf. Jo-Jo also loved soft, feminine things, like her white pearls and pink-flowered dresses. I was happiest when wearing one of my Goth outfits of boots, jeans, and a T-shirt. The look matched the darkness in my heart, along with all the pain and sorrow that dwelled there—

"Sophia?" Jo-Jo asked in a soft voice, pulling me out of my musings.

I shrugged. "One more body in the trunk won't hurt."

It was the longest sentence I'd spoken all day, and the harsh syllables grated against my ears the way they always did. Every word I uttered strained my vocal cords, which had been ruined long ago—not to mention the awful noise of me actually speaking. My voice sounded like a rusty engine that whined and whined and just wouldn't start, no matter how hard you turned the key in the ignition. And that was on a good day.

The old, familiar sadness sparked in Jo-Jo's eyes as she listened to me. She had repeatedly offered to use her Air magic to fix my broken voice, but I always refused. My ruined vocal cords were my mark of survival, just like the spider-rune scars branded into Gin's palms were hers. My voice and her scars might not be pretty, but they were reminders of what we'd been through, of everything we'd suffered through and come out the other side stronger from.

"I'll get to work," I rasped.

Jo-Jo gave me a grim smile, as if she knew exactly what I was thinking about. "Yes, it's time for all of us to get to work."

Jo-Jo and Finn concentrated on cleaning up the glass and other debris, while I got down on my knees and tackled the smears and splashes of blood on the kitchen floor.

I still had on the heavy black coveralls I'd donned at the Pork Pit before I'd gone out to load up the bodies of the carjackers Gin had killed, so a little more blood on them wouldn't hurt. I had dozens of pairs of coveralls just like these, and all of them had had someone's blood on them at one point or another. Usually, more than one person's at a time, thanks to Gin's prowess as the Spider.

While Jo-Jo and Finn swept, straightened, and talked in low voices, I stretched out my right hand and reached for my Air magic. I'd always thought of my power as a heavy black cloud, one that swallowed up all the ugliness I saw and replaced it with something fresh, clean, and good. Like a cold March wind blowing in a fierce thunderstorm and just as quickly pushing it on out, leaving behind a clear blue sky and a beautiful spring day.

Back and forth and back and forth, I moved my right index finger over every bit of blood that coated the floor. Slowly, the crimson puddles dried up, as though they'd been on the floor for days instead of just a few minutes. The stains turned a rusty brown, then got darker and brittle-looking as I used all the natural gases in the air to break down the blood into minuscule molecules and then sweep them away. It didn't take long. Like Gin and Jo-Jo, I was strong in my magic.

When the floor was spick-and-span, I moved on to the counters and the cabinets, giving them the same attention until the whole kitchen looked like it had been professionally cleaned from top to bottom. Only one thing left to do: get rid of the dwarf's body, along with those of his carjacker friends.

"Dump time," I told Jo-Jo.

She nodded. "I'll rustle up some breakfast for when you get back."

I walked through the house and stepped out onto the front porch, where I'd put the dwarf's body so it wouldn't be in the way while we cleaned the kitchen. Finn followed me. I tossed him my car keys, then bent down and hefted the dead dwarf over my shoulder. Finn opened the trunk of my black convertible and let out a low whistle at the five bodies already stuffed inside.

"Good thing some of them were dwarves," he said. "Otherwise, they might not have all fit in there."

"Mmm-hmm," I agreed.

I threw the dead dwarf on top of the other carjackers, then arranged his arms and legs in such a way that I could close the trunk lid. When that was done, I went around to the front of the car and slid into the driver's seat.

"Do you need some help?" Finn asked, handing me the keys. My skull-and-crossbones key chain glinted a ghostly silver in the moonlight. "Want me to drive you or something?"

I shook my head. I always preferred to do this part alone.

"Okay, then," he said, stepping back and shutting the car door. "Happy body dumping."

I grinned at him, then cranked the engine and drove away.

I steered my convertible with its trunkful of dead men over to the old Ashland Rock Quarry. The abandoned quarry was a popular place to dump bodies, not just with me but with a lot of folks, since it was full of rocky outcroppings and hidden caves. You could slide a body into some of them, and it wouldn't be found for years, if ever. Plus, you could always drive up to the top of the quarry and heave someone over the side. The fall and resulting splatter made it tougher for the coroners to determine exactly how someone had died—and who they were to start with, if you wanted to obscure your victim's identity.

The quarry might be one of the best places to get rid of the bad folks Gin killed as the Spider, but I didn't use it exclusively. That was the beauty of living in Ashland. There were hundreds of hidden hollers, secret trails, and other quiet spots that made perfect graves.

And I knew them all.

I parked my convertible about half a mile out from the quarry, under a stand of maple trees, and then spent the next two hours hauling the bodies over to the spot I wanted, a deep crevice in the rocky ground that would hide the dead men from sight. A few scraggly pines had stubbornly staked out their claims on the rim of the rocky opening, and their sad, drooping branches would further camouflage the bodies. The moon was full, so I didn't need to risk using a flashlight to see what I was doing. It was cold too, and even the animals were quiet tonight, safe and warm in their nests and dens.

When I'd gotten the bodies where I wanted them, I climbed down into the crevice, stripped off the dead men's clothes and shoes, and put them into a garbage bag I'd brought along for the purpose. The cotton, leather, and rubber would all get burned in our old woodstove when I got back to the salon. I also fished the cash out of their wallets and slid it into an envelope, which I tucked into a pocket inside my coveralls. I'd anonymously donate the money to one of the local homeless shelters, just like I always did. Lots of folks in Ashland needed a helping hand, and these men certainly couldn't spend the money wherever they were going.

When I was done, I climbed up out of the crack and peered down at the men, making sure I hadn't left anything behind. Some folks might have taken the time to throw some dirt over the bodies, but I figured the animals deserved to eat too. I'd come back in a few weeks when the bones were stripped bare and use my Air magic to dissolve them into powder that the wind would whisk away, just like I did to all the other bodies I'd gotten rid of over the years, first for Fletcher and now for Gin.

It was the least I could do after everything Fletcher had done for me—after he'd rescued me from the awful thing that had happened, after he'd risked himself to save me. Jo-Jo and I had both been so grateful that we'd pledged our Air magic to Fletcher for life, Jo-Jo to heal him and me to clean up after he eliminated someone as the Tin Man. It was a pact, a promise, that I'd never regretted.

When Gin had taken over the assassination business from Fletcher, we'd switched our services over to her. She wasn't quite on the same path that Fletcher had been on, doing the same good that he'd done, but she'd get there soon enough. Jo-Jo had told me that she'd seen it in her dreams.

I didn't have dreams of the future like my sister did. Not exactly. Instead, I got flashes off people, the living and most especially the dead, flashes of who and what they'd been in their lives, of all the things they'd done, and of all the things they *would* have done if they'd still been breathing.

As I looked down at the men, a tangle of images filled my mind. The men laughing, their hands curled into fists, the sharp sounds of glass breaking and a woman screaming. And I knew that the dead men would have severely beaten that woman, and her young daughter too, maybe even killed them, if Gin hadn't come along tonight—just the way they'd done to all the other people they'd carjacked in recent months.

The images faded away, but I stayed where I was, listening to the echoes of the screams in my head. Or maybe they were the memories of my own screams, back before my voice had been ruined. It was hard to tell sometimes.

Either way, these men were dead, and they'd never hurt anyone again. A smile curved my lips at the thought.

"Good riddance," I rasped, and walked back to my car.

By the time I left the rock quarry and returned home, the sun was rising over the eastern ridges of the mountains. I parked my convertible in the driveway, got out, and stopped a moment to admire the pleasing purples and graceful grays that streaked the sky like fingers slowly brushing aside the darkness.

The dawn always gave me hope that someday the darkness in me would finally lighten too.

I stepped inside the house. The smell and sizzle of frying bacon filled the air, along with the clanking and clattering of dishes.

"Breakfast in ten minutes," Jo-Jo called out.

She'd timed things perfectly, the way she always did, thanks to her Air magic. I went upstairs to one of the bathrooms, stripped off my boots and bloody coveralls, and took a hot shower. I pulled my wet black hair back into a ponytail and threw on a fresh pair of black socks, boots, and jeans.

I topped off my outfit with a black T-shirt covered with pink puckered lips and a pink leather collar studded with crystal hearts. I also covered my lids with a glittery pearl-pink shadow that brightened up my black eyes and put a similarly colored gloss on my lips. Maybe it was knowing that Gin had saved that woman and little girl from being beaten by the carjackers, but I felt strangely cheerful this morning, as warm and bright as the cracks of sun slicing in through the windows.

I headed downstairs to the kitchen. Finn was already sitting at the butcher's block table, sipping a steaming cup of chicory coffee. I arched an eyebrow at the sight.

"While you were dumping the bodies, I took the liberty of going out and buying a new coffeepot," he said, grinning. "It's not as good as the one Jo-Jo broke, but it will do for now."

"Mmm." I gave him a noncommittal grunt, although I leaned over and rumpled his walnut-colored hair.

Finn grinned a little wider and sipped some more coffee.

I sat down next to him, and Jo-Jo slid a plate piled high with scrambled eggs, bacon, and chocolate-chip pancakes in front of me, along with a glass of pomegranate juice. I breathed in, enjoying the sweet and salty scents mixing with the dark caffeine warmth of Finn's coffee.

"Any problems with the bodies?" Jo-Jo asked, fixing her own plate and taking a seat across from me.

"Nope."

I'd just picked up my fork when footsteps sounded, and Gin stepped into the kitchen. She'd taken a shower as well, washing off all the blood from last night, and was wearing a clean pair of sneakers, along with jeans and a long-sleeved blue T-shirt that featured the Pork Pit logo of a pig holding a platter of food.

"Mmm-mmm-mmm. Something smells good," Gin said.

"Help yourself, darling," Jo-Jo said. "I thought I'd do you a favor and fix breakfast this morning."

Gin dished out some eggs, bacon, and pancakes, then joined Finn, Jo-Jo, and me at the table. We all focused on our food, but once the first helpings had been gulped down, Gin turned to me.

"Any problems with the bodies?" she echoed Jo-Jo's earlier question.

I huffed in amusement. I'd been getting rid of bodies far longer than she'd been killing people as the Spider.

"So that's a no," she murmured. "What about the last guy? The sixth carjacker who ran away? Any sign of him?"

Finn and Jo-Jo exchanged a guarded glance, but my lips twitched with amusement. Nope, no signs of him. Not now, after I'd sandblasted the kitchen clean with my Air magic and dumped his body somewhere it would never be found. I had no doubt that the crows and other critters in the rock quarry were already taking care of all the carjackers' bodies and having just as fine a breakfast as we were. All in all, it had been a good night's work.

"Don't worry," Finn piped up, a grin creasing his handsome face. "It's all been taken care of."

"Taken care of?" Gin asked, a suspicious note creeping into her voice. "How?"

"Oh, Sophia and I found the last guy's body a few streets over from the Pork Pit," Finn lied in an easy tone. "You must have done more damage than you'd thought, because he'd already bled out by the time we got there."

Gin frowned. "But I don't remember so much as nicking him with one of my knives."

Finn shrugged. "Well, you must have, because he was dead. Looked like you caught him in the leg and severed an artery. Sophia loaded him into the trunk of her car with the other bad guys, drove them all off to parts unknown, and did her thing. Problem solved."

Gin's gray eyes narrowed, and I could almost see the wheels turning in her mind. Finn kept grinning at her, completely unconcerned by her cold, suspicious stare. That boy could lie better than anyone I'd ever seen. Sometimes I thought he could smile and talk his way out of anything, even his own death.

Jo-Jo kept cutting her pancakes up into small, dainty bites, as though she didn't have a care in the world. I followed her example and crunched down on another piece of crispy, salty, smoky bacon. Mmm. So good.

"Well, problem solved, I suppose." Gin shrugged and started eating again.

When she got up and went over to the stove for seconds, Jo-Jo, Finn, and I all shared a conspiratorial grin, the secret of what had really happened tangling up in the threads of all the others we shared and binding us that much closer together.

As friends—and as a family too.

Tangled Schemes

This story takes place after *Venom*, book 3.

Bria Coolidge

"Tell me everything you know about the Spider."

Hildie Mallas popped another pretzel into her mouth. She took her sweet time chewing the salty snack, then knocked back a long swallow of beer. Hildie smacked her lips to get rid of the foam that speckled them and reached for another pretzel, like she hadn't even heard my question.

I grabbed the plastic bowl of stale pretzels and pulled them away from her. "I want to know everything you know about the assassin the Spider—*right now*."

Hildie looked at me through bleary, bloodshot eyes that stood out like brown marbles in her pale face. Her dull blond hair hung in flat, limp strands around her face and just brushed the collar of her shiny, black vinyl jacket.

We were in a bar not too far away from Southtown. Hildie had suggested we meet here, and the establishment was exactly what I'd expected it to be: small, cramped, and seedy.

Even though it was just after three in the afternoon, the dingy plastic blinds on the windows were closed, shutting out the weak December sun and making it seem much darker and later in the day than it really was. Twangy country music alternately wailed and sputtered from a battered, flickering jukebox in the back corner. Most of the patrons lounging at the scarred wooden tables wore leather pants and jackets that marked them as bikers, although a few sported cowboy hats and boots instead. Almost everyone had a drink in one hand and a cigarette in the other, and smoke hung in thick blue clouds over the wooden bar that ran down one wall.

Once I was sure that no one was more interested in our conversation than they should be, I turned back to Hildie. "You didn't answer my question."

She shifted on her stool and took another swig of beer. Hildie Mallas was an informant, a small-time petty crook who occasionally snitched on others when the price was right. A couple of days ago, she'd contacted me claiming that she had information on the Spider. Everyone in the city was talking about the Spider these days, ever since the assassin had declared war on Mab Monroe, the Fire elemental who was the head of the city's underworld.

As a detective with the Ashland Police Department, I had a sworn duty to find the Spider and bring her to justice for all the crimes she'd committed. No matter what.

But I didn't know what to do, or especially how to *feel*, about the fact that the Spider also happened to be my older sister, Genevieve Snow. The girl I'd seen Mab torture the night the Fire elemental had murdered our mother, Eira, and our older sister, Annabella. The girl I'd thought Mab had killed that night, just like the Fire elemental had wanted to kill me.

Guilt churned in my stomach the way it always did whenever

I thought of that awful night—and the cowardly thing I'd done to survive it.

"Just relax, will ya, Detective Coolidge?" Hildie replied in a low, raspy voice. "I told you that I don't know anything but that my friend does. She'll be here soon, and she'll be expecting the cash reward you've been promising for the info."

Her eyes glittered with greedy interest, and I bit back a tired sigh. In other words, the mystery woman expected to be paid, probably for false information, and Hildie no doubt expected a cut as well. But it was my own fault, really. I wanted to find the Spider, wanted to find *Genevieve*, so badly that I'd started offering cash for any information about her. My own money, taken from the trust fund my adoptive parents had set up for me years ago.

So far, I'd gotten exactly nothing for my time, trouble, and money. No leads on whom the Spider was masquerading as, where she might strike next, or why she'd decided to go after Mab Monroe. Of course, I imagined that Genevieve wanted to kill Mab for murdering our family, as that was the most logical conclusion, but I wasn't sharing that information with the crooked cops on the force.

Knowing that my sister was the Spider and that we both had a grudge against Mab would make me even more of a target with the other members of the police department than I was already. Good, honest cops like me were a rarity in Ashland. From the newest rookies to the most seasoned officers, almost everybody on the force preferred to take money to look the other way and ignore all the criminals who crossed their paths. Cowards and traitors, the lot of 'em.

But my most pressing problems were that I didn't know what Genevieve looked like now, what name she might be using, or where she might be living in the city. It was like she was a ghost who just magically appeared, killed Mab's men, and vanished into thin air. Genevieve had always been smart, but she'd taken it to a whole new level as the Spider.

I didn't know whether that was good or bad.

Hildie must have sensed my frustration, because she grinned, revealing the small gap between her front teeth. "Don't worry, Detective," she repeated. "My friend will be here soon, and then she'll answer all your questions about the Spider."

I unclenched my tight fists and slowly smoothed my hands down my jeans, resisting the urge to grab Hildie and demand that she tell me everything she knew right now—if she even had any information to start with.

Still impatient, I plopped down on a stool at the corner of the bar not too far from where Hildie was sitting and signaled for the bartender to bring me a beer. I had no intention of drinking anything, but it was better to blend in. As much as I could, anyway, what with all the biker leather and cowboy hats.

The bartender put a dirty glass in front of me, his sharp movements making beer slosh over the side and fill in the jagged grooves in the wood. I laid a ten-dollar bill next to the spilled beer. The bartender swiped my money and headed on down the line to the next customer. He didn't offer me any change. Of course not.

I scooted the beer away and studied my reflection in the cracked mirror behind the bar. Blond hair, blue eyes, rosy skin, a navy coat worn over a matching sweater. Maybe it was the dim light or the clouds of choking smoke, but I looked tired— and I *felt* tired. I had for days now, but I was determined to see this thing through to the end, even if this meeting with Hildie and her mysterious friend was probably another waste of my time, energy, and money.

I made sure that my back was to the wall and that I had a clear view of everyone in the bar. Once that was done, there was nothing else to do but sit here and ignore the suspicious looks coming my way until Hildie's friend showed up.

Not for the first time, I considered how ironic it was that

Genevieve was using her childhood pendant as her assassin moniker. A spider rune, the symbol for patience.

Because me? I *hated* waiting.

It had all started with a plain brown envelope several weeks ago.

Someone had scrawled *Detective Bria Coolidge* across the envelope. Nothing unusual about that—except the fact that it had been delivered to my home in Blue Marsh and not the police station where I worked in Savannah, Georgia. I kept my home address private, for obvious reasons, so I looked closely at the spindly, spiderlike handwriting. I could have sworn I'd seen that same handwriting somewhere before, but the memory just wouldn't come to me.

Curious, I closed the front door, stood in the foyer, and carefully examined the envelope, wondering if someone had sent me a nasty surprise, since there was no return address. It had happened before. More than one criminal had thought they could scare me off a case by sending me photos of myself with a red bull's-eye painted on my forehead or by stuffing a dead rat into a box and wrapping it up to look like a present.

I ran my hands along the envelope. There wasn't much in it. A couple of sheets of paper, at most. No dead rats today. Hurray for small favors.

I went into the kitchen and pulled on the pair of rubber gloves that I kept by the sink so I wouldn't contaminate the envelope's contents with my fingerprints. Then I grabbed a knife out of one of the drawers and used it to slice open the end of the envelope.

A single photo was nestled inside. I pulled it out the wrong way and found myself looking at the back of the picture.

More handwriting was scribbled there: *This was taken in*

August in Ashland. She needs you, Bria, and you need her. It's time to come home.

It wasn't the most ominous note I'd ever gotten. In fact, there was nothing threatening about it at all. But for some reason, it made my heart pound and my palms sweat.

I flipped over the photo, and everything just . . . *stopped.*

A woman's right hand stretched out in the photo, her fingers splayed wide, like she'd been trying to block the camera, like she hadn't wanted to have her picture taken. But the angle of the shot gave me a crystal-clear view of the scar in the center of her palm. A small circle surrounded by eight thin rays.

A spider rune—my older sister Genevieve's rune.

All the air whooshed out of my lungs, and my knees buckled. I sagged against the kitchen counter, then slid down to the floor. The dirty dishes in the sink rattled at my sharp, sudden movements.

For the last seventeen years, I'd thought that Genevieve was *dead,* that Mab Monroe had killed her just like the Fire elemental had murdered our mother and older sister. I'd seen what Mab had done to Genevieve that night, how the Fire elemental had made my sister hold on to her own rune while Mab superheated the silverstone and branded it into her palms.

I'd heard Genevieve's screams, and I'd smelled the stench of her burning flesh. I'd thought no one could survive that much pain, not to mention the collapse of our house afterward, but this photo proved otherwise. I would have known Genevieve's spider rune anywhere—*anywhere.*

Metal dug into my palm, snapping me out of my memories. I was clutching my own rune, a primrose, the symbol for beauty. I wore the silverstone pendant on a chain around my neck, just like the rest of my family had worn theirs. My mother Eira's rune had been a snowflake, representing icy calm, while Annabella's curving ivy vine had symbolized elegance.

I forced myself to release the pendant and looked down at

my shaking hand. Three silverstone rings glinted on my left index finger. Snowflakes ringed one band, while ivy vines curled through another. The third ring had a small spider rune stamped into the middle of it. I wore the rings every single day, just like I did my own primrose pendant. It was my way of remembering and honoring my murdered family.

Except now I knew that Genevieve was alive—my sister was *alive*.

Legs trembling, I surged to my feet and rummaged through one of the junk drawers in the kitchen until I found a magnifying glass. Using the glass, I peered at the photo from every possible angle, trying to see every little detail and glean every single clue that I could from it.

But there wasn't much to see. All I could make out in the background was the blurry curve of a smile. None of Genevieve's other features was visible. Not her hair, not her clothes, nothing unique or distinctive. Whoever had taken the photo had been very careful to only show the scar on her palm and nothing else.

Frustration burned like acid in my stomach. Was my sister okay? Was she safe and warm? Did she have a place to live, enough food to eat? Did she even remember me and what had happened to our family?

Did she miss me like I missed her?

The questions filled my mind, more and more of them until they crowded out everything else. But of course, I didn't have answers to any of them—not a single one. I didn't even know who had sent me the photo or why. Why *now*, after seventeen years? What did this mysterious person want? What was I supposed to do now that I knew Genevieve was still alive?

I looked at the scrawled message on the back of the picture again. *She needs you, Bria, and you need her. It's time to come home.*

Home. Such a small, simple word, but it meant so many

things—and not all of them were good. I'd once had a home and a family who'd loved me, until Mab had destroyed them with her Fire magic.

But most of all, I'd had Genevieve. The two of us had been an inseparable team. Annabella had been older and more interested in boys than anything else, while Mother had often seemed busy, distracted, and worried, but Genevieve had always had time for me.

Memories flooded my mind. The two of us playing hide-and-seek and having pretend tea parties with my dolls and stuffed animals. Genevieve helping me shake the snow globes that our mother collected, as we tried to make the snow inside them all swirl up at the same time. Genevieve fixing me hot chocolate with extra marshmallows just the way I liked it. Genevieve letting me crawl into bed with her late at night whenever I had a bad dream.

My heart squeezed in on itself with each memory, with every bittersweet reminder of what I'd lost when Mab Monroe had decided to destroy the Snow family.

I reached down and twisted Genevieve's ring around on my index finger. The spider rune set into the middle of the silverstone gleamed with the motion, almost like it was a real creature crawling along the metal. Suddenly, I knew exactly what I was going to do, what I *had* to do.

I was going back to Ashland. I was going home to find my sister and make Mab pay for what she'd done to us.

No matter what.

I got lucky. A spot had just opened up in the Ashland Police Department, since a detective named Donovan Caine was looking to leave the city. I contacted Caine, and we arranged a simple swap—he'd take my job in Savannah, and I'd take his in Ashland. No muss, no fuss, not too much bitching from our supervisors.

Donovan Caine sounded tired when I called him to make the final arrangements.

"Are you really sure you want to come to Ashland, Bria?" he asked for the fourth time just on this call. "It's not like what you're used to down in Georgia."

"What do you mean?"

Donovan sighed. "Ashland is an extremely tough place to try to enforce the law. Sometimes it seems like there are more criminals than decent, honest people." He sighed again, the sound deeper and more despondent than before. "And some of the cops aren't much better than the criminals they occasionally arrest. My partner was one of those. Actually, he was worse, and he did a lot of bad things to a lot of innocent people."

"I grew up in Ashland," I replied. "I know how violent the city is and how Mab Monroe has her fingers in everything."

Maybe I hadn't been truly aware of it when I was a kid, at least not until Mab had paid her late-night visit to my house, but everyone knew that Ashland wasn't exactly the safest city. Most of the cops I knew in Savannah, Blue Marsh, and beyond thanked their lucky stars that they didn't work in Ashland, and no one could understand why I wanted to move there.

I hadn't told anyone about getting Genevieve's photo in the mail. My friends on the force would just try to convince me that someone was playing a sick game with me. Maybe they were, but I had to find out for myself. If there was even the slightest chance that Genevieve was still alive, then I was going to find my sister.

"So why would you want to come here?" Donovan asked.

"It's a family matter. I'm coming back home to track down a relative I haven't seen in years. Now, here's my question for you. Why do you want to leave so badly? Other than the sky-high crime rate and crooked cops?"

He hesitated a moment before answering. "There's a woman I need to get away from."

I frowned. "What woman? And why do you need to get away from her?"

Donovan let out a bitter laugh. "I hope you never find out. Good luck to you, Bria. You're going to need it."

He hung up on me.

A few days later, we officially made the swap, and I was back in Ashland.

I immediately set out to find Genevieve, but I had nothing to go on. I'd had the forensics department take a look at the photo before I'd left Blue Marsh, but there hadn't been any fingerprints on it, and there was nothing special about the paper, ink, or envelope that had been used. So I started digging through the Ashland police reports and all the other official records I could get my hands on, but there were no mentions of a woman with spider runes branded into her palms ever having come through the city as either a victim or a criminal.

I expanded my search to orphanages and foster homes, thinking that perhaps Genevieve had been adopted like I had, but I came up empty again.

And again, and again.

It was like Genevieve Snow had just ceased to exist after the night of the fire. Nothing gave me any clue about where she might have gone or where she might be now, and I was at a dead end before I even got started.

Oh, the other cops told me plenty of outlandish stories—rumors, really—about some assassin who went around the city calling herself the Spider. Supposedly, she was the best in the business and could get to anyone, anywhere, anytime. For the most part, I ignored the stories, since they couldn't possibly be about Genevieve. She would *never* kill anyone, much less be a notorious assassin who murdered people for money. Not my sweet, gentle, kind, thoughtful big sister.

Donovan Caine had been right about the other cops, though. My partner, a giant named Xavier, was a good guy, but many folks on the force were far more interested in taking bribes and padding their already fat wallets than in helping people and putting criminals behind bars where they belonged.

Still, despite the many obstacles, I did the best job I could, although my honesty quickly got me labeled as a coldhearted bitch who wasn't a team player. Like I cared about such petty insults. I hadn't come to Ashland to be popular—I was here to make a difference and help those who needed it. That's the oath I'd sworn when I'd graduated from the police academy, and that's what I was determined to do.

Since I couldn't find Genevieve, I focused on my other reason for returning home: taking down Mab Monroe.

I dug through old reports, questioned witnesses, and started building my case against the Fire elemental. I didn't know if I could get Mab for murdering my family, but I was damn sure going to try. I would happily nail her for whatever I could, even if it was just a minor traffic violation. It was a place to start, at least.

The other cops tried to warn me off in a variety of friendly and not-so-friendly ways, but I let it be known that nothing was going to make me back down. The word *suicidal* quickly got tagged onto *coldhearted bitch.*

Then came the night Elliot Slater broke into my house.

The giant worked for Mab as her top enforcer, the guy who permanently disposed of anyone who made too many problems—like me. I'd been expecting Mab to send someone after me since I was digging up all her dirty laundry, but Slater and his men stormed into my house and got the upper hand. I was gut-shot, and they were about to kill me when a strange woman wearing a ski mask appeared in my living room and took them out—with silverstone knives.

At first, I thought *she* was the suicidal one. Who could possibly kill a roomful of giants with just a couple of knives? But one by one, she cut them down, and I realized that those rumors about an assassin named the Spider weren't so farfetched after all, especially when she sent Elliot Slater running for his life.

I thought she might kill me too, but instead, she actually wanted to talk to me—almost like she *knew* me. That should have been my first clue to who she really was, but I was in so much pain at the time that it took everything I had just to keep standing.

"What are you then?" I asked her at one point. "Some sort of guardian angel?"

"The angel of death, maybe," she drawled in a light tone. "People who have guardian angels generally don't need my services."

I passed out shortly after that, and when I woke up, I was completely healed, and all the blood and bodies had vanished from my house like they'd never even been there to start with. Someone had used Air elemental magic to put me back together and clean my house, and I could feel the faintest remnants of the power crackling in the air like static electricity about to shock me. The sensation put me on edge, especially since the lingering power felt so different from my own Ice magic.

But I didn't have time to wonder about the assassin and why she'd saved my life, because Elliot Slater had another target: Roslyn Phillips, a beautiful vampire whom Slater was obsessed with.

Xavier, my partner, was in love with Roslyn, which complicated matters, as did the fact that Roslyn refused my help and pretended nothing was wrong. But things came to a head after an ugly scene where Roslyn told everyone on board the *Delta*

Queen riverboat casino about how Slater was making her pretend to be his girlfriend and how much he disgusted her.

Roslyn disappeared after that. I wanted to help her press charges against Slater for stalking, so I did my best to find her, but I didn't have a single lead—until someone called in an anonymous tip about a bunch of bodies at Slater's rustic mansion in the mountains above Ashland.

Xavier and I rushed up there to find a bloody, bruised Roslyn and several bodies not only in the mansion but in the surrounding woods as well. Roslyn told a story that was eerily similar to mine. Slater had abducted Roslyn and was going to beat her to death, but a masked woman had intervened, killing the giant and the rest of his men instead.

Word quickly leaked to the media, and I was standing outside with the reporters and other cops when someone triggered an explosive device, and a rune appeared, burning in the stone of Elliot Slater's mansion.

A circle surrounded by eight thin rays. A spider rune—Genevieve's rune.

And just like that, so many things made sense. Why the assassin had saved me, why she had saved Roslyn, why she had killed Elliot Slater, why she was announcing her presence with everyone watching, including Mab Monroe.

I stood there and stared at the spider rune until it burned out and its silvery light finally faded away, but I couldn't deny the truth any longer.

My big sister Genevieve Snow was indeed alive—and she was the notorious assassin the Spider.

After that night, I redoubled, tripled, quadrupled my efforts to find Genevieve, but I didn't have any more luck this time around. I still had no leads, other than the photo, and no idea where to find any new clues. So I'd put the word out on the street that I was offering cash for information that would get me to the Spider. If I couldn't find Genevieve, I figured I'd track down her alter ego instead.

But no one knew who the Spider was, what she looked like, or where her home base might be. No one even seemed to know how you went about contacting and hiring her. She just seemed to magically appear, kill whomever she wanted, whenever she wanted, and then magically disappear again. And now she had her deadly sights set on Mab Monroe.

The harder and longer I looked and the more money I doled out for useless information, the angrier I got—at Genevieve.

My sister had saved me from Elliot Slater, so she knew—*she knew*—that I was back in Ashland. Hadn't she recognized me? Why didn't she contact me? I could understand not wanting a face-to-face meeting, since I was a cop, but she could have called me at the very least.

Didn't she want to see me? Didn't she care about me? Or had saving me from Slater just been a coincidence? Did she even remember me? Or had Mab burned all the memories of our family out of her heart that night so long ago?

I didn't know the answers to any of my questions, and it was driving me crazy.

A finger poked my shoulder, snapping me out of my memories. I looked over at Hildie, who had drained two more beers and emptied another bowl of pretzels while I'd been daydreaming.

"What?" I growled.

She held up her phone. "My friend just called me. Didn't you hear it ring?"

I shrugged, not bothering to explain what I'd really been thinking about.

"Anyway, my friend's waiting outside," Hildie said.

"Why doesn't she come into the bar?"

Hildie shrugged. "She doesn't like crowds, especially this kind of crowd."

I looked out at the folks huddled over their drinks. The bikers and the cowboys eyed each other with open hostility, and the tension between the two groups was as thick as the blue smoke hanging over the bar.

"Fair enough," I said.

I slapped some more money down on the bar to cover Hildie's watery beers and stale pretzels, and then we both left the bar.

Hildie led me outside, down the street, and into an alley at the end of the block.

A woman leaned one shoulder against the wall, smoking a cigarette. She wore a fitted Fiona Fine pantsuit that cost more than everything I had on put together. The expensive fabric was a rich amber color that matched her hair, which was pulled back into an elegant twist. She was quite beautiful, with high cheekbones, perfect tan skin, and bright hazel eyes. A delicate gold chain ringed her neck, and a thick gold watch circled her left wrist.

Nice clothes, expensive jewelry, striking face. The woman wasn't what I'd expected, which made me even more uneasy. What would someone who looked so polished and put together have to do with Hildie, who was the very definition of small-time?

The woman must have sensed my wariness, because she smiled, revealing two small fangs that marked her as a vampire.

"This is Cynthia," Hildie said.

I pushed my coat aside so Cynthia could see the gold detective's badge and the gun clipped to my belt. She grinned, as though my being a cop amused her.

"Hildie says you have information about the Spider," I said.

"You tell me what you know, and I'll decide how much it's worth. If I like what I hear, you get a few bucks."

Cynthia took another drag of her cigarette, then flicked it away. It sparked a moment before dropping down and drowning in a puddle of oily water. The vampire pushed away from the wall and sauntered over to me. Instead of stopping in front of me, she circled around, examining me from all angles. When her inspection was done, she stopped, gave an approving nod, and looked over at Hildie.

"You did good finding this one," Cynthia said in a husky voice. "She'll fit in nicely with the other girls."

My eyebrows shot up. Fit in nicely where? And with what other girls?

Cynthia saw my questioning look. She let out a low chuckle and smiled at me again. "You have no idea what's really going on, do you? Well, let me explain it to you, honey. I have a business a few streets over, right in the heart of Southtown. Lots of girls work for me, a few guys too. But a couple of my clients, well, they have a certain type, and they want some fresh meat."

A police report popped into my head, something that had crossed my desk earlier in the month, right before Elliot Slater and his men had been killed by the Spider. Someone was going around downtown Ashland kidnapping women, grabbing them right off the streets on their way home from school or work or overpowering them in parking garages. Most of the women were found in alleys just like this one a few days later. The ones who weren't beaten to death or didn't die from exposure had been pumped full of so many drugs they could barely remember their own names, much less what had happened to them.

"So you've been kidnapping women and handing them over to sick bastards to be abused? Well, you picked the wrong cop to mess with, *honey*," I growled, anger and disgust roaring through my body. "Because I don't take bribes."

Cynthia's smile grew a little wider, and her fangs gleamed like white razors in her mouth. "Oh, honey, I don't want to bribe you. A business associate suggested that I convince you to work for me—one way or another."

So someone had set me up to be kidnapped by Cynthia. Probably Mab Monroe, trying to eliminate me yet again.

"With all that pretty blond hair and those big blue eyes, I can make enough off you to live in fine style," Cynthia continued. "For a month or two, anyway, given my rather expensive tastes."

For the first time, I realized I was only talking to Cynthia. Where was Hildie?

Out of the corner of my eye, I spotted the other woman sneaking up on me. Hildie raised her hand, and something flashed silver in the afternoon sun. I whirled around and caught her wrist right before she would have jabbed a syringe into my neck. Hildie must have had some dwarven blood, because even though she was shorter than me, she was much stronger.

We seesawed back and forth for several seconds before I finally managed to drive my boot into Hildie's shin. She howled with pain, and I shoved her away. Hildie stumbled back against the alley wall, and the syringe fell from her hand and skittered across the concrete.

I reached for my gun, but strong arms wrapped around me from behind, pinning my hands to my sides.

"Just hold still, honey," Cynthia murmured in my ear, her breath reeking of cigarette smoke. "You won't feel a thing. Hildie, get that syringe over here right now!"

Even more anger and disgust roared through me than before. Bria Coolidge didn't take bribes, and I never, ever gave up.

I still couldn't grab my gun, but I was far from helpless, even against a vampire who was physically stronger than me. Because in addition to our silverstone rune pendants, the women in the Snow family had another thing in common: we all had elemental Ice magic.

I reached for my magic, relishing the feel of the cool power rippling through my veins. As an elemental, I could create, control, and manipulate Ice any way I wanted to, including making objects with it. Maybe it was because I'd been thinking about Genevieve so much lately, about the Spider and all the people she'd killed, but it only took me a second to form a long, jagged Ice knife in my right hand.

I raised my foot and smashed my thick, heavy boot down into Cynthia's instep, right on top of one of her fancy Bella Bulluci pumps. The vampire snarled, but she didn't release me. I didn't really expect her to, but her grip on my arms loosened just enough for me to bring my hand up.

Then I snapped my hand down and rammed the Ice knife into her thigh as deep as it would go.

The vampire screamed, high and loud enough to make me wince. Cynthia lurched back, and the Ice knife pulled free from her leg. I whirled around and slashed out with it. The cold shard sliced across Cynthia's chest, tearing through her jacket and drawing blood. It wasn't a deep wound, but it would certainly sting.

"Bitch!" she screamed. "You ruined my suit!"

I dropped the Ice knife, surged forward, and drove my fist into her face. *Crunch.* Cynthia's nose broke with a satisfying sound, her head snapped back against the alley wall, and she slumped to the asphalt unconscious.

A soft scuff sounded, and I looked over my shoulder. Hildie was standing behind me, once again clutching that syringe. When she saw that I was still standing and that her friend Cynthia wasn't, Hildie's mouth gaped in surprise, and she started backing away.

I yanked the gun out of the holster on my belt and aimed it at Hildie's heart. She froze.

"I've already got quite a lot of blood on me," I said in a cold, furious voice. "But I'd be happy to add yours to the mix. So I'd stand still if I were you."

Hildie decided to stand still.

Dark satisfaction filled me. I might not be as deadly as Genevieve had become as the Spider, but I could take care of myself when push came to shove.

I used my phone to call the situation into the station. The other cops took their sweet time getting here, but eventually, several folks showed up, and Hildie and Cynthia were carted away. I went to the station to fill out the necessary paperwork and clean up. I was just getting ready to leave for the day when Xavier stopped by my desk.

At around seven feet tall, Xavier was a giant with a strong, imposing body, and his shaved head gleamed like polished ebony under the station's harsh lights.

"I just heard about the bust. Nice work, Bria." Xavier grinned. "Lots of folks will sleep a little easier tonight knowing that Cynthia is off the street." The grin dropped from his face. "But you should have called me for backup."

I raised an eyebrow. "I'm a big girl, Xavier. I can take care of myself—and Cynthia has the stab wounds to prove it."

"I know," he replied. "But Southtown is still dangerous, no matter if you're a dwarf, a giant, a vampire, or an elemental. You need to remember that. What were you doing over there, anyway? You weren't scheduled to work today."

"I was following up on a lead on the Spider."

Some emotion flickered in Xavier's dark eyes, although I couldn't quite tell what it was. "Did you find out anything?"

I let out a frustrated sigh. "Of course not. Hildie and Cynthia didn't know anything about her. They just lured me over there so Cynthia could use me like she did those other women she drugged and kidnapped. The Spider is still a ghost."

Maybe it was my imagination, but something that looked a lot like relief flashed across Xavier's face before he covered it up with another grin. Suspicion filled me. Xavier seemed like a good guy, but sometimes I wondered whose side he was really on—because I didn't think it was necessarily mine.

"Are you headed home now?" he asked.

"Actually, I'm starved. I thought I'd swing by the Pork Pit and get something to eat first. You want to come? My treat."

That weird emotion flickered in Xavier's eyes again. "No, that's okay. You go on ahead. I should check on Roslyn."

I nodded. I didn't know how long Xavier had been in love with Roslyn, but the giant had barely left her side since her ordeal at Elliot Slater's hands. I admired Xavier's devotion. Maybe if I was lucky, someday I'd find a guy to love me the way he loved Roslyn.

Finnegan Lane's face popped into my mind, but I pushed the image away. Lane might be attractive in a cocky, smarmy kind of way, but the investment banker was about as far from honest, loyal, and devoted as you could get, and I had no desire to be just another conquest to him.

"Bria?" Xavier asked. "What are you thinking about?"

"Nothing," I said, trying to ignore the surprising longing I always felt whenever I thought about exactly how green Finnegan Lane's eyes were. "Nothing at all."

Xavier walked me outside, and we said our good-byes. Thirty minutes later, I slid into a booth in the Pork Pit.

The barbecue restaurant was just a few blocks over from the bar where I'd spent the afternoon with Hildie and Cynthia, but the Pork Pit was a world apart from the seedy, run-down bar.

Sure, the restaurant's blue and pink vinyl booths might have a few decades on them, and the blue and pink pig tracks on the floor that led to the men's and women's bathrooms could use a fresh coat of paint. But no matter how worn it was, everything was clean and polished, from the tables to the chairs in the middle of the restaurant to the long counter that ran along the back wall. And the smell was absolutely *divine*—sugar and spices mingled in the air until I could almost taste the sweet, smoky barbecue sauce that was the restaurant's claim to fame.

It was just after six, and the dinner rush was going strong. The waitstaff bustled through the restaurant, carrying plates piled high with steaming barbecue beef, pork, and chicken sandwiches, while a dwarf dressed all in black dished up bowls of baked beans behind the counter. Sophia Deveraux, I think her name was. My stomach rumbled, and I stared out the storefront windows and waited for someone to notice me.

"Rough day, Detective?" a familiar voice murmured.

I looked up to find Gin Blanco standing next to my booth. Gin was the owner of the Pork Pit, a slender but strong-looking woman with dark brown hair and eyes that seemed more gray than blue. She wore a blue work apron over a pair of dark jeans and a long-sleeved black T-shirt.

I didn't know quite how I felt about Gin, especially since we hadn't gotten off to a good start. Someone had severely beaten Gin while she was leaving class one night at Ashland Community College. I'd caught the case, but Gin had refused to tell me who had attacked her. Word on the street was that it had been Elliot Slater for some slight that Gin had committed against Jonah McAllister, a lawyer who worked for Mab Monroe.

I was interested in anyone who was mixed up with Mab and her minions, and I'd set my sights on Gin, hoping to get her to press charges against Slater or whoever had attacked her in hopes of building my case again Mab.

Gin had refused, but I'd run into her again after Roslyn's confrontation with Slater on the *Delta Queen* riverboat. I'd had a hunch that Gin might know where Roslyn was hiding from Slater, so I'd come to the Pork Pit. I'd tried everything I could think of to get Gin to tell me where Roslyn was, but Gin had put me in my place and claimed she didn't know a thing—a claim Roslyn had later backed up.

I'd apologized to Gin, of course, and she'd said she'd forgiven me.

On the surface, Gin Blanco seemed nice enough, but I always got the feeling that she treaded carefully around me—like she was hiding something, although I had no idea what it might be.

"Detective?" Gin asked again. "Rough day?"

I gave her a tired smile. "You might say that."

"Well, some good hot barbecue will fix you right up. So what'll it be?"

I ordered a barbecue chicken sandwich, along with baked beans, potato salad, onion rings, and a blackberry iced tea. Gin scribbled down my order on her pad, then went back behind the counter to fix my food.

I watched her work through the crowd of customers and waiters between us. Gin's movements were smooth and fluid, whether she was dumping fries onto a plate or handing a customer his change. She had an easy grace that I admired, moving more like a ballet dancer than a cook. Just looking at her made me feel clumsy.

Gin also reminded me of Genevieve.

It had taken me a while to figure it out. At first, I'd thought Gin reminded me of my college roommate, but lately, I'd realized that I was really thinking about Genevieve instead. Gin had the same coloring that I remembered Genevieve having—the same dark brown hair and light eyes—and she was in her early thirties, the same age my sister would be now.

Then again, so were thousands of women in Ashland.

Of course, I knew that Gin wasn't my sister. She couldn't be. I'd dug into Gin's background when I was investigating who might have beaten her, so I knew that she had been orphaned as a kid and that a distant cousin, Fletcher Lane, had taken her in. She'd inherited the Pork Pit from Fletcher after he was killed a few months ago. In an interesting quirk of fate, Gin also happened to be Finnegan Lane's foster sister.

Still, I couldn't help the small pang that pierced my heart at knowing that Gin wasn't Genevieve. It would be . . . *nice* to belong to a place like the Pork Pit, someplace so warm and inviting. Maybe that was why I ate at the restaurant so often, because it had the homey feel that my own house didn't, ever since Elliot Slater and his men had stormed inside and tried to kill me—

"Here you go."

Gin put my food on the table, along with a large slice of cherry pie topped with vanilla-bean ice cream that was just starting to melt. That was another weird thing about Gin: she was always bringing me extra food. A slice of cake, cookies, a square of homemade fudge. I didn't know why she gave me more than what I ordered. Unlike the other cops in Ashland, I didn't expect freebies everywhere I went.

I shook my head. "I didn't order the pie—"

Gin waved her hand, cutting me off. "I know, but we had extra, and you looked like you could use something sweet to help drown out a bitter day. Enjoy, Detective."

She winked at me and headed over to the counter to tend to some more customers. Then Gin sat down on a stool behind the cash register and picked up the book she was reading. I couldn't see the title from here, although a framed copy of *Where the Red Fern Grows* was mounted on the wall near the cash register. Gin saw me watching her and gave me a little wave before she started reading.

I stared at Gin for another second before turning my attention to the food on the tabletop. Instead of picking up my sandwich, I grabbed my fork and dug into the cherry pie. I couldn't help myself; I'd always had a weakness for sweets. I took a bite and sighed with happiness. The warm fruit was the perfect blend of sweet and tart, and the ice cream was a cool, creamy, vanilla ribbon mixed in with the warm, flaky, buttery crust.

I noticed Gin watching me, and I gave her a thumbs-up. She grinned and returned to her book.

I ate another bite of pie. Despite my terrible day, Gin was right: I felt a little bit better about things. Oh, I might not have learned anything new about the Spider, but I'd taken Cynthia and Hildie off the streets. That was a victory. Now I was eating a good meal in a good restaurant. I was better off than a lot of folks out there.

All that was left to do was find Genevieve, the Spider, or whatever she was calling herself these days. What I was going to do after that, if I was going to turn her in for being an assassin, well, I hadn't quite decided that. But I *was* going to find my sister—and soon. I could feel it in my bones.

No matter what.

Spider's Nemesis

This story takes place after *Tangled Threads*, book 4.

Chapter One

Mab Monroe

The assassin just wouldn't die.

No matter what I did, no matter how hard I had my men look for her, no matter whom I hired to kill her, the Spider just wouldn't die. Once again tonight, she'd escaped the trap I'd set for her—and embarrassed me in the process.

I *hated* being embarrassed. It wasn't good for business or, more important, my image.

It was two days before Christmas, and I was standing in the old Ashland train yard. My property, which was currently littered with bodies.

The cops were already here, the blue and red lights on top of their city-issued sedans spinning around and around, throwing garish flashes of color everywhere. The bright pools of light illuminated the railcars that stood in the yard and made the rusty metal tracks gleam like bronze ribbons. The cops had already broken out the yellow crime-scene tape, stringing it up from one railcar to the next.

I always wondered why they bothered with such asinine things after the fact. My men were dead. Cordoning off the area wasn't going to do the dead giants any good, and there wouldn't be much evidence to collect. The Spider never left anything important behind at the sites of her kills.

Just that damn rune.

Tonight she'd drawn it into the loose gravel underfoot, like a chicken scratching in the dirt. A circle surrounded by eight thin rays—a spider rune.

I stared down at the mark at my feet, my hands curling into fists and a bit of steam rising off my clenched fingers. I would have liked nothing more than to unleash hot, pulsing wave after wave of my Fire magic until that damn rune and all the ground around it were charred to ash. But I couldn't do that, not while other people were watching.

Reporters from the city's newspaper and the TV and radio stations, along with various social-media outlets, clustered in groups behind the crime-scene tape, their phones and cameras all aimed in this direction, filming the cops as they loaded the bodies onto gurneys to slide into the coroner's vans that had been dispatched to the scene.

And folks thought *I* was evil. At least I wasn't a media vulture. Sure, I killed people for money, whim, pleasure, or simply to make a point, but I didn't film the process—or the aftermath.

A few of the reporters noticed me staring in their direction and took that as an invitation to start squawking at me.

"Ms. Monroe! Mab! Mab! Can you give us a statement about what happened? Is it true that the Spider killed several members of your security detail?"

The reporters' questions all ran together, like a swarm of mosquitoes whining in the background. I ignored them and stared at the rune on the ground again. I wondered the same thing I always did whenever I saw the symbol.

Why a spider rune? Out of all the runes out there, why had she chosen such a simple one to leave behind as her mark?

The rune nagged at me, like a pin pricking my skin over and over again. I *knew* I'd seen the symbol before, but I couldn't quite place where or whom it had belonged to. Someone I'd killed, most likely, since the Spider always cheerfully crowed about payback during the brief phone conversations I'd had with her. But who could it be? I'd long ago lost count of all the fools I'd eliminated over the years.

You didn't get to be the head of the Ashland underworld by being a shy, retiring type, and I'd risen through the ranks faster than most. Of course, I'd had some help from certain colleagues who preferred to remain hidden in the shadows, but I'd clawed my way to the top of the criminal food chain in no small part due to my own ruthless determination and especially my Fire magic.

The elemental power burned inside me, as though my veins were filled with lava instead of blood. Oh, sure, other elementals had Air, Ice, or Stone magic or pitiful offshoots of those areas like electricity, water, or metal, but *nothing* could compare to the feel of my Fire magic, to that molten heat that was always lurking just below the surface of my pale skin, ready to be used in the most vicious, painful, creative way possible.

The snowflakes swirling in the cold December air hissed and steamed away as they came into contact with my copper-colored hair. I was one of those elementals who constantly gave off waves of power, even when I wasn't actively using my Fire magic to let someone know exactly how unhappy I was with them. Right now, I would have loved nothing more than to show the Spider just how displeased I was with her—and that you tangled with Mab Monroe at your own bloody peril.

Once again, my gaze traced over the rune at my feet. Obviously, the spider rune referred to her assassin name, but I felt like there was much more to the symbol than that. It had to have *some* personal meaning to her, and if I could only figure out what that meaning was, then I'd know exactly whom I was up against—and how best to find and kill the bitch. A task that had morphed from an amusing pastime into a growing necessity.

Footsteps crunched on the gravel behind me, but I didn't turn around. I knew who it was. He was the only one brave—or foolish—enough to approach me after such an embarrassing defeat. Any defeat, really.

Jonah McAllister, my longtime lawyer, stepped up beside me. McAllister wore a long, heavy, black overcoat over a slick gray suit, and the flashing lights from the police cars made his elegant coif of silver hair take on cool blue and then garish reddish tones. His hair looked decidedly at odds with his ageless face. The tan skin there was so smooth and tight you could have bounced a quarter off his cheekbones.

"The official tally is four giants dead and, of course, Elektra LaFleur," Jonah said, a note of regret creeping into his voice, since he'd been fucking her while she'd been in Ashland.

"LaFleur," I muttered in disgust. "I never should have hired her. The only thing she excelled at was running her mouth. What a waste of time and money."

My gaze slid from the spider rune over to the dead woman lying on the ground next to it. She'd once been quite pretty, with her bob of glossy black hair. Now her pale skin had taken on a waxy quality, and her green eyes were open wide with shock, pain, and more than a little fear.

Elektra LaFleur. Supposedly the best assassin money could buy, with powerful electrical magic that she used to fry her victims to a smoking crisp. I'd hired LaFleur to come to Ashland, track down the Spider, and kill her, but LaFleur hadn't been up to the task, as evidenced by the stab wound in her chest and the blood that had pooled underneath her body.

"Well, at least the Spider didn't burn down anything else

while she was here," Jonah said, trying to put a positive spin on things.

"No, Jonah," I snapped. "She took care of that the last time she was here. Or have you forgotten what she did to my train depot?"

I stabbed a finger at the blackened remains of the depot. A few days ago, the Spider had snuck into the train yard to rescue a girl I'd had kidnapped and was holding as motivation for her father. The assassin had started a fire in the depot as a distraction, and the whole structure had burned to the ground.

Jonah swallowed and took a step back, appropriately wary of the venom in my voice.

I turned away from him, reached down, and picked up something else the Spider had left behind tonight: a white orchid. The petals were cold in my hand, like delicate slivers of ice. The orchid was Elektra LaFleur's signature, something she used to decorate the bodies of her victims, just like the Spider did with her quaint little rune.

Assassins and their stupid symbols. I'd never understood why some folks felt the need to mark their kills. Knowing that your enemy was dead should be satisfaction enough.

It always was for me.

"What do you want to do about Bria Coolidge?" Jonah asked, wisely changing the subject.

"That depends. What's she telling the other cops and the press?"

He shrugged. "That Elektra kidnapped her, put her in a railcar, and threatened to torture her. That she heard a struggle and didn't see anything until someone opened the railcar. Coolidge claims that by the time she got outside, Elektra and the giants were dead and the Spider was gone."

"Do you believe her?"

Jonah shrugged again. "It fits some of the other eyewitness accounts about the Spider, but I think there's more to Coolidge's story than what she's saying. She knows that you want her dead, Mab, and that you sent Elektra to do the job."

This time, I shrugged. "I don't care what she knows or whom she tells it to. Coolidge can't touch me. No one can. I bloody *own* this city."

I looked across the train yard. Detective Bria Coolidge sat in the back of an ambulance that had its doors open and was letting an EMT take her blood pressure while another one cleaned out the scrapes on her face.

Xavier, the giant who was her partner on the force, stood nearby, keeping an eye on Coolidge and talking to one of their superior officers. Xavier was one of the few folks in the police department who wasn't on my payroll. A shame. He seemed much tougher and far more competent than the people who did report to me.

Coolidge was pretty enough, with her shaggy blond hair, rosy skin, and blue eyes, but I focused on her necklace, a silverstone pendant shaped like a primrose.

I'd seen Coolidge wearing the pendant before when our paths had crossed, but for some reason, I couldn't stop staring at the rune tonight. A primrose, the symbol for beauty.

I started thinking about all the other symbols I'd seen tonight. The Spider's rune. LaFleur's orchid. And now Coolidge and her primrose.

It took a few seconds, but the memories bubbled up to the surface of my mind, erupting like a volcano. And suddenly, I remembered another girl and another necklace . . .

Chapter Two

Years Ago

"Why are you wearing a snowflake necklace?" I asked.

The girl looked at me with her big blue eyes. "Because it's my rune. A snowflake for icy calm. The symbol of the Snow family."

The girl's name was Eira Snow, and we were sitting at a table that had been set up in my enormous playroom. Lemonade, cookies, cupcakes, and more covered the white wooden table, along with some of my mother's fine china and stacks of white linen napkins. Stuffed animals, puzzles, and other toys crowded the floor, while glossy books were stuffed into the shelves that lined one of the walls.

Even though Eira was a teenager and several years older than me, we were supposed to be playing together, but I didn't have any interest in the food or the toys. I'd already used my Fire magic to melt three of the cups and singe most of the fur off the stuffed animals, leaving only their glass eyes intact. I'd even used my finger like a blowtorch and scorched my name in cursive writing into the top of the wooden table.

Eira had looked at me with wide eyes when I'd done that, and she'd nervously fiddled with the end of one of her long golden pigtails, like she wanted to tell me to stop. But she hadn't, and she wouldn't—if she knew what was good for her. I was only seven, but I'd already discovered that it was much more fun to use my elemental magic on people than on my stuffed animals.

I knew a lot more than everyone thought I did, especially about what my family really did and where our money came from. My dad, Marcus, was a mob boss, just like in all the old movies I watched on TV. I didn't know exactly what that meant, except that people did what my father said when he said it. And if they didn't, he used his Fire magic on them until they cried and begged him to stop. He'd let me watch the last time he'd used his power on someone, telling me it was time that I learned exactly what my Fire magic was good for.

It had been . . . *exciting*.

"Where do you think my mom is?" Eira asked in a tense, worried voice.

I shrugged. "Probably still talking to my dad."

The older girl started chewing on her fingernails. Eira and her mother had arrived at our estate this morning, along with several giant bodyguards. My father had welcomed them inside, and I'd heard him say something about a family feud and finally making peace before Eira and I had been brought here to my playroom while the adults talked.

That had been *hours* ago. I didn't understand what was taking so long or why my father didn't just tell Eira's mother what he wanted her to do. That would be the end of things, as far as I was concerned.

Eira shifted in her chair and took a small sip of her lukewarm lemonade. The movement made the silverstone pendant at her throat gleam again. It was a snowflake, delicate and pretty, with six sharp points. I loved silverstone, because the magical metal had the same sort of hunger that I had—the hot desire, the aching *need* to have everything that I wanted as soon as I wanted it.

Eira carefully set her cup down, and her pendant glimmered again, even brighter than before. Jealousy surged through me. Despite all my toys, I didn't have a necklace like that, and I wanted one. I wanted *hers*. Right now.

I got to my feet, walked around the table, and held out my hand. "Give me your necklace. I want to look at it."

Of course, I had no intention of ever giving it back to her, but I didn't tell Eira that. She would just cry big, fat, sniveling tears.

Eira shook her head and wrapped her hand around the snowflake rune, as if that would protect it—and her—from me. "No. It's *my* necklace. My mother gave it to me. Get your own."

My eyes narrowed, and anger flared in my heart. "No, I want *yours*. Give it to me. Right now. Or I'll tell my dad that you won't."

Her face paled a little at my threat, but she sat up straight in her chair. "And I'll tell my mom that you tried to take it from me."

For a moment, I didn't know what to do. Nobody ever said *no* to me. Not my dad, not our servants, not even the giant bodyguards who went everywhere with us. Usually, they all hurried to give me everything that I wanted, especially now that my dad had said that I could use my Fire magic to hurt and burn people just like he did.

Eira kept staring at me, her eyes cold and wary now. Well, if she wouldn't give the necklace to me, then I would just take it, the way I took everything else I wanted.

I grabbed for the pendant, but Eira slapped my hand away. I

lunged for the pendant again, but she got to her feet and backed up, so that she was standing on the other side of the table.

"Give me your necklace," I commanded. "Or I'll take it from you—and I'll make it *hurt*."

I reached for my Fire magic. Red sparks filled the air, and flames began to crackle and burn on my fingertips. I held the flames out to her and smiled, letting her imagine exactly what I would do to her pretty face with them.

Instead of being afraid of me, Eira held out her own hand, and a faint blue glow flickered in her palm before turning into a solid ball of elemental Ice. She had magic too, but her chilled, frosty power felt *awful*, nothing like the molten heat running through my veins. I shuddered at the horrible icy sensation and reached for even more of my magic. I didn't know why, but I wanted to burn the other girl with my Fire now more than ever.

We stood there in the playroom, facing off across the table.

"Leave me alone," Eira said. "And I'll leave you alone."

"Not until you give me your necklace," I snapped. "Give it to me *right now*."

She shook her head.

Nobody told me no, especially not this . . . this *girl*. My anger burned a little brighter, flaring up into full-on hate. I reared my hand back, reached for even more of my power, and threw my Fire magic at her.

Eira's eyes widened, and she ducked out of the way. My ball of Fire flew through the air and smacked into the wall behind her. Smoke boiled up, and an alarm started blaring, the same alarm that sounded whenever I used too much of my magic inside the house.

Eira turned and raced toward the closed door at the far end of the playroom.

"Oh, no, you don't!" I hissed and chased after her.

I grabbed the back of her white dress just before she reached the door. Eira spun around and slapped my hands away. I lunged at her, and we both fell to the floor, rolling around and around, both of us screaming, Eira telling me to stop and me telling her to give me her necklace or else.

Heavy footsteps sounded, and I was dimly aware of the door banging open and hitting the wall. A few seconds later, hands pulled me off the older, larger girl. I kicked and lashed out, but the hands trapped my arms down at my sides. I looked up at my father, who held me firmly against his legs.

"Enough, Mab!" my father snapped. "That is *enough!*"

I wasn't afraid of much, but I knew better than to disobey my father given the commanding tone in his voice, so I stayed still.

"Eira, honey, are you all right?" a soft feminine voice called out.

A woman hurried into the playroom and helped Eira onto her feet. She looked just like Eira, all golden hair and big eyes with a faint blue glow. The woman was an Ice elemental, just like Eira was.

In that moment, I hated the mother just as much as I hated the daughter.

I shifted on my feet, but my father kept his hands on me, holding me in place, almost like he knew what I wanted to do, how I yearned to lash out with my Fire magic and burn the other two elementals to ashes.

Eira's mother grabbed her daughter's hand and faced me and my father.

"I think we should go now," the mother said. "Thank you for your . . . hospitality, Marcus."

My father nodded at her. "Thank you for meeting with me, Elisabetta."

The Ice elemental nodded back at him, then looked over at me. Her eyes narrowed in thought for a moment before she led Eira out of the room. The other girl stared back over her shoulder at me, and I caught a final glimpse of her snowflake pendant before she stepped into the hallway and vanished from sight.

That was the first time I fought with Eira Snow—but it wasn't the last.

Three days later, my father gave me a present. I unwrapped the box, popped off the top, and looked at what was nestled inside the white tissue paper: a dozen wavy golden rays strung together and surrounding a large ruby.

"It's a sunburst rune, the symbol for fire," my father said in a proud voice. "I had this necklace made special just for you, Mab. Now, isn't it much better than that silly snowflake you wanted?"

"Yes," I whispered, stroking the shiny gold with my fingertips. "It's so much prettier than *her* puny necklace."

My father nodded, satisfied by my answer. He helped me put on the necklace, then stepped back so I could admire myself in the mirror over the vanity table.

Red hair, black eyes, pale skin, and now a necklace around my pale throat. The light streaming in through the windows hit the golden rays, making it seem like they were flickering, like I was wearing a ring of fire around my neck.

"I love it," I said, smiling up at my father.

He smiled back at me, elemental Fire flashing in his own black eyes. "Good."

He left me in my bedroom, and I sat there in front of the mirror and studied my necklace from every angle. My father was right. My sunburst was so much prettier than that stupid snowflake. So much fiercer, so much *stronger*. Just like my Fire magic was better than any Ice elemental's measly power.

Still, I wasn't going to forget what had happened with the

other girl. How she'd told me no. How she'd humiliated me in front of my father.

Someday, I vowed, I would have Eira Snow's rune necklace, even if I had to melt it right off her throat.

Chapter Three

Years Ago

"She's going to kill you," an old, slightly wheezy voice said.

"Really?" I murmured, trying to find a place to sit down that wouldn't stain my white pantsuit. "Well, I wish her luck in trying."

I shoved a pile of twenty-year-old gardening magazines off a lumpy black velvet sofa and took a seat there, perching on the very edge of the moldy cushion. Dust puffed up as the magazines hit the floor, the motes shimmering in the sunlight streaming in through the window. I swallowed a sneeze and tried not to wonder how long it had been since fresh air had circulated through the room. Ten years, fifteen, maybe even longer than that.

I sat in what was quite possibly the filthiest house in all of Ashland. Overstuffed furniture that was fifty years out of date crowded into the small, square living room, along with clothes that were even older and were so worn that they were little more than stacks of threads strung together.

Grimy, cracked jars held a variety of buttons, safety pins, and dried tea leaves, among other things, and more than a few gnarled bones nestled on the tabletops, right next to the glass figurines of the animals they represented. Books, magazines, and newspapers were also strewn throughout the room, most of them spattered with distinctive brown splotches of dried blood. Little paths wound through the whole mess, looking like the small, cramped tunnels in a rabbit's warren—or a rat's nest. I never could decide which description was more fitting.

An actual pigsty would have been cleaner than this room, and the rest of the house was just as bad. In the bathroom, the kitchen, and the bedrooms, piles of dirty dishes, rotten food, and other debris littered every single surface from the counters to the tables to the floor. Some of the piles towered five, six, and even seven feet in the air.

Disgusting, absolutely *disgusting*, but I couldn't get rid of the mess, short of burning the whole house to the ground. An option I'd considered more than once, but I wouldn't take that drastic step just yet. I still needed Magda and her visions— for the moment. Once my hold on the Ashland underworld was complete and I was finally able to kill some of my more dangerous, demanding colleagues, well, then I would revisit the issue—and dear old Magda along with it.

"She's going to kill you," my aunt repeated in a firmer voice.

I dragged my gaze away from the filth and focused on my father's aunt, my great-aunt. Magda Monroe was a short woman, barely taller than a dwarf, and she was as thin and hunched over as a blade of grass bowed down by heavy morning dew. Her salt-and-pepper hair stuck out in frizzy wisps around her head, and her tan skin was lined and splotchy with age. Her black eyes were still sharp, though, as sharp and hard as mine. Magda might be over ninety, but nothing was wrong with her mind—or her Air magic.

Magda crouched over the corpse of a freshly killed chicken in the back corner, which was the only relatively clear part of the living room. She had already sliced up the chicken and was peering at its bloody entrails, looking at something that only she could see or understand. Her black eyes glowed, burning like hot coals in her wrinkled face, while her Air magic brushed up against my skin like a sticky, humid breeze, but the sensation didn't bother me. Air and Fire were two elements that complemented each other. It was Ice and Stone magic that I couldn't stand, and the cold, hard waves of power that came along with them.

"She's going to kill you," Magda said for the third time.

A tiny spider crawled out of the stack of magazines that I'd tossed onto the floor and darted across the warped floorboard in front of me. I used the toe of my black stiletto to grind it into the wood, enjoying the small *crunch* it made, before crossing that leg over my other one.

An annoyed sigh escaped my lips. "And just who is this mysterious person who's going to kill me?"

I'd made the trip to this forsaken holler high in the mountains above Ashland because Magda had called and insisted that I come, saying she'd seen some vision that just couldn't wait. Using Air magic to see the future wasn't an exact science, and Magda dabbled in other things as well, like the blood of the dead chicken on the floor. But my aunt tended to be right more often than not, so I humored her requests and made sure she had a steady supply of poultry.

Listening to Magda's visions and advice had allowed me to expand my father's business interests a few years before, when I'd assumed my rightful place as the head of the Monroe family empire. My father hadn't wanted to step aside, of course, but he hadn't had much choice. Oh, Marcus had put up a good fight, even challenging me to an elemental duel, but he'd realized that his days were numbered. He'd known that my magic was stronger than his—stronger than almost anyone else's power—but he'd challenged me anyway.

I'd almost regretted burning him to ash in his own study. At the very least, I should have done it outside, where what was left of him would have just blown away cleanly instead of dusting up my favorite chair.

"Snow," Magda whispered, interrupting my thoughts. She ran her finger through the chicken's blood and then used the sticky mess to draw on the floor. "Death by Snow."

My whole body tensed, and I leaned forward, eager to know what nebulous thing she'd seen in the cluster of blood, bones, and feathers.

"Snow?" I asked in a sharp tone. "Do you mean Eira Snow?"

The Ice elemental was still alive and still making trouble for me. Eira and I had been enemies ever since the first day we'd met in my playroom, and our feud had only grown over the years. The fragile truce that our parents had negotiated between our families had crumbled long ago.

For the most part, we'd stayed away from each other while I'd been growing up, especially given the age difference between us. Although I had considered killing Eira when she married a man I had my eye on, Tristan Mitchell, a Stone elemental. I hadn't had any real feelings for Tristan, but he'd been handsome and rich, and, most important, I'd thought his magic would be an interesting one to pass on to my own daughter someday. I'd pursued him, but he had actually loved Eira and had married her instead of me. Sentimental idiot. But it was just another way Eira Snow had embarrassed me without even trying.

Love. Such a foolish emotion.

Still, that emotion and the grief that had followed had kept Eira out of my hair for the last several years, after her beloved Tristan had been killed. Well, that and the three brats she was busy raising. All girls and all Ice elementals, just like their cursed mother.

But Eira had once again become a thorn in my side as of late. Apparently, I'd killed one of her friends, along with the woman's family, over a gambling debt that the husband couldn't pay. I had no real malice toward the Graysons, but I was securing my hold on the last of the gambling operations in the city, and I'd needed to make an example of what happened when you didn't pay Mab Monroe and her bookies. Burning the Graysons' house to the ground with them locked inside had seemed like the easiest way to make my point. I hadn't had any problems with late payments since then.

Plus, it had just been *fun*.

But Eira had taken it personally, the way she took everything. Over the last few weeks, I'd heard whispers that she was pressuring some city officials to look into my businesses, even though she knew I already had most of the cops, judges, and district attorneys in my pocket. Still, Eira persisted with her nonsense, to the point that it was starting to annoy me.

And people only ever annoyed me once.

I realized that Magda was staring at me, so I repeated my question.

"You think that Eira Snow is going to kill me?" I let out a merry laugh. "That's absurd. Her magic isn't *nearly* as strong as mine, and we both know it. That's the reason she hasn't challenged me to an elemental duel for killing that friend of hers. *Nobody's* magic is as strong as mine. You've told me so yourself—many, many times."

Magda grinned, showing me a mouthful of stained yellow teeth that looked like tiny knives. "And that was true, until Eira had a girl with both Ice *and* Stone magic. Her power's growing even as we speak. That girl, that's the Snow I mean. She'll be the equal of you someday, Mab. Eventually, she'll be even stronger than you. And then she will kill you, just like you've killed so many other elementals."

My eyes narrowed. "How do you know that?"

Magda gestured at the floor. "The signs have shown it to me."

I got to my feet, stalked over, and stared down over her shoulder. Magda had used the chicken's blood to draw a series of runes on the floor. Snowflakes. Small circles with thin rays radiating from them. One after another, she'd drawn them on the floor, making a ring of them around the chicken's body, as well as her own.

I frowned, bent down, and looked at the marks a little more closely. No, not snowflakes. Not exactly. Snowflakes didn't have eight points on them. Then again, Magda's hands weren't as steady as they used to be. She'd probably put the extra marks there by mistake.

I shouldn't have paid any attention to Magda's prophecy. After all, she was occasionally wrong. Besides, I *knew* that I could kill Eira, that I could fry her to a crisp anytime I wanted to with my Fire magic. We'd come to blows more than once over the years, and each time, I'd known that my power was greater than hers. I could *feel* it deep down in my bones, and I trusted my instincts a whole lot more than I trusted the remains of a dead chicken.

But a girl with both Ice *and* Stone magic . . . now, that could be problematic. Being able to tap into two elemental areas was a rare gift. I'd wanted to potentially give that ability to my own daughter, using Tristan and his Stone magic, but Eira and her daughter had gotten that power instead. Once again, Eira Snow had lucked into something that I'd wanted, something she'd gotten without even *trying*, without even planning or plotting or working so hard for it like I had.

That old, familiar hate flared up in my heart, burning away everything else.

"Which one?" I asked in a harsh voice. "Which one of Eira's brats has dual powers?"

Magda dipped her fingers into the chicken's blood, and her

Air magic gusted through the filthy room again, like a hot breeze blasting against my face. After a few seconds, the sensation faded away, and Magda started rocking back and forth on her knees, making her bones pop and crack. She started muttering something I couldn't understand, something about *spiders and webs*, and *stings and stones*, and she kept dipping her fingers into the chicken's blood and using it to draw those lopsided snowflakes all over the floor.

Sometimes Magda got like this and became trapped in the twisted visions of her Air magic. Disgust and annoyance shot through me, and I sighed and reached for my Fire power. Hot, hungry flames danced on my fingers, eager to leap off my hand and consume every single thing they could. I curled my hand into a fist, then reached down and smashed it and the flames into Magda's face.

Magda shrieked with pain and toppled over onto her side. Her head cracked against the floor, but the sharp, painful motion jolted her out of the magical trance that had seized her mind. I watched her buck and writhe on the floor while she rode out the waves of pain and power rippling through her body. It wasn't the first time I'd hit or burned her, and I'd do it again to get some answers.

"So what do I have to do to stop this prophecy of yours?" I asked when she'd finally calmed down and sat upright again. "The ludicrous idea that this little Snow brat is going to kill me?"

Magda peered up at me, a fist-sized burn on her left cheek. The leathery skin there had already blistered and swollen up. She shook her head. "There's nothing you *can* do to stop it," she rasped. "Not this time. Not this girl. She'll be the death of you, Mab. Mark my words. She'll be stronger than you—she'll be stronger than anyone for a long, long time to come."

Despite the hot, stuffy air in the living room, a cold shiver swept down my spine. I didn't have Air magic like Magda did, so I didn't have any sort of precognition or insight into the future, but I felt like someone had just walked over my grave all the same, all because of Eira Snow and her three brats.

Anger and disgust filled me again. I straightened up and paced back and forth, moving as quickly as I could through the narrow, twisting paths that snaked through the rotting garbage that filled the house. Thinking. Finally, I stopped and stared down at Magda once more.

"Your vision didn't tell you which one of Eira's daughters it is?" I asked. "Which girl has both Ice and Stone magic?"

Magda shook her head. "I didn't see that for sure, but it's probably the youngest one. That's how these things usually work."

I didn't know if Magda's prophecy would ever come to pass or not, but there was something in her voice, something in the way she looked at me, that made me uneasy. Like she'd already seen my death and was just marking time until it happened.

I hadn't killed my own father and spent the last several years clawing my way to the top of the Ashland underworld to let someone threaten me now, to let someone destroy everything I'd worked so hard to get in the first place, even if she was just a girl. Children were simply tools, things that could be used to manipulate and motivate other people. I felt no more for them than I did for anyone else, which was nothing at all.

"Well, then," I said in a cold voice, "if you don't know exactly which girl it is, I'll just have to kill them all—and their mother, for good measure."

Magda cackled her approval and drew another warped snowflake on the floor.

"What do you mean the assassin said *no kids*?" I barked at Elliot Slater.

The giant shrugged his massive shoulders. "He had almost agreed to do the job, but he balked when he realized that you wanted the three kids dead too, along with their mother. I even offered to triple his fee just like you told me to, but he wouldn't hear of it. Apparently, he has a thing about not killing kids. Can you believe that?"

We sat in my study, drinking whiskey and discussing how best to arrange the deaths of Eira Snow and her three daughters. Elliot lounged in the red leather chair across from me, swirling the amber liquid around in his crystal glass. He was tall and powerful, even for a giant, although his chalky skin, thin blond hair, and hazel eyes gave him a pale, washed-out appearance.

Elliot had been working for me for several years, steadily rising through the ranks, until now he was the head of the giant bodyguards I employed. He'd proven himself to be loyal, dependable, and as vicious as I was in his own way. Elliot enjoyed stalking beautiful women and then beating them to death when they didn't return his twisted affections, and I made sure he had a steady supply of them, just like I did with Magda and her chickens. So far, both of us were pleased with the arrangement. Elliot also knew that if he failed to keep on pleasing me, he'd be as dead as his predecessors.

"What was this assassin's name again?" I asked.

"The Tin Man," Elliot replied. "Not much is known about him, but he's supposed to be the best in the business. Credited with lots of kills over the years, although he's smart about not having anything traced back to him. I had to go through three cutouts just to make contact, and I still don't have a clue who he really is or if he's based here in Ashland or somewhere else."

I leaned back in my chair, took a sip of whiskey, and enjoyed the sweet, slow burn of the liquor in my mouth and throat. Not nearly as heady as using my Fire power, but the whiskey had its own kind of magic.

"What about other options? Other assassins?"

Elliot shrugged again. "Everyone I talked to said this Tin Man is the best. If he won't do it, he won't do it. I say you just let me and my boys go over to this elemental's house and take care of business ourselves like usual."

I shook my head. "Eira Snow would turn your men into ice cubes. She's not as strong as me, but she's no pushover with her magic. Besides, she still has friends and influence in Ashland. If an attack by your men were to fail, everyone would know that I was behind it. And if Eira survived, she would cause even *more* trouble. I wouldn't mind that so much, but of course, my friends in the Circle would frown on such unwanted attention being drawn to our organization. Mason Mitchell might have finally given me the green light to kill Eira, but I need to be somewhat discreet about it. That's why I wanted it done by an assassin, so there would be no way to trace the attack back to me."

Elliot leaned forward and stared at me. "Then perhaps you should handle it yourself and *discreetly* let everyone, including Mason, know just how strong you are, just how untouchable."

I arched an eyebrow. "And what would that get me?"

The giant leaned back in his chair. "The respect of the few remaining underworld bosses we've been having problems with. And if not their respect, then something even better: their fear."

I took another sip of whiskey and considered Elliot's idea. I'd been quietly amassing power for years, ever since my father's death. A piece here, a piece there, until I almost had the whole pie.

To many folks in Ashland, I was a wealthy, benevolent businesswoman who donated millions of dollars to various charities every year. Those fools didn't realize that those charities were merely fronts for my organization and that I had my hands in every illegal business in the city. My father had been an underworld prince, sharing power with others, but I was going to be a bloody *queen* and answer to no one.

The more I thought about the giant's idea, the more I liked it. Eira was a powerful elemental, wealthy, influential, and respected. Her death would send shock waves through Ashland, and everyone would wonder if they might be next if they pissed off the wrong person—me.

Still, I wasn't going to be *too* blatant about things. It was one thing to have people suspect you of murder, but it was quite another for them to know that you actually did it. Most of the time, the suspicion was all you needed, especially given how painful I planned to make Eira's and her daughters' deaths.

"Fine," I said. "I'll do it myself, and if Mason doesn't like it, then too bloody bad. It'll be more fun, anyway. It always is."

Elliot nodded his approval. "What do you want me to do about the assassin? He's returned the fee that he requested."

"As if that would be enough to save him for saying no to me," I scoffed. "Find out who this mysterious Tin Man really is and kill him."

"I'll get Douglas on it," Elliot said.

I nodded. Douglas was one of Elliot's more capable men. He'd track down the assassin and eliminate the mysterious Tin Man. And if Douglas didn't, then I'd keep sending men until one of them succeeded. Giants were disposable that way. Everyone who worked for me was disposable that way, even Elliot, even if he didn't realize it.

I settled back a little deeper in my chair and sipped some more of my whiskey. A smile curved my lips as I started thinking about the most painful, pleasurable way to kill Eira Snow.

Chapter Four

Years Ago

Killing Eira was easier than I'd thought it would be.

Breaking her daughter was much, much harder.

It was ridiculously simple for Elliot and his men to overcome the bodyguards Eira had hired to protect her mansion and her daughters. Most of the guards barely had time to scream before Elliot bashed their heads in with his massive fists. He did the same to a few of the servants as well before someone sounded the alarm, and the others fled into the woods that surrounded the house.

Then Eira jumped into the mix, using her Ice magic to cover the servants' escape and kill as many of the giants as she could. I trailed behind Elliot and his men, more than content to let them handle the frontal assault. Let Eira fritter away her magic, trying to save the people who'd abandoned her. The more she used now, the less she would have later, when I finally confronted her.

It took half an hour before Elliot and his men drove Eira

into a hallway in the downstairs part of the mansion where she decided to make her last stand.

The giants fell back, and I stepped forward to face my oldest enemy. Eira's eyes narrowed, her blue gaze cold and frosty with the glow of her Ice magic.

"I should have known it was you, Mab," Eira snarled, creeping back toward the living room that lay behind her.

I smiled, matching her slow retreat step for step. "Yes, you should have. My only regret is that I didn't do this a long time ago. The first day we met, actually."

Her mouth flattened out into a thin line, and her hand crept up to clutch the snowflake pendant hanging around her neck. She still wore it, all these years later. "You tried, remember?"

"Well, tonight I'm finally going to succeed. Look at you, Eira. You're a scared, sweaty mess. You've already used up most of your Ice magic trying to help people who ran at the first sign of trouble. You won't last a minute against my Fire power."

Doubt flickered in her eyes, but she dropped her hand from her snowflake rune and straightened her shoulders in defiance. "We'll see."

And then we dueled.

It took a little longer than I'd expected, but my plan worked. Eira had squandered so much of her Ice magic trying to get others to safety that she barely had any left to fling at me. I could have killed her immediately, but it was much more satisfying to let my Fire creep closer and closer to her, cutting through all the pitiful Ice that she managed to create.

Eira knew she was dead. At the very end, she didn't even look at me. Instead, she turned her head to the side, glanced up, and said . . . something. I wasn't sure what.

I never found out her last words, because my Fire washed over her a second later. One moment, Eira was fighting me. The next, the ashy remains of her body crumpled to the floor.

The sight made me smile like nothing else ever had. Not my father's death, not the other underworld bosses I'd dispatched, not all the other enemies I'd eliminated over the years.

A few seconds later, Eira's oldest daughter ran down the stairs and crouched by her mother's side. She wasn't nearly as strong in her magic as Eira had been, and it only took one ball of Fire to turn her into a pile of smoking ash.

Two down, two to go.

But the other two brats turned out to be a little luckier or perhaps even a little smarter than I'd expected. It took Elliot about twenty minutes of searching before he caught the middle brat sneaking through the house. He dumped her unconscious body at my feet.

"I thought you'd want to do it yourself," he said.

I nodded. "And the youngest daughter? The one with both Ice and Stone magic?"

The giant shook his head. "Haven't found her yet. This one led my men on a merry chase through the house, though. I think she might have hidden her sister somewhere. That, or the youngest brat realized what was going on and hid herself."

I stared down at the middle girl. She was young, maybe twelve or thirteen, with a wild tangle of brown hair instead of Eira's smooth golden locks. She looked like a broken doll splayed at my feet, like one of my toys that I'd long ago smashed to bits. The only thing left to do was burn her alive, just like I already had done to her mother and older sister.

I had raised my hand and started to do just that when I noticed something gleaming around her neck. Curious, I bent down and shoved her hair aside.

The girl wore a silverstone pendant, just like Eira had when she was younger. Just like the Ice elemental had until I'd killed her less than an hour ago.

A strange sort of fury filled me then. I ripped the necklace from around the girl's throat and closed my fingers over the pendant, not even bothering to see exactly what the symbol was. The silverstone was cold and smooth, and the round shape of it dug into my palm, along with several rays radiating out from the center. Another damn snowflake, most likely, just like the one Eira had worn.

I'd torn the pendant off Eira's burned body and done the same thing to the ivy vine her oldest daughter had been wearing, to keep as a reminder of my triumph tonight. But two pendants were enough, and I didn't need any more trophies.

My fingers tightened around the silverstone. I grabbed hold of my Fire magic and started to melt the metal—

Elliot cleared his throat. "Mab?" he asked. "What do you want to do now?"

The giant's voice penetrated my odd rage, and I looked down at the girl again. Thinking.

"Tell your men to keep searching for the youngest daughter," I replied. "You're going to stay here and help me with this one."

"Why?" he asked. "Kill her and be done with it."

"No," I said, smiling again, my fingers tightening around the pendant in my hand. "That would be too easy, just like killing Eira was too easy. The mother might be dead, but I can still make her daughters suffer—starting with this one."

Sometime later, the girl jerked awake with a start.

I lounged on a nearby couch and watched her, enjoying her confusion, then her panic, then her terror, as she realized that she was tied to a chair and that I'd had Elliot duct-tape her precious silverstone rune between her hands.

Even more delicious was the fact that the girl couldn't see what was going on, since I'd had the giant blindfold her as well. A trick I'd learned from my father. People were *so* much more easily frightened when they couldn't see what horrible thing was about to happen to them. The anticipation alone was enough to break most folks.

Still, after a moment, the girl pushed aside her terror and started struggling, trying to break free of the heavy ropes that Elliot had lashed around her body. I got to my feet, went over, and leaned down so that my mouth was close to her ear.

"There's no use in struggling," I purred. "I've made sure those ropes are quite secure."

I trailed a fingernail down her cheek, letting her feel my Fire magic. The girl yelped and jerked away, but of course she had nowhere to go. I started questioning the girl, asking her where her sister was, but the little brat refused to talk, even when I threatened her with my Fire magic.

I stared at her, at the stubborn set of her chin and the hardness of her mouth. This one was her mother's daughter, after all, determined to be a thorn in my side until the very end.

"So brave, so young, so very stupid. Have it your way then," I said.

I stepped back and reached for my Fire magic, concentrating my power on the pendant trapped between the girl's hands. It was easy for me to direct my magic into the bauble, to focus my Fire on that one area and slowly, agonizingly heat and melt the silverstone until the magical metal seared itself into her tender palms.

The girl screamed and cried and thrashed against the ropes, but surprisingly, she still didn't tell me what I wanted to know, not even when I knew she could smell her own burning skin. The stench of it filled the air, mixing with that of Eira and the oldest girl.

Finally, I grew tired of torturing the middle brat and left her alone, still weeping and wailing. She wasn't going anywhere, and she wasn't the one I wanted dead, anyway. Her younger sister was—the one Magda believed had both Ice and Stone magic. Bria was her name. Which made the middle brat, the one I'd just tortured, Genevieve, according to the information Elliot had gathered for me.

I found the giant crouched down in the kitchen, opening the cabinet doors and peering at the pots and pans, as if Bria might actually be hiding in such a small, cramped space.

"You still haven't found her?" I asked in a sharp voice.

Elliot looked over his shoulder at me. "We're doing the best we can. It's a big house, and she's a little kid. There are a lot of places she could be hiding. Or she might have darted off into the woods. But don't worry. We'll find her sooner or later—"

A scream sounded, a sharp, high-pitched wail that radiated with terror. A few more screams followed that first one.

Elliot grinned and got to his feet. "See? I told you they'd find her sooner or later. Now all we have to do is go get her—"

Another scream sounded. This one was also full of pain and terror, but something else dominated the sound, something that made even me take heed.

Fury—pure, raw, elemental *fury*.

The girl's magic ripped through the house in much the same way mine had slammed into Eira earlier—intense and unstoppable. The blast of power slashed through the whole mansion, gaining force with every second, and the girl's magic sliced into my skin like an ice-cold whip, one that had a granite core.

And I felt something I hadn't felt in a very long time: fear.

"Magda was right," I whispered. "She *is* strong."

The scream faded away, and for a moment, there was an eerie silence. Then, one by one, the stones under our feet began to splinter. No, not splinter. That was too slow. The stone simply *shattered*, and I knew it was because of her scream, because of *her* elemental power.

Not mine.

The whole mansion began to shake and buck and heave,

and I staggered back, clutching a counter for support. Jagged cracks zipped through the ceiling, and chunks of plaster started falling like raindrops.

"Let's get out of here!" Elliot shouted above the growing roar of destruction.

I was already sprinting toward the nearest door, throwing it open, and stumbling outside. Elliot was right behind me. We staggered to the edge of the woods, then turned and looked back at the house.

It was like something out of a disaster movie. Piece by piece, room by room, floor by floor, the mansion simply collapsed in on itself. Dust, smoke, and other debris filled the air. Glass shattered, wood snapped, and fires bloomed like orange orchids in the mess. What had once been an immaculate mansion had been reduced to rubble by a girl who hadn't even come into her full power as an elemental yet.

A shiver rippled down my spine, and once more, I felt like someone had just walked over a grave—my own.

"Well," Elliot said when the noise and dust finally settled down. "I guess you don't have to worry about finding the other brat now. Nobody could have survived that. Not even the elemental who caused it. Whoever was in that house is dead now—dead and buried."

He was right. Genevieve, the middle brat, the one I'd left tied up in the mansion, was certainly dead, killed by her own sister's magic. Even I couldn't have survived something like that, such sudden, massive destruction.

"Come on," Elliot said. "Let's see if any of my men made it out of the mansion on the other side. I know how you hate to waste resources."

The giant started skirting around the edge of the ruined structure, calling out for his men. I followed him. Just before I rounded a corner on the back side of the mansion, I stopped and looked over my shoulder.

The fires were rapidly spreading, consuming all the wood, glass, and plaster and leaping from one mound of rubble to the next. The flames would eat up whatever hadn't been destroyed by the house collapsing. Elliot was right. Eira Snow and her three daughters were dead and buried—forever.

So why couldn't I shake this nagging feeling of dread?

Chapter Five

A Few Months Ago

O nce word of the deaths of Eira Snow and her daughters hit the news, things got much easier for me. No one could point a finger at me and say that I'd caved Eira's own house in on her, but most folks figured that I'd had *something* to do with her death.

Either way, it worked out well for me. The few remaining pockets of resistance in the underworld melted away, and I took control of the city just the way I'd always planned, just the way I'd always dreamed.

I finally had everything I had ever wanted—and it was *wonderful*.

Oh, I still had minor problems here and there over the years. An Air elemental named Alexis James thought she could embezzle from her father's company after I took it over, although someone killed her before I could get around to doing it myself.

An assassin managed to take down Tobias Dawson, someone who thought he was a business associate of mine. That same assassin also had the audacity to kill Jake McAllister, Jonah's son, during a party at my mansion. Plus, I still hadn't found a way to eliminate some of my more demanding colleagues in the Circle, including Mason Mitchell, who still thought I worked for him instead of the other way around.

Still, everything was more or less under control—until the day Detective Bria Coolidge came to Ashland.

Elliot was the one who broke the news to me, and we discussed it one night while having dinner at Underwood's, the city's most expensive restaurant. Really, there was nothing to discuss. Somehow, some way, Bria Snow, now Bria Coolidge, had survived the destruction of her family's mansion, and now she had returned to Ashland.

Magda's prophecy, the one I'd all but forgotten about, came rushing back to me, and I felt the same uncomfortable dread and annoying touch of fear that I had experienced all those years ago when I'd first heard Bria's elemental scream of rage, pain, and fury.

"Kill her," I ordered. "Tonight."

But Elliot didn't manage to do it. He slunk back to my mansion, telling some ridiculous tale about a masked woman— an assassin—who'd killed his men and saved Bria Coolidge.

Normally, I would have burned his skin from his bones for spouting such a ridiculous story. Only . . . his story wasn't quite as ridiculous as it first seemed.

Alexis James. Tobias Dawson. Jake McAllister. This was one setback too many, and I started wondering if there was more to Alexis's, Tobias's, and Jake's deaths than I'd originally thought.

Then came the night that Elliot himself was killed, and I got a call from a woman I'd met once before—in my own bathroom, right after she had killed Jake McAllister and dumped his body in the bathtub, although I hadn't realized what she'd done at the time.

She'd crowed at me a little before finally getting down to business. "You're finished in this town, Mab. You and all your cronies and minions. I'm putting you on notice. I'm going to take down your organization one piece, one player at a time, until you're the only one left. And then I'm coming for you."

I'd countered her threats with some of my own, and she'd spouted back some nonsense about leaving her calling card on the side of Elliot's mountain mansion.

"That fucking spider rune?" I'd asked, staring up at the symbol burning in the stone. "Why a spider rune? It's so simple, so weak."

She'd hesitated a few moments. "Why a spider rune? Because it's the symbol for patience. And I can wait however long I have to until I get you. So look at the rune, Mab, memorize it, and remember it well. Because you'll be seeing it again real soon, sugar. Including the second before you die."

Then she'd hung up on me.

My gaze flicked over to Bria Coolidge, wondering if it could have been her I'd been talking to, but the detective was staring up at the burning rune just like everyone else was. She wasn't even holding her phone.

She wasn't the one who'd killed Elliot and the rest of my men.

For the first time in a very long time, I had a real enemy— one who was just as vicious and deadly as I was.

Chapter Six

Present Day

"Mab?" Jonah asked, breaking into my jumbled thoughts and pulling me back to the here and now. I blinked, and the last of my memories faded away, like the snow still melting in my hair. Yes, I had an enemy, and now she'd killed the assassin I'd hired to kill her.

I stared down at Elektra LaFleur, my gaze once again going to the spider rune that had been scratched into the gravel beside her body. The snow had picked up speed while I'd been lost in my memories, the individual flakes swiftly filling in the spider rune—

And then I remembered.

Eira's snowflake necklace flashing around her throat when we were young. The snowflakes Magda had drawn when she'd first told me about her vision that a girl with both Ice and Stone magic would kill me. The strange, lopsided snowflakes that had eight points instead of six. The feel of the middle brat's silverstone rune in my hand and all those rays radiating out of that one solid circle.

"Not snowflakes," I whispered. "They were *never* snow-flakes. They were spiders and webs instead. Spiders and webs, and stings and stones, just like Magda said."

"Mab?" Jonah asked again. "What are you talking about? Of course they're snowflakes. They're all around us."

I ignored him, my mind racing in a dozen different directions, putting all the puzzle pieces together. It didn't take long. Now that I finally remembered, I knew *exactly* what I had to do.

I stared down at the white orchid I was still clutching. My fist exploded with elemental Fire, and the beautiful flower instantly disintegrated. I opened my fingers and let the smoking ash float away on the cold winter wind. Like Elektra LaFleur, the orchid was of no further use to me.

Jonah skittered to the side like a cockroach. He always got nervous whenever I so casually unleashed my Fire power. He'd seen me kill too many people with it over the years to be anything but wary around me. It was the only quality I admired about him.

"I know who she is," I said in a satisfied voice. "I should have realized it immediately, but it was such a long time ago, and I've killed so many people since then. But I know *exactly* who she is now. More important, I know how I can find her and hurt her like she hasn't been hurt in a long, long time—not since the last time we met, as a matter of fact."

Jonah blinked. "You know who the Spider is?"

I nodded.

"Who—*who* is it?"

"Nobody important," I replied. "Just a lost little girl I should have killed a long time ago, along with her baby sister. But I'll rectify that situation very, very soon."

Jonah's silver eyebrows drew together in confusion, although the rest of his face didn't move along with them. "How are you going to do that?"

I outlined my plan. He listened to me intently, his perfectly smooth features betraying nothing of what he was really thinking. Sometimes I thought that was the reason Jonah got all those Air elemental facials, so he could better hide his true feelings from me.

"It will take a few weeks to arrange everything," Jonah said when I was finished. "Especially if you want to lure quality talent to Ashland and cast a net over the whole city."

"Take however long you need to, and spend as much money as necessary. I don't care what it costs. Just make sure the job is done *properly* this time. Because Jonah?"

"Yes?"

I let him see the black fire burning in my eyes. "This is your last chance."

The lawyer pressed his lips together, swallowed, and nodded his head.

I stalked through the train yard and headed toward my waiting limo. The driver hurried to open the back door. Before I slid inside the car, I stopped and looked over my shoulder.

Bria Coolidge was staring at me, along with her partner, Xavier. Both of them had calculating looks on their faces, clearly wondering what I was up to, where I was going, and what I might be plotting against them and their mysterious friend. I gave them a dismissive glance and slid into the back of the limo. The driver shut the door and hurried around to the front.

I reached forward, opened the bar, and poured myself a glass of whiskey. Outside, Bria and Xavier kept staring at my limo. Even though they couldn't see me through the tinted windows, I raised my glass to them in a silent toast, then drained all the whiskey inside.

Let them wonder. Let them worry about what I was up to. They'd find out soon enough.

Because it wouldn't be long until Bria Coolidge was dead— and her sister, Genevieve Snow, the Spider, along with her.

Haints and Hobwebs

This story takes place after *Tangled Threads*, book 4.

Chapter One

Gin Blanco

The first time I saw the haint was in the cemetery.

Shocking, I know, a ghost hanging out in a graveyard, but the pale, wispy figure still caught my eye, if only because it was the first one I'd ever seen.

You'd think I would have been visited by more haints in my time, given the fact that I was a semiretired assassin and that I'd helped a lot of people move on from this life to the next with a slice or two of my silverstone knives.

I had come to Blue Ridge Cemetery to place some forget-me-nots on the grave of Fletcher Lane, my murdered mentor. The old man had taken me in off the streets when I was a teenager, trained me to be an assassin like him, dubbed me the Spider, and then set me loose on the greedy, corrupt citizens of the Southern metropolis of Ashland.

Good times.

I had been crouched over Fletcher's grave for about ten minutes, brushing the dry, withered remains of the autumn leaves off his granite gravestone and arranging the blue forget-me-nots in an empty soda bottle I'd brought along for the purpose. The slick green glass was the same color as Fletcher's eyes.

It was a bitterly cold January day. The sun looked like it was submerged under dingy dishwater clouds rather than hanging in the sky, and its weak rays didn't even come close to melting the thin patches of crusty snow that littered the ground like shreds of tissue paper.

But I didn't pay much attention to the cold—I was too busy talking to Fletcher. I'd been catching the old man up on everything that was happening in my life, from the reappearance of my baby sister, Bria, back in Ashland to my ongoing war against Mab Monroe, the Fire elemental who'd murdered my mother and my older sister when I was thirteen.

Fletcher's grave was my own private confessional, a place where all my whispered secrets and worrisome weaknesses would be whipped away by the biting winds that whizzed across this particular ridge of the Appalachian Mountains.

Weaknesses that I had to hide as Gin Blanco—and most especially as my alter ego, the Spider.

I had just finished telling Fletcher about my deepening feelings for my lover, Owen Grayson, when a flash of movement caught my eye. I immediately palmed one of the silverstone knives hidden up my sleeves. I might be mostly retired from being the Spider these days, but I still had plenty of enemies who wanted me dead, namely Mab, now that I was openly gunning for her.

My fingers curled around the knife's hilt, and a small symbol stamped into the metal pressed into a larger matching scar embedded in my palm. Both of them spider runes, a small circle surrounded by eight thin rays. The symbol for patience. The same rune, the same scar, was branded into my other palm. It was my assassin name and so much a part of who and what I was.

Knife in hand, I turned my head, ready to face whatever danger might be lurking in the cemetery—and to put it down, if necessary, in the bloody, permanent fashion I was fond of and so very good at.

And that's when I first saw the haint.

She hovered over a gravestone about twenty feet away from where Fletcher was buried. I'd never given much thought to ghosts before. They were dead, after all. It was the living you had to watch out for—the people who could still screw you over six ways from Sunday the second they got the chance.

Still, it surprised me how translucent she was, like a shadow cast by the moon. Everything about her was pale silver, from her sweet, old-fashioned gingham dress to the wild, wavy hair that cascaded down her back like a waterfall. Her features were sharp, though, painfully so. Big eyes, full lips, a crook of a nose. She wasn't what I would consider pretty—her features were too angular for that—but something in her face made you take a second look at her.

All put together, she looked like an old-timey mountain girl, someone who had once lived in one of the hundreds of forested hollers that clutched around the city of Ashland like thin, green, grasping fingers.

Besides, haints or not, only mountain girls went around barefoot in the winter. Like Jo-Jo Deveraux, the Air elemental who healed me whenever I needed patching up. I eyed the ghost's toes, which rested on a patch of snow. I wondered if she could even feel the cold in whatever half-life she was clinging to.

I had told Fletcher everything that was troubling me, at least for today, so I slid my knife back up my sleeve and focused on the ghost. It took me a minute to realize that she was trying to clean off the gravestone, just like I'd done with Fletcher's. I didn't know if she could really brush aside the glittering cobwebs that swooped from one side of the gravestone to the other with her silvery fingers, but the tight set of her mouth told me that she was sure determined to try.

I got to my feet and walked over to the grave. The haint didn't stop her phantom brushing, much less look at me. I supposed that she was used to being ignored. So was I. As the Spider, I had spent a good portion of my life creeping through the shadows and being as invisible as possible—until the moment I chose to strike.

I watched the haint work for a while. Maybe it was just my imagination, but the thick, sticky cobwebs seemed to quiver, shiver, and slowly break apart one tangled thread at a time under her relentless touch. Maybe she really *could* brush them away if she focused hard and long enough. And what was time to a haint?

My gray gaze traced over the faint markings on the smooth stone.

Thomas P. Kirkwood, beloved son, 1908–1929.

Maybe it was because I had been thinking about Owen so much lately and trying to come to terms with my feelings for him, but I didn't think the long-dead Thomas was the haint's son. No, I thought, only a lover could inspire that kind of devotion, even among ghosts and, most tellingly, all these years later.

Curiosity was one trait that Fletcher had instilled in me above all others, so I crouched down in front of the gravestone, then reached forward and ran my fingers across the weather-worn words.

The stone radiated sorrow.

People's actions and feelings sink into their surroundings over time, especially into stone. As a Stone elemental, I could sense those psychic vibrations in whatever form the element took around me, from the proud whispers of a beautiful jewel to the harsh cries of a concrete floor spattered with blood.

The gravestone's sad murmurs filled my mind, along with

soft, whistling notes that told of the crumbling passage of time and how the sun, wind, rain, and snow had slowly worn away the hard, pointed edges of the marker. Not unusual emotions in a cemetery. The same feelings would eventually sink into Fletcher's gravestone as the years rolled on by.

What surprised me was the rage.

It pulsed through the stone like a cold, black, beating heart—slow, steady, and unending.

Thump-thump-thump-thump.

Somehow I knew it was the haint's rage. After all, if she'd died around the same time as Thomas, then she'd probably been haunting the cemetery since the 1920s, which meant that she'd had decades for her feelings to sink into the gravestone.

But who was the haint so angry at? Thomas? Had their love affair somehow gone wrong?

I concentrated on the rage, listening to the harsh mutters buried deep, deep down in the stone. I got the sense that the ghost's anger was directed at someone else, someone who'd taken Thomas away from her. Sharp, anguished shrieks of helplessness also trilled through the stone, punctuating the rage and mixing with faint whispers of guilt.

Whatever had happened to Thomas, there was nothing the haint could do about it now, and it was eating her up inside. If she even had an inside anymore. Maybe that was why she hadn't faded away into the afterlife yet. Maybe she *couldn't* until things were set right. At least, that was what always seemed to happen in the stories I read for the various literature classes I took in my spare time at Ashland Community College.

Guilt, rage, helplessness—I could relate to all those emotions since I'd felt every single one of them every single day since Mab Monroe had murdered my mother and my older sister. Really, they were the driving forces of my life—and would probably be the death of me when I finally went up against the Fire elemental.

So I took pity on the ghostly mountain girl. I leaned forward and spent the next few minutes brushing off all the cobwebs that decorated the gravestone.

No one had touched the marker in years, decades probably, and the webs were so thick and sticky that they clung to my skin like grayish glue. Hobwebs, Fletcher would have called them. When I was younger, he used to tell me stories about how little hobgoblins would start hiding in the silky strands if I didn't clean the cobwebs out of the corners of my bedroom. I smiled at the memory and kept working.

In addition to getting rid of the hobwebs, I also dusted off all the dried leaves and snapped twigs that the wind had carried this way.

When I was finally done, I looked over at the haint. "There," I said. "Better now?"

I must have surprised her, because for a moment, she zipped around me like moonlit lightning. I blinked, and there she was, shimmering a few feet away. The mountain girl's eyes met mine. When she realized that I was actually looking at her, that I could actually *see* her, her mouth rounded into a perfect O. After a moment, she crept forward and waved her hand in front of my face.

"What?" I asked, brushing away her cool, ghostly fingers. "If you're trying to make me cold, I don't think it will work. I'm an Ice elemental, you see. Ice and Stone, actually. I can create Ice cubes with my bare hands that are colder than you are. And if you're trying to scare me, well, you should know that I've spent a good part of my life being an assassin and killing people—bad, bad people. So I don't scare easy."

The mountain girl dropped her hand. She backed up a few steps, crossed her arms over her chest, and considered me, her silvery gaze taking in every little thing about me, from my heavy fleece jacket to my chocolate-brown hair to my pale skin and gray eyes that were almost as cold as hers.

I stood there and let her stare. As an assassin, I was used to being patient, used to waiting for my targets to become vulnerable, no matter how long it took—minutes, hours, days, weeks, months. Or in Mab's case, years.

But even I couldn't compete with a haint. She had all the time in the world, and I had things to do, specifically a restaurant to run.

"Well," I said, "I hope you find what you're looking for. Peace, revenge, whatever. Maybe I'll see you the next time I come here to visit Fletcher."

The haint didn't speak, of course, but I didn't really expect her to. Still, the mountain girl stood next to Thomas's forgotten grave and watched me disappear into the darkening twilight.

Chapter Two

Gin Blanco

"I think I'm being haunted," I said the next day.

Finnegan Lane, my foster brother and partner in murder, mayhem, and mischief, arched an eyebrow. Amusement filled his bright green eyes, which were the same color as those of Fletcher, his father. "Really? Has one of your previous dark and dirty misdeeds come back to bite you in the ass?"

"Nothing as dramatic as that. I seem to have brought home a haint from the cemetery."

I jerked my head to the right. Finn stared at the spot, but he didn't see the mountain girl spinning around and around on the stool next to him, a small, silly smile on her face. I wasn't quite sure how she could spin like that and the stool not move, but then again, haints weren't my specialty. Killing people was. So I just sighed and leaned my elbows down on the counter.

It was almost closing time at the Pork Pit, the barbecue restaurant I ran in downtown Ashland, and my Gin joint was largely deserted. I'd already sent the waitstaff home for the day, and the only people inside were me, Finn, and Sophia Deveraux, the dwarf who was the head cook.

Well, us plus the haint.

I'd first noticed the mountain girl when I opened up the restaurant this morning. I didn't know how she'd tracked me from the cemetery to the Pork Pit, but she had. I'd found her wandering around inside, looking at the well-worn but clean vinyl booths, the peeling blue and pink pig tracks on the floor that led to the men's and women's restrooms, respectively, the long counter in the back of the restaurant, even the bloody framed copy of *Where the Red Fern Grows* that hung on one of the walls.

She'd perked up when I came into the restaurant, her ghostly figure pulsing a brighter silver. I'd tried to talk to her, to ask her what she was doing here and what she wanted, but all she did was stare at me with big eyes that almost glowed with hope.

I had no idea why. I wasn't one to inspire hope in people—more like fear, followed quickly by terror, blood, and death.

The mountain girl had hung out in the restaurant the rest of the day, always keeping me in sight. When I went over to a booth to take someone's order, she tagged along. When I went into the alley in the back of the restaurant to dump the day's trash, she stayed two steps behind me. She even followed me into the bathroom, until I shooed her away and told her that I liked to do my lady business in private.

But none of the folks who'd come into the Pork Pit noticed her hovering over their shoulders, wistfully eyeing their thick, juicy barbecue beef and pork sandwiches, steak-cut fries, and baked beans coated with Fletcher's secret barbecue sauce. Apparently, I was the only one who could see her.

Well, me and Sophia.

I supposed it made sense. Sophia was an Air elemental, which meant she could create, control, and manipulate all the natural gases in the air the same way that I could in the stone around me. No doubt, she sensed the psychic vibrations the ghost was giving off. Not that Sophia would say anything about it, since she didn't talk much. Still, every once in a while, she would stare at the mountain girl out of the corner of her eye.

And the mountain girl stared right back at her. That was because Sophia wasn't just a dwarf—she also happened to be a Goth. Sophia wore black from the bottoms of her heavy boots to her jeans to her T-shirt, which featured a white, grinning pirate skull-and-crossbones. A matching silverstone skull dangled off the black leather collar that ringed her neck. Her hair and eyes were black too, although her lips were a bright, glossy pink in her pale face.

Sophia's clothes stood out in stark contrast to Finn's slick gray designer Fiona Fine suit and my simple long-sleeved blue T-shirt and jeans.

"And why do you suppose this particular haint has decided to haunt you?" Finn asked, taking a sip of the chicory coffee he favored. "You didn't kill her, did you? Or someone she cared about?"

"No. According to the gravestone she was floating around, she probably died long before I was even born."

Finn perked up. "Gravestone, eh? What was the name on it?"

In addition to being an investment banker, Finn also had a network of spies throughout Ashland and beyond. To him, digging up dirt on other people was an amusing hobby, as was seducing whatever woman happened to be strolling by at the time. I'd never been able to decide what Finn liked best— money, secrets, or women. But his unashamed pursuit of all three was one of the many things I loved about him.

This time, I raised my eyebrow. "You really want to research this for me? It's just a ghost."

"A ghost who's haunting you," Finn pointed out. "She's got

to have a reason, right? Otherwise, why not just stay in the cemetery and hang out for another hundred years or so?"

He had a point. Truth be told, I was kind of curious myself about why she'd latched onto me. Oh, I could tell that the haint wanted *something*—I just didn't know what it was or why she thought I could give it to her. As a semiretired assassin, I wasn't known for my kind and generous nature. Quite the opposite, in fact.

"All right," I said. "See what you can find out."

I told him Kirkwood's name, along with the year he'd died.

Finn toasted me with his coffee mug, downed the rest of his brew, and left to get started on his mission. On his way out the front door, Finn passed someone coming into the Pork Pit.

Owen Grayson.

A smile creased my face at the sight of the sexy businessman, and all sorts of warm feelings flooded my veins—feelings that I didn't want to examine too closely. Owen and I had been lovers for several weeks now, and it always surprised me how much I'd come to care about him in such a short time.

But the really crazy thing was that he seemed to care about me just as much.

Owen knew all about my violent, bloody past, present, and future as the Spider, but it hadn't made him run screaming in the other direction—yet. He never shied away or ignored who I was and what I did as an assassin, mainly because he'd done his own share of dirty deeds over the years to protect his younger sister, Eva.

Owen's complete acceptance of me was one of the things I liked most about him, along with the fact that he always gave me the time and space I needed, whether I was stalking a target or trying to come to grips with our blossoming relationship.

Still, despite all we'd been through, some small, cynical part of me couldn't help but wonder when it would end. When Owen would get tired of the danger I put myself in and all the nights I came over to his house with blood spattered on my clothes. When he'd tell me we were through. Sure, Owen cared about me, but I didn't know that we were meant to last forever.

I wanted us to, though—far more than I should have.

As the woman Gin Blanco, my deepening feelings for Owen were unsettling enough, since I'd never been the type to wear my heart on my sleeve. As the assassin the Spider, they were downright disturbing, since I knew just how very easily someone could take Owen away from me forever. I'd already lost so many people—my mom, Eira; my older sister, Annabella; Fletcher. I didn't want to lose Owen too. Not now, not ever.

I smoothed out my features and kept the troubling turmoil out of my eyes. "Hey there, handsome," I drawled.

"Hey there, yourself," Owen rumbled.

He leaned across the counter and gave me a quick kiss that made me wish we could skip the dinner reservations he'd made and go straight to his house for dessert.

He drew back, and I realized the mountain girl had stopped her spinning and was staring at him. No surprise there. Oh, Owen wasn't as handsome as Finn—few men could compete with my foster brother's perfect features and smarmy smile— but something in Owen's face had attracted me right from the start.

I'd never been able to figure out if it was the slightly crooked tilt of his nose or the thin scar that slashed underneath his chin. Or maybe it was his piercing violet eyes, which were further set off by his blue-black hair and tan skin. Either way, once you looked at Owen, you didn't want to stop. At least, I didn't want to stop.

"You ready?" he asked. "Our reservation is at eight. I figured we'd swing by my place first so you could shower and change."

I arched an eyebrow. "Shower, eh? You know, I never end

up showering alone at your house. Why do you think that is?"

A devilish grin spread across his face, and heat sparked in his eyes. "Well," he said, matching my earlier drawl, "I wouldn't want you to get lonely in there. Besides, you need someone to wash your back, and I'm more than happy to volunteer for *that* particular job."

I laughed. "Well, how can a gal refuse such a generous offer? Just let me close up for the night and get my bag."

Owen made a low, formal bow. "As you command, my lady. Now and always."

His voice dropped to a raspy murmur on the last word. The intense look in his eyes made my heart quiver with longing, but I pushed the wistful feeling aside. For what seemed like the thousandth time, I told myself not to care too much for Owen Grayson, even if I knew it was already too late.

Sophia helped me turn off all the appliances before grabbing her own things and leaving through the swinging doors that led to the back of the restaurant. The dwarf would close up behind her, which left me to lock up the storefront.

I was so busy laughing and talking with Owen that I forgot about the mountain girl until I stepped outside and turned to pull the front door shut behind me. She stood there in the doorway, and I hesitated, wondering how rude it would be to reach through her translucent body to grab the doorknob.

The mountain girl's silvery eyes flicked to Owen, then to me. An aching sadness filled her face for a moment before her mouth flattened out into that determined line again. She reached over and touched the brick that lined the door of the restaurant, pressing her ghostly fingers into the stone as best she could. Then she looked at me again, raising her eyebrows in a silent question.

I frowned, then reached over and put my hand on top of hers, so that we were both touching the brick.

As always, my Stone elemental magic let me hear the

clogged, contented murmurs of the brick—the ones that matched the stomachs and arteries of so many of my customers after eating at the Pork Pit. But there was something else in the brick now, some other faint emotion mixed in with the usual pleasure.

I closed my eyes and concentrated, focusing on that sound, pulling it out of the stone, and trying to make some kind of sense of it.

Help him, a soft voice whispered in my mind. *Please.*

Startled, I dropped my hand from the brick. My eyes snapped open, and I found the mountain girl staring at me once more.

Who was *him*? Thomas? And why did she want me to help him? Thomas was dead and buried in the cemetery, just like Fletcher. There was nothing I could do for either one of them now. I killed people—I didn't bring them peace after the fact.

"Gin?" Owen asked. "Is something wrong?"

"No," I said, plastering a smile on my face. "Everything's just fine."

Her ominous plea delivered, the mountain girl stepped back inside the restaurant. I hesitated a moment, then leaned forward, grabbed the knob, and pulled the door shut.

My hand trembled the faintest bit as I slid the key into the lock and turned the dead bolt. I looked inside at the haint once more. The mountain girl's sad silver eyes were the last thing I saw before Owen put his arm around me and pulled me away from her for the night.

Chapter Three

Gin Blanco

"She's definitely a haint, all right," Jo-Jo said two days later. "Definitely a haint and not a ghost."

"What's the difference?" Bria asked.

I was curious about that myself. Fletcher had always used the words *haint* and *ghost* like they were interchangeable, and so had I.

"Well," Jo-Jo said, leaning over to put another coat of magenta polish on Bria's nails, "for the most part, ghosts are just troublemakers. Mean old souls who like to scare the living. They rattle chains, moan and groan, break mirrors, and generally make pests out of themselves. But haints, now, haints have a specific purpose. A *mission*, if you will. They're clinging to this life for a reason, and they can't or won't let go until that mission is completed, no matter how long it takes."

Well, that told me the mountain girl wanted something from me, but it still didn't tell me what that something was.

"Why do you think *I* can see her?" I asked. "I thought only

Air elementals like you and Sophia could see haints or ghosts. Not someone with Ice and Stone magic like me."

Jo-Jo shrugged. "It might be because you're supposed to help her with her mission. It happens like that sometimes, no matter what kind of elemental magic you have or even if you have none at all."

I looked to my left. The haint was here today, of course, pacing back and forth across the room. She'd been shadowing me for three days now. Every time I turned around, there she was—including when I'd been in the shower with Owen a few nights ago.

I would have knifed her for that little intrusion if I could have. She must have seen the murderous glint in my eyes, though, because she backed off a little after that. I hadn't seen her again until the next morning, when I opened Owen's bedroom door and found her slumped against the wall outside. Ever since then, though, she'd been my constant, silent companion.

Now the three of us—well, four, if you counted the haint— were in Jo-Jo's beauty salon, located in the back of her large antebellum house.

Jolene "Jo-Jo" Deveraux made her living as a self-pro-claimed *drama mama*. In addition to healing wounds, Air elemental magic was also great for fighting the ravages of time, and Jo-Jo used her power to do everything from smoothing out crow's feet to getting rid of pesky sunspots to putting various body parts back up to where they had been ten years and twenty pounds ago.

Scissors, combs, tweezers, blow dryers, curling irons, and every other tool that could be used to cut, wax, pluck, or exfoliate could be found in Jo-Jo's salon, along with cherry-red chairs, stacks of beauty magazines, and dozens of bottles of pink nail polish. Rosco, Jo-Jo's basset hound, snoozed in a wicker basket in the corner.

Like her sister, Sophia, Jo-Jo was also a dwarf, although

she was as light and sugary-sweet as cotton candy compared to Sophia's darker Goth nature. Jo-Jo's white-blond curls were perfectly arranged on top of her head, she wore a pink dress covered with enormous pink daisies, and a string of pearls dangled from her neck. Even though it was January and the salon floor was cool to the touch, Jo-Jo's feet were bare.

Mountain girls, I thought, and smiled.

Jo-Jo had offered to give Bria and me manicures and pedicures so we could spend some time together. Bria Coolidge might be my long-lost baby sister, but she was also a detective for the Ashland Police Department, and one of the few honest cops on the force. A few weeks ago, Bria had not only found out that I, Gin Blanco, was really her big sister, Genevieve Snow, but she'd also discovered that I was the assassin the Spider.

Needless to say, Bria had had more than a few problems with my former profession and occasional pro-bono deeds for the good citizens of Ashland. Still, we were trying to have some kind of relationship, trying to get to know each other again, and it was more than I had ever dared to hope for.

Jo-Jo had already finished my nails and was now working on Bria's. I wasn't much for manicures. As an assassin, I always kept my nails short, since it made it easier to get rid of the blood that settled underneath them. But Bria had always loved playing with our mother's makeup when we were kids, so I'd come to the salon and sat through Jo-Jo's ministrations. The dwarf had also trimmed Bria's blond hair, shaping it into a bob that was sleek and tousled at the same time.

"I heard of a few haints when I was living in Savannah," Bria said. "But nothing like what Gin's describing. What do you think this one wants? What do you think her mission is?"

I shrugged. I hadn't told anyone about the whispered words the haint had sent me through the brick at the Pork Pit, but they'd echoed in my head ever since.

Help him. Please.

"Well, I don't know exactly what she wants, but I know who she is," Finn called out from the doorway.

My foster brother swaggered into the salon, a cup of steaming chicory coffee in one hand and a thick manila folder in the other. He pulled up a chair so that he was sitting between me and Bria, then turned and gave my sister his most charming smile.

"Love the new 'do, Detective," Finn murmured. "It really brings out your bone structure."

Bria snorted, but a spark of interest shimmered in her blue eyes. Finn had laid a very public, very passionate kiss on my baby sister a few weeks ago during a Christmas party at Owen's house. Ever since then, the two of them had been engaged in their own sort of mating dance, with Finn running after Bria the way he did when any beautiful woman crossed his line of sight and Bria just as easily resisting him.

I didn't know what the final outcome would be, but so far, it had been entertaining to watch their battle of wills.

After another moment of eyeing Bria, Finn turned his attention to me and held up the file.

"You know, I didn't expect this to be quite the challenge it was," he said. "I actually had to go over to the newspaper office and bribe one of my sources to let me into their morgue."

"Poor baby," I murmured with false sympathy.

Bria snickered at my tone. Finn glared at her a second before turning his attention back to me.

"Seriously, Gin, do you know what a pain in the ass it is to go through microfilm? It took me *hours* to find the information. Hours I could have spent in the arms of a good woman—like sweet Bria here."

Bria rolled her eyes, and this time, Jo-Jo snickered.

"You were the one who volunteered." I plucked the folder from his hand. "So lay it out for me."

Finn batted his eyes at my baby sister one more time. "The guy who's buried in the cemetery is one Thomas P. Kirkwood."

"I already knew that."

I opened the folder and found a black-and-white picture on top of a stack of papers. Thomas Kirkwood had been a handsome man. Thick, curly hair, kind eyes, nice smile. Even a couple of dimples in his cheeks. I could see why the haint had been drawn to him. Most women would have been.

The mountain girl floated over to me. She bit her lip and stretched out her fingers, caressing Thomas's face, even though it was only a photo. A silver tear slid out of the corner of her eye, streaking down her face like a falling star.

"Yes," Finn said in a smug tone. "But you don't know how he died. You don't know how he was *murdered*."

"Murdered?" Bria asked, bristling. "When?"

"Relax, Detective," Finn said. "This was back in the nineteen twenties, well before you were a twinkle in anyone's eye. Apparently, there was something of a feud going on between Thomas and another man, Homer Graves."

Jo-Jo stiffened at the name.

"Do you know him?" I asked.

The dwarf looked at me with her clear, almost colorless eyes and nodded. "I do. He's a vampire. Probably around three hundred years old or so. Lives up on top of one of the ridges not too far from Warren Fox's store, Country Daze."

Her words were innocent enough, but concern filled her middle-aged face. Whoever Graves was, he was a bad person— bad enough to worry even Jo-Jo, who was one of the strongest elementals around.

"Anyway," Finn continued, "Thomas was in love with a girl named Tess Darville. By all accounts, she was in love with him too, but her parents wanted her to marry Graves instead."

My eyes flicked over to the haint. She looked at me and nodded.

Tess, I could almost hear her say. *My name is Tess.*

"So what happened?" Bria asked.

"Well, everyone thought that Tess and Thomas just up and ran off together." Finn hesitated. "Until their bodies were found two weeks later. They'd both been tortured. Mutilated, really, with their throats slashed from ear to ear. But the worst part was that their, um, hearts were cut out of their chests and never found. Of course, Homer Graves was the prime suspect, but the cops could never prove anything. They just didn't have the forensic science back then that they do now. It's all there in the copies I made of the newspaper clippings."

Bria frowned. "Their hearts were cut out of their chests? Where were the bodies found?"

Finn looked at her. "Out near the old Ashland Rock Quarry. Why?"

My sister's face tightened. "Because I got called out to a body dump there three days ago. Two victims, a young couple, both eighteen. They'd been missing for almost two weeks."

"And let me guess—their hearts were cut out of their chests," I finished.

Bria nodded. "I need to call in about this. See if Graves has any connection to my two victims."

She barely waited until her nails were dry before getting to her feet. She pulled out her cell phone and called Xavier, the giant who was her partner on the force, filling him in. Finn trailed my sister out of the salon, insisting that he was going with her, that he could tell her even more.

I waited until I heard the front door of the house shut behind them before I turned to Jo-Jo. "What else do you know? I saw how you tensed up when Finn said Graves's name. He's rotten, isn't he? Rotten to the core."

She hesitated. "There was some other talk about Graves as well. Not only that he murdered that poor couple way back when but about how he did it."

My eyes narrowed. "What kind of talk?"

"That he was an Air elemental in addition to being a vampire," Jo-Jo said in a low voice. The dwarf raised her clear eyes to mine. "That he . . . that he actually *ate* their hearts. Fried them up like hamburgers, put them on a bun, and everything. Supposedly, cutting out their hearts helped him suck their souls out of their bodies. Eating them, well, I think he did that just for fun."

I'd seen a lot of bad things in my time as the Spider, and I'd done more than my fair share of dark deeds myself. But that turned even *my* stomach.

"Can you . . . can you even *do* that with Air magic?" I asked. "Tear someone's soul out of their body?"

Jo-Jo slowly nodded.

I rubbed my chest, which was suddenly aching, and glanced over at Tess Darville. The mountain girl floated over and took Bria's chair. For a moment, her features blurred, and she looked exhausted.

Just . . . *exhausted.*

I had no doubt that Graves had murdered her and Thomas Kirkwood out of jealousy or spite or both. But I still had so many questions.

Had the Air elemental vampire really sucked out Tess's soul? Was that what I was looking at right now? And where was Thomas? Where was his soul or spirit or whatever? If he'd loved Tess as much as she loved him, then why wasn't he here with her, even if they both had been murdered?

Tess stared at me, and I could tell exactly what she was thinking.

See? This is why I've been haunting you. Because you're the only one who can help me. Because you're the only one strong enough to do what needs to be done.

Suddenly, I knew exactly what Tess wanted and why she'd latched onto me that day in the cemetery. It was my own fault, really, for telling her who I was and what I did. I should have known better than to open my mouth, even to a haint. Fletcher had taught me to be smarter than that.

But the old man had also taught me that it was okay to help folks who couldn't help themselves—and that sometimes the only way to do that was with the point of one of my knives.

I stared at the mountain girl. After a few seconds, I nodded. Tess blinked at me in surprise for a moment before she nodded back.

"Gin?" Jo-Jo asked, looking first at the haint, then at me. Since Jo-Jo was an Air elemental, she could see Tess just like Sophia could. "What are you going to do?"

"What I do best," I said. "What I've done so many times before as the Spider. I'm going to kill that murderous son of a bitch Graves so Tess here can finally rest in peace."

Chapter Four

Gin Blanco

Jo-Jo gave me directions to Homer Graves's place. I grabbed a bag of tools that I kept stashed in her house just for these sorts of situations, got into my car, and headed out.

Normally, I would have been more cautious, would have waited to do some recon at the very least before going in with knives slashing. But there was no time. Not with Bria sniffing around. She'd do the right thing, the cop thing, and get a warrant before she went to question Graves.

I already knew Graves was a murderer who liked to torture his victims. I didn't want my baby sister anywhere near him, especially if he was a soul sucker like Jo-Jo thought.

Besides, Tess had waited so long already. I figured she was anxious to get on with things. Even a haint could only be so patient.

I got as close to Graves's rugged, remote property as I could, then pulled my car off the side of the road, shouldered my bag of supplies, and hiked the rest of the way in on foot.

Tess floated beside me the whole time, her face tight with worry, her hands fisting in the ghostly folds of her gingham dress. I didn't know why. I was the one sticking my neck out here—hers had already been cut long ago by Graves. Still, her concern touched me.

According to Jo-Jo, Graves lived at the top of a holler in the mountains above Ashland. I followed her directions up a faint hiking trail, then stopped when I crested a forested ridge and spotted Graves's house through a screen of trees. Above me, the bare skeletal branches *creaked* and *cracked* back and forth as the wind tangled through them. The faint whispers almost seemed to be warning me.

Stay away . . . stay away . . . stay away . . .

I pushed my unease aside and used the binoculars I'd brought along to peer at the house in front of me. It could have been a replica of a hundred others I'd seen in hollers like this one—white clapboard that had long ago turned dingy with age, a porch with warped, weathered, sagging boards, and a dull tin roof dotted here and there with black mold. Charming.

Whatever else he was, Graves definitely didn't care what kind of disrepair his property fell into. Still, his neglect would make my job easier. It was only around three in the afternoon, and he would have easily seen me creeping through his yard if the grass hadn't been as high as my waist and choked with winter weeds and black briars.

Once again, that feeling of unease crept up on me. Maybe it was because the area was so completely lifeless. No birds fluttered in the trees, no rabbits scurried through the fallen leaves, nothing moved at all but the wind, with its relentless whistle of cold air.

"Okay, Tess," I whispered, turning to the haint. "Time to earn my pro-bono services as the Spider. Where's Graves most likely to be? I want to do this quick and quiet-like, before he even knows I'm here."

Tess bit her lip, then pointed to the left side of the house. Still keeping inside the tree line, I put my binoculars back into my bag and skulked in that direction.

A small shack was attached to the back side of the house, made of the same dingy clapboard as the main structure. I got down on my belly and left the trees behind, crawling through the grass and masking my furtive movements with the gusts of wind that blew across the overgrown yard.

Five minutes later, I reached the side of the shack and eased back up into a standing position. I peered in through one of the windows, but an inch of grime covered the glass. All I could see inside was a faint glow, like someone had left a bare bulb burning.

The windows were too small for me to go through, so I dropped my bag on the ground, palmed one of my silverstone knives, and tiptoed over to the door. And then I waited, counting off the seconds in my head.

Five . . . ten . . . fifteen . . .

Five minutes later, I was still waiting, and I hadn't heard a peep from inside the shack. No rustles of clothing, no soft footsteps, no whispers of movement. Graves wasn't here.

"All right, Tess," I said in a low voice. "He's obviously not in there. So where to now? The main house?"

The haint shook her head and pointed at the door. I sighed and started to move away, but she darted in front of me, stomped her bare foot into the ground, and stabbed her finger at the door again. Whatever was in there, Tess wanted me to see it.

"Getting bossed around by a haint," I muttered. "Finn will never let me live this down."

I hesitated a moment, then reached out and tried the knob. To my surprise, it turned, so I eased the door open and slipped inside. I thought it would take a few seconds for my eyes to adjust to the semidarkness, since the windows were smeared with dirt, but there was plenty of light in the shack.

Hundreds of lights, actually—all trapped in glass snow globes.

The globes sat on shelves that covered all four walls of the shack from floor to ceiling. A large stone table was set into the middle of the packed dirt floor. Even from here, I could see that the table was crusted with dried black blood, and I could hear the harsh, ragged screams that raged through the stone.

Bad things had happened on that table—some very bad things indeed.

This was where Graves had tortured Tess and Thomas and who knew how many other innocent people over the years, including the two bodies the cops had discovered in the rock quarry. This was where he'd cut out their hearts.

This was where Graves had stolen their souls.

I'd never given much thought to my immortal soul before. As an assassin, I figured I'd already booked a front-row seat on the express bus downstairs a long time ago. But somehow I knew what was in the globes: souls. It was the only explanation that made sense. The lights were the same pale silver as Tess, the same pale, translucent silver that I'd never seen anywhere else.

Two of the lights bounced around inside their globes like tennis balls, as if they could somehow knock the globes off the shelf, break the glass, and free themselves. But the others—*all* the others—had sunk into the bottoms of their globes, and they barely glowed at all.

My mother had collected snow globes before she died. It was bone-chilling to see something so harmless used in such an evil way.

It was one of the most disturbing things I'd ever seen.

"Graves brought you here and hurt you, didn't he?" I asked Tess. "Because you didn't love him like he loved you. Graves kidnapped and tortured you and Thomas because you two were in love. You and Thomas both died, but somehow you kept Graves from getting your soul. Thomas is trapped here somewhere, isn't he? In one of the globes. That's why you needed my help. To kill Graves. To free Thomas . . . and all the others."

Tess gave me a haunted look and slowly nodded. She floated over to the back wall and hovered there in front of a globe. Judging from the thick hobwebs wrapped around it, this snow globe had been in the shack longer than all the others. For a moment, the light inside perked up and glowed at Tess's appearance. Then it settled back down into the bottom of the globe and winked out like a firefly.

Tess wrapped her fingers around the globe, trying to pick it up, but of course, she couldn't. She might be able to brush away a few leaves, but something this heavy was beyond the haint's abilities.

The longer I stood in the shack looking at all those trapped souls, at all the people Graves had murdered over the years, the angrier I got, until my rage matched what I'd felt when I touched Thomas's gravestone.

"That soul-sucking son of a—"

That was all I got out before I noticed Tess waving frantically. I heard footsteps behind me and immediately whirled around, but I was already too late. I turned my head just in time for someone to smash me in the face with a shovel.

I was out cold before I even hit the dirt floor.

When I came to, I was strapped down on the stone table that I'd seen when I first came into the shack. Thick ropes lashed my legs and feet, while two more held out my arms as if I was crucified. Not too far-fetched an idea, given what I knew about Homer Graves.

"You're finally awake," a smooth voice said. "Excellent."

Footsteps sounded, and a man came into view.

Homer Graves was not what I'd anticipated. Given the decrepit state of his house and yard, I'd expected a run-down man who wasn't too big on personal hygiene. But Graves's black hair was carefully styled and slicked back from his high forehead, and he'd just shaved, because I could smell his lemon-scented cologne. A fitted black suit draped over his thin body, and a silver tie had been artfully knotted at his skinny neck.

All put together, he looked like an undertaker—mine, if I wasn't careful.

"So you're the big, bad Air elemental vampire who gets his kicks by cutting out people's hearts and stealing their souls. I thought you'd be taller."

I made the words as light and mocking as I could, considering how hard my head was pounding. Graves had whacked me but good with that shovel, and I felt scattered and hollow inside, like a piece of me was already missing. I slowly moved my jaw and blinked my eyes. My vision was okay, but I could taste hot, salty blood in my mouth. I wasn't in the best shape of my life, but I was still a long way from dead.

Graves regarded me a moment, then held up something where I could see it—one of my knives.

I bit back a curse. Of course he'd searched me while I was unconscious and found them. Two up my sleeves, one in the small of my back, and two more tucked into the sides of my boots. The vampire probably thought he was going to carve me up with my own blades, but I'd be damned if I let that happen.

Instead of responding to my taunt, Graves smiled, revealing two gleaming white fangs. Then he leaned forward and drew the knife across my stomach. The swift strike wasn't deep enough to kill me, but it definitely got my attention.

Blood immediately soaked into my shirt and jeans. Underneath me, the stone of the table started to wail. It knew what was coming next—more cuts, more blood, more pain.

So much more pain.

I ignored the stone's cries, sucked in a breath, and focused on pushing away the burning fire of the cut.

The vampire cocked his head to the side. "So you're not a screamer, then. Well, that's disappointing. Before I kill you, though, I suppose I should ask the basic questions. Who are you? And why did you come here?"

Despite my precarious position, Graves wasn't going to be breathing much longer, so I saw no reason not to tell him the truth. Besides, I wanted to rattle his cage a bit. Rattled people often made mistakes, and I needed the vamp to make one right now, so I could cut myself free before he started in on me with my own knife again.

"Tess sent me. Tess Darville, the woman you murdered in the nineteen twenties."

For a moment, Graves's hazel eyes widened, and he looked as shocked as he could, what with his hangdog face. Then his features smoothed out into a pleasant mask once more.

"Tess? Tess sent you? Is she . . . is she here now?" He licked his lips and looked around the shack.

Suddenly, I knew what he wanted—what he'd *always* wanted. Tess's soul, trapped in one of those snow globes along with all the others.

"That's why you killed all those other couples, isn't it?" I whispered. "Because Tess somehow got away from you."

Graves shrugged, but he kept staring around the shack, a sharp, sick, hungry look in his eyes now. Since I was tied down, I couldn't see if Tess was here, but I hoped she wasn't. I didn't want Graves to trap her too.

"I had already killed Tommy Kirkwood," Graves said. "I left the shack just for a second to go put on a clean suit. I wanted to look my best for Tess before I took her soul. She was special, you see. So special to me. The first woman I ever loved, the first woman I ever killed. But when I came back, she was gone. She'd somehow gotten free. She didn't get far, though. I found her just inside the trees, but she was already dead, and her soul was already gone . . ."

His voice trailed off, and I could tell that he was lost in his memories. A lot of vamps were like that. They lived so long that the past and the present often blurred together for them. After a moment, Graves came back to himself. He looked at me and smiled.

"You know, I never could lure Tess back in here, not even when I used Kirkwood's soul as bait. But I'm sure she'll come for *you*, since she sent you here in the first place. I'm sure when she hears you screaming, she'll come running, and then my collection will finally be complete."

Graves stepped closer and tightened his grip on my knife. "Tell me, where would you like me to make the first incision? I used to be a doctor during the Civil War, so I always give my patients a choice about where I cut them first."

He'd been a doctor during the Civil War? Okay, this was getting creepier by the second. I supposed that explained why Graves liked to butcher people, though, since surgery had been quite barbaric back then. Well, that and the fact that he was just a sadistic son of a bitch.

Graves brought the knife up again. He gently drew the bloody blade down my cheek, then my neck, before finally stopping the knife right over my heart. He pressed down, and the blade pierced my shirt and nicked my skin.

I felt the hot blood well up over the knife, roll across my left breast, and start trickling down my side.

"I think I'll start with your heart," he murmured. "Everyone screams during that. It's sure to bring Tess flying straight to you."

Graves drew back, and I tensed myself for what was to

come. I'd only get one shot to take him down, and I had to make it count—

"You're not going to do a damn thing to her," a loud voice boomed.

Graves whirled around just like I had a few minutes before.

Owen stepped into the shack, threw himself forward, and crashed into the vampire.

Chapter Five

Gin Blanco

The two men fell to the dirt floor, punching, kicking, and grunting.

"Owen," I whispered.

Soft wonder warmed my heart at the fact that he'd come for me without my even asking him for help. I let myself revel in the emotion and its heady power for a sweet, sweet second before I pushed it out of my mind. Owen had given me the opening I needed to free myself—something I had to do, or we were both dead.

Graves had taken away my silverstone knives, but that didn't mean I was helpless. Far from it.

I was an elemental, after all, so I reached for my Ice magic. A cold silver light flared in my right palm, centered on the spider-rune scar there, and a second later, I was holding a jagged Ice knife. I had to bend my wrist at an awkward angle, but I managed to slice through the rope that tied one hand down. I used the Ice knife to cut the rest of the ropes and sat up.

The wound in my stomach stung with every movement, but I hissed through the pain and used my magic to make a second Ice knife. They weren't as strong as my regular blades, but they'd do the job.

I'd make sure of that.

By this point, Owen was on top of Graves. He drew his fist back to punch the vamp, but Graves brought up his hand. The vampire's eyes burned like topaz torches in his face, and a blast of wind exploded from his palm and blew Owen off him.

Owen flew through the air, crashed into the doorjamb, and fell to the ground. The globes on the shelves closest to him rattled like dry bones at the vibration, and the lights brightened, shocked out of their slumber by the sudden bout of violence.

The spider-rune scars branded into my palms itched and burned at the influx of the vamp's elemental magic, but I forced the sensation aside, hopped off the table, and put myself between Graves and Owen, who was groaning and struggling to get to his feet.

The vamp saw my weapons and let out a polite, cultured laugh. "Ice knives? Really? Do you really think those pitiful blades will beat me? Silverstone is so much better, so much sharper."

I smiled. "That's the thing about me, Graves. I always make do with what's available."

This time, I was the one who sent out a burst of magic with my hand—but it wasn't Ice. I was the rarest of elementals, gifted in not one but two areas, and this time, I put my fingers down on the edge of Graves's butcher's block and used my Stone magic to shatter the table into a thousand pieces.

Chunks of bloody rubble blew back onto Graves, who lost his footing and went down on the floor.

I was on him a second later.

I cut and cut and cut him, making Ice knife after Ice knife as they broke and shattered in my hands, but the vampire just wouldn't *die*. He wasn't even *bleeding*, no matter where or how deep I cut him, and I couldn't figure out why. All that appeared on his skin were these thin silver lines, like I had dipped my fingers into a bucket of liquid silver and painted stripes all over him.

I let out a low growl of frustration, and Graves just laughed in my face.

"Let me know when you get tired," he said. "I'll be happy to kill you then."

A ghostly hand waved at me, and I turned my head to see Tess standing in the middle of the shack, right where the table had been. She held her hands out wide and whirled around and around, the faint shimmer of her body reflecting like moonlight off the snow globes. It took me a second to realize what she was trying to tell me.

"The souls," I whispered.

Somehow Graves was drawing his power from the trapped souls. That was why I couldn't kill him—because he couldn't *be* killed until they were all free.

Graves saw me hesitate, then used his Air magic to blast me off him the same way he had blasted Owen. I let him. I crashed into one of the shelves, then slumped down onto the floor and stayed there.

Graves got up, straightened his tie, and stepped toward me. "And now I think it's time for you to die, my dear."

I ignored him. Being smug was a quick way to get dead in my experience. Instead, I stretched up a hand, reaching for the closest globe. It only took a second for me to use my magic to make it Ice over. I kept concentrating, and my elemental Ice quickly spread from one globe to the next. In seconds, the Ice had coated all of them, and the shack looked like a snowstorm had suddenly erupted inside.

"What are you . . . what you are doing?" Graves asked, but it was already too late.

"Killing you," I snarled.

I sent out a final brilliant burst of Ice magic and shattered each and every one of those damn snow globes.

Chapter Six

Gin Blanco

For a second, nothing happened. Then, one by one, the globes erupted like miniature volcanoes, until the smashing symphony of glass was all I could hear.

Well, that and Graves's screams.

As the globes broke, all the trapped souls spilled out. One by one, they woke from their long slumber and winked back to life, until the whole shack pulsed with their bright, beautiful lights.

And then they went after Graves.

It was like watching a swarm of killer bees attack a wounded animal. One after another, the lights—the souls—slammed into Graves until they covered his entire body.

The vampire screamed and screamed, but the souls kept attacking. He fell to his knees and then onto his back, but the souls kept on with their psychic swarm, feasting on him the same way the vamp had once feasted on them.

I couldn't really see what was happening, but I got the

impression that the souls were taking back whatever pieces of themselves Graves had stolen in the first place.

It seemed to go on and on, although it couldn't have lasted much more than a minute, two tops. Finally, the souls started to peel off. In ones and twos, they flew out of the shack, escaping up into the atmosphere—to the stars, to heaven, or maybe someplace else entirely.

Either way, they were finally *free*.

And when it was over and the last of the silvery souls was gone, I got to my feet, dug one of my knives out of the rubble, and walked over to where Graves lay spread-eagle on the floor.

The vampire was a mere husk of his slick self—literally. However he'd used his Air elemental magic to trap the souls in the first place, however they'd been sustaining his existence over the years, all that power was gone now—and him along with it.

His skin was dry, splotchy, and shriveled, like he was severely dehydrated. His black hair slid out of his scalp in clumps, and his formerly white fangs were now brown and brittle-looking.

I'd seen photos before of vampires who'd been starved, who'd been denied the blood they needed in order to survive. That was what Graves looked like now. It was nothing less than he deserved and far kinder than what he'd inflicted on his victims.

Soft whimpers rasped out of the vampire's throat, and he looked like he was about a minute away from dying. As the Spider, I was good at judging things like that. His desperate gaze fixed on me, and I leaned over him just like he'd done to me earlier.

"You know what the difference is between you and me, Graves? I don't give people a choice about where I cut them," I said. "I know it's not very sporting, but one slice is usually all I need."

Then I leaned over a little more and cut the bastard's throat, just to be sure.

This time, he bled, and his blood was just as red as mine.

Once I was sure that Graves was dead, I helped Owen to his feet, and the two of us stumbled out of the shack and into the yard. We found a rickety iron bench half hidden in the weeds, and the two of us sat down until we got our breath back.

Owen picked glass and other debris out of his hair, while I lifted up my shirt and looked at the wound on my stomach. Still bleeding, but I'd be all right until I got to Jo-Jo and she healed me.

I turned to Owen. "Jo-Jo called you, didn't she? And told you where I was going?"

He winced. "She said she had a feeling you might need help and sent me after you. Are you mad at her? Or . . . me? For coming after you? I know you like to . . . work alone."

I might have been angry before, back when I'd been the Spider full-time and still killing people for money. But since then, I'd learned that it was okay to rely on other people—sometimes, anyway.

If anything, today proved that Owen's feelings for me were *real*—and so were mine for him. Owen had come after me when I needed him to, and I knew that if I didn't find a way to kill Graves, the vamp would have sucked out Owen's soul and stuck it in one of those eerie snow globes. And that upset me more than anything had in a long, long time.

"I don't want to crowd you, Gin," Owen said, taking my silence for disapproval. "But I'm always going to come for you, no matter how much danger you're in, and no matter how much danger that puts me in. I hope you know that. I hope you know just how much you mean to me. You're just . . . *everything*."

The intensity burning in his violet eyes took my breath away. I reached over and squeezed his hand in mine, trying to put all my feelings into that one simple gesture. Owen squeezed back, telling me that he understood—and that he always would.

"I do know that," I said in a soft voice. "And I feel the same way about you. I'm glad Jo-Jo told you what I was doing. Believe me, I was happy you showed up when you did."

Owen grinned. "You know, we make a pretty good team. I come in as the distraction, and then you take care of the bad guy. Or something like that."

I shook my head and laughed. We sat there, holding hands and resting, for a few more minutes. I was just about to suggest that we hike down the holler to my car when a shimmering light caught my eye and Tess strolled out of the shack.

And this time, she wasn't alone.

The mountain girl was holding hands with a man who was just as pale and translucent as she was. Thomas Kirkwood. I recognized him from the photo Finn had shown me at Jo-Jo's salon.

The two of them drifted away from the shack, then stopped. Thomas stared down at Tess, and she beamed right back at him.

"Wow," Owen whispered.

I eyed him. "You can see them?"

"I can," Owen said in a low voice. "They look so . . . happy. So . . . in love."

And they did. Thomas gently brushed a strand of Tess's hair back over her shoulder, his fingers lingering there like he couldn't believe she was real, like he couldn't believe they were finally together again after all these long years apart.

Tess clamped her hands over her mouth like she was trying not to cry, then threw her arms around Thomas's neck. She rained kisses on her lover's face, and a silver star exploded with each press of her lips against his skin. Thomas turned his head and caught Tess's lips in his, and a whole shower of stars flickered and danced around them.

"Wow," I whispered, echoing Owen's sentiment.

We sat there and watched the two lovers.

Finally, Owen spoke again. "Do you think that'll be us in a hundred years?"

I arched an eyebrow. "You mean, will we finally be reunited after you've spent almost a century being a soul-sucking vampire's power source and lightning bug? I sincerely hope not."

Owen bumped me with his shoulder. "You know that's not what I mean."

"I know," I said, laughing.

I turned my attention back to Thomas and Tess. They had their arms wrapped around each other. Somehow I knew that they'd never be apart again.

Tess saw me staring and gave me a happy wave. Her smile was so wide and bright that I thought she'd never stop glowing. Maybe she never would, in whatever afterlife she was headed to now that she'd been reunited with her long-lost love.

"I don't know if that will be us or not," I said, my voice thick with all sorts of emotions that I didn't want to think about too much right now. "But it's a nice thing to hope for, isn't it?"

"Yes, it is," Owen murmured. "Yes, it is."

He slipped his arm around my shoulder and pulled me close. I laid my hand on his heart and rested my head on his shoulder.

Quiet, still, bruised, and bloody, we sat there on the bench until the sun set and Tess and Thomas finally faded away for good. Finally at peace and with each other as they belonged, as they were always meant to be—and as they'd always stay from now on.

Now and always.

Parlor Tricks

This story takes place after *Deadly Sting*, book 8.

Gin Blanco

"A carnival? Really?"

Detective Bria Coolidge looked at me. "You don't like carnivals?"

"Not particularly," I said. "There are already enough people around here looking to con you without you having to actually pay for the privilege."

Bria rolled her eyes. "That's just a stereotype. Not all carnivals are looking to cheat folks."

"I know that," I said. "But I also know that this is Ashland. So if there was any place for a carnival to be crooked, this would be it."

Bria didn't answer me. She knew as well as I did that corruption was a way of life in our sprawling Southern city, along with violence, magic, avarice, and greed. Cheating, beating, and even murdering your enemies wouldn't get you jail time in Ashland as much as applause, admiration, and respect—and someone immediately plotting to take you down the same way you had taken down your enemies.

My baby sister and I stood at the entrance to the Ashland Fairgrounds, a wide, grassy clearing that was nestled in among the Appalachian Mountains, which ran through and around the city. Tree-covered ridges towered over the clearing, giving the landscape a bowl-like shape. The fairgrounds hosted a variety of events throughout the year, everything from livestock shows to sporting tournaments to camps for kids. On this warm June evening, it was the site of *The Carnival of Wondrous Wonders!* At least, that's what the banner stretched above the entrance said.

Bria had parked her sedan in the gravel lot, and we'd eased into the stream of people heading for the fence that cordoned off the clearing. Most of the other carnival-goers were families with young kids or sullen teenagers looking to escape from Mom and Dad's watchful eyes for a few hours. Bria looked a little out of place with her jeans, her blue button-up shirt, and the gold detective's badge glinting on her belt, right next to her holstered gun. So did I with my boots, jeans, and long-sleeved black T-shirt.

"Well, look at it this way," Bria said in a cheery voice. "The odds of anyone here knowing you are pretty slim. If nothing else, you can just relax and not have to worry about anyone trying to kill you tonight."

Heh. I wouldn't count on it.

By day, I was Gin Blanco, owner of the Pork Pit barbecue restaurant. By night, in the shadows, I was the Spider, Ashland's most notorious assassin. Actually, I suppose these days, I was more infamous than notorious, since most of the underworld thought—or at least suspected—that I was the Spider, the woman who'd killed powerful Fire elemental Mab Monroe back in the winter. As a result, many of the crime lords and ladies had sent men after me, trying to take me out, these past few months. With Mab's death, all of the underworld movers and shakers were grappling for power, and some of them thought that murdering the Spider would go a long way toward cementing their position as the city's new head honcho.

"Gin?"

"Okay, okay," I grumbled. "You're right about that. I doubt any of the crime bosses and their goons will be here tonight."

A country-fried clown wearing blue-and-white gingham coveralls, a blue shirt, and brown boots that were about five sizes too big waddled over to us. Bits of straw stuck out of the pockets of his coveralls, and a battered straw hat was perched on top of his curly red wig. White pancake makeup covered his face, although it had started to run in the heat. His painted-on, oversize red lips were curled up into a garish grin, although red and blue tears also covered his face, as though he didn't know whether he wanted to laugh or cry. I'd definitely cry if I had to walk around in that getup. Or kill the person who'd made me wear it. That would definitely turn my frown upside down.

Bria smiled at him, which the clown took as an invitation to dance around us, mock-tripping over his enormous boots. Finally, he reached inside his coveralls. I tensed, ready to tackle him if he came up with a weapon, but he was only going for a red balloon stashed away among the straw. He spent the better part of two minutes not-so-comically huffing and puffing, trying to blow it up, before he eventually succeeded. Then he danced around us again and started twisting the balloon into the shape of a man. When he was finished, the clown sidled up to me, probably hoping to get me to smile and laugh like Bria was.

"Go away," I growled. "Or you'll be crying real tears when I make you eat that balloon."

The clown frowned, not quite sure whether I was joking, but I let the coldness seep into my gray eyes, and he got the message. He tucked his balloon man under his arm and quickly scurried away from me.

"Did you have to do that?" Bria asked, exasperation creeping into her light voice. "He's a clown. He was just trying to do his job and entertain you."

"No, I didn't have to do that, but I don't like clowns."

"Is there anything about carnivals that you *do* like?"

I thought about it, then brightened. "Corn dogs. If they're not too greasy."

Bria shook her head in exasperation.

"Look, I'm sorry. But when you said you wanted me to help you with something, I didn't expect this. Why are we here, anyway?"

"Because I got a report about a missing girl, and this is the last place she was seen." Bria reached into the back pocket of her jeans, drew out a photo, and handed it to me. "Her name's Elizabeth Robbins. Sixteen. Parents died in a car accident six months ago. She lives with her aunt, Fran, who's one of the police department dispatchers. Fran said she dropped Elizabeth off here with some friends last night. The friends and Elizabeth got separated, and no one's seen her since."

"What else does Fran say?"

"She says Elizabeth's been acting out a little lately, cutting classes, things like that," Bria replied. "But she says Elizabeth always checks in and lets Fran know where she is, and it's not like her to just disappear."

"I'm guessing your fellow boys in blue weren't too concerned about a missing girl," I said. "At least, not one who isn't related to someone wealthy and important, even if her aunt does work for the police department. They probably labeled her a runaway."

She nodded. "You know it."

Like almost every other institution in Ashland, the police department had more than its share of corruption. Most members of the po-po took bribes to look the other way, but my sister was one of the few good, honest cops on the force.

I stared at the photo. Elizabeth Robbins was a pretty girl. In fact, with her blond hair and blue eyes, she looked a lot like Bria. She was even wearing a necklace, the way Bria always did, although Elizabeth's was a small diamond heart rather than Bria's silverstone primrose rune. But the camera had captured the tightness in her young features and the shadows that clouded her gaze. This was a girl who was still grieving for her parents. I knew the feeling, since my mother and older sister had also died when I was young.

I started to hand the picture back to Bria, but she shook her head.

"Keep it. I have a copy." She reached into her back pocket and drew out another photo.

I arched an eyebrow. "So you knew I'd help you after you showed me her picture. Have I ever told you how much you excel at emotional manipulation?"

Bria grinned.

"Well, let's get started," I said. "Before that clown comes back."

We spent the next hour roaming from one side of the fairgrounds to the other, looking at all the carnival attractions. Game booths, concession stands, a Ferris wheel, and other spinning, whirling rides lined both sides of a long thoroughfare. Smaller paths branched off the main drag and led to other areas, including a house of mirrors, a tent where a magician did tricks, and a petting zoo. Like the clown, everything had a Southern feel to it, from the boiled and roasted peanuts sold in the concession stands, to the slow, twangy drawls of the carnival workers, to the Mountain High roller coaster, which really wasn't more than ridge-high in these parts.

But the carnival really did have some wondrous wonders,

thanks to all the magic users on staff. Fire elementals made flames shoot out of their fingertips before forming balls out of the flickering Fire and then juggling them. Crowds of kids squealed with excitement as an Air elemental took a group of colorful animal balloons and made the creatures float up and down and do loop-the-loops in the breeze, as though the plastic blue and pink bears, lions, and tigers were engaged in old-fashioned aerial combat. Dwarven and giant strongmen and strongwomen hefted small cars full of carousing clowns over their heads. There was even a drinking contest for vampires to see who in the crowd could down the most pints of blood in two minutes. The winner got a giant stuffed bat.

I let Bria take the lead. She showed the missing girl's picture to the carnival workers, but they all shook their heads and said they didn't remember seeing Elizabeth. Nothing unusual there. It was Friday night, and the carnival grew more crowded by the minute. The workers were all rushing to get folks their food, get them on the rides, and get them involved in—and shelling out dollars for—the games.

But the more people Bria asked about the girl, the more convinced I became that something was wrong.

For one thing, everyone was just too *friendly*. Instead of being pissed that Bria was interrupting them, they all smiled and politely nodded at her. Sure, she was a detective, but they had customers to see to and money to make. They should have been more upset that she was cutting into their profit margins.

Then there was the fact that staff members were passing signals to one another. As soon as Bria started to move on to the next booth, the worker she'd left behind would either pull out his cell phone and text something on it or make a hand gesture to another carnival member standing nearby. Now, that could have been standard stuff: be nice to the po-po or anyone else asking questions, but warn one another all the same. Still, the most telling thing was the way all the workers' eyes slid away from the photo and how the smiles dropped from their faces the second Bria turned her back to them.

Oh, yes. Something was *definitely* wrong here.

Bria finished talking to the vampire running the ring toss. He moved off to give some metal rings to a group of kids to throw at the poles that were the targets. She watched him for a few seconds, then turned to me.

"Do you get the feeling all these folks know more than they're telling?" she asked in a low voice.

"Absolutely," I replied. "Not to mention the fact that they're all watching us."

Bria's gaze cut left and right as we walked down the thoroughfare. Her face tightened as she noticed all the furtive looks that came our way from the workers, especially since they stared at her more than at me, their features dark, troubled, and twisted with fear. I wondered if it was because of the badge on her belt or for some other reason. Maybe they were nervous because she was a cop. Or maybe they were worried she'd figure out what happened to Elizabeth Robbins—and their part in it.

Either way, Bria kept showing the girl's picture and asking about her. I watched my sister's back, ready to reach for one of the five silverstone knives I had on me—two up my sleeves, one against the small of my back, and two in my boots. My weapons of choice as the Spider. But everybody remained just as sugary-sweet as the cotton candy they were selling, and no one made any sinister moves. Still, I thought it was just a matter of time before someone tried something, and I would be ready for them when they did.

Finally, around nine o'clock, a bugle sounded, and everyone headed toward the center of the fairgrounds, where a series of wooden bleachers had been arranged around a circular stage. Bria grabbed one of the pink fliers the country clowns had been passing out, and she read through the colorful, splashy type.

"It says this is the main show," she said as we climbed to the top row. "And that we should be prepared to be awed and amazed."

"Awed and amazed. Check."

We sat down, and the red-, blue-, and green-tinged spotlights focused on the stage dimmed, and shadows fell over the fairgrounds, causing the crowd to slowly hush. A lone white light snapped on, illuminating the center of the stage. A low drumroll started, slowly growing louder and louder until my brain pounded from the ominous sound—

BANG!

The sharp, sudden explosion was even louder than the thunderous drumroll, and the noise reverberated through the fairgrounds, echoing up the ridges that surrounded the clearing and back down again. For a moment, everything went dark, making more than a few folks scream in surprise. Then the lone spotlight snapped back on. Pale green smoke billowed up into the starry night sky, and a woman appeared in the center of the stage to the strains of triumphant music.

Ta-da.

The woman wore a short red ringmaster's coat over a ruffled white silk shirt and black satin short-shorts. Black tights encased her lean, long legs, while a pair of black stiletto boots gave her a few more inches of height. She bowed low, removing her tall black top hat and showing off her hair, which was a rich strawberry blond and piled on top of her head in an artful array of soft curls.

"I thought this was a carnival, not a circus," I muttered to Bria.

"Shhh."

The woman straightened up. She waved her hand, and a summer breeze gusted through the clearing, whipping away all the wispy strands of green smoke that were hovering over the stage. So she was an Air elemental, then—a strong one, judging from the sharp burst of power rolling off her.

I was an elemental myself, gifted with Ice and Stone magic. Since my elements were the opposite of hers, the woman's Air power felt like invisible needles stabbing into my skin. Her magic also made the scars embedded in my palms itch and burn. Each of the marks was shaped like a spider rune, my rune, the symbol for patience. Something I would need a lot of if this show was as cheesy and over-the-top as the rest of the carnival.

I shifted in my seat, trying to get away from the uncomfortable sensation of the other elemental's power, although I knew it would vanish as soon as she quit using her magic. Beside me, Bria did the same thing, since she had Ice magic as well. She didn't like the feel of Air power any more than I did.

"Greetings, kind friends!" the woman proclaimed in a voice that was almost as loud as the smoke explosion had been. "I am Esmeralda the Amazing, and I'm here to welcome you to our wonderful carnival!"

The crowd politely clapped. Esmeralda beamed and bowed low again, accepting the applause.

"And now," she purred, "be prepared to be awed . . . and amazed!"

Zippy, cartoonish music blared to life, and the colorful spotlights zoomed this way and that, as a variety of performers ran, tumbled, cartwheeled, and pratfalled across the stage. For the next half hour, Esmeralda narrated the action as carnival members performed trick after trick. Clowns goofed off and tried to escape from the strongmen and -women who tossed them back and forth like rag dolls. Acrobats tumble-tumble-tumbled before forming swaying human pyramids, while a guy coaxed a black bear to roll back and forth on top of an oversize red ball embossed with white stars. There was even a woman dressed up like a superhero—Karma Girl, I think— who got shot out of a cannon.

All around me, folks laughed and cheered and clapped and whistled. But I tuned out the cacophony and looked past the bright lights and blur of movement onstage. My eyes scanned the shadows and all the workers behind the scenes manning the lights, sound system, smoke cannons, and all the other things that went into such an elaborate production.

I wondered if this was where Elizabeth had been taken.

It would be easy to snatch someone out of the crowd. With night already settled in and all the spotlights focused on the stage, deep, dark shadows surrounded the bleachers. All you'd have to do was wait for someone to go get a drink or a snack, follow them under the bleachers, and either rob, murder, or spirit them off to parts unknown. Since Elizabeth's body hadn't been found, I was assuming whoever had grabbed her had gone with the third option.

I wondered what they'd wanted with the girl. Lots of terrible things happened in Ashland on a daily basis. Beatings, robberies, murders. Maybe Elizabeth had caught the eye of an unsavory character. Maybe someone had tried to mug her and she'd fought back. Maybe she'd seen something she shouldn't have. Any one of those or a dozen other scenarios could have taken place, and I had no way of knowing which one.

The only thing I did know was that *something* was going on at this so-called Carnival of Wondrous Wonders. The workers had all been too polite to Bria and too prepared to say that they hadn't seen anything at all, almost like they'd been expecting those very types of questions about a missing girl. In fact, the whole thing seemed like a drill they'd gone through many times before, right down to their quick, pat denials.

Finally, the clowns, the dancing bear, and the other performers left the stage, and Esmeralda was alone once more.

"And now for our final performance of the evening," she said.

The stage went dark. The bombastic music swelled for a few seconds before giving way to that low, booming drumroll. The lights dimmed again, then—

BANG!

"The Wheel of Death!" Esmeralda called out.

A spotlight snapped on, illuminating a large white wheel with four spokes on it, two at the top and two at the bottom. The crowd oohed and aahed right on cue.

Esmeralda held out her hand, and another spotlight lit up the stage. "Please welcome Arturo the Most Magnificent Bladesman!"

BANG!

More noise, more smoke, more theatrics. Esmeralda used another blast of her Air magic to sweep the smoke away, and a man appeared in the second spotlight—a giant who was almost seven feet tall, with pale skin, slicked-back black hair, and a long, drooping black mustache that curled up at the ends. He was dressed in a sleeveless green silk shirt and black pants, but the most interesting thing about him was the black leather sash he had slung over his wide, muscular chest, one that practically bristled with knives.

I perked up. I liked knives.

Bria noticed my sudden interest in the show. I couldn't hear above the crowd noise, but I thought she snorted, either in disgust or amusement. I wasn't sure which one.

"And now, ladies and gentlemen," Esmeralda proclaimed, "watch in awe and wonder as I brave the Wheel of Death!"

The crowd oohed and aahed some more as Arturo took Esmeralda's arm and escorted her over to the wheel. She threw her top hat into the crowd, blew everyone a kiss, then turned and put her back against the wheel. She reached up and grabbed the two spokes at the top while she rested her stiletto boots against the two spokes at the bottom, forming a star shape with her body. One of the clowns got back up onstage and started turning a hand crank to make the Wheel of Death go 'round and 'round.

Arturo and Esmeralda bantered back and forth for a minute before the giant pulled one of the knives from his sash. He used it to slice an apple that another clown handed to him, supposedly proving how razor-sharp the blade was, then turned his attention to Esmeralda. Arturo held his knife out and frowned, his bushy black eyebrows drawing together in exaggerated concentration, as though this were the very first time he'd ever done this shtick.

Thunk!

A knife landed beside Esmeralda's right arm, inches away from her dainty wrist.

Thunk!

Another knife, this one close to her left wrist.

Thunk!

Thunk!

Two more knives, one on either side of her legs.

And on and on it went, the crowd gasping at every safe throw, until Arturo had used all the knives in his sash and the Wheel of Death looked more like a pincushion than the cheap plywood it was. Finally, the contraption stopped, and Esmeralda got off. This time, she was the one who plucked a knife from the wood. She turned to face Arturo, and the crowd collectively sucked in an excited breath as folks realized what she was about to do. Esmeralda paused and furrowed her lovely brow with the same dramatic effect Arturo had used before, then threw the weapon at him.

The giant caught the knife between his teeth.

Ta-da.

I knew it was a trick, misdirection and sleight of hand, but I had to admit that they pulled it off well. I might have even believed it was real if I hadn't felt another gust of Esmeralda's Air magic sweep across the stage, blowing a bit of smoke over

Arturo and obscuring him at just the right moment to help with the illusion.

She took Arturo's hand, and they both bowed low before—*BANG!*—disappearing in another puff of green smoke.

Everyone in the crowd surged to their feet, clapping, whistling, and cheering. Even I joined in and politely applauded.

"Don't tell me the Wheel of Death finally impressed you," Bria said as we trudged down the bleachers with everyone else.

"Parlor tricks are all well and good if flash is all you're going for," I said. "But we both know that I use my knives for more . . . practical purposes."

Bria snorted again, but she gestured at the stage. "Come on. Since it looks like Esmeralda is the big attraction around here, let's go see if she knows anything about Elizabeth."

"Don't hold your breath."

She shrugged. "If I ask enough people enough questions, somebody will let something slip. They always do."

I followed her to the stage. Esmeralda and Arturo had reappeared and were autographing carnival fliers and posing for pictures. Bria and I stood by and waited until they finished with their fans. I eyed the knives, which had been tucked back into Arturo's sash. They looked like decent blades, if a bit thin, but I could tell by the way the edges glinted that they were as sharp as he'd claimed them to be onstage. The giant himself was extremely muscular and showed off his enormous strength by picking up a couple of kids and bench-pressing them over his head, one in each hand, while their parents took pictures.

Finally, all the autographs had been signed, all the photos had been taken, and the crowd drifted away, leaving Esmeralda and Arturo alone together. My sister stepped up to them and plastered a polite smile onto her face.

"Hi, I'm Detective Bria Coolidge with the Ashland Police Department. I was wondering if I might have a few moments of your time . . ."

She told them about Elizabeth and showed them the missing girl's picture. Arturo gave it a cursory glance and shrugged, but Esmeralda took the photo from Bria and studied it carefully. Then she too shrugged and handed it back.

"Sorry, Detective," Esmeralda said. "I'm afraid I haven't seen her. As you can see, we get quite a few teenagers in here—hard for one of them to stand out. Why, we had such a large group from Cypress Mountain that they practically took over the whole fairgrounds a few nights ago."

Bria nodded. That was pretty much the same line all the other workers had given her, although it sounded much smoother and far more sincere coming from Esmeralda. She definitely knew how to sell her act.

The ringmaster looked at Bria and smiled. "But you, on the other hand, are quite striking. Has anyone ever told you what lovely skin you have? Why, it's practically *flawless*."

"Um, thanks," Bria said.

Esmeralda kept staring at my sister, as though Bria were a sculpture she was admiring. Up close, I could see that the ringmaster was pretty flawless herself, actually. Her skin was as pale and smooth as freshly fallen snow. Rich red highlights shimmered in her blond hair, while her eyes were a dark hazel, with flecks of gold flashing in the whiskey-colored depths.

Arturo noticed his boss's interest in Bria, and he peered at my sister a little more closely before glancing at Esmeralda. He raised his eyebrows in a silent question. She winked at him, and he nodded.

The quick exchange made me wonder what they were up to. I tensed a little, once again ready to reach for one of my knives if Arturo came at us, but he turned and headed toward the main thoroughfare. I wondered where he was going, but I didn't follow him. Keeping Bria in my sights was much more important.

Esmeralda didn't say anything to me. In fact, she didn't so

much as glance at me, but I was used to that. My dark chocolate-brown hair and gray eyes weren't nearly as striking as Bria's classic features.

Finally, Bria cleared her throat. "Anyway, thanks for your help. I appreciate it and how nice all your workers have been, taking the time to look at the photo."

Esmeralda waved her hand. Her long nails were the same bloodred as her jacket. "No problem at all, Detective. You look thirsty. Be sure to get something to eat and drink before you head home for the night. The carnival stays open until midnight. Tell Cathy that Em sent you, and she'll give you a discount. I always like to help out local law enforcement. Why, it's just disgraceful, the poor salaries they pay such decent, honest, hardworking folks like you."

I had to bite my lip to keep from laughing. She obviously didn't know how corrupt the police were in Ashland. With all the bribes they took, crooked cops around here did just fine. Some of them even had mansions up in Northtown, the rich, fancy, highfalutin part of town.

"Thanks," Bria said, managing to keep her face smoother than mine. "We'll do that."

Esmeralda gave us another beaming smile and moved over to talk to one of the acrobats, but she kept her gaze fixed on Bria the whole time.

"Let's get out of here," I murmured to my sister.

"Yeah," Bria said. "This place is starting to weird me out."

"It's taken this long?"

She shrugged. We left the stage area and walked down the main drag back toward the entrance.

"Come on," Bria said. "I missed dinner, so we might as well eat before we leave. I'm starving."

We got in line at one of the concession stands that bore the name *Cathy's Sweets*, although it looked like Cathy was serving up the usual carnival fare—burgers, fries, and all the greasy fixings in between. Smoke from the grill drifted out from the stand, mixing with the smells of sizzling meat, fresh-cut lemons, and cinnamon. I breathed in, enjoying the flavorful aromas, and my stomach rumbled in anticipation. Finally, it was our turn to order.

"What can I get you?" The woman behind the counter gave us a tired, uninterested look.

"I'll have a grilled chicken sandwich, onion rings, and a sweet iced tea," Bria said.

"And you?" The woman looked at me.

"Give me a lemonade, two corn dogs with spicy mustard, fries, a cinnamon-sugar pretzel, and a cone of cherry cotton candy," I replied.

Bria blanched a little at my choices, but she pulled some money out of her jeans pocket and handed it over the counter. A few minutes later, we sat down at a blue plastic picnic table to the right of the stand. Since the main show of the night was over, the crowd had thinned out quite a bit, and we were the only ones sitting in the shadows. I scanned the area. Once again, I felt the eyes of the carnival workers on me, but since it didn't seem like any of them was going to be stupid enough to approach us, I took a sip of my lemonade, then picked up one of my corn dogs.

"Do you know how disgusting that is?" Bria asked, wrinkling her nose. "Not to mention what it's going to do to your heart and arteries."

"It's meat on a stick, batter-dipped and deep-fried," I said. "If Finn were here, he'd say it was nature's perfect food."

My sister smiled at the mention of Finnegan Lane, who happened to be her significant other as well as my foster brother. "Yeah, well, Finn doesn't need to eat that stuff any more than you do."

Instead of answering her, I dipped the corn dog in the mustard and took a big bite of it. The spicy heat of the mustard tickled my tongue, while the cornmeal batter on the meat was crispy on the outside but soft and fluffy on the inside.

I was as hungry as Bria, and we both downed our food. I even managed to persuade her to eat some of the pretzel and cotton candy. She grumbled about all the sugar going straight to her ass, but she sighed with contentment after she took the first bite of the light-as-air cotton candy.

"This was actually pretty good," Bria said when we'd finished.

She stood, grabbed her empty greasy plates, and dumped them in a nearby trash can. She turned back to me and then stopped, slapping at something on her neck. A second later, she crumpled to the ground.

"Bria? Bria!"

I leaped to my feet and started to go over to her, but something stung my arm. I looked down. A red-feathered dart stuck out of my bicep. I cursed and immediately yanked out the dart, even though I knew it was already too late.

"Damn . . . tranquilizer . . . darts," I mumbled as the realization of what had happened flitted through my mind.

I whirled around, searching for my attacker, but everything was fuzzy and distorted, as though I were staring at it through one of those freaky carnival mirrors. Still, I stumbled forward, heading toward Bria so I could see whether she was still breathing. Even as I tried to get to her, I was aware of someone slinking through the shadows, moving closer and closer to us. I blinked, and Arturo came into focus. The giant was holding a small gun in his beefy hand.

"Get them out of sight." Esmeralda's voice drifted out of the darkness. "Quickly."

That bitch had Arturo drug us, probably with the same tranquilizers they used on the dancing bear. She was going to pay for that—in blood. Even as I tried to palm one of my knives to fight back, everything grew even fuzzier.

The ground rushed up to meet my face. My eyes closed, and the world went black.

I woke up with my neck twisted at an awkward angle. At first, I thought I was at home in bed, but then the night came rushing back to me. Carnival. Missing girl. Questioning the workers. Esmeralda and her Wheel of Death. The dart stinging my arm.

Since I didn't know where I was or who might be watching, I kept still, although I cracked my eyes open.

I was in a cage.

Someone had tossed me into a cage, although the bars were made of thick wood instead of metal. My body was sprawled across a bed of hay, which reeked of some animal, probably one of the goats from the petting zoo. The musty stench made my nose itch and twitch, but I held back my sneeze. Unconscious people did not sneeze.

I didn't hear any movement, so I risked opening my eyes a little more. It looked like I was in some sort of makeshift barn. Old, weathered boards formed the walls before arching up to create the roof. A few more wooden cages like the one I was in sat inside the building, but the rest of them were empty. Tools and other odds and ends covered the walls, and I spotted the dancing bear's big red ball slowly listing from side to side in the corner.

But the most important thing in the barn was Bria.

My sister was a few feet away from me, propped up in one of the clown cars. I watched her for a few seconds. Her chest rose and fell with a steady rhythm, and some of my worry eased. She was still breathing, which meant that everything else that might have been done to her could be fixed. All I had to do was get us out of here.

Too bad I didn't have my knives to help me with that. Arturo must have searched us, because I spotted my silverstone knives sitting on a wooden table a few feet away from the clown car. Bria's gun and badge were also lying there—

A low moan sounded, and I slowly turned my head to the side. Elizabeth Robbins lay in another clown car off to my left. She barely resembled the young, pretty girl in the photo Bria had given me. Her skin was waxy and gray, and her face had a hollow, gaunt, sunken look, as though she was on the verge of death. Her blond hair was matted, and large clumps of it had fallen out. The golden strands littered her slumped shoulders like the hay in my cage. The only reason I knew it was her was because she was wearing the same diamond heart necklace as in the photo Bria had shown me.

What had happened to the girl? I didn't know, but I was going to get her and Bria out of here before things got any worse. I had started to reach for my Ice magic to create a set of lockpicks so I could get out of my cage when the barn door opened and Esmeralda and Arturo stepped inside.

"I don't think this is a good idea," Arturo said as he hurried after the ringmaster. "I mean, this chick is a cop. Not some moody teenage girl."

"Are you kidding me? Did you not see her? She's *perfect*," Esmeralda said.

I kept my eyes open just wide enough to watch the ringmaster lean down and stare at my sister once more. She stroked Bria's cheek, lightly digging her nails into my sister's flesh.

"All that lovely, lovely skin," Esmeralda murmured, then clucked her tongue. "Youth truly is wasted on the young."

"But someone's sure to come looking for her," Arturo said. "Who knows how many people she told she was coming here tonight? Not to mention all those knives the other chick had on her. You don't carry quality blades like that unless you know how to use them. You're taking a big risk with them."

Esmeralda turned to glare at him with cold eyes. "And so

are you, for even daring to question me. So shut your mouth and lock the door. It's time to get started. We need to be gone from here in the morning."

Arturo stabbed his index finger at Elizabeth, who hadn't stirred since letting out that one moan. "And what about her? I thought you were going to drain her the rest of the way tonight."

Esmeralda shrugged. "Not now, not when I have such a fine specimen here. Crack her skull open and dump her body in some cave in the woods like you usually do. I don't care—just make sure she disappears. At least long enough for us to get out of town."

Drain her? What were they talking about? Esmeralda was an elemental, not a vampire.

I watched Esmeralda crawl into the clown car right next to Bria. She spent a few moments fussing, moving first one way, then the other, as though she needed to be as comfortable as possible for whatever foul thing she was planning. Finally, Esmeralda took Bria's hand, and her hazel eyes began to glow with her Air magic.

And I watched while she took my sister's life and made it her own.

The rosy, healthy flush in Bria's cheeks slowly faded away, replaced by a dull, sickly pallor, and her face started to take on the same gaunt look Elizabeth's had. Esmeralda sighed with contentment, and I realized that her skin was growing brighter, warmer, almost as if she was taking the glow from Bria's cheeks and putting it into her own.

My eyes narrowed. That was *exactly* what she was doing.

My friend Jolene "Jo-Jo" Deveraux was an Air elemental, one who used her magic to heal folks. Jo-Jo grabbed hold of oxygen and all the other natural gases in the air and used those molecules to clean wounds, restore vitality, and put ripped skin back together. Esmeralda had the same sort of power, only she was using her Air magic and all those molecules to pull Bria's health and well-being into her own body. Draining the life out of my sister like a vampire sucking someone dry of blood, until there would be nothing left of Bria and she would die.

I wondered how many girls Esmeralda had done this to over the years. The carnival was the perfect cover for something like this. No doubt, Esmeralda had Arturo snatch up a girl or two at every town the carnival visited, drained them, disposed of their bodies, then packed up and moved on before anyone realized exactly what had happened. A nice little murderous scheme.

Well, it was going to stop—right now.

Arturo was busy watching Esmeralda, so he didn't see me wrap my hands around two of the wooden bars on my cage. Forget the lockpicks, and screw being subtle. Not with these monsters. I reached for my Ice magic, letting the cool power bubble up from the deepest part of me. Cold silver lights flared, centered on the spider-rune scars embedded in my palms, and I pushed the power outward. It took me only a second to completely coat the bars with an inch of elemental Ice, pushing it into all the tiny holes and cracks in the wood.

Esmeralda must have sensed me using my magic, because her head turned in my direction. She realized that I was awake and trying to break free. She snapped her fingers at Arturo.

"Get her!" she hissed, tightening her grip on Bria's hand.

"Don't worry," I snarled. "I'm coming out."

I sent out a burst of magic, shattering the elemental Ice that had been driven deep into the wood. The cage bars snapped like matchsticks under my fingers.

Arturo hurried over to the cage, but I was quicker. I crawled out and stayed on the ground, waiting until he was in range. Then I lashed out with my foot, catching the giant in the knee. His leg buckled, and he put a hand on the ground to keep from falling flat on his face. He staggered upright, and I got to my feet and darted forward so that I stood right in front of him.

Then, looking him in the eyes, I grabbed one of the knives out of his leather sash and stabbed him in the chest with it.

He screamed. I smiled and twisted the knife in deeper, just as I had done a hundred times before as the Spider. Blood spurted from the wound, spattering onto my hand, face, and clothes, but I didn't care. The giant would be bleeding a whole lot more before I was through with him—and so would his sick, twisted bitch of a boss.

Arturo screamed again and swung his fist at me. This time, I reached for my Stone magic and used it to harden my skin into an impenetrable shell. The giant's fist plowed into my chin. The sharp, strong blow didn't break any of my bones, thanks to my magic, but there was still enough force behind Arturo's punch to throw me off him.

I slammed into the dancing bear's ball and bounced off it, but as soon as I hit the floor, I scrambled right back up onto my feet, still clutching his knife.

Arturo and I faced each other, about twenty feet of empty space between us. Apparently, the giant thought this was going to be a repeat performance of what he'd done onstage earlier. He reached for the knives in his sash and started throwing them at me—only this time, he wasn't looking to miss. No, this time, he aimed for my heart.

Thunk!

Thunk! Thunk!

Thunk!

Since I was still holding on to my Stone power, I didn't bother ducking Arturo's knives. The blades bounced harmlessly off my magic-hardened skin and clattered to the barn floor, tumbling every which way.

Instead, I ran toward the giant even as he backed up. But he wasn't paying attention to where he was going, and he bumped up against another one of the clown cars. Arturo's arms windmilled, and he ended up with his ass in the bottom of the car and his long legs dangling over the side. He raised his hands, trying to fend me off, but I smashed my Stone-hardened fist into his face, snapping his head back.

"Catch *this* between your teeth," I growled.

Then I rammed the bastard's own knife into his throat. Arturo arched back, clawing at the blade in his windpipe, so I obliged him by ripping it out. Blood sprayed everywhere, as bright, thick, and runny as the greasepaint the clowns wore.

Wheezing all the while, the giant clutched his throat with both hands, as if that would save him from the brutal, fatal wound. But after several seconds, his hands slipped off his bloody throat, and his dark eyes grew blank and glassy—

A blast of Air magic threw me across the barn.

It was like being picked up and hurled by a tornado, but I managed to hold on to my Stone power as I smacked into the far wall. The tools there rattled from the sudden, violent disruption, but they stayed on their pegs. Another gust of wind picked me up and tossed me against the wall again before turning me around and holding me there, two feet off the ground.

I glared at Esmeralda, who climbed out of the clown car and slowly approached me, one hand held out in front of her to help her control the gusts of Air swirling around me. The ringmaster's eyes glowed a bright hazel as she used her magic to keep me right where she wanted me.

"I'll kill you for daring to interfere with Esmeralda the Amazing!" she bellowed.

"Oh, don't make promises you can't keep, sugar," I drawled.

I pushed back against her magic with my own Ice and Stone power, raised my arm, and chucked the knife I was still holding at her.

Esmeralda shrieked, threw her hands up, and sent out a haphazard burst of Air magic. The sharp gust of wind knocked the knife off course, and the weapon sailed harmlessly off to the left. But my toss had ruined her concentration, and the feel of her Air magic quickly died down to a mere whisper of a breeze. I slid down the wall onto my feet, then grabbed another one of Arturo's knives from where it had landed on the floor and headed in her direction.

But Esmeralda recovered fast. She tossed another blast of Air magic my way, forcing me back while she sprinted for the barn door. I started after her, but my feet got tangled up in a pile of oversize clown boots. Cursing, I broke free of the mess, even though I knew I wasn't going to be quick enough to catch her before she ran outside—

Click.

Esmeralda knew that sound as well as I did. She froze, then slowly turned around. Bria had one hand braced on the side of the clown car to hold herself upright. With her other hand, she pointed her gun at the ringmaster's chest.

Sometime during the fight, my sister had woken up, climbed out of the clown car, and stumbled over to the table where her gun was. Sloppy, sloppy, sloppy of Esmeralda not to have put the weapon somewhere more secure. Then again, she hadn't planned on Bria ever waking up to use it.

Bria leveled the gun at the ringmaster's heart. "Needless to say, you are under arrest," she growled.

Esmeralda stayed where she was, although I could see her trying to think of a way to escape. I moved over to stand beside my sister, careful not to get in her line of fire.

"You okay?" I asked.

Bria nodded. "Other than feeling completely exhausted, I'm fine. What did she do to me?"

"The same thing she did to Elizabeth and I'm guessing a lot of other girls," I said. "She was using her Air magic to pull the life out of you."

Esmeralda laughed, the ugly sound bouncing around inside the barn. "Not the life, you idiot. The *beauty.*"

"And what would you need with my beauty?" Bria asked. "You have plenty of your own."

Esmeralda let out another harsh laugh, then gestured at her own face and body. "Please. You have no idea how long and hard I've worked to look this way. The diets, the face creams, the makeup. And when I was finally perfect, do you know what happened?"

Neither Bria nor I answered her, but we didn't have to.

"Old age," Esmeralda hissed, as though it were the vilest thing ever. "Gray hair, wrinkles, sagging skin. Nobody wants to see that. Nobody pays to see the old crone at the carnival. They all want to stare at the pretty young woman in the center of the ring. But I figured out a way to stop it—to stop all of it."

"Yeah," I said. "And all you had to do was kill a bunch of innocent girls."

Esmeralda shrugged. "Youth is wasted on the young—and so is beauty. If they weren't strong enough to keep theirs, then that was their fault, not mine."

"Well, it's over," Bria snapped. "You're going to jail, where you belong. I wonder how long it will take for all that stolen beauty of yours to fade. What do you think, Gin? Six months?"

"Nah," I said. "Not with all that magic she wasted trying to kill me. I'd give her a month, two tops, before she looks her real age, whatever that is. It won't be pretty, though, will it, Esmeralda? Sad, since we know that's all you really care about."

Panic filled the ringmaster's eyes, and her gaze darted left and right, but there was no way out and nowhere for her to run. The witch had finally been caught, and soon everyone would see her exactly as she was—warts, wrinkles, and all.

"I'd rather die!" she screamed.

Esmeralda reached for her Air magic to throw at us. I tightened my grip on the knife in my hand and headed toward her, determined to end the ringmaster once and for all—

Crack! Crack! Crack!

Bria shot her in the chest three times.

Esmeralda's eyes bulged in pain and surprise. Her mouth opened wide, as though she were going to scream, but the only sound that escaped her lips was a soft rasp, like the air leaking out of a balloon. She toppled over onto the floor, blood soaking into the hay around her.

I waited until my ears quit ringing, then looked at my sister. "What did you do that for? I would have taken care of her."

"I know," Bria replied in a grim voice. "But who knows what else she might have tried to do to you with her Air magic? She might have tried to suffocate you with it or something worse. I didn't want to take that chance, and I especially didn't want her to hurt you like she hurt me—like she hurt all those other girls."

I nodded. Bria protecting me, caring about me, fighting side by side with me, was something I was still getting used to, after her being gone for so many years. But keeping your family safe no matter what was a need I understood all too well. Sometimes I thought it was the *only* thing I understood. Well, that and retribution. And sometimes they were one and the same.

Bria grabbed her badge off the table while I tucked my knives away in their usual slots. Then we both walked over to look at the ringmaster—at least, what was left of her.

Death had snuffed out the magic that had sustained Esmeralda, and her body was already starting to deteriorate. Wrinkles grooved her once-smooth skin, gray streaked her hair, and her perfect bloodred nails had come free from her gnarled, knotted fingers. She looked like she'd been dead for months instead of just a few minutes.

"How old do you think she was?" Bria asked.

I shrugged. "Doesn't much matter now, does it? Because she's as dead as can be."

While Bria pulled her phone out of her jeans and called her fellow boys in blue to report what had happened, I went over to the clown car where Elizabeth was lying.

I put my hand on her forehead. She was cool to the touch, but she was still alive. Jo-Jo could take care of the rest. Elizabeth jerked awake at the feel of my hand on her skin, her eyes wide with panic and fear. I gently squeezed her shoulder, letting her know that everything was all right. After a moment, when she realized that it wasn't Esmeralda looming over her, the girl's face relaxed.

"It's okay, sweetheart," I said in a gentle voice. "You're safe now."

Elizabeth nodded, and her eyes slid shut in exhaustion once more. "I used to like the carnival," she muttered. "Not anymore."

I smiled, even though she couldn't see it. "I know the feeling."

Bria and I were at the carnival late into the night. In addition to calling the cops, Bria also contacted Fran, the girl's aunt. I watched as Fran got out of her car, ran over to where Elizabeth was resting in the back of Bria's sedan, and hugged her niece tight. Jo-Jo would be here in a few minutes to fully heal her, and the girl would be right as rain again soon enough.

Bria said something to them, then headed in my direction. I was sitting on top of the fence that lined the clearing, and she hopped up next to me.

"Elizabeth should be fine in a few days," she said. "It looks like Esmeralda didn't do any lasting damage. I talked to Jo-Jo on the phone. She said that since Esmeralda didn't fully drain Elizabeth, it's sort of like Elizabeth is suffering from severe dehydration. Some Air magic and a lot of fluids, and she'll be okay."

I nodded. "Good."

"I also called Finn and asked him to do some research into the carnival," Bria said. "He found an old newspaper article from the early eighteen hundreds that talked about a traveling Carnival of Wondrous Wonders. The main attraction was a knife-throwing act that featured a particularly beautiful woman."

"Esmeralda the Amazing."

She nodded. "There's no telling how many people she murdered over the centuries to keep herself young. Dozens, maybe even hundreds. We've already started contacting law-enforcement agencies in other towns the carnival passed through so we can look into all the missing-persons reports."

I'd figured it would turn out to be something like that. "What about the other carnival workers? Were they all involved in it?"

Bria shook her head. "Apparently, Arturo was the only one who actually helped her abduct and kill the girls. The other workers were never allowed into that barn, which they set up at every carnival site, so they never actually saw what Esmeralda did to the girls. The workers were suspicious, but mostly they were too afraid of Esmeralda to really look into it. I need to get back and finish interviewing them. It shouldn't take too much longer."

"I'll wait for you," I said.

Bria nodded, hopped off the fence, and moved back into the crowd of cops. The carnival workers also milled around, looking shell-shocked. I wondered what would happen to the carnival now, if it would continue on or if the workers would have to find another one to join. I had a feeling that the wondrous wonders would be no more, just like Esmeralda and Arturo.

Since Bria was busy, I left my perch on the fence and wandered back through the carnival. Finally, I wound up at the main stage. I climbed the steps and looked out at the bleachers.

They were empty now, but I could almost hear the roar of the crowd, feel the heat of the spotlight, see everyone's eager eyes fixed on me. Esmeralda had loved this so much that she'd murdered for it. Well, I supposed people have murdered for less—including me.

I was about to leave the stage when I noticed a tin pail of apples sitting next to the Wheel of Death. I looked around, but no one was in sight, so I walked over and grabbed an apple. I skewered the fruit on a piece of plywood that had splintered on the wheel—right where Esmeralda's heart would have been if she had been on the contraption.

When I was satisfied the apple would stay in place, I cranked up the Wheel of Death until it was spinning around and around at a dizzying pace. Then I walked to the opposite side of the stage, several feet behind where Arturo had stood.

I palmed one of my silverstone knives. I hefted it in my hand for a moment, then tossed it up, caught it by the blade, and threw it at the spinning wheel.

Thunk!

The apple exploded into pieces.

Ta-da.

I grinned. The wheel slowed down, and I went over and pulled my knife out of the plywood. I flipped the blade up into the air before catching it with ease and giving a low bow to the empty bleachers.

"This old girl's still got it," I murmured, straightening back up. "Parlor tricks and all."

Whistling, I slid my knife back up my sleeve and left the Wheel of Death and the stage behind.

Spider and Frost

Spider and Frost takes place after ***Last Strand***, book 19. It is a crossover novella between the **Elemental Assassin** and the **Mythos Academy** series.

Chapter One

Gin Blanco

"I'm going to kill Finn," I growled. "Slowly. Deliberately. Painfully. Really take my time. Really make it *hurt*."

A disbelieving snort echoed out of my phone, and the woman on the screen shook her head, making her shaggy blond hair fly around her shoulders. Despite my ominous threat, she laughed, which made her blue eyes sparkle and her rosy skin glow.

Detective Bria Coolidge, my baby sister, smiled at me. "As much as I hate to admit it, Gin, the situation isn't Finn's fault," she said. "Not this time—"

Bria's voice cut off, and she disappeared from the screen. A moment later, a man popped into view, with Bria hovering behind him. With his walnut-brown hair, green eyes, and tan skin, the man was as handsome as my sister was pretty, and the two of them made a striking couple.

Finnegan Lane, my foster brother, peered at me through the phone screen. "You cannot possibly blame this little snafu on *me*," he said in an indignant tone. "Like Bria said, it's not *my* fault that some sort of rockslide is blocking the road. Or whatever is holding up traffic."

"No," I replied. "But it *is* your fault that I'm stuck here at the train station by myself. *You're* the one who told me to go ahead and leave the hotel and that you, Bria, and Owen would meet me here."

"Hey, don't blame me because your significant other just *had* to have blueberry muffins this morning," Finn replied. "Why, I would say it's entirely *Owen's* fault that you're at the train station alone. Not mine—"

His voice cut off, and he too disappeared from view, much like Bria had done a minute ago.

When the phone stilled again, another man was staring through the screen at me. The early-morning sunlight brought out the blue highlights in his black hair, as well as his violet eyes and tan skin. His nose was slightly crooked, and a white scar slashed across his chin, but the tiny imperfections only added to his rough, rugged appeal, and I thought he was the handsomest man I'd ever seen. Then again, love could make anyone biased, even a bitter, jaded assassin like me.

Owen Grayson, my significant other, grimaced with guilt. "Finn's right. *I* was the one who wanted to get some blueberry muffins from that great little café we ate at yesterday."

He held his hand up, revealing a large white paper bag dangling from his fingers before slowly lowering it again.

"On the bright side, I got enough muffins for everyone, along with some whipped cream cheese. I know that's your favorite, Gin."

Some of my annoyance faded away, and a smile crept across my lips. Blueberry muffins slathered with cream cheese *were* one of my favorite breakfast treats, and it warmed my heart that Owen had remembered that small fact and gone out of his way to get me said muffins, even if it was keeping us apart right now.

"What am I supposed to do?" I asked. "The train is leaving in fifteen minutes. There's no way you all will make it to the station by then—"

The loud shriek of a whistle drowned me out.

Bria, Finn, and Owen might currently be stuck on the side of the road, but I was standing smack dab in the middle of the Pine Crest train station. A few days ago, the four of us had left Ashland to take a much-needed vacation and escape the myriad problems and clever criminals that populated our violent, dangerous city.

Finn had had his heart set on exploring Pine Crest, a charming little town tucked away in the Appalachian Mountains in North Carolina that catered to skiers in the winter and tourists in the summer. Distance-wise, Pine Crest wasn't all that far from Ashland, but in some ways, it might as well have been a completely different realm.

Instead of run-down, graffiti-covered buildings, colorful storefronts filled the downtown area, which boasted everything from cafés and bakeries, to antiques shops and bookstores, to artisan workspaces where you could learn how to blow glass, sculpt clay, and carve wood. In addition to shopping, we'd spent the last three days at the Pine Crest Resort, taking advantage of its luxurious spa and gourmet restaurants. Even though it was late March, a winter storm had recently swept through the area, leaving behind cold temperatures and plenty of snow for some late-season ice skating and sledding.

This morning, we were supposed to take a scenic train ride from Pine Crest over to the nearby town of Cypress Mountain. In addition to the beautiful scenery, the trip also featured a stop at a historic train depot, where lunch would be served.

The train ride was the grand finale of our trip, one last chance to relax before we drove back home to all the usual problems waiting for us in Ashland—demanding underworld bosses, old enemies lurking in the shadows, new rivals rising up and trying to take us down.

Fighting for my life was practically a monthly occurrence for me, Gin Blanco, the notorious assassin the Spider. Now that I had finally defeated Mason Mitchell, my evil uncle and the head of the Circle, the secret society responsible for much of the crime and corruption in Ashland, I was the official, undisputed queen of the city's underworld. We'd only been gone a few days, but I was sure that a dozen new problems and even more enemies were already waiting for me back home.

But right now, I only had one problem: the fact that I was here, and Bria, Finn, and Owen were stuck elsewhere.

I sighed. "I could always take the shuttle back to the resort and wait for you all there. We have to get our luggage anyway before we leave for home."

Earlier this morning, Owen had slipped out of bed so that I could sleep late, although he had texted me about his plan to grab some muffins and other snacks before coming to the train station. The resort shuttle had dropped me off at the station about five minutes ago, which was when I'd realized the others weren't already here. I'd called Bria to find out where they were.

The answer? Stuck on the opposite side of Pine Crest. Apparently, the clipper storm that had dumped enough snow here for us to go skating and sledding had also caused some rockslides in the area, including on the main road that led into town. Hence my being stranded miles away from my loved ones.

"Don't be ridiculous," Finn said, his face popping into view over Owen's shoulder. "Go on the train ride. Relax, eat, enjoy the scenery. I already paid for the tickets, and I sent yours to your phone last night."

"Yeah," Bria chimed in, shoving her face in next to Finn's. "There's no reason why you should miss out on the fun."

"Think of it as a test run," Owen said, still in the center of the screen. "If you like it, then maybe we can come back and ride the train again. Maybe in the fall, when the leaves are changing colors. That would be nice."

I knew they were right, but I still hesitated. "Well, if you're sure you don't need me to call for a ride and head that way . . ."

Finn rolled his eyes. "We're fine, Gin. It's just a little traffic jam. It's not like black-clad villains are running around wild and we're all in mortal danger again."

Bria shoved her elbow into his side, making him hiss with pain. "Don't jinx us. We're still on vacation until the end of the day, remember?"

Finn gave her a sour look and rubbed his ribs, but he didn't say anything else.

"Finn's right," Owen chimed in. "Go on the train ride, and we'll be waiting at the Pine Crest station to pick you up this afternoon. And if the food isn't as good as advertised, then at least you'll have some blueberry muffins to look forward to, right?"

He waggled the paper bag, and I smiled back at him.

"Okay, then, I'll see you all in a couple of hours. Oh, and Finn?"

"Yeah?" he said, leaning toward the screen.

"If you eat all my blueberry muffins—"

Finn huffed, cutting off my warning. "I know, I know. You'll kill me. Slowly. Painfully. Deliberately. Really take your time. Really make it *hurt*."

"So you *were* listening earlier," I drawled. "Excellent. I do so hate having to repeat myself."

He huffed again. "I wonder if I'm the only person who has to deal with death threats from their sister the assassin on a regular basis."

I snorted. "In Ashland? Please. There are more family feuds in our city than customers at the Pork Pit."

Finn tipped his head in agreement. "Either way, enjoy the trip. Oh, and Gin?"

"Yeah?"

He winked at me. "Try not to kill anybody today, okay?"

I glanced around at the cutesy shops lining the storybook-looking street that ran in front of the train station. "Somehow I don't think that will be a problem. This place is about as far away from Ashland as we could get and still be in the Appalachian Mountains."

Finn chuckled at my words, as did Bria and Owen. I joined in with their laughter, but a small, nagging part of me wondered if Bria was right—and if Finn had just jinxed us all with his talk of villains and killing.

I ended the call, slid my phone into the back pocket of my jeans, and headed inside the train station. Just like the rest of Pine Crest, the station was colorful, charming, and immaculate, with beige brick, glossy black wooden beams, and stained-glass windows featuring, you guessed it, trains. Black wrought-iron chandeliers shaped like train wheels and studded with bare bulbs dangled from the high ceiling, while old-fashioned lampposts shaped like pine trees stood at the ends of the wooden benches that lined the walls.

Dozens of people were milling about in the main lobby, checking their phones and drinking coffee, and everyone seemed happy, relaxed, and cheerful. But I knew how deceiving looks could be, so I took up a position in the far corner, close to one of the wide archways that led into the back of the station, and studied everyone around me. I didn't spot any immediate, obvious threats, so I reached out with my magic, listening to the brick walls.

People leave emotional vibrations behind in whatever stone

is around them, and as a Stone elemental, I can hear and interpret all those feelings, from amusement to annoyance to murderous rage. But the brick walls only whistled about all the trains that had rumbled through the station over the years, along with the hurried, harried passengers who were eager to board and get to their next destination, wherever it might be.

A woman opened a metal door marked *Employees Only* and stepped through one of the archways close to the corner where I was standing. She was about my age, early thirties, with dark brown eyes and tan skin. Her blond hair was sleeked back into a low ponytail, and she was sporting an old-fashioned conductor's uniform of a black suit jacket with shiny gold buttons over a ruffled white shirt and black pants with a thick gold stripe running down each leg. The only thing that ruined her polished, professional look was her footwear. Instead of shiny black wing tips to match the rest of her spiffy uniform, the conductor was sporting scuffed, stained, brown hiking boots.

A brimmed black hat trimmed with gold thread topped the conductor's head, and she stopped and tugged it down, as if something had knocked it askew. She also ran her hands down her jacket, smoothing it into place.

The woman spotted me, and she turned and smiled. "You here for the trip, ma'am?"

I nodded. "Yep."

Her smile widened, and she nodded back at me. "Excellent. I'm Winifred. I'll be your conductor today. See you on board."

I nodded at her again. She flashed me another smile, then stepped through the archway, moved deeper into the station, and vanished from view.

"Attention, passengers. Now boarding. The ten o'clock Lunch and Look tour," a voice announced through the station's crackling intercom system. "Please have your tickets ready and start making your way out to the tracks, and we'll be under way shortly."

I plucked my phone out of my pocket, pulled up the text and ticket info that Finn had sent me, and got in line with everyone else. As the group slowly snaked toward the archways, I noticed a girl standing alone in the opposite corner and surveying the people in the lobby, just as I had done earlier. And just like me, she had her arms crossed over her chest, and a wary look filled her face.

The girl couldn't have been more than eighteen, but she seemed far more suspicious than excited about the trip. She reached up and ran a hand down her dark brown hair, although her thick locks immediately frizzed out to where they had been before, despite her halfhearted attempt to tame them. A gray messenger bag was slung across the girl's chest, and something odd was sticking up out of the side. Did she play some kind of sport? Was that a hockey stick? I squinted, but I couldn't quite make out exactly what the shape was—

The person ahead of me stepped forward, and suddenly, I was at the front of the line.

"Ticket, please," Winifred chirped in a bright voice.

"Here you go."

I showed her my phone, which she zapped with a handheld scanner. A cheery *beep* sounded, a light on the scanner turned green, and the conductor gestured for me to step forward through the archway into another, much smaller waiting area. The other passengers were already opening the glass doors in the far wall and heading outside to the tracks. I moved out of the way of the folks coming up behind me and looked back over my shoulder, but the girl had vanished.

I glanced around, but I didn't see her anywhere in the main lobby. A bit of unease trickled down my spine. There was no way any of my old enemies from Ashland could have possibly tracked me here, much less sent some girl I had never seen before to spy on me.

But that didn't mean *other*, new enemies weren't lurking

around somewhere, just waiting to strike.

If Finn were here, he would have said I was being paranoid, which admittedly was my usual state of mind. Oh, yes. Finn, Bria, Owen. They all would have told me to relax and enjoy the ride and not even *think* about enemies or danger or anything else untoward.

But I couldn't do that. I hadn't been able to do that since my mother and older sister were killed when I was thirteen, and I certainly couldn't do it now, given everything that had happened to me as both Gin Blanco and the Spider over the years.

A compromise, then.

As I pushed through a door and stepped outside to board the train, I told myself I was going to do my very best to relax— and still be on the lookout for trouble in the meantime.

Chapter Two

Gwen Frost

"I don't like this," I muttered. "Not one little bit."

"Oh, stop worrying, Gwen," a voice with a biting English accent piped up. "Everything is fine, and so far, everything is going exactly according to plan."

I glanced down at the sword sticking up out of the top of my messenger bag. Instead of being plain and featureless, half of a man's face was inlaid into the sword's silver hilt. An arched eyebrow, a sharp cheekbone, a hooked nose, even the round bulge of an eye. The features were as familiar to me as my own face, as was the sword's larger-than-life voice and confident, boisterous personality.

I shook my head. "I still don't like this."

Vic, my talking sword, rolled his purple eye. "You never like anything having to do with artifacts."

That was certainly true. During my time at Mythos Academy, I had encountered far too many artifacts that had been used, wielded, or worn by various mythological gods, goddesses, warriors, and creatures over the centuries. And I had witnessed all the damage the magical weapons, armor, clothing, books, jewelry, and other items could do, especially to the people I cared about. But I was an Oracle, someone who had been gifted with magic by the gods, as well as the Champion of Nike, the Greek goddess of victory, so it was my duty to protect artifacts from anyone who wanted to use them to do bad, bad things.

A while back, I had helped defeat Loki, the Norse god of chaos, and the Reapers of Chaos, people who willingly served the evil god. Once Loki was imprisoned, I'd thought that would finally be the end of all the death, danger, and destruction that had plagued me at Mythos Academy, but it hadn't been—not by a long shot.

Okay, okay, so things weren't quite *that* dire. Many of the Reapers had either been killed or captured during the Battle of Mythos Academy or had gone into hiding afterward, but there were still plenty of Reapers and other bad folks running around who would do anything to get their hands on mythological artifacts that would give them amazing abilities—and let them hurt and manipulate innocent people.

A long, loud, weary sigh escaped my lips. Sometimes I thought I would *never* get done saving the world.

My phone beeped, and I pulled it out and read the text message from Logan Quinn, a Spartan warrior who was also my boyfriend.

"Logan says the convoy is still stuck on the side of the road and Coach Ajax is trying to clear the rockslide so the vehicles can get through. He's going to text me again when he knows more. Logan also says some female cop from another town is poking around, asking questions and trying to figure out what's going on. Nickamedes and Professor Metis are talking to the cop right now."

Vic snorted. "Regular mortals have no clue about the mythological world. Don't worry, Gwen. Nickamedes and

Metis will send that nosy cop on her way, and Logan, Ajax, and the others will move those rocks soon enough. Everything will be fine, and we'll get the artifacts back to the academy in one piece just like we intended. After all, no one even knows we're here."

That was the plan, which worried me more than I cared to admit.

A couple of weeks ago, a group of Reapers had broken into the Crius Coliseum after the museum had closed for the day and made off with dozens of artifacts. Linus Quinn, Logan's dad and the head of the Protectorate, the mythological police force, had asked me and my friends to track down the Reapers and recover the stolen weapons and other items, but the thieves had seemingly vanished—until three days ago.

Daphne Cruz, my Valkyrie best friend, was a total computer genius. Using security and traffic cameras, along with some other footage, she'd spotted a couple of the Reapers leaving a nearby casino, and she'd eventually tracked them all the way back to a remote mountain cabin on the outskirts of Pine Crest.

Clever of the Reapers to hide so close to Mythos Academy, especially since we'd all expected them to get far away as fast as possible. But this group of Reapers had been much smarter and sneakier and far more patient than most, and they had spent the last two weeks lying low, just waiting for the search to die down so they could slip out of the area. If not for some of the less cautious Reapers partying at the casino, we never would have found them.

At dawn, my friends and I had raided the cabin hideout and recovered the artifacts with no resistance. The only problem was that we hadn't found the Reapers along with the items they'd stolen.

Nickamedes, Professor Metis, and Coach Ajax all thought the Reapers had fled, but I wasn't so sure. The artifacts they'd stolen were worth millions of dollars on the black market, and

I'd never known any thieves to just give up a major score like that. Especially not now, when so many of the Reapers had been exposed, were on the run, and were desperate for enough money to disappear to some deserted tropical island where the Protectorate couldn't find them.

Adding to my worries was the fact that these artifacts were much more dangerous than most, which is why we'd split them up. Earlier this morning, Nickamedes, Metis, and Ajax had overseen the packing of some of the smaller artifacts into wooden crates, which had been loaded onto the train to be whisked from Pine Crest over to Cypress Mountain, where the academy was located. I'd stayed behind here at the station to keep an eye out for Reapers, while everyone else had returned to the cabin to load the rest of the larger, heavier artifacts into several SUVs.

The plan had been for Nickamedes, Metis, and Ajax to drive those vehicles back to the train station and drop off Logan and Daphne, along with Carson Callahan, Oliver Hector, and Alexei Sokolov, some other Mythos students. Together, my friends and I were going to pretend we were just on the train for the Lunch and Look tour and guard the artifacts until we reached the Cypress Mountain station, where Nickamedes, Metis, and Ajax would meet us. But of course, the rockslide had derailed our careful plotting, and now here I was, stuck at the train station all by myself, except for Vic—and the other artifact in my messenger bag.

I reached down and patted the side of my bag, just as I'd done a dozen times in the last ten minutes. My fingers traced over the shape of a long, slender box, although I couldn't feel the artifact nestled inside—Minerva's Dagger.

Supposedly, the dagger granted the wisdom of Minerva, the Roman war goddess, to whoever held it. On the surface, it didn't sound like a big deal, but often, the most innocent-sounding artifacts were the most dangerous. Besides, wisdom could be used in a variety of ways, from solving a crossword puzzle to winning a fight to figuring out how to steal even more artifacts from other museums. Either way, the dagger was simply too powerful and valuable to store with the other crated artifacts in the train's baggage car, so Metis had given me the weapon, and I'd slipped it into my bag to transport it back to the academy.

From Logan's text, it sounded like the rockslide was a natural occurrence and not some clever, devious Reaper trap, but that knowledge didn't make me feel any better, only more anxious.

"Attention, passengers. Now boarding . . ." The announcer's voice boomed through the speakers attached to the walls.

I gnawed on my lower lip. "Do you think I should get on the train like we planned? Or wait here for Logan and the others?"

"And stay here at the station all alone? With no one else around?" Vic's hilt quivered, as though he was shaking his half of a head. "No. At least there will be plenty of people on board the train. Surely the Reapers won't be daring enough to attack you out in the open like that."

I huffed. "Do you not remember the last time we were on a train? When we went to the academy in Snowline Ridge, Colorado? Because I distinctly remember several Reapers attacking us right in the middle of the ride in broad daylight."

Vic rolled his eye again. "Okay, so *maybe* the Reapers won't be daring enough to attack us this time."

"We both know that Reapers don't care who they hurt, only that they get what they want."

Vic's hilt quivered again, as though he was trying to nod his half of a head in agreement.

"Besides, I think I spotted one of them already," I said. "Did you see the way that one woman was staring at me earlier?"

"The woman in the black fleece jacket?" Vic replied. "Yeah,

I noticed her too. But just because she was staring at you, that doesn't mean anything. Maybe she thought you were someone else. And we both saw her glancing around the train station, like she was looking for someone."

"Yeah," I muttered. "Maybe she was looking for *me*, and especially Minerva's Dagger."

My hand curled a little more tightly around the strap of my messenger bag. I didn't see the mysterious woman anymore, so I moved away from the corner and headed toward the front doors. I didn't know who that woman was, but she seemed dangerous, and I didn't want to get on the same train as her. I hated leaving the other artifacts in the train's baggage car, but protecting the dagger was the most important thing right now.

As I neared the exits, I tried to remember where the closest coffee shop was. I'd walk down the street, hole up in the first one I came to, and drink hot chocolate until Logan and the others arrived.

I had reached out to push one of the glass doors open when a black SUV zipped up to the curb outside the station and screeched to a stop. I froze, my hand still stretched out in front of me.

One of the SUV doors opened, and a guy got out of the back of the vehicle. He was about my age, eighteen or so, and wearing a long black overcoat over a black T-shirt, jeans, and boots. With his blond hair, brown eyes, and tan skin, he was super cute, and the sight of him made my heart pound and my breath catch in my throat, but not in a good way.

The guy's name was Brayden Vitales, and he was a Reaper.

Brayden was a Roman warrior, which meant that he was gifted with supernatural speed, just like Amazons were. According to the information that Daphne had dug up in the last few weeks, Brayden was the head of the Dolos Crew, named after the Greek god of trickery, treachery, deception, and more. The group of thieves also included Valkyries and Vikings, all of whom were exceptionally strong.

Together, Brayden and the rest of the Dolos Crew specialized in stealing artifacts from museums, libraries, and even secure Protectorate storage facilities, although the recent heist at the Crius Coliseum was their biggest, splashiest, and most daring so far.

On all their previous jobs, the Dolos Crew had vanished without a trace—until they popped up somewhere new and stole some more artifacts. Reapers were usually so careful, so I found it really weird that Brayden and his friends would risk partying someplace like a casino, which had dozens of security cameras that could potentially be used to identify and track them down. But I supposed even the smartest criminal slipped up on occasion.

Two older, thirty-something adult men and a woman also got out of the SUV. Brayden looked at his phone, then gestured with his hand, pointing up and down the street, and the adults peeled off, as if they were searching for someone—me, most likely.

So much for our plan to split up the artifacts. Somehow the Reapers had tracked the objects here anyway, which meant that I was once again in serious, serious danger.

I muttered a soft curse and moved away from the doors before Brayden spotted me. I glanced around, but everyone was heading toward the back of the lobby, and there was only one place for me to go: on board the train.

"You have to get on the train, Gwen," Vic said, echoing my thoughts. "The Reapers will see you if you try to leave."

He was right. I couldn't slip away from the station without Brayden and the other Reapers outside potentially spotting me, and I couldn't stay here in the empty waiting area either. Maybe the train would be marginally safer, even if that mysterious woman was on board.

Either way, it was the only choice I had, so I pulled up my ticket on my phone and got in line with everyone else.

I showed my phone to the female conductor, stepped outside, and boarded the train.

The train was an old, vintage model that had been lovingly restored, and everything looked like it had just been cleaned, waxed, and polished, from the wide picture windows, to the glossy wooden benches topped with thick red cushions, to the brass rails that served as handholds and cordoned off the groups of seats from the main aisle. Even the air smelled faintly of some fresh, lemony cleaner.

I glanced down at my phone and quickly found my seat assignment, right in the middle of one of the cars. I grimaced, knowing that I was far too exposed here, in everyone's line of sight, but I was trapped until all the other passengers sat down. Maybe then I could find a more out-of-the-way seat, perhaps by one of the doors, with my back to the corner, where I could see any potential Reapers who might be on board and creeping up on me.

"Is this seat taken?" a soft feminine voice asked.

Startled, I looked up. The woman in the black fleece jacket, the one who'd been watching me earlier inside the station, stood in the aisle, a pleasant smile fixed on her face. Up close, she was quite pretty, with dark brown hair and pale skin, but the thing that caught my attention was her eyes. At first, I thought they were a weak, watery blue, but on a closer look, I realized they were actually a deep, wintry gray. The color reminded me of the sly, wicked gleam of Vic's blade.

"Is this seat taken?" the woman repeated, giving me another pleasant smile. "I know the seats are assigned, but my friends didn't make it, and I don't want to sit by myself. Besides, you look like you could use some company too."

Company was the very last thing I wanted, but I just shrugged in return. Making a fuss about the seat would draw unwelcome attention, which I wanted even less than I wanted her dubious company.

The woman took my shrug as an invitation to sit down on the bench facing mine. I tensed, and my hand drifted over to my messenger bag, which was resting on the seat beside me.

In addition to her black fleece jacket, the woman was wearing a royal-blue T-shirt with some sort of pink pig logo on it, along with dark jeans and black boots. Somehow she made the casual clothes look cool, even though she was a bit underdressed, considering that most of the other passengers were wearing either suit jackets and ties or pretty sweaters and dresses. Then again, I was no fashionista myself, since I was sporting a worn purple hoodie over a long-sleeve gray T-shirt, gray jeans, and my favorite and most comfortable purple-and-gray plaid sneakers.

The woman tugged down the sleeves of her jacket, then leaned forward and stuck her hand out to me. "My name is Gin Blanco. You can call me Gin, like the liquor."

I flinched and had to stop myself from visibly recoiling at the polite gesture. Thanks to my psychometry magic, I *never* shook hands with strangers, and I rarely did more than bump fists with my friends.

Touch magic, some people called it. Basically, I got flickers of memories and flashes of feelings off just about any object I touched with my bare skin. Oh, I was safe enough drumming my fingers on the red seat cushion or clutching the brass railing, since those were common, ordinary, everyday objects that hundreds of people had used over the years. Besides, no one had any special feelings for or big attachments to things like seats and rails.

But touching someone else, especially this mysterious,

suspicious woman . . . well, that was almost guaranteed to open a window into her memories and give me a front-row view of everything that had ever happened to her and all the things she had done in return—good, bad, and ugly.

I usually didn't get flickers or flashes off people unless I was physically touching them, but sometimes my psychometry magic gave me other small hints about folks. And right now, a little voice in the back of my mind was whispering a warning that I very much did *not* want to touch this woman and see what was lurking in her heart.

"My name is Gwen," I said, finally answering her question. "Gwen Frost."

I studied her closely, but no recognition flared in her eyes, indicating that she wasn't part of the mythological world. Pretty much everyone, from the youngest Mythos student to the oldest Protectorate member to the cruelest Reaper, knew *exactly* who I was. Gwen Frost, Nike's Champion, the girl who had defeated and imprisoned the powerful god Loki. I was rather famous for saving the world—or infamous, depending on your point of view.

The woman, Gin, kept staring at me. When it became apparent that I wasn't going to shake her hand, she slowly dropped it to her lap and gave me a puzzled look, which made me feel a little guilty.

"Sorry," I said, trying to explain. "But I don't want to shake your hand. I, uh, just got over a cold. I might still be . . . germy."

Gin's forehead crinkled like she didn't believe my lame excuse. Yeah, I wouldn't have believed me either. But after a few seconds, she nodded.

"I don't particularly like shaking hands either," she drawled. "Especially when the other person's hand is warm and wet, like a limp fish. Or when they try to crush your bones to show you how strong and superior they are."

Despite my best intentions, a laugh escaped from my lips,

and I found myself smiling at her.

Gin grinned back at me, then relaxed back in her seat. "Well, we might as well get comfortable, Gwen Frost. We have a long ride ahead of us."

Her tone wasn't the least bit dark and sinister, but something about her words made a shiver skitter down my spine. I didn't mind the ride being long. I just hoped that the Reapers wouldn't find me and that this wouldn't be the last trip I ever took.

Chapter Three

Gin Blanco

I was pretty sure the girl was in trouble.

Finn would have claimed that I was being paranoid yet again, but something about the girl seemed slightly . . . *off.* Oh, there was nothing wrong with Gwen Frost herself, and she seemed smart, strong, and capable. But the way she eyed everyone in the train car, especially me, as if she was just waiting for someone to leap up out of their seat, brandish a weapon, and reveal their true evil intentions, reminded me of . . . well, *myself.*

I was always waiting for new and old enemies alike to appear and try to kill me and my loved ones. Story of my life.

So when I'd seen Gwen board the train through one of the windows, I'd left my assigned seat in another car, entered this one, and plopped down across from her. Gwen's trouble wasn't any of my business, but I just couldn't sit by and let someone get hurt. Especially not a girl who seemed as weary and wary, and as haunted and hunted, as I always felt, even now, when I was on vacation.

But perhaps the most curious thing was that Gwen didn't seem particularly *afraid* of whatever trouble she was in, just resigned to the fact that something bad was going to happen sooner or later. Her resolute resignation made me even more curious about what might be going on. Besides, I had to do something to occupy my time until the train stopped for lunch.

I studied the girl again. Frizzy brown hair, pale skin, a few freckles sprinkled across her cheeks. Her features were quite pretty, but one thing stood out: her eyes. At first, I thought they were blue, but a second look revealed that they were really a lovely shade of violet.

My gaze flicked over to her bag. It too was perfectly ordinary, although some sort of longish box was bulging up against the side of the gray fabric. Of course, I couldn't tell what the girl might be hiding in that box, but I could clearly see what was sticking up out of the top of the bag.

"Is that a sword?" I asked.

Gwen's hand curled around the bag in a protective gesture, and I got the distinct impression that she wanted to hide the weapon from sight. "Yeah. I go to Mythos Academy. It's for, uh, fencing class."

I didn't know nearly as much about swords as I did about knives, but even I knew that wasn't a fencing sword. The weapon was much too broad and thick for that, and the hilt was all wrong. Instead of being smooth silver, the hilt was shaped like half of a man's face, as though an actual person was trapped somewhere deep inside the metal. Curiouser and curiouser.

"Mythos Academy, huh?" I murmured, still eyeing the sword.

"Have you heard of it?"

I shrugged. "Just in passing. It's in Cypress Mountain, right?

That fancy private boarding school where all the rich kids go?"

Gwen kept staring at me, as though she expected me to say something else. But after a few seconds, she slowly nodded. "Yeah. That fancy private boarding school for rich kids."

My gaze flicked over her clothes. A hoodie, T-shirt, jeans, and scuffed sneakers didn't exactly scream *rich kid*, but I knew even less about clothes than I did about swords. For all I knew, she was wearing a Fiona Fine designer hoodie and Bella Bulluci sneakers that cost more than the five silverstone knives I was carrying—one secured in the small of my back, two tucked up my sleeves, and two more nestled in the sides of my boots.

"So, Gin, where are you from?" Gwen asked.

Most people probably would have thought she was just making polite conversation, but her eyes narrowed, and she stared at me as though she was going to weigh my answer very, very carefully.

"Ashland," I replied. "I run a barbecue restaurant called the Pork Pit. Maybe you've heard of it?"

She shook her head. "Sorry, but I haven't."

"That's okay."

I reached into my jacket pocket. Gwen tensed, and her hand drifted over to the sword, as though she was going to yank the weapon out of the top of the bag. Wary and skittish. Yep, she was most definitely in some sort of trouble.

I kept my movements slow and easy as I pulled a small white card out of my pocket and held it out between us. Gwen hesitated, but she reached out and took the card. She blinked, and I could have sworn that magic flared in her violet eyes, even though I didn't sense any elemental power rippling off her. No Air, Fire, Ice, or Stone and no offshoot elements like electricity, acid, water, or metal. Nothing like that at all.

Still, some . . . *force* gathered around her, like a blast of wind about to whistle in my direction, and it seemed like she saw something else besides the small white card in her hand.

Gwen blinked again, and the force—or whatever it was—abruptly vanished. She stared down at the card and rubbed the thick paper in between her fingers. "*The Pork Pit, Gin Blanco, Proprietor and Purveyor of Ashland's Finest Barbecue*. Cool. I've never met anyone who owned a barbecue restaurant before."

She gave me a cautious smile, and I grinned back at her. That was the magic of barbecue—talking about it almost always broke the ice with other people.

Then, out of the corner of my eye, I spotted a flash of purple, and I glanced over at her bag. For a moment, I didn't understand what I was looking at or where the odd bit of color was coming from. Then I realized that the sword's round, bulging eye was open—and that the very bright, very purple eye was staring straight at me.

"Barbecue, eh? Well, that's not *nearly* as tasty as Reaper blood and bones, but I have been known to enjoy a good barbecue sandwich on occasion."

Shock jolted through me like an electric current. Not only did the sword seem to be talking to me, but it was also speaking in a cool English accent. But that simply wasn't possible.

Swords couldn't talk . . . could they?

I blinked and blinked, trying to come up with an explanation for what I was experiencing. Maybe I'd drunk too much hot chocolate at the resort this morning and was having a weird sugar-induced hallucination. Maybe someone in the train station had discreetly doused me with a powerful mind-altering poison. Or maybe there was much more to Gwen Frost and her sword than there appeared to be.

I opened my mouth to ask the sword a question, but from one instant to the next, the sword's eye was closed again, along with its mouth, and it was still and inanimate once more. I watched it closely, but the weapon—he?—didn't move or speak again.

Had I just imagined the sword talking to me? I rubbed my head, which was suddenly pounding. Maybe Finn was right. Maybe my constant paranoia was finally getting the better of me and making me see things that weren't really there. That seemed far more plausible than a talking weapon.

Gwen stuck her arm in front of the sword, shielding it from my line of sight. Then she gave me a bright smile and tucked my business card into her hoodie pocket. "Tell me about your barbecue restaurant."

I got the feeling that she was desperately trying to change the subject, but I decided to play along—for now. At least until I could wrap my mind around the idea of a speaking sword.

"Well, the Pork Pit is located in downtown Ashland, and it's my pride and joy . . ."

The last of the passengers boarded, the whistle screamed, and the train pulled out of the Pine Crest station. Winifred, the conductor, ambled along the aisle, smiling and stopping to speak to everyone, including Gwen and me.

"We're going to climb up to the very top of Pine Crest Mountain, where the old historic depot is located," she said in a conversational tone. "That's where lunch will be served, so sit back and enjoy the scenery in the meantime."

Gwen and I both murmured our thanks. Winifred tipped her black hat to us, then moved on to repeat her spiel to the folks in the next section of seats a few feet away.

I stared out the window. As its name implied, Pine Crest Mountain was covered with pine trees, all of which were outlined in a picturesque coating of ice and snow. A couple of inches of snow also covered the ground, adding a clean white sheen to the landscape, although the sparkling crystals were quickly melting away under the clear blue sky and bright March sunshine.

As the trees and snow slid by and the train slowly chugged up the mountain, I kept talking to Gwen, asking question after question and trying to find out more about her.

The girl was polite, if exceptionally vague. Still, I learned a few things. In addition to attending Mythos Academy, Gwen also had an after-school job in the academy's library, which she referred to as the Library of Antiquities, as though it held more than just old reference books and dusty encyclopedias. Her grandmother lived in a nearby town and worked as some sort of fortune-teller, although Gwen kept referring to her grandmother as an Oracle, as though the term meant something special.

"What about your parents?" I asked.

"My dad died a long time ago. I don't even remember him." Gwen's face hardened. "My mom died a couple of years ago when I was sixteen."

Her cold, flat tone indicated there was a lot more to the story than that, but she clearly didn't want to talk about it. And who was I to make someone else talk about their feelings? Especially since that was always the very last thing I wanted to do myself.

I nodded in understanding. "My parents are both gone too. I don't remember my dad much either, but my mom died when I was thirteen. It was . . . tough."

That was an understatement, but I wasn't about to share how Mab Monroe had murdered my mother, Eira Snow, and my older sister, Annabella, and burned our mansion to the ground with her elemental Fire magic. That was way too heavy a conversation for what was supposed to be a fun, relaxing train ride.

My gaze dropped to my hands, and I massaged the scars embedded in my palms, which were suddenly aching. The marks had been a parting gift of cruel torture from Mab the night she'd murdered my family, and each silvery scar was shaped like a small circle surrounded by eight thin rays—a spider rune. The symbol for patience, something that had influenced my life in so many ways, especially as an assassin.

I was also wearing a silverstone pendant shaped like a spider rune, although I had tucked the necklace and matching chain under my T-shirt. Normally, the slight weight of the pendant against my skin comforted me, but right now, the spider rune was as heavy as an anvil pressing against my heart.

That was the funny thing about grief. No matter how much time passed, no matter how happy I was now, every once in a while, that heavy, heavy grief would sneak up on me like, well, an assassin in the night, twist the broken shards of my heart that belonged to my mother and sister, and remind me of everything I'd loved—and lost.

Gwen frowned. "Are you okay? What are those marks on your hands?"

My fingers clenched into fists, my nails digging into the scars embedded in my palms. My first instinct was to hide the marks, but she was just asking a simple question, and I didn't see a reason not to answer. Besides, if I opened up to her, then maybe she would trust me enough to let me help with whatever trouble she was in.

So I stretched my fingers wide and held out my palms where she could see them. "Just a couple of old scars. Sometimes they ache. They're spider runes, actually. The symbol for patience."

Her frown deepened, but she didn't seem to recognize the marks or what the symbols truly meant. She opened her mouth to ask another question, but the whistle screamed again, cutting her off, and the train slowed, sputtered, and ground to a halt.

"All right, folks," Winifred called out from the front of the car. "We've arrived at the original Pine Crest station. Lunch is going to be served inside the historic depot. If you will all follow me, please."

The conductor plodded down the stairs, opened the door, and got off the train. Gwen grabbed her messenger bag, stood up, and moved into the aisle, and I fell in step behind her.

The train had stopped at the very top of the mountain, although the town of Pine Crest was still visible in the valley several miles below. From this height, the colorful shops, clean streets, and surrounding stands of evergreen trees looked like miniatures that had been carefully nestled inside a snow globe.

Another sharp shard of grief twisted into my chest. My mother had collected snow globes, and Bria and I used to spend hours shaking them when we were young. I admired the pretty, panoramic view a moment longer, then shoved my grief aside and followed the rest of the passengers.

Winifred and the other employees herded us across a wide wooden platform, through some glass doors, and into the station. Historic black-and-white photographs showing both the inside and the outside of the old depot, along with various trains, adorned the white brick walls, and glass display cases containing tools, bits of metal, and other objects were scattered around the main lobby. Round dining tables covered with green linens were set up in the middle of the area, while long rectangular buffet tables lined one of the walls.

Most folks made a beeline for the food, but a few people wandered over to the far side of the lobby, where a wide, waist-high table ran the entire length of that wall. Tiny mountains, pine trees, and gray stones jutted up from the tabletop, along with several small houses and businesses, and several electric trains careened around the tracks in endless loops, occasionally belching out some low, rumbling *choo-choos*.

Gwen glanced around curiously, then headed over to the buffet tables. I trailed after her. We each fixed a plate of food and grabbed a seat at a table. Gwen slung her messenger bag down onto the chair beside her and arranged it so that the sword was propped up and staring out over the table, almost like it was a real person sitting here with us. Weird.

A waiter came around and poured lemonade into our empty glasses.

I held mine out. "A toast to a safe trip?"

A shadow passed over Gwen's face, but she clinked her glass against mine. "I'll drink to that."

We both dug into our food. Hot roast-beef-and-cheddar paninis studded with apple slices, all of it encased in thick, crusty grilled sourdough bread. Crispy fried baby potatoes seasoned with dill and loads of Parmesan cheese. Dried figs stuffed with blue cheese and wrapped with brown-sugar-glazed bacon and then baked to perfection.

Everything was excellent—except for the desserts. I cut into a cranberry-orange scone that was as dry as dust, while the chocolate chip brownies were almost as hard as the brick walls.

I huffed in annoyance and pushed my plate away, refusing to eat the rest of the scone and the brownie. "I make better desserts than this at the Pork Pit."

Gwen laughed. "Now you sound like Grandma Frost. She loves to bake, and she's always complaining if we get dessert at a restaurant and it's not as good as what she makes at home."

"Your grandma sounds like a nice lady."

A bright light filled Gwen's eyes. "She's the best."

She seemed genuinely happy when talking about her grandma, and I was glad she had at least had one parental figure in her life. After my mother and sister were killed, I'd spent some time living on the streets, so I knew how hard it was to think that you were alone and that no one would ever help you or watch out for you. I didn't know what would have happened to me if Fletcher Lane, Finn's dad, hadn't taken me in and trained me to be an assassin.

We got second helpings of everything except the desserts.

Gwen told me a little more about her grandmother, while I talked about Bria, Finn, and Owen and all the fun things we'd done while on vacation.

Eventually, the luncheon started winding down, and Winifred, the conductor, wandered over to our table. "How was the food?"

"It was great," Gwen replied. "Will we be leaving soon?"

"Yep," Winifred replied. "In about thirty more minutes."

Gwen nodded, pushed back from the table, and stood up. "Great. I'm going to look around before we leave."

She smiled at me, grabbed her messenger bag, and headed toward the electric-train diorama in the front of the lobby. I stayed at the table and sipped the last of my lemonade, content to people-watch. Everyone was talking, laughing, eating, and admiring the photographs and displays, and no one was doing anything suspicious.

So why were the brick walls muttering?

The low, sinister notes washed over me like a tide slowly rising along a sandy shoreline and threatening to drown anyone who didn't get out of the way. According to what Finn had said, the old historic depot was only used for special events, so it sat empty most of the time. Yet the stones were teeming with emotional vibrations.

Something was wrong.

I scanned the crowd again, but everything was the same as before. Passengers talking, laughing, eating, and ambling around the exhibits, waiters refilling drink glasses and offering coffee to those who wanted it, a few other workers putting out a final round of food. I reached out with my Stone magic, wondering if I was mistaken, but the bricks kept right on muttering, the dark whine an annoying hum that reverberated through my head loudly enough to make my teeth ache.

Then I realized what else was wrong. Gwen wasn't in the main lobby anymore.

I stood up, getting a better view, but she had vanished. I didn't know for certain that the muttering walls had anything to do with her, but I hadn't stayed alive this long by ignoring my instincts. So I set down my lemonade and circled around the lobby, as though I was admiring the historic photos and displays along with everyone else.

I still didn't spot Gwen, but I did come across two corridors that led away from the main lobby. One went left, and the other went right. I went down the right one and came across a couple of bathrooms, but they were all empty, so I kept going and eventually wound up in a kitchen.

A few workers gave me curious looks, but I smiled and nodded at them all, moved through the kitchen, yanked open a wooden door, and stepped through it.

I found myself at the front of the station, which featured another wide wooden platform with several sets of steps that led down to the ground. A gravel parking lot stretched out for about a hundred feet before giving way to a two-lane road in the distance. Gwen wasn't out here, although a black SUV was haphazardly parked nearby, more in the snow-crusted grass than on the bare gravel, as though someone had been in such a rush to reach the depot that they didn't care how dirty their tires got.

Even outside, I could still hear the mutters of the brick walls, and the sounds were growing increasingly loud and violent. Someone around here was definitely up to no good, and I would bet every dollar in the Pork Pit cash register that Gwen Frost was somehow involved.

I pulled my phone out of my pocket and texted Bria. *Train stopped for lunch. Might be some trouble with the ride. Find me as soon as you can.*

Bria texted me back almost immediately. *What?!?! We're on our way!*

I sent her a thumbs-up emoji, then set my phone on silent

and slid it back into my pocket. Bria, Finn, and Owen wouldn't get here in time to stop whatever bad thing was brewing, so I was on my own yet again.

I was okay with that.

Instead of wasting time backtracking through the kitchen, I stalked along the wooden platform, peering through the windows that fronted the station. I spotted another, smaller kitchen, along with some more display rooms and one area with an enormous video screen and several benches. A few folks were sitting on benches, watching a documentary about the historic depot. Even through the window, I could hear the narrator's booming, solemn tone, along with the sharp shriek of a train whistle and the loud, continued *chug-chug-chug* of the engine on the screen.

I moved on. Finally, at the far end of the platform, I looked through a window into a storage area. Chairs were stacked along the walls, with several large cardboard boxes and other odds and ends haphazardly strewn about. No framed photographs or video screens adorned the walls, and only a couple of bare bulbs dangled from the ceiling, casting out far more sinister shadows than the few they banished.

Gwen was standing in the middle of the storage area, texting on her phone. She was so focused on her device that she didn't notice the guy tiptoeing through the brick archway behind her. The guy was young, eighteen or so, like Gwen, with blond hair and dark eyes. He was wearing a long black coat over dark clothes, but the sword belted to his waist glinted a bright silver.

In my experience, people didn't carry weapons unless they were planning on using them.

I glanced back over my shoulder, but no one was creeping up behind me on the platform, and no other vehicles had entered the parking lot. Had the guy with the sword come here alone? If so, it was going to be the last mistake he ever made. I didn't know what sort of trouble Gwen Frost was in, but I was going to help her get out of it.

I followed the platform around the corner of the building and came to another door. The knob turned easily in my hand, and I slipped back inside the depot. This door led into a short corridor, and voices murmured nearby, so I quickly moved in that direction. I stopped at the archway I'd seen through the window, eased up to the opening, and peered inside the storage area.

Gwen was standing with her back to one of the walls. She must have shoved her phone back into her jeans pocket, because both her hands were clenched into fists.

The blond guy was standing a few feet away from her, his sword now clutched in his hand. I snorted. Fencing class. Right.

Two older men were flanking the young guy, along with a woman, and all three of them were also clutching swords. A weird sense of déjà vu washed over me, and for a moment, I felt like I was back at the Winter's Web Renaissance Faire, which had taken place in Ashland a couple of months ago. Only these people weren't dressed in knight and pirate costumes, and those swords definitely weren't wood or plastic. Even more telling, everyone looked like they knew *exactly* how to use the sharp, pointed weapons, especially the young guy, who seemed to be the leader, despite his age.

"Gwendolyn Frost," the guy drawled. "Nike's Champion. The girl who saved Mythos Academy. I thought you'd be taller."

He chuckled at his old, tired, cliché joke, as did his three friends.

"Brayden Vitales," Gwen replied in an icy tone. "I thought you'd be smarter than to face me in person."

I grinned. The girl had some serious gumption. Even though she was surrounded and outnumbered, Gwen was still standing her ground and eyeing her enemies like she was plotting the best way to take them all down. I admired her courage, although four against one wasn't the best odds.

Good thing I was here to help with that.

"Let's skip all the usual threats and other violent chitchat," Brayden said. "We came here to recover the artifacts that you and your friends stole from our cabin, and you're going to tell us where they are—every last one."

Gwen's chin lifted in defiance. "I don't know what you're talking about."

"Don't play dumb with me," Brayden replied, a bit of anger creeping into his voice. "We had security cameras hidden in the woods, and we saw you and your Protectorate friends storm inside the cabin and take our artifacts."

He dug his hand into his coat pocket. I tensed, getting ready to leap into action, but he only pulled out a phone. "Besides, we tagged the most valuable artifacts, and the tracking app led us straight here."

He waggled the phone at Gwen, then slid it back into his pocket.

"What are you planning to do with the artifacts?" Gwen asked. "Use them to start another war?"

Brayden laughed again, but it was a low, bitter sound. "Please. The Reapers are *finished*, especially now that Covington and his followers failed to take over the academy out in Snowline Ridge. As for me and my crew, well, we've decided to do the smart thing and get while the getting is good."

"You're going to sell the artifacts on the black market, take the money, and disappear." Gwen shook her head in disgust. "Typical Reapers, running away whenever things don't go exactly like you all planned."

Brayden shrugged off her harsh accusation. "More or less. I'll admit that it was clever of you and your friends to split up the artifacts, but it also gave us a chance to cut you off from the rest of them."

She jerked back in surprise. "*You* caused the rockslide on the highway?"

Brayden gave her an evil grin. "Yep. Well, the other part of my crew did. I told them to recover the artifacts and kill your friends."

Gwen's face paled, but her hands curled into even tighter fists. "If you hurt Logan or anyone else, I'll—"

"You'll do what?" Brayden sneered at her. "Cry? Well, not for long, because we're going to kill you, Oracle, just like the other half of my crew is killing your Spartan boyfriend and the rest of your friends right now."

Oracle? Spartan? It had been a while since I'd read any mythology books, but I remembered the two types of ancient warriors, as well as Nike, the Greek goddess of victory. Unless I was gravely mistaken or these folks were engaged in some weird fantasy role-playing game, Mythos Academy was much more than just a fancy boarding school for rich kids, and Gwen and the rest of these people were far more powerful and dangerous than they appeared to be.

"But like I said, enough idle threats and chitchat," Brayden said. "Where are the artifacts, exactly? Where is Minerva's Dagger? Did you leave the artifacts on the train or did you stash them here at the depot?"

Gwen shuffled back, and I realized that her messenger bag was sitting on the floor behind her, as though she'd dropped it and then stepped in front of it to guard whatever was inside. Even from this distance, I could still see the faint outline of that long rectangular box pressing up against the thick gray fabric. That bulge looked like just about the right size and shape to hold a dagger. So Gwen was carrying this so-called Minerva's Dagger in her bag, but where were the other artifacts Brayden had mentioned?

"Reaper scum," a voice with an English accent muttered.

Startled, I glanced around, wondering where that voice had

come from, but none of the adults had opened their mouth, and I didn't see anyone else in the storage area. Gwen shifted on her feet again, and a flutter of movement caught my eye.

The sword sticking up out of her messenger bag was sort of . . . *vibrating*. The sword's eye was also wide open, revealing its brilliant color, which was the same violet as Gwen's eyes.

"You'll never get away with this," the English voice sounded again, and the sword's mouth moved in perfect sync with the angry, muttered words.

Wait a second. Was her sword . . . actually . . . really . . . truly . . . *talking*?

I blinked and blinked, once again wondering if I was hallucinating or if my lemonade had been spiked with something or if my rampant paranoia was making me see things that weren't really there. But the sword's eye remained open, and no one else seemed surprised by the words coming out of its—his—mouth.

Brayden sneered down at the weapon. "Don't worry, little toothpick. We'll take you too. You'll fetch a few dollars on the black market, even if we have to muzzle you."

"A few dollars?" The sword sniffed, and the entire weapon vibrated with righteous indignation. "I'll have you know that I am worth *far* more than a few measly dollars. Why, a talking sword is one of the rarest and most valuable artifacts of all! I'm bloody *priceless*!"

"You're not helping, Vic!" Gwen hissed, glaring down at the sword.

Vic? So the sword had a name. Okay. I thought I'd seen some weird stuff in Ashland over the years, but talking weapons and sword-toting villains were a whole new experience for me. I'd been right before. Gwen Frost was up to her eyeballs in trouble—and it was up to me to get her out of it.

I studied Brayden, along with the two men and the woman. Besides the swords in their hands, it didn't seem like they had any other weapons, and I didn't see anyone else lurking around, waiting to jump into the fight.

Oh, sure, I could have palmed one of the silverstone knives hidden up my sleeves and sidled forward until I got close enough to strike. But sometimes the best approach was the most direct one, especially given the fact that Brayden looked like he was about three seconds away from lunging forward and slashing his sword across Gwen's chest. So I loudly cleared my throat, then stepped around the archway and strode forward, my boots *tap-tap-tap-tapping* out an ominous beat on the stone floor.

The two men whirled around, although the woman kept her eyes on Gwen. Brayden turned to the side so that he could see both Gwen and me at the same time.

Brayden frowned. "Who are you?"

"Your worst nightmare, sugar," I drawled.

His blond eyebrows creased together in obvious confusion. "I didn't realize that any of the nightmare gods and goddesses had Champions."

I shook my head, just as confused as he was. "Trust me. I'm nobody's Champion. I just always wanted to say that to an enemy."

Brayden glanced over at his friends, and they all shrugged back at him. Even Gwen was staring at me with a bewildered expression, as was Vic, her talking sword, and I got the distinct impression that everyone thought I was a few barbecue sandwiches short of a picnic.

Anger sparked in my chest, joining my own increasing confusion. *I* was fine. *They* were the ones spouting gibberish about mythological warriors and artifacts and whatnot.

"Forget about Champions," I growled. "Here's the deal. Lower your swords, and move away from my new friend Gwen."

"Or else what?" Brayden asked the inevitable question.

A cold, thin smile spread across my face. "Or else I'll kill every single one of you."

Brayden studied me a little more closely, but he didn't seem overly concerned about my threat. "I don't know how you'll be killing any of us, lady, since you don't even have a sword."

He chuckled, as did his three adult friends. Idiots. Just because they couldn't see my weapons didn't mean that they weren't there.

"Trust me, pal," I said. "You don't want to mess with the Spider."

Once again, confusion filled Brayden's face, along with everyone else's. "So you're the Champion for a spider goddess?"

I threw my hands up in consternation. "Will you stop babbling about gods and goddesses?" I jerked my thumb at my chest. "*I'm* the Spider. Me. Gin Blanco. No one else involved."

Not so much as a hint of recognition sparked in his or anyone else's eyes.

"Do you think she tripped and hit her head?" Vic asked, breaking the tense, awkward silence. "Or maybe she's been drugged. Gwen, did you see anyone slip her anything on the train?"

More frustration filled me. Having to explain exactly who I was and what I did was rather annoying. I much preferred it when my enemies automatically quaked in their boots at the mere whisper of my assassin name.

"*I'm* the Spider," I repeated, my voice even sharper than before. "The notorious assassin who runs a barbecue restaurant in her spare time. The queen of the Ashland underworld, feared by crime bosses near and far."

More blank looks all around. For once, my reputation did *not* precede me.

"Oh, yeah," Vic piped up. "She's definitely been drugged."

I sighed. "I killed Mab Monroe and Mason Mitchell and a whole bunch of other bad folks. Seriously, none of this is ringing a bell?"

Brayden shrugged, not the least bit impressed with my credentials, such as they were. "Never heard of you." An evil grin spread across his face. "As for being an assassin, well, we're Reapers. We know all about killing people."

The two men also grinned, while the woman smirked at me and twirled her sword around in her hand, as if she just couldn't wait to cut me down with the sharp, silver blade.

Gwen shook her head. "You need to get out of here, Gin. Assassin or not, you've never dealt with Reapers before."

"Don't worry about me, sweetheart. I can take care of myself. Been doing it for a long time now."

I crooked my index finger at Brayden. "What are you waiting for? If you're such a badass, then come on over here and try to kill me with that fancy sword. I'll be more than happy to take it away and gut you with your own weapon."

Perhaps it was my confident purr, but for the first time, a bit of doubt flickered across his face. "There are four of us and one of you."

"First of all, I can count just fine, sugar," I drawled. "And second, those are terrible odds—for you and your friends."

A flush swept up his neck, and anger bloomed like ugly red roses in his cheeks. Brayden opened his mouth, probably to snarl some insult right back at me, but a voice cut him off.

"What's going on in here?"

I glanced to the left. Winifred, the conductor, strode into the storage area, an odd look on her face. She stopped about ten feet away from me, Gwen, and the Reapers, or whatever weird term these people were calling themselves.

Brayden flashed her a wide smile. "Nothing's wrong. We were just having a little private chat with our new friends. That's all."

Winifred's forehead crinkled in confusion, and her gaze flicked from one person's sword to the next. She stepped forward, as if to get a better view of everyone, and I did the same thing, putting myself in between her and the Reapers.

Winifred stopped and gave me a puzzled look. "Are you . . . trying to protect me?"

"Something like that," I replied. "Stay behind me, Winifred."

She frowned and shifted backward. A soft *skitter-skitter* sounded, and my gaze dropped to her feet. The laces on her right boot were loose and dragging along the floor, hence the odd noise.

I started to lift my gaze, but once again, I noticed how her scuffed brown boots didn't match the rest of her sleek black uniform. Not only that, but her pants were also too long, as were the sleeves of her jacket, almost like . . . she was wearing someone else's clothes.

Like she had killed the real conductor, donned their uniform, and taken their place on the train.

As soon as the thought popped into my mind, I opened my mouth to shout a warning to Gwen, but Winifred was quicker than me—much, much quicker, as though she had some sort of supernatural speed.

Winifred yanked a gun out of her pants pocket, aimed it at me, and pulled the trigger.

Crack!

The bullet punched straight into my chest, and I dropped to the floor.

Chapter Four

Gwen Frost

"**N**o!" I yelled. "No! No! No!"

I started to rush over to Gin, who was crumpled on the floor, but Brayden stepped up and brandished his sword at me.

"Ah, ah, ah," he said. "You stay right there, Gwen."

I had no choice but to freeze. How had things gone so terribly wrong so quickly? Ten minutes ago, I'd slipped away from the luncheon and the displays in the main lobby and snuck into this storage area to have some privacy while I texted Logan for an update. He hadn't answered me, so I'd texted Daphne next and then Carson, but no one was responding, not even Oliver or Alexei. I'd been so worried and focused on my phone that I hadn't heard Brayden creep up behind me until it was too late. I hadn't even had a chance to grab Vic to try to cut down any of the Reapers.

My gaze dropped to Gin, who was sprawled across the floor like a broken doll, and my heart squeezed tight with worry, dread, and a heaping dose of guilt. Now a woman was dead because of my lack of awareness. And Logan, Daphne, and the rest of my friends might be dead too, if Brayden was telling the truth about the rest of the Reapers causing that rockslide to steal the artifacts that Nickamedes, Professor Metis, and Coach Ajax had loaded into the SUVs.

Winifred, the fake conductor, kept her gun trained on Gin. I glanced back over my shoulder, but no one came to investigate the commotion. The documentary blaring in the nearby room must have drowned out the sound of the shot.

After a few seconds, when Gin didn't move, Winifred lowered the weapon to her side and glared at Brayden.

"I thought you idiots were going to grab the girl quietly," she hissed. "Not make a scene and let one of the passengers sneak up on you."

"We *did* do things quietly," Brayden protested. "It's not *my* fault that some random person decided to play hero. She even said she was an assassin, as if any mere assassin would be a match for Reapers like us. Can you believe that?"

He laughed, and the rest of his crew joined in with his hearty chuckles. Anger surged through my body, and my hands clenched into fists again.

Winifred kept glaring at Brayden, not at all amused. "Well, I don't care who she is, little brother. Only that you messed up—*again.*"

Little brother? I glanced back and forth between Winifred and Brayden. Same blond hair, same dark brown eyes, same straight nose and pointed chin. The resemblance between them was obvious, and I mentally kicked myself for not seeing it before.

The Protectorate had compiled a detailed file on Brayden Vitales, just as they did on all known Reapers, and I remembered one of the documents mentioning that he had an older sister, an Amazon, with the same sort of amazing speed that he had, although I hadn't thought much of it at the time. But of course, his sister would be just as evil as he was, and apparently, she was the brains behind the Dolos Crew, its actual leader. Smart of Winifred to let her brother be the front man and thus the focus of the Protectorate investigation, while she stayed safely hidden in the background.

Brayden waved off his sister's harsh words. "I didn't mess up anything. Yeah, we had someone try to play hero, but she's dead now. Problem solved."

Winifred shook her head in exasperation. "Problem solved? Please. I had to swoop in and clean up your mess, just like I *always* do. Why, you wouldn't have even realized that the Protectorate had found your little mountain cabin if *I* hadn't set up those security cameras in the woods. You'd all be twiddling your thumbs in Protectorate custody right now if I hadn't gotten an alert on my phone and warned you to leave the artifacts behind and get out."

At her sharp, chiding tone, the other three Reapers dropped their heads and shifted on their feet, but Brayden huffed and rolled his eyes.

"And I have thanked you for that, numerous times," he snapped. "Now, let's get what we came here for. Agreed?"

Winifred shot him another angry look. The two of them might be brother and sister, but there was little love lost there. Yeah, I was totally Team Winifred, and I would have gotten tired of keeping Brayden from screwing up too.

"Fine," Winifred muttered. "I've searched the depot. There's nowhere to hide the artifacts in here, so she must have stashed them on the train. Let's go. *Quietly* this time. We can't afford any more mistakes."

Brayden rolled his eyes again, but Winifred ignored him and waved her gun at me. "Get your bag, Champion. Now."

I didn't have a choice. She could easily shoot me before I managed to get my hands on Vic. So I slowly leaned down, grabbed my messenger bag from the floor, and hoisted the strap onto my right shoulder. The bottom of the bag bumped against my hip, along with the box inside that contained Minerva's Dagger.

It was only a matter of time before the Reapers searched my bag and found the weapon and Winifred figured out that the other artifacts were stored in the train's baggage car. I had to figure out a way to escape before the Reapers realized that I was utterly expendable, or Gin would have died for nothing.

"We're going to get on the train, and you're going to tell us exactly where the rest of the artifacts are," Brayden said. "And if you're still feeling a little reluctant, well, just look at your new friend lying on the floor."

He gestured over at Gin, and my heart squeezed tight again. She'd been so strong, so calm, so confident in herself and her skills. Had she really been an assassin? I would probably never find out.

I frowned. Wait a second. The last time I'd looked at Gin, I could have sworn that her right hand had been flat on the floor. But now her fingers were curled inward, almost like she was hiding something in her palm, although I didn't know what, if anything, that meant. Winifred had shot her in the chest, and not even a Spartan like Logan could survive something like that.

"You two, stay behind and get rid of the body," Winifred ordered, pointing at the two men. "Dump our would-be heroine in the woods at the edge of the depot, then get on the train. With any luck, the animals will come and pick her bones clean. I've heard rumors that there are some wild Fenrir wolves in the area. Maybe even some Nemean prowlers too."

I shuddered at the thought of the oversize wolves and panther-like prowlers tearing into Gin's body, but there was nothing I could do to stop the Reapers.

The two men nodded and slid their swords back into the

scabbards on their belts, but Brayden brandished his blade at me again.

"Let's go," he growled.

I managed one more guilty glance down at Gin, who was still lying on the floor, before he shoved me forward and forced me out of the storage area.

We marched down the corridor back toward the main part of the depot. Brayden and the female Reaper sheathed their swords and stored the weapons under their long black overcoats. Winifred also shoved her gun into her pants pocket, hiding it from sight.

We quickly reached the lobby. The luncheon was over, and folks were heading outside to the wooden platform that lined the back of the station.

Brayden clamped his hand around my upper arm. "Come along quietly, and don't make a fuss," he warned. "Or we'll start killing the passengers."

His eyes gleamed, and a cruel, sadistic grin creased his face. "Actually, make a fuss if you want to, Gwen. I wouldn't mind cutting down a few mortals. Staying off the grid and planning heists is pretty boring. It's been a long time since I've had any real practice—or fun—with my sword."

I glared at Brayden, who just cackled in return.

Once again, I didn't have a choice, so I let him steer me past the stragglers, who were all still cluelessly talking, laughing, and taking photos with their phones. Brayden gestured for me to open one of the glass doors, and we stepped outside, crossed the wooden platform, and boarded the train. Winifred and the female Reaper followed us.

"I have to keep up appearances as the conductor," Winifred said in a low voice. "Brayden, you stay with Gwen in here.

Rosie, you keep an eye on them, and make sure the girl doesn't try to bolt or warn the other passengers what's going on."

Rosie, the other Reaper, nodded and dropped into a nearby seat.

"I don't need a bloody babysitter," Brayden muttered.

"Considering I just had to shoot a woman, and we still don't have our hands on the artifacts, I'm not taking any chances," Winifred snapped back. "Now, be a good boy, and try not to screw up any more today, okay? I'm going to start looking for the artifacts. They have to be on board somewhere."

Brayden glared at Winifred, who ignored him, spun around, and left the car. Rosie grabbed a magazine about the tourist town of Cloudburst Falls, West Virginia, that someone had left behind on a nearby seat and thumbed through it, although she kept glancing over at me.

"Okay, Gwen," Brayden hissed in my ear. "You're going to sit down and behave, or I'm going to make you wish you had cooperated—"

"Excuse us," a voice called out.

Brayden and I both froze and looked over our shoulders. An elderly couple was waiting for us to move out of their way so they could walk down the aisle and find their seats. Rosie tensed and slowly lowered the borrowed magazine to her lap.

Brayden flashed the couple a friendly smile and tightened his grip in warning, his fingers digging painfully into my upper arm. "Oh, sure. Sorry about that. My girlfriend and I were just talking about how good lunch was."

I wanted to punch him in the face for daring to call me his girlfriend, but I forced myself to smile at the couple, knowing that Brayden would kill them if I didn't play along.

"That's right," I chirped in a bright voice. "The food was so good."

The man and woman frowned, as though they could hear the blatant lie in my voice, but I kept my fake smile plastered on my face. They murmured about how good the food had been, then moved past us.

The second they were out of the way, Brayden shoved me forward and pushed me down into my seat, then took the one across from me where Gin had been sitting earlier. Another wave of guilt and sadness washed over my heart. Whether she'd been an assassin or not, Gin Blanco hadn't deserved to die just because she'd had the misfortune to try to save me from a bunch of greedy thieves.

Brayden leaned back in his seat. To a casual observer, he probably looked like he was relaxing, but he shoved his coat aside and curled his hand around the hilt of the sword belted to his waist. I knew that he would draw the weapon, lunge forward, and gut me without hesitation if I did anything he didn't like. A few seats away, Rosie also dropped her hand to her own sword.

"Reaper scum," Vic hissed in a low voice, still sticking up out of the top of my messenger bag.

Brayden rolled his eyes at the sword's snarky words, then focused on my bag, which I'd propped up in the seat beside me. I'd tried to turn it so that the bulge of the box wasn't so obvious, but his gaze locked onto it anyway. Drat.

"So that's where you're hiding the dagger. Of course. Hand it over. Now."

I glared at him, but Brayden casually patted the hilt of his sword.

"Hand it over, or I'll start stabbing people," he replied. "A few of them might escape, but they won't all get off the train before I kill them."

Yet again, I had no choice but to do as commanded, so I reached into the dark depths of my bag, drew out a long, rectangular gray velvet box, and passed it over to him.

Brayden glanced around, but other than Rosie, no one was paying any attention to us, so he slowly cracked open the box.

His eyes brightened, and he let out a low whistle of appreciation. "Now, *that* is an artifact."

Most of the mythological weapons I'd seen were rather plain, and the power hidden inside them was far more important and valuable than any adornments attached to the outside.

Not this dagger.

Minerva's Dagger was crusted with jewels. A stunning array of rubies, topazes, citrines, and white diamonds covered the hilt, forming a pretty mosaic pattern, while smaller, matching jeweled chips were embedded in the gold blade itself. Given the plethora of gemstones, the dagger looked like it was intended for more decorative and ceremonial purposes rather than being used in battle, although I would have dearly loved to snatch it away from Brayden and see just how sharp and strong the blade was by plunging it into his rotten heart.

Brayden tossed the box onto the empty seat beside him, then carefully grabbed the dagger by the blade and held it up to the bright afternoon sunlight streaming in through the windows. The mosaic pattern on the hilt featured a circle with several jagged rays radiating out of it, making it look like a dazzling jeweled sun. Strangely enough, the pattern reminded me of the scars I'd seen on Gin's palms earlier. What had she called them? Oh, yes—spider runes, whatever that meant.

A fresh wave of guilt and sadness crashed through my chest, and I made a silent vow to myself—that Brayden, Winifred, and the other Reapers were going to pay for what they'd done to Gin Blanco.

Brayden let out another low, appreciative whistle. "Just the jewels on the hilt alone are worth several hundred thousand dollars. We could always pry them off and sell them one gemstone at a time. Or maybe we'll sell the intact dagger to a mythological collector for even *more* money." A greedy grin creased his face. "I'm not too picky as long as I get my cut of the score."

The whistle shrieked, making me flinch, and Winifred stepped back into the car. She slowly moved along the aisle, still playing the part of the friendly conductor, nodding and smiling as she reminded everyone that the train was departing and to please take their seats.

She stopped beside Brayden and gave him a sharp look. "Put that dagger away before someone else sees it!" she hissed.

He huffed with annoyance, but he lowered the dagger to his side. Winifred walked on, and Brayden glowered at her back.

"Seems like you have some issues with your big sister," I said.

"Winifred is fifteen years older, so she thinks that automatically makes *her* the boss," he grumbled, a sour expression twisting his face. "She might be the brains of our crew and plan all our heists, but *I'm* the boss."

He puffed up and jerked his thumb at his chest, and I had to resist the urge to roll my eyes at the petulant tone in his voice. Brayden wasn't the boss of anything, except being a whiny brat.

Winifred reached the end of the car, then turned around and headed back this way. She stopped and asked Rosie something, but the other Reaper shook her head, as though she didn't know the answer. Winifred plastered another smile on her face, but it was a tight, worried expression. She chatted with a few more passengers, then strode over, bent down, and looked at Brayden, as though she was just making casual conversation.

"Where are Dennis and George?" she asked. "They haven't texted me, and I didn't see them get on board the train."

"I'm not their mom," Brayden replied, his voice even more petulant than before. "How should I know? They're probably just in another car."

Winifred shot him a nasty look, but she straightened up and moved on. She opened the door at the front of the car and stepped over to the next one. The whistle shrieked again, and the train slowly chugged away from the platform, heading down the backside of Pine Crest Mountain.

The other passengers, including Rosie, peered out the windows at the pretty scenery, but Brayden leaned forward and fixed his dark brown gaze on me. "Now, let's get down to business. Where did you hide the rest of the artifacts?"

I bit my lip, thinking about the best way to get out of this mess. I didn't want to reveal the artifacts' location, but Winifred would figure it out soon enough. Besides, I didn't dare fight the Reapers while innocent people were around, so maybe I needed to go where there were *no* innocent people around.

"Where do you think they are?" I snapped. "Where on this train is big enough to hide anything? What's the one place that is not full of passengers?"

He gave me a blank look.

"The artifacts are in the baggage car, you idiot."

Anger stained his cheeks a dark, mottled red. I *cluck-cluck-clucked* my tongue, mocking him. "Your sister's right. You are definitely *not* the brains of the crew."

Brayden growled, leaned forward, and swiped Minerva's Dagger across the back of my left hand. Given his Roman speed, he was simply too quick for me to stop, and I didn't even have time to try to dodge the blow. One moment, Brayden was glaring at me. The next, he was slicing the dagger through the air, the blade glinting a bright, sinister gold.

Even though it was adorned with jewels, the dagger still bit deep into my skin, and blood welled up out of the wound. I hissed in pain and surprise and started to jerk back, but Brayden clamped his fingers around my left hand. He tightened his grip and twisted, making even more pain explode in the wound, but that was a small misery compared with the sudden, overwhelming surge of my psychometry magic.

The second his skin touched mine, I saw everything there was to know about Brayden Vitales.

Images flickered through my mind one after another, almost too fast to follow. A young Brayden scurrying along after a much older Winifred, trying to keep up with her longer strides. Brayden watching with wide-eyed fascination as Winifred swung a sword and cut down a girl in front of her. Brayden struggling to lift his own sword while Winifred circled around and barked out instructions. Brayden trying to obey her directions but always tripping over his own feet or losing his grip on his sword or doing something else clumsy. Winifred mercilessly mocking every single mistake Brayden made and then mocking him even more as angry, frustrated tears slid down his cheeks . . .

"Not so tough now, are you, Gwen?" Brayden hissed.

He dug his fingers even deeper into my skin, and a fresh wave of pain and memories bloomed in my mind—including one of Minerva's Dagger.

I reached out with my magic and latched onto that image. Brayden was in the Crius Coliseum, standing in front of a glass artifact case and staring down at the dagger, which glimmered like liquid gold.

"Soon, baby," he murmured, stroking his fingers across the glass. "Soon you'll be all mine, along with the other artifacts. Then I'll have enough money to leave Winifred and the rest of these losers behind and finally start my *own* crew . . ."

Brayden abruptly shoved me away. I fell back against my seat, sweating, clutching my wounded hand, and gasping for breath. He smirked and waggled the dagger at me again, and my stomach roiled at the sight of my own blood glistening on the blade. Maybe it was my imagination, but the jewels embedded in the hilt seemed to glow a little more brightly than before, almost as if they approved of the pain and violence the Reaper had inflicted on me.

"Maybe that will teach you to keep your smart mouth shut." He glared at me, although his anger quickly congealed into a cold, sadistic grin. "Although I'm happy to give you another lesson, Gwen, just in case you didn't get the point this time around."

His low, evil chuckles scraped against my skin like razors, and my wound throbbed in response. I glanced over at Rosie, and the other Reaper smirked, clearly enjoying my suffering.

Brayden's laughter slowly died down. He glanced around, but no one had noticed what he'd done except Rosie, and he jerked his head at me.

"Wrap that up," he ordered. "I can't have you dripping blood all over the place for the mortals to see."

Under his sharp, watchful gaze, I dug into my messenger bag, shoved my hand past a stack of *Karma Girl* comic books, and grabbed a roll of purple gauze. Nyx, the Fenrir wolf I was taking care of, had recently decided that she loved to chase strings, so I'd been using the gauze as a sort of toy for her.

I wrapped the gauze around the wound as tightly as I could manage with one hand and shoved the end underneath the other layers to hold it all together. My blood swiftly seeped through the purple gauze, staining it an ugly brown, but there was nothing I could do about that right now.

The other passengers kept murmuring to each other, pointing at the various trees and rocks they spotted through the windows, and generally oohing and aahing over the snowy scenery, but a tense silence descended over Brayden and me. A couple of minutes later, his phone beeped, and he pulled it out of his coat pocket and stared at the message on the screen.

"Winifred says the other employees are finally taking a break, so it's time for us to get the rest of the artifacts." He jerked his head at Rosie, who got up, came over, and dropped into the seat next to him.

"Watch her," Brayden ordered, sliding Minerva's Dagger into his coat pocket. "I need to text Winifred and let her know the artifacts are hidden in the baggage car."

Rosie nodded, pushed her jacket aside again, and curled her hand around the hilt of her sword. She never took her eyes off me as Brayden started typing on his phone.

Every button he hit was like a grain of sand trickling through an hourglass, and I was rapidly running out of time to figure out how to defeat Brayden and the other Reapers, protect the artifacts, and get off the train alive.

Chapter Five

Gin Blanco

The thing no one ever tells you about getting shot is that it bloody *hurts*, more than just about any other kind of injury. And over the years, I had been shot, stabbed, choked, cut, punched, crushed, burned, and bludgeoned enough times to know. Yep, that was me, Gin Blanco, wound expert. Sometimes I thought I should just quit the assassin business and start training to become a nurse. Because I certainly had a lot of experience dealing with injuries.

Like the massive, puffy bruise that was aching in my chest right now.

Winifred had been going for a kill shot, and her aim had been true. Her bullet would have blasted straight into my heart—if I hadn't used my Stone magic to harden my body into an impenetrable shell. Even then, the bullet had still hurt, as though someone had hit me in the chest with a sledgehammer.

The force of the blow had knocked the wind out of me, and I'd crumpled to the floor, although no one had seemed to notice that I wasn't bleeding all over the stone. Sloppy, sloppy, sloppy of Winifred and the other Reapers not to check and make sure that I was really down for the count.

So I lay there with my eyes closed, listening to my enemies plot, as well as Gwen's answers to their questions. Sweet of her to be so worried about me, but I could take care of myself, and it sounded like she could too, given all the things she said.

Although I still wasn't sure why Gwen kept calling them Reapers. To me, they were just your run-of-the-mill thieves, but I wasn't about to quibble over semantics. It didn't matter what fancy name they gave themselves. Winifred, Brayden, and the others had tried to kill me, so I was going to return the favor. Only I wouldn't be so foolish as to let any of them live, even if I wasn't a Champion for some mythological goddess . . . or whatever Gwen Frost truly was.

"You two, stay behind and get rid of the body," Winifred ordered her minions. "Dump our would-be heroine in the woods at the edge of the depot, then get on the train. With any luck, the animals will come and pick her bones clean . . ."

The other Reapers murmured their agreement, and several sets of footsteps sounded, including the squeaking of Gwen's sneakers, along with a couple of heavier thumps. My enemies were splitting up. Excellent. That would make it easier for me to kill all of them.

The last of the footsteps faded away, but I remained still and silent on the floor, as though I truly was dead, instead of about to make a whole bunch of other people that way.

"I can't believe Winifred is making *us* get rid of the body," one of the men grumbled. "She shot the woman, so *she* should have been the one to haul the body outside. Or made her stupid kid brother do it. Not dumped the job on us just because we're Vikings and stronger than she is."

"No kidding," the second man muttered his agreement. "I don't mind getting rid of a body, but tracking down the girl and retrieving the artifacts was supposed to be an easy payday. So far, nothing about this has been *easy*."

Aw, being a criminal was *so* hard these days. I hid a grin. If he only knew how much harder—and bloodier—it was about to get.

"Come on," the first man grumbled again. "Let's carry her outside and be done with things. We still need to get on the train before it leaves."

Some more footsteps scuffed across the floor. One of the men must have squatted down, because his sour breath wafted over my cheek, and I could smell the burned coffee he'd drunk earlier in the day. My fingers tightened around the knife I'd palmed on my way down to the floor during my supposed death. The spider rune stamped into the silverstone hilt pressed into the larger matching scar that adorned my palm, and a sense of calm resolve and deadly purpose settled over me. Nothing steadied me like the cold, hard feel of a knife in my hand.

The coffee drinker dug his fingers into my right shoulder and rolled me over onto my back. My eyes snapped open, and I gave him a bright, sunny smile.

"Boo!" I hissed.

The man flinched and jerked back, but I surged up, fisted my hand in his coat, and yanked him right back down toward me—and my knife.

The silverstone blade punched into his chest, making him yelp with pain. The man lashed out again and again, trying to swat me away like a pesky bug. I didn't know anything about Vikings, but he was as strong as he had claimed to be, and his brute force easily rivaled that of a giant or a dwarf. But I used my Stone magic to harden my skin again, and his hard, heavy blows didn't do any real damage to my face, neck, and arms.

The man pitched over onto his side, and I followed the motion, maneuvering around so I was on top of him. Then I ripped my knife out of his chest and slashed it across his throat, and his pain-filled yelps morphed into desperate, choked gurgles.

This guy was already more dead than alive, so I scrambled to my feet and whirled around, searching for the second man.

A glint of metal caught my eye. On instinct, I ducked, and a sword zipped through the air where my head had been. The second man—the Reaper—snarled in frustration and whirled around. He lifted his sword and came at me again.

I waited until he was in range, then reached for my magic. This time, I tapped into my elemental Ice power, and I snapped up my hand and blasted the Reaper with a cloud of Ice daggers. The cold jagged chunks punched into his face, neck, and chest, bruising and cutting his skin. The man growled in pain, but he kept charging forward, so I whipped up my knife to block his blow.

Clang!

His sword crashed into my knife, and the blow rocked my entire body, hard enough to make me bite down on my own tongue. This guy was even stronger than the first one had been. I wondered if that was what made him a Viking, or maybe even a Reaper too, but it didn't much matter. Strong or not, I was about to make him dead.

The man snarled and drew his sword back for another swing, but I darted forward and spun past him. Then I whirled back around and lashed out with my boot, driving it into the side of his left leg. He grunted in surprise, even as his knee buckled, and he toppled to the ground.

I didn't give him a chance to get back up.

I surged down and forward and rammed my knife into his back, making him scream. Then I yanked the blade out, dug my fingers into his hair, pulled his head back, and cut his throat.

This guy's screams also morphed into desperate, choked gurgles. I released his hair, and he thumped to the floor, quickly bleeding out, just like the first man had.

I straightened up, my gaze sweeping back and forth across the storage area, searching for more enemies to fight. But the other Reapers had left, taking Gwen along with them, and I was all alone. No footsteps pounded in this direction, and it didn't seem like anyone had heard the sounds of the fight—

A phone beeped.

Curious, I tucked my knife back up my sleeve, then crouched down and rifled through the first man's pockets. I pulled out his phone and read the message from Winifred.

Hurry up. Train leaving in five minutes.

I slid the dead guy's phone into my jeans pocket, right alongside my own phone, then straightened up. Winifred was right.

I had a train to catch.

I quickly dragged the dead men off to one side of the room, then haphazardly piled some of the cardboard boxes on top of the bodies, hiding them from sight as best I could. Then I hurried out of the storage area.

By the time I made it back to the main lobby, the luncheon was officially over, the waiters had packed up all the leftover food and disappeared into the kitchen, and everyone else was already on board the train. I opened one of the glass doors, scurried to the left, and darted behind one of the wide brick columns that supported the platform roof. Then I peered through the train windows, trying to spot my enemies.

No . . . no . . . no . . .

There they were.

Gwen and Brayden were sitting across from each other in one of the cars, with Rosie, the Reaper woman, perched a few seats away. And of course, Winifred was ambling along the aisle, smiling and nodding as though she really were a conductor instead of just a murderous pretender. It was a smart disguise. The conductor had free rein of the entire train, and she could do just about anything she wanted while she was wearing that stolen uniform.

I pulled my phone out of my pocket, but I didn't have any messages from Bria, Finn, or Owen. Weird. I would have expected Bria to have sent me a string of texts by now, asking where I was and what was happening, along with more and more frowny faces. My sister loved emojis just as much as Silvio Sanchez, my personal assistant, did.

I sent my friends a group text explaining what was going on, along with the fact that the real conductor was probably dead somewhere back at the main Pine Crest station. I finished by saying that the train was about to leave and asked them to meet me at the Cypress Mountain station, then slid my phone back into my pocket.

I looked through the windows again. Gwen, Brayden, and Rosie were all still in the same car, but Winifred had moved on to a different one.

The whistle screamed, the engine clanked, the wheels churned, and the train slowly pulled away from the station. I held my position, not wanting any of the Reapers to spot me. If they realized I was still alive, then they might hurt Gwen or some of the other passengers. Winifred certainly seemed determined to get her hands on whatever artifacts were on board, and I had no doubt that she would kill every single person who got in her way.

I waited until the car with Gwen, Brayden, and Rosie had moved past my position. Then I stepped out from behind the column and started running, my boots slapping against the platform's thick wooden planks. The train was swiftly gaining speed, and I had to time this just right, or I would be left behind, and Gwen would probably wind up dead.

So I pumped my arms and forced my legs to move even

faster as I rushed toward the end of the platform. I picked up my pace a little more, took one final step, and then leaped forward as far as I could, stretching my arms out wide, wide, wide . . .

For a moment, I hung in the air, like a spider swinging on a strand of its own web. Then my chest crashed up against the back of the caboose. Gravity took over, pulling me down, down, down, even as I flailed out with my hands, searching for something, anything, that I could grab onto . . .

My fingers closed around one of the rungs on the ladder attached to the back of the caboose. My body jerked to an abrupt stop, wrenching my left shoulder. The sharp, painful motion almost made me lose my grip, but I used my Stone magic to harden my fingers and forced myself to hang on.

I dangled there for a few more seconds, my brain sloshing around inside my skull. The world slowly stopped spinning around, and I was finally able to reach up and grab the rung with my other hand, as well as anchor my boots on another rung below.

I glanced down, watching the metal tracks whiz by below my feet. Not even my Stone magic would have saved me if I'd fallen off and somehow been sucked under the train's chugging wheels. I shuddered at the thought, then quickly pushed it away.

I'd caught the train—literally. Now I needed to get back inside and help Gwen. So I looked up, reached for the next rung on the ladder, and started climbing.

Chapter Six

Gwen Frost

Try as I might, I just couldn't think of a way to take down Brayden and the other Reapers. At least, not without a whole lot of innocent people potentially getting hurt in the process. So I decided to bide my time, stick to my original plan, and wait for the Reapers to take me to the baggage car. Besides, every second Brayden wasted texting on his phone was another second for Logan, Daphne, and the rest of my friends to escape the Reapers' trap, get past the rockslide, and come find me.

That's what I kept telling myself, over and over again, instead of dwelling on the possibility that Logan, Daphne, and the others might already be dead.

An image of Logan lying by the side of the road, blood coating his chest, his eyes empty and fixed on the sky, filled my mind, but I shoved it away. Logan freaking Quinn was a Spartan and one of the best warriors in the mythological world. It would take a whole lot more than a rockslide and a Reaper ambush to kill him. Not to mention all the other smarts, skills, and magic that Daphne, Carson, Oliver, and Alexei had, along with Nickamedes, Professor Metis, and Coach Ajax. They were going to be fine. My friends were going to be just *fine*.

And if they *weren't* fine . . . well, I would at least take down the Reapers who had a hand in hurting them—starting with Brayden, Winifred, and Rosie.

Brayden finally put his phone away. A couple of minutes later, Winifred stepped back into the car and jerked her thumb over her shoulder. Brayden nodded back at her, as did Rosie.

He grinned at me. "Time to find the pot of gold at the end of the Protectorate rainbow." His grin faded away, and a cold light filled his eyes. "Get up and head toward the front of the car. And don't try anything stupid, or I'll shove this dagger in your back and watch you bleed out."

Once again, I didn't have a choice, so I reached over and grabbed my messenger bag. I slung the strap onto my shoulder, making sure that Vic's hilt was within easy reach of my right hand. Rosie stood up, stepped out into the aisle, and backed up. Brayden clamped his hand around my upper arm again, then hauled me to my feet.

I glanced around, but the other passengers were busy talking, admiring the scenery, and taking photos with their phones and cameras. Rosie gave me a cold look, her hand darting into her coat and curling around the hilt of the sword belted to her waist. Like Brayden, she wouldn't hesitate to gut me if I didn't do exactly as the Reapers commanded.

"Come along, baby," Brayden crooned for the benefit of any-one listening. "Let's go see what the view is like from another car."

Baby? Ugh! I glared at the Reaper. My fingers curled into a tight fist, and I had to resist the urge to punch him in the face.

Brayden smirked at me, then dragged me along the aisle, heading toward the door at the front of the car. Once again, I had no choice but to go along with him, but as soon as I got the chance, I was going to grab Vic and take down Brayden, Rosie, and Winifred—for my friends, and especially for Gin.

With that dark vow beating in my heart, I plastered a smile on my face and let Brayden lead me to his doom.

Brayden forced me through one car after another. They were all filled with people, but no one paid any attention to us. A few times, we had to stop to let other folks move in front of or past us as they returned to their seats, but everyone smiled and nodded, and no one had any idea about how much danger they were in.

We left yet another car behind, and Winifred was waiting on the small platform outside. I glanced around, wondering if I could shove at least one of the Reapers off the train, but a waist-high metal railing lined the platform to prevent things like that from happening. Too bad.

"I just checked," Winifred called out, raising her voice to be heard over the train's continued *chug-chug-chug*. "The baggage car is empty. Follow me."

She turned around, opened the door on the next car, and stepped through to the other side. Brayden tightened his grip on my arm and dragged me along behind him. Rosie followed us, then closed and locked the door behind her.

A wide aisle ran down the center of the baggage car, and metal shelves lined the walls, stretching from the floor up to the low ceiling. Several suitcases of various shapes, sizes, and colors were sitting on the shelves, and a couple of open cardboard boxes containing packs of cheese crackers, bags of trail mix, and cartons of soft drinks were squatting next to each other on the floor.

My gaze skipped past the suitcases and snacks and landed

on the wooden crates nestled together on the shelves near the center of the car. Each crate featured a large symbol stenciled in black—two gryphons sitting side by side, just like the statues that perched on the steps outside the Library of Antiquities on the Mythos campus. My heart sank. I'd hoped the Reapers might at least have to search through the luggage for the artifacts, but the crates might as well have had *Property of Mythos Academy* painted on them in big, bold letters.

Brayden let out a loud whoop of excitement, then dropped my arm and hurried toward the crates like a Nemean prowler bounding straight toward a rabbit. Winifred also hurried forward, although Rosie remained behind me, her hand still on her sword, blocking the exit.

I reached out and took hold of one of the metal shelves, as though I was using it to steady myself against the train's rocking motion. Rosie kept staring at me, still wary and suspicious. I sighed and dropped my head, as though I was utterly defeated, although I kept watching her out of the corner of my eye.

Rosie stared at me a few more seconds, then shifted her focus over to Winifred and Brayden. The second she was distracted, I discreetly brought up my right hand and curled it around Vic's hilt. For once, the talking sword was silent, although he vibrated slightly against my fingers, telling me he was ready to strike whenever I was.

Winifred tried—and failed—to pry the lid off one of the crates. "Help me with this."

"You got it," Brayden replied.

He yanked his sword out from underneath his long black coat, then wedged the blade underneath the lid. It took him a few tries, but eventually, he tore the lid off with a long, harsh *screech.*

Winifred grabbed the wooden slab and set it aside, and then both she and Brayden leaned forward, staring down into the crate. A couple of weapons were nestled inside the shredded brown packing material, along with a few other objects.

"The Sword of Eris, the Scroll of Seshat, the Arrows of Osiris . . ." Brayden's voice trailed off as he picked up first one item, then another, and set them all back down inside the crate. "Yep, these are some of the goodies we stole from the Crius Coliseum. And lucky for us, they're the more powerful and valuable artifacts, along with Minerva's Dagger, of course."

Brayden grinned, yanked the dagger out of his coat pocket, and flashed it at Winifred, who grinned back at him. Apparently, getting her hands on valuable artifacts made her much more agreeable. Rosie grinned as well, although she still had her hand on her sword, just like I did.

Winifred's grin widened. "Now that we've found the arti-facts, all we have to do is stay in here until we reach Cypress Mountain. Then we'll grab as many artifacts as we can carry and slip away from the train station. We'll be long gone before the Protectorate even realizes what's happened—"

The train lurched, as though the engine was suddenly having trouble dragging the rest of the cars along behind it. Winifred and Brayden both stumbled around, since they weren't holding on to one of the shelves like I was. So did Rosie, who was still guarding me.

The second the Reaper staggered away from me, I yanked Vic free and let my messenger bag fall to the floor. Then I raised the sword high and whirled around. The train lurched again, and I let the momentum carry me all the way over to Rosie, who was now standing in the very back of the car, right in front of the door. Her eyes widened at my approach, and she dropped her gaze, trying to yank her own sword free from its scabbard.

Too late.

I swung Vic out in a vicious arc and slashed his blade across Rosie's chest, making her scream and stagger backward. She slammed into the door, and her head hit the metal with a loud, sickening *crack*. Rosie's scream abruptly cut off, and she slumped to the floor, blood rapidly pooling underneath her body.

"Yeah!" Vic said, his mouth moving underneath my palm. "Take that, Reaper scum!"

Rosie wasn't getting up again, so I whirled around, facing the front of the car again. Brayden and Winifred had both regained their balance. Brayden was still holding Minerva's Dagger, while Winifred was clutching the Sword of Eris, which had belonged to the Greek goddess of discord and strife. The sword greatly increased the strength of whoever wielded it.

The two Reaper siblings grinned at each other, then brandished their blades at me. I didn't need to touch them or use my psychometry magic to realize they were looking forward to hurting me.

White-hot fury exploded in my heart at everything the Reapers had done—stealing the artifacts, threatening me, and especially killing Gin Blanco. I didn't care what weapons or magic they had or how much danger I was in. Brayden and Winifred were going to pay for their crimes, even if it was the last thing I ever did. So I tightened my grip on Vic and widened my stance, trying to find better balance and some more stability, given the train's continued abrupt jerking motions.

"Please." Brayden sneered at me. "There are two of us and one of you. Face it. Your time is up, Champion. Get ready to die."

"Actually, you got the odds wrong—again," a familiar voice drawled.

A shadow detached itself from the wall near the front of the car and stepped out into the light. I gasped, along with Brayden and Winifred.

Gin Blanco snapped off a mock salute to the Reapers, then looked over at me. "Hey, Gwen. Sorry I'm late."

Chapter Seven

Gin Blanco

"How—how are you standing here right now? I *shot* you," Winifred growled. "In the chest!"

"Oh, sugar," I drawled. "It takes more than a bullet to the heart to keep me down for long."

Her gaze dropped to my chest. "You have on a bulletproof vest?"

"Something like that," I agreed.

I didn't bother trying to explain my Stone elemental magic to her. I doubted she'd believe me, especially since no one else had believed anything I'd said so far today.

"How did you get back on the train?" Winifred demanded. "You weren't on board when we left the old depot. I *know* you weren't, because I checked."

I shrugged. "I grabbed the ladder on the back of the caboose and climbed up to the roof. Fun fact: each car has an access hatch with a nice little window embedded in the ceiling, so it wasn't too hard for me to move around and keep an eye on things.

Once I saw your little group start heading in this direction, I figured you were going toward the baggage car, so I ran across the tops of the other cars and got ahead of you. Then I used another hatch to get down in here."

I shook my head. "Even on a train, no one ever thinks to secure anything that's above their heads and out of their line of sight. It's sad, really. Such a rookie mistake."

The two Reapers looked at each other like I was speaking gibberish, and a confused look filled Gwen's face too. Maybe I *was* weird, talking about easy access points at a time like this, but they had always been some of my favorite things as the Spider. Over the years, I'd managed to sneak into dozens of places I shouldn't just because someone hadn't bothered to lock their second-story doors and windows. Or in this case, the access hatches embedded in all the train-car roofs.

"Are you a member of the Protectorate?" Winifred asked, her dark brown eyes narrowing in thought. "Some sort of secret shadow bodyguard for Nike's Champion?"

An annoyed, exasperated sigh escaped my lips. Why wouldn't these people just *listen*? I'd told them time and time again that I was an assassin, but they *still* didn't believe me. It was like they were trying to force me to fit into their weird mythological worldview, or whatever it truly was.

"It doesn't matter who she is," Brayden snarled. "She's still going to die, just like Gwen is."

He stepped forward and brandished a weapon at me.

"Oh," I purred, a wide grin spreading across my face. "I just *adore* knives. I have several of my own. Wanna see one?"

I flicked my wrist and palmed the knife hidden up my right sleeve. Brayden sucked in a surprised breath, as did his sister, and uncertainty flickered across both their faces, as if they were just now realizing that I was as big a threat as I claimed to be.

"Who *are* you?" Winifred demanded.

"Like I said before, I'm the Spider. And I don't much like it when people threaten my friends."

Winifred jerked her head at her brother. "You kill the Champion. I'll handle the assassin."

He nodded back at her, then turned toward Gwen, who lifted her bloody sword and firmed up her fighting stance. Given the Reaper woman lying on the floor in the back of the car, Gwen Frost could take care of herself. Good to know.

I left Gwen to deal with Brayden and focused all my attention on Winifred again. For a moment, I thought she might pull out the gun she'd shot me with earlier, but instead, she hefted her sword a little higher, then snarled and rushed toward me. Winifred used her dizzying speed to close the distance between us in the blink of an eye, and I barely had time to whip my knife up to defend myself.

Clang!

Her blade crashed into mine, and the force of the blow almost ripped my silverstone knife right out of my hand. Winifred was even stronger than the two Viking Reapers in the old depot. Even more troubling was the fact that her sword was glowing with a bright bronze light, as though the weapon contained some sort of magic that was giving Winifred supernatural strength, as well as enhancing her own already incredible speed.

Gwen and the Reapers had been talking a lot about artifacts, but I'd thought they were just referring to pottery, statues, and other pretty antique decorations. I was finally getting an inkling of what *artifacts* truly meant—and the enormous power such things possessed.

Clash-clash-clang!

Winifred hammered her sword at me over and over again, each blow hard enough to rattle my entire body, and it was all I could do to counter her blows and not lose my grip on my knife.

The train jerked forward, and the unexpected motion sent

me staggering all the way over into the door at the front of the baggage car. My hand slammed into the metal, and I lost my grip on my knife, which hit the floor and tumbled away.

In the back of the car, Gwen was still battling Brayden, and she too lost her balance and staggered to the side. Her arm slammed into one of the metal baggage shelves, and she hissed with pain, even as her sword fell through her fingers.

"Can't believe you bloody dropped me in the middle of a fight . . ." Vic grumbled, before the talking sword's annoyed words were lost in the continued groan and churn of the train's engine and cars.

Given all the loud noise and clanging commotion, I was starting to think *restored train* meant *on its last wheels*. But the engine kept chugging, and the baggage car shuddered back and forth and back and forth, as if trying to settle into some sort of rhythm and equilibrium with all the other cars on the tracks. I clung to one of the metal posts that supported the shelves, trying to keep my balance, and Gwen and the Reapers did the same thing.

After what seemed like forever but couldn't have been much more than a minute, two tops, the ride smoothed out, and we were all able to release our handholds.

I glanced around, searching for my silverstone knife. Somehow it had slid all the way to the back of the car where Gwen was, while her talking sword had ended up close to my side of the car.

Winifred growled and stalked toward me. She was still clutching that sword, which started glowing even more brightly than before, as if the Reaper's rage was further fueling its magic.

I considered palming the knife hidden up my left sleeve, but I couldn't keep blocking Winifred's blows for much longer. Sooner or later, she would use her superior strength and speed to force her way past my defenses and gut me. At the very least, I needed a larger, sturdier weapon to knock that glowing bronze sword out of her hand.

"First my Champion dropped me, and then she let me rattle around all over the bloody place," Vic muttered. "Gwen just polished me the other day, and I was looking all nice and shiny. But that's all ruined now . . ."

My gaze locked onto the still-grumbling sword. Despite his incessant chatter, Vic was an impressive weapon, and he should hold up nicely against the Reaper's enchanted blade.

Winifred growled and quickened her pace, drawing her sword back for yet another strike.

I was out of time and options. When in Rome, as the old saying went. Or in this case, the wild, weird world of Mythos Academy.

I lunged for the talking sword.

Chapter Eight

Gwen Frost

I was still trying to find my balance when I saw Gin dart toward Vic, who was lying on the floor near the front of the car and still chastising me for dropping him. As if it had been *my* fault that the train kept lurching forward like an old, wheezing truck that was about to run out of gas.

Winifred charged forward and swung her sword at Gin.

"Look out!" I yelled.

Gin dodged Winifred's attack, spinning in the other direction and moving away from the Reaper. Then, just as quickly, Gin whirled back around, put her shoulder down, and plowed into Winifred. The Reaper lost her balance and staggered backward, although she bounced off one of the shelves and charged right back at Gin again.

Gin stepped forward, hooked the toe of her black boot under Vic's blade, and kicked the sword up into the air. She easily caught Vic with one hand, then smoothly whirled all the way around to block Winifred's blow.

It was seriously one of the coolest things I had ever seen.

Even Logan, a Spartan who could pick up any object and automatically use it as a weapon, would have been impressed.

But I had my own Reaper to battle, so I dragged my gaze away from Gin. Brayden had also regained his balance, and he stalked toward me, still clutching Minerva's Dagger. I backed up, and my sneaker hit something, making it skitter across the floor. I glanced down and realized Gin's knife had somehow ended up by my feet.

"Time to die, Gwen," Brayden hissed, still stalking toward me.

My eyes darted back down to the knife. I *should* scoop it up and use it to defend myself before Brayden tried to kill me with his weapon again, but I hesitated. From the easy, skillful, familiar way Gin had wielded her knife against Winifred, I was guessing that she had a very deep, very personal attachment to the blade, which meant my psychometry magic would kick in the second I touched the knife—and I would see all the people Gin had killed with it over the years.

I had already witnessed enough blood, death, and destruction at Mythos Academy to last three lifetimes, but I didn't have any other options, so I braced myself, then leaned down and plucked the knife up off the floor.

Just as I expected, my psychometry kicked in, and the memories slammed into me like a tidal wave, threatening to knock my legs out from under me and drown me in the flickers and flashes of feelings.

There were *so* many memories, so many more than I had expected, each showing a different place and time.

Gin palming the knife with cold, ruthless, expert precision in what must have been her barbecue restaurant, given the blue and pink booths and the matching pig tracks covering the floor. Gin throwing herself out of the back of a bullet-riddled van, then killing a couple of tall, muscled women—giants, maybe?—with the blade. Gin clutching the weapon and facing down another tall, muscled woman, along with several men, at what looked like a wedding.

But one memory was a little clearer and sharper than all the rest: Gin standing outside a beautiful mansion, part of which had been crumbled, as though someone had taken a wrecking ball to one side of the structure and knocked off parts of it. Clouds of dust cloaked the air, but Gin stalked through the swirling fog, her knife clutched in her hand. She stared down at a man trapped underneath some rubble on the ground—a man with the same wintry gray eyes she had—then coolly, calmly leaned forward and cut his throat.

I flinched, expecting to start screaming at the awful memory, as I so often did. But instead of horror or rage or some other terrible emotion, soft, soothing relief flowed through me instead—Gin's relief that she had *finally* killed this man, this dangerous enemy who had caused her so much pain, and that he would never hurt her friends and family again.

I knew that feeling all too well. It was the same sort of relief I had felt when I'd realized that Agrona Quinn, Logan's evil ex-stepmother, was dead. And that Vivian Holler, Loki's Champion, was trapped in her own mind and my memories and no longer a threat. And of course, that Loki himself was imprisoned and would never again menace the mythological world—

"You might as well give up, Champion." Brayden's voice jarred me back to the here and now, and mine and Gin's memories faded away, if not the feelings that went along with them. "You can't beat me, Gwen. Not when I have Minerva's Dagger. I can *feel* its magic flowing through me, the power, the wisdom, the history. There is literally *nothing* you can do, no attack you can make, that I haven't seen before."

He brandished the dagger at me, and the jewels embedded in the gold blade glittered like drops of ruby, topaz, citrine, and diamond blood. Even though I wasn't touching the blade, my psychometry roared to life again, and suddenly, I could feel the *hunger* emanating from the dagger, its burning thirst and deep, dark, unquenchable desire to be in yet another battle and add the knowledge of that fight to all the others that were already stored inside it. The dagger wasn't so much a weapon as it was a greedy *parasite*, sucking up all the life and blood that crossed its blade. My magic recoiled, and my stomach twisted with revulsion.

But Brayden was right—I couldn't beat him. Despite all the battles I'd been in against Agrona, Vivian, and the other Reapers, I was still just eighteen. I simply hadn't been a warrior long enough to counter all the wisdom and knowledge that had accumulated in Minerva's Dagger over the centuries.

Brayden grinned and twirled the dagger around in his hand in a showy, taunting motion. I flinched again, and my fingers tightened around Gin's knife. The metal was strangely cool against my skin, and something slid up against my palm. I loosened my grip and glanced down.

A symbol was stamped into the knife's hilt—a small circle with eight thin rays, the same symbol that had been branded into both of Gin's palms. What had she called it? Oh, yes, a spider rune, the symbol for patience. Now that I was holding her knife, I knew that every word she had said before had been true.

Gin Blanco *was* the Spider.

I couldn't beat Brayden on my own. Not with my limited skills and training. But I wasn't on my own right now. No, right now, I was holding a knife that had been used by the best assassin in all of Ashland.

So I reached out with my magic, my psychometry, and all those memories flickered through my mind again. All the bad, bad people Gin had faced down, all the life-and-death battles she'd been in, and especially all the ways she'd found to defeat her enemies over the years.

Brayden stalked toward me, slashing Minerva's Dagger through the air. I watched him come, a cold calm settling over me—the same cold calm Gin had felt countless times before. Using my psychometry, I truly, fully, completely embraced that quiet emotion, that eerie stillness, that utter certainty, until it blotted out everything else, including my own worry that I wasn't smart, strong, or skilled enough to win this fight.

Because I knew that Gin *was* smart, strong, and skilled enough, and I was holding a piece of her in my hand and even more of her in my mind and heart.

Brayden stopped, grinned, and flipped the dagger end over end in his hand. "You know what? I might keep this dagger. It's certainly been useful in this fight. It would be nice knowing that no enemy could ever stand a chance of beating me, not even Nike's Champion."

I didn't respond to his taunts. Instead, I kept focusing on that cold calm and all the memories of Gin that were still flashing through my mind.

Brayden's grin widened, and he lunged forward, trying to cut me with the dagger. But I—or maybe Gin—had been expecting the blow, and I sidestepped his charge, whipped around, and sliced the knife across his upper arm.

Brayden hissed with pain and staggered back. He glanced down at the blood that was clearly visible through his cut coat and the T-shirt underneath. "You sneaky little bitch!" he snarled. "You're going to pay for that!"

I held up my crudely bandaged hand. "Just paying you back for cutting me earlier. What's wrong, Brayden? You can dish it out, but you can't take it? Yeah, that's how it usually goes with arrogant Reaper bullies like you."

Brayden growled and charged forward, slashing out with the dagger over and over again. He wasn't playing around now, and each blow was meant to be a deadly strike, but I dodged his attacks and lashed out with Gin's knife in return.

I managed to cut Brayden's other arm, then opened up a deep gash in his left thigh. He staggered away from me, struggling to find his balance.

"Minerva's Dagger might make you smarter, but it doesn't make you any more graceful," I taunted him. "Why, you're as clumsy and awkward as a Black roc with its wings tied together."

Rage sparked in his eyes, making them glimmer even more brightly than the dagger's gold blade, and Brayden charged forward. I braced myself for his attack, but he wasn't watching where he was going—or especially where he was putting his feet down. One of his boots landed on the wooden lid that he and Winifred had removed from the artifacts crate earlier, and he skidded to the side, his arms windmilling wildly as he fought to stay upright.

I waited until he teetered in my direction, then lunged forward, shoved his flailing arm out of the way, and buried Gin's knife in his heart.

Brayden's eyes bulged, and he screamed with pain. He raised Minerva's Dagger to try to kill me, but I ripped Gin's knife out of his chest and used it to knock the artifact out of his hand. The dagger landed on the floor, and the golden glow of magic quickly winked out, faster than a star giving way to the approaching dawn.

The train jerked yet again, and Brayden toppled forward, hitting my chest and forcing my entire body to the side. My head smacked into one of the metal shelves, and gray and purple stars erupted in my eyes.

I managed to hang on to Gin's knife, but my legs slid out from under me. I hit the floor hard, causing more stars to erupt in my eyes. Brayden dropped down onto me like the deadweight that he was, punching the air out of my lungs. Even worse, his warm, sticky blood stained my skin and seeped into my clothes.

In the front of the car, Gin was still battling Winifred. I tried to move, to yell, to tell Gin to be careful, but a third wave of stars filled my eyes, growing darker and darker until they blotted out everything else.

Chapter Nine

Gin Blanco

I didn't know what kind of training Reapers usually had, but Winifred could definitely fight. She was smooth, skilled, and fast with that sword, and whatever power the blade possessed also made her incredibly strong. But Vic was strong too, and the talking sword easily blocked all of Winifred's hard, heavy, hammering blows.

The only disconcerting thing was that Vic kept talking through the whole fight. Somehow, despite the fact my hand was clamped around the sword's hilt, and thus over his mouth, he *still* found a way to keep talking. His lips tickled the spider-rune scar in my palm time and time again, which was weird enough, but his shouted encouragements made the sensations stranger still. I didn't hear all his muffled words, but I got the gist of what he was saying.

". . . take her down . . . kill Winifred . . . defeat this Reaper scum . . ."

I grinned. The sword was even more bloodthirsty than I

was. So nice to meet a kindred spirit, even if that spirit was encased in metal.

Clash-clash-clang!

Winifred and I broke apart after a furious exchange, and she studied me with dark, narrowed eyes.

"You really *are* an assassin," she accused, as if I hadn't made it crystal clear who and what I was all along. "You should come work for me, for the Reapers. I'll make it worth your while." Winifred jerked her head to the side. "See those crates over there? They contain hundreds of thousands of dollars in mythological artifacts. Help me get them off this train, and I'll cut you in on the deal—"

Brayden let out a bloodcurdling scream, drowning out the rest of her offer. I knew that sound. I'd heard it more times than I could remember. Gwen had hit something vital, and Brayden was well on his way to being dead.

Winifred glanced over at her brother. Instead of worry, dread, or fear, an annoyed look creased her face, and she huffed out an exasperated breath, as if Brayden couldn't even die right. For a moment, I thought she might go over and try to help him, but instead, she faced me again.

"You can have a bigger cut now," she said. "All you have to do is help me eliminate Nike's Champion."

My eyebrows shot up. "Your brother just got killed, and you're still offering to make a deal with me?"

"Brayden was always a thorn in my side, always thinking that *he* ran things, when *I* did all the planning." Winifred's eyes glittered with anger. "The only reason we even lost the artifacts in the first place was that Brayden and the rest of those Reaper losers just *had* to sneak out and go out partying at a casino. I told Brayden time and time again that we all had to stay at the cabin and lie low until the Protectorate heat died down and I had a buyer lined up for the artifacts. But he didn't listen, which is why I'm on this bloody tourist train in the first place, instead of already counting my money. Well, now that he's gone, I don't have to worry about his stupid mistakes constantly tripping me up anymore."

More anger filled her eyes, although her expression quickly turned cold and calculating. "But I can always use a good fighter like you, Gin. So help me kill the girl, and you can have Brayden's cut of the money after I sell the artifacts."

A laugh bubbled up out of my lips. "Sugar, a few weeks ago, I gave away fifty million dollars to charity. A couple hundred grand in lousy antiques isn't going to tempt me."

"You're making a mistake. My offer is genuine."

"Oh, I'm sure it is," I replied. "Just like I'm sure you would stick that fancy bronze sword in my back the second you got the chance. Especially since you didn't bat an eye at your baby brother getting killed. Not much for family, are you?"

Winifred shrugged. "Family is useful—until it's not."

And that was one of the many, many differences between the two of us. Because if I'd just seen Bria get cut down, I would have been doing everything in my power to kill the person who'd killed my baby sister. Not trying to make a deal with an enemy to save my own skin and make a few bucks on the side. Vic was right. Winifred really was Reaper scum.

The train jerked yet again, catching me off guard. I staggered to the side, and Winifred saw an opening. She charged forward and lifted her sword high, ready to bring it down and finally end me once and for all.

This time, instead of fighting the train's helter-skelter motion, I went along with it, dropping to my knees and ducking Winifred's swing. Her sword whistled through the air where my chest had been a moment before. The train jerked again, and for the second time, I went with the momentum, letting it pick me up and set me back onto my feet.

Then I followed the surging motion all the way over to Winifred—and buried Vic's blade in her stomach.

"That's what I'm talking about!" the sword crowed, his lips moving underneath my palm again. "Way to go, Spider assassin lady!"

I grimaced at the oddly ticklish sensation and yanked the sword out of Winifred's stomach. She reached out and tried to grab one of the shelves, but her hand slipped off the metal, her legs buckled, and she slid down to the floor.

She didn't move after that.

Once I was sure that Winifred was well on her way to bleeding out, I stepped over her body and hurried to the back of the car, where Gwen and Brayden were sprawled on the floor, both of them deathly still.

"Gwen?" I asked. "Gwen! Are you okay?"

She grunted, lifted her head, and shoved Brayden away. He landed on his back, his sightless eyes staring up at nothing. Blood stained his arms, along with one of his legs, and a larger patch of it was centered right over his heart. Another grin stretched across my face. Nice. I couldn't have done a better job of killing him myself.

Gwen slowly sat up. Her brown hair was a tangled, frizzy mess, and a purplish bruise was already forming on her temple, but she seemed to be okay.

I leaned down and held out my arm. She hesitated a moment, then grabbed my hand. I pulled her up, and we stood there, locked together.

Gwen stared at me, her violet eyes big and bright and glowing with even more magic than what the Reapers' weapons had possessed. But even more disconcerting was the look on her face, like she was peering deep, deep down into my heart and seeing everything I had ever done, thought, felt, and experienced.

I froze, not sure what to do or say and not wanting to interrupt her trance . . . or whatever she was doing with her magic right now.

After a few seconds, Gwen shook her head, released my

hand, and stepped back. That strange, bright glow had vanished from her eyes, and she gave me a look that was equal parts impressed and sad. Once again, I had the feeling she had seen a lot more of me than I'd wanted her to—a lot more than I would ever want anyone to see.

I cleared my throat, carefully took hold of Vic's bloody blade, and held the sword out to her. "Thanks for letting me use Vic. He came in pretty handy."

Vic sniffed, and his violet eye swiveled around to glare at me. "I *always* come in handy when there are Reapers to kill."

Gwen grinned and shrugged at me. I grinned back at her, then exchanged her sword for my knife.

"Thanks for the knife," she said. "It came in handy too, especially since I was up against Minerva's Dagger. That arti-fact gives whoever wields it the wisdom of the Roman war goddess Minerva, including how to win whatever battle they are currently engaged in."

Gwen gestured at the knife in my hand. "But I got plenty of wisdom from you, Gin. You saved my life."

I wasn't sure what she meant by that, but I decided not to ask any questions. It had already been a strange enough day with Reapers and talking swords and everything else that had happened. Sometimes it was just better to go with the flow and not think too much about the small details. So I moved on to more practical matters, as I so often did.

"What are we going to do about all of this?" I asked, ges-turing at the three dead Reapers sprawled across the floor. "Be-cause the train will be stopping soon, and it's only a matter of time before someone comes in here. Normally, I would call my friend Sophia Deveraux to come and make all these bodies disappear, but she's miles away in Ashland."

Gwen gave me a mysterious smile. "Don't worry, Gin. I have my own friends, and they are also very good at covering things up."

Chapter Ten

Gwen Frost

I tucked the Sword of Eris back into the crate with the other artifacts and replaced the lid. I also grabbed Minerva's Dagger, which had landed on the floor close to Brayden's body, and slid it back into my messenger bag, along with Vic.

Gin and I left the bodies in the baggage car, and she used some sort of Ice magic to lock the door behind us so no one could get inside. After that, we took turns ducking into a bathroom to clean ourselves up, then returned to our original seats. Everyone was still busy talking and taking photos of the scenery, and no one paid any more attention to us than they had during the rest of the ride.

Gin asked to see Minerva's Dagger, so I fished it out of my bag and passed it over. She twirled it back and forth in her fingers, getting a feel for the weapon.

"Sharp blade, nice balance, but all that bling is just asking for trouble," she said. "In Ashland, some folks would kill you for the jewels alone."

She shrugged and handed the dagger back to me. I slid the weapon into its box, which Brayden had left on the seat, then stuffed the whole thing back into my messenger bag.

"Well, I agree with the assassin," Vic piped up from his spot by the window. "I don't care what kind of power the dagger has. All those jewels make it look like a cheap trinket. Why, back in my day, you didn't need any fancy jewels on your hilt to prove that you were a *real* weapon . . ."

And he was off, talking about how a proper sword didn't need any frou-frou decorations.

Gin eyed him, then looked at me. "Does he always talk so much?" she whispered.

"Oh, yeah. You get used to it after a while."

"Vic should meet my foster brother. Finn also loves to hear the sound of his own voice." Gin laughed, and I joined in with her chuckles.

Vic eventually wound down, announced that he was taking a nap, and shut his eye. Soon soft snores were rumbling out of his mouth, although the continued *chug-chug-chug* of the train mostly drowned them out.

"So you're an Oracle," Gin said. "What does that mean? That you can see the future?"

I nodded. "Something like that, but every Oracle's power is a little different. Grandma Frost can see the future, and she works as a fortune-teller, like I told you before. My mom, Grace, could tell whether people were lying just by listening to their words. But I have psychometry magic, which means that I see . . . other things."

"Like what?"

I drew in a breath, then slowly let it out. "Whenever I touch something that someone has a strong, personal connection to, like a family ring or a favorite T-shirt or a beloved book, then I see all the memories that are attached to the object—good, bad, and . . . bloody."

Understanding filled Gin's eyes. "So when you picked up my knife, you saw all the people I'd killed with it over the years." A grimace twisted her face. "Sorry about that. All those battles were bad enough for me to endure. You shouldn't have had to witness them too, Gwen."

I hesitated, wondering if I should ask the question that had been on my mind ever since I had grabbed her knife, but since we were sharing secrets, I decided to see if she would reveal some more of hers.

"I saw several old battles, but mostly, I got drawn into a more recent memory. You were standing in front of this big, ruined mansion, and this guy was lying on the ground, half buried in the rubble in front of you." I drew in another breath and wet my lips. "Who—who was he?"

Gin's grimace deepened, and lines of pain bracketed her mouth. "My uncle. Mason Mitchell. Several months ago, I found out that he was the head of the Circle, a secret society that did a lot of bad things in Ashland. I also found out that he killed his twin brother, Tristan, my father, when I was a kid. He also ordered my mother's and my older sister's murders, and he was threatening me and my friends."

Those lines of pain smoothed out. Gin's face hardened, and her eyes glittered like bits of gray ice in her face. "So I killed him."

Her tone was cold, flat, and matter-of-fact, but her words didn't bother me. I'd felt her overwhelming relief when she'd killed Mason, and I knew that she'd taken him down to protect herself and her loved ones—the same way I had battled Loki, Agrona Quinn, Vivian Holler, and all the other Reapers who had tried to hurt me and my friends.

"I'm sorry," she said in a low voice. "Watching that must have been difficult for you."

I shrugged. "Yeah, seeing the battles and everything you went through was terrible, but those memories also helped me—*saved* me. I wouldn't have been able to beat Brayden and Minerva's Dagger without your assassin skill and prowess."

"So you're saying that I know more about fighting than some ancient wisdom and war goddess?" A wry smile curved her lips. "Well, that's certainly good for my ego."

Gin glanced over at Vic, who was still napping. "What will happen to Minerva's Dagger and the other artifacts?"

"Hopefully, my friends will be waiting at the Cypress Mountain station, and we'll take the artifacts to the academy. They'll be cleaned up, cataloged, and put in storage for a while, and then eventually some of them will be displayed in the Library of Antiquities."

"Your library sounds really cool."

A smile spread across my face. "It is. You should come see it sometime."

Gin grinned at me. "It's a deal—but only if you come to the Pork Pit, along with your friends. I especially want to meet Logan, the Spartan boyfriend."

A blush burned in my cheeks at her teasing, but I grinned back at her. "It's definitely a deal."

About thirty minutes later, the train finally slowed and pulled into the Cypress Mountain station. I grabbed Vic and my messenger bag, and Gin and I got off the train along with everyone else.

I scanned the wooden platform, but I didn't see my friends. I checked my phone, but no one had texted me, and I still had no idea what had happened during the rockslide or if Logan and the others were okay.

Gin laid a comforting hand on my shoulder. "Don't worry. If Logan is as good a fighter as you said, then I'm sure he's fine. Just like I'm sure my folks are fine. Let's go see if they're waiting inside the station."

I bit my lip, worry churning in my stomach, but I followed her inside. Even though Gin was acting perfectly normal and natural, she walked with a smooth, strong, confident stride, and people instinctively scrambled back to get out of her way. I felt like a guppy trailing along behind a shark.

We ended up standing in a corner, staring out over the sea of people moving through the main lobby. Most folks were heading outside, but a few were going against the flow and streaming inside to take the train back over to Pine Crest.

I stood on my tiptoes and scanned the crowd, but I still didn't see Logan, Daphne, or anyone else from Mythos Academy.

Gin must have sensed my worry, because she jerked her thumb toward the doors. "Let's check outside. They might be waiting in the parking lot."

By this point, my stomach had tied itself into tight knots, but I nodded and followed her, trying not to think about what it would mean if the others weren't outside.

We crossed the lobby, pushed through a set of double doors, and ended up at the edge of the paved lot that fronted the train station. I scanned the vehicles in front of me, but I didn't see any of the black SUVs that had been used to transport the artifacts.

My heart sank, and my stomach tied itself into a few more knots. Maybe my friends hadn't escaped the Reapers' trap. Maybe the rockslide had crushed their vehicles. Maybe they had all died while I'd been fighting Brayden on the train—

"Hey there, goddess girl," a familiar voice drawled behind me. "Did you miss me?"

I whirled around, and there he was—Logan freaking Quinn, with his black hair, pale skin, and ice-blue eyes. His face crinkled into a teasing smile, and he opened his arms.

I dropped my messenger bag, surged forward, and hugged him tight. "I was so worried about you," I whispered in his ear.

"I was worried about you too," Logan whispered back.

"But we both made it through another battle, and that's all that matters, right?"

"Right."

I drew back and pressed my lips to his. My psychometry kicked in, and I reveled in the feel of Logan's love for me, in the warm spark of emotion that burned so brightly and fiercely deep inside his heart. That spark perfectly matched the one burning in my own heart, and I knew those two flames would never be extinguished.

We broke apart, and Logan grinned at me, his hands still on my waist.

"Wow. If that's how you're going to kiss me every time you take a train ride and we have to fight a few Reapers, then we'll have to do this more often."

I rolled my eyes. "Uh-huh. Don't get too cocky, Spartan."

His eyes gleamed with mischief. "Only with you, goddess girl. Only with you."

Gin pointedly cleared her throat.

"Oh! Sorry. Let me introduce you two. Logan, this is Gin Blanco. Gin, this is Logan Quinn."

They shook hands, and Gin gave him an appraising look. "So this is the Spartan boyfriend."

A bit of shyness swept over me, but I threaded my fingers through Logan's. "Yeah."

She grinned. "I approve. Now let's see if we can find my people."

"Oh, I think they're over there." Logan paused. "Talking to Nickamedes."

Gin's eyes narrowed at his hesitation. I raised a questioning eyebrow, but Logan shook his head.

"Trust me. You need to see this for yourself," he replied.

Logan grabbed my messenger bag and slung the strap onto his shoulder. Vic was still napping inside, and the sword yawned, smacked his lips, and murmured something about killing Reapers before starting to snore again. Still holding Logan's hand, I moved forward, with Gin following along behind us.

Logan headed for the far end of the lot, where a couple of SUVs were parked together. A man with the same black hair, ice-blue eyes, and pale skin as Logan's was standing beside one of the vehicles. He was wearing a blue sweater vest over a matching shirt, along with black corduroy pants and wing tips.

A blond woman was standing in front of him, with her arms crossed over her chest. A gold detective's badge was clipped to her black leather belt. My heart squeezed a little. My mom, Grace, had been a detective too.

" . . . I assure you that we have the situation firmly under control." Nickamedes's voice drifted over to me.

The woman snorted in disbelief. "Well, it seems to me that this situation is completely *out* of control."

Gin looked at the woman with a combination of love and relief. I didn't need my psychometry magic to tell me that she had been as worried about her friends as I had been about mine.

"Your sister?" I asked.

"Yep, Detective Bria Coolidge, being a hard-boiled badass like usual," Gin replied, pride and affection filling her voice. "I'm guessing that's the fussy librarian you told me about earlier?"

I nodded. "Yep, that's Nickamedes, Logan's uncle."

"I don't care how smart you think you are or which elite boarding school you work for, Mr. Nickamedes," Bria snapped. "If I don't see my sister in another minute, two tops, then I'm taking over this whole operation. Is that clear?"

Nickamedes glared down his nose at her. "This operation is not *yours* to take over, Detective Coolidge."

Bria lifted her chin and glared right back at him. "Well, I would have to disagree, especially since my friends and I kept you and your convoy from getting killed by those people in the creepy black cloaks and rubber masks who wanted to skewer you all with their swords."

Nickamedes bristled. "As I have said *numerous* times now, we had the situation completely under control." He paused and cleared his throat, as if what he was about to say next left a sour taste in his mouth. "Although we are grateful for the assistance of you and your friends."

Bria rolled her eyes. She opened her mouth and stabbed her finger at Nickamedes, as though she was going to lay into him some more, but then she caught sight of Gin, and she immediately hurried in our direction.

"I'm so glad you're okay!" Bria said, hugging Gin tight.

"I'm always okay," Gin replied, hugging her sister back. "Although the train ride turned out to be a lot more exciting than I expected."

Bria drew back and gave her a knowing look. "Aren't things always more exciting whenever you're around?"

Gin laughed and slung her arm around her sister's shoulders. "You can say that. Where are Finn and Owen?"

Bria waved her hand. "Finn is still down the mountain, along with some of Nickamedes's friends. Some guy named Ajax and a woman named Metis. As for Owen—"

"I'm right here," someone said.

A tall, muscled man with black hair stepped around the side of the SUV and came over to us. He curled his arm around Gin's waist and drew her close, and their love for each other shone on their faces for everyone to see.

Gin pressed a quick kiss to Owen's lips and drew back. "Hey, you."

He grinned back at her. "Hey, you too. Sorry it took us so long to get here."

"Better late than never," Gin teased.

Owen's grin widened. "I have something for you." He lifted

his arm, showing off the white paper bag in his hand. "Your blueberry muffins, as promised."

Gin clutched a hand to her heart and let out a dramatic sigh. "My hero."

She opened the paper bag, grabbed a muffin, and sank her teeth into the sweet treat. Gin and Owen started talking, while Bria and Nickamedes kept arguing over who had jurisdiction to deal with the Reapers, both the dead ones on the train and at the historic depot and the others who had been captured or killed during the rockslide ambush.

Logan leaned down. "What happened on the train, Gwen? Who is that woman, really?"

"She's the woman who saved my life. And I think Vic and I saved hers too. So I guess you could say we all saved each other."

Logan frowned, not understanding my cryptic words, so I hooked my arm through his.

"Come inside the station and buy me a hot chocolate, and I'll tell you all about it."

An hour later, we were all still at the Cypress Mountain station. Professor Metis and Coach Ajax had finally arrived, along with Daphne, Carson, Oliver, and Alexei. So had Finnegan Lane, Gin's foster brother.

The introductions had been made all around, and once everyone realized we were all more or less on the same side, the hostility and distrust had gone way, way down. Bria, Owen, and Finn had all looked a little confused when Professor Metis had drawn them aside and explained the mythological world, but Gin had just nodded, as if it all made perfect sense to her.

For their part, Gin and her friends had tried to explain Ashland to us, with all its elementals, vampires, giants, and dwarves, and then it was our turn to be confused. Funny how our two cities could be so close to each other and yet still be in completely separate worlds. But I decided to treat the whole thing like it was a time-travel plot in one of the comic books I loved to read. In other words, I decided not to think too long and hard about it, lest I get caught up wondering what cosmic vortex or flap of a butterfly's wings or fantasy author's whim had caused all of this to happen.

"Are you sure we aren't entitled to a finders' fee?" Finn asked, eyeing the crate of artifacts Coach Ajax was loading into an SUV to take back to the academy. "After all, Bria, Owen, and I helped you all take out those Reapers on the road. And Gin totally kicked some Reaper ass on the train."

Coach Ajax finished loading the crate, then drew himself up to his full height and crossed his arms over his chest. The afternoon sun glinted off his black hair and made his dark eyes and onyx skin gleam. "You need a finder's fee for doing the right thing?"

Finn eyed Ajax's impressive biceps and sidled back a step. "Well, when you put it like that, I suppose not." He sighed, as though the weight of the world was yoked on his shoulders. But just as quickly, his face brightened again. "But let me look at all those jewels on Minerva's Dagger again. Just one more time. Pretty please?"

Daphne Cruz stepped up beside me. The Valkyrie was wearing a pink leather jacket over a matching shirt and black jeans, and neon-pink sneakers adorned her feet. Her blond hair was sleeked back into a high ponytail, and pink eyeshadow and gloss brought out her black eyes and amber skin.

Daphne waved her hand, and a few pink sparks of magic shot off her fingertips and flickered in the air like fireflies. "That Finn guy does not give up easily."

"No kidding," Vic piped up from his spot in the SUV's back-seat. "I'm just glad he didn't try to take *me* home with him."

I actually thought Vic and Finn would be perfect for each other, especially since Finn seemed to love to talk as much as the sword did, just like Gin had said, but I kept quiet.

"I'm just glad we're all okay," Daphne replied, more sparks flickering in the air around her.

Gin, Bria, Finn, and Owen had been discreetly eyeing the pink sparks of magic streaming out of the Valkyrie's fingertips, although they hadn't come right out and said anything about them. Bria, in particular, kept opening and closing her mouth, obviously dying to ask questions, but she restrained herself.

Professor Aurora Metis walked over to me. Her black hair was sleeked back into a high, tight bun, and silver glasses covered her green eyes. The lenses also reflected a bit of sunlight down onto her bronze skin. "We've got everything loaded up. We should get the artifacts back to the academy where they'll be safe."

I nodded. "Give me a minute, please."

Metis moved off to talk to Ajax. My friends started climbing into various vehicles, while Bria, Finn, and Owen got into their own SUV.

That left me and Gin standing alone in the parking lot. I hesitated, wondering what to say. In some ways, today had gone exactly as I'd expected, with Reapers, double crosses, artifacts, blood, and death. But in other ways, so many things had happened that I *hadn't* expected, including meeting Gin, although I was so very, very glad our paths had crossed.

Gin smiled at me, as if she knew exactly what I was thinking. "It's harder to say good-bye than I thought it would be."

I nodded. "For me too."

She held out her arms, and I stepped forward and hugged her. Gin hugged me back, then we broke apart.

"Take care, Gwen," she said. "And if you ever need anything, anything at all, I'm just a phone call and a train ride away."

I laughed at her black humor. "I'll try to stick to the phone call. I haven't had the best luck with trains."

She joined in my laughter, but then her face turned serious. "I'm so glad I got to meet you and be a part of your world, even if it was only for a day."

"Me too. And I'm going to take you up on that offer of a free meal at the Pork Pit. I want to come see what Ashland is like."

Gin tilted her head toward the open SUV door. "Just be sure to bring your talking sword. He'll probably come in handy again."

"According to Vic, he *always* comes in handy, remember?"

We both laughed, then stared at each other again.

"Good-bye, Gwen."

"Bye, Gin."

The assassin nodded at me, then stuck her hands into her jeans pockets and ambled away with that smooth shark-like stride, heading over to the SUV where her friends were waiting.

Logan stepped up beside me. "You ready to go?"

I watched Gin slide into her vehicle and shut the door behind her. The soft *thump* echoed through the parking lot, but it didn't sound like a good-bye to me. No, it was more like a promise of further adventures to come—for both of us.

I turned to Logan and smiled. "Yeah. Let's go home."

Logan held out his hand, and I threaded my fingers through his again. Together, we headed toward the Mythos convoy. I stopped at the open SUV door and glanced back over my shoulder.

Gin was sitting in her vehicle with the window rolled down. The assassin winked at me, then the engine rumbled, and the SUV cruised away.

I waved at her until the vehicle was out of sight, then slid into my own seat, with Vic on one side of me and Logan on the other.

"Well, I, for one, am looking forward to getting back to the academy and taking my afternoon nap," Vic said. "You wouldn't *believe* how that Spider assassin lady manhandled me today. I know she's a really good warrior, but she didn't even bother to oil me or shine my blade after she got through with me . . ."

I let the sword's words wash over me. In the front, Carson was driving, while Daphne was fiddling with the radio, trying to find a song she wanted to listen to. Behind me, Oliver and Alexei were talking in low voices.

The Reapers had been defeated, the artifacts were safe, and I was surrounded by my friends. So I leaned my head back against the seat and soaked up everything that was happening around me, especially the warmth and strength of Logan's fingers intertwined with my own.

It was good to know that some things would never change, whether I was in Mythos Academy, Ashland, or somewhere else.

About the Author

Jennifer Estep is a *New York Times*, *USA Today*, and internationally bestselling author who prowls the streets of her imagination in search of her next fantasy idea.

Jennifer is the author of the **Elemental Assassin**, **Mythos Academy**, **Galactic Bonds**, **Section 47**, **Crown of Shards**, **Gargoyle Queen**, and other fantasy series. She has written more than forty-five books, along with numerous novellas and stories.

In her spare time, Jennifer enjoys hanging out with friends and family, doing yoga, and reading fantasy and romance books. She also watches way too much TV and loves all things related to superheroes.

For more information on Jennifer and her books, visit her website at www.jenniferestep.com or follow her on Facebook, Instagram, Twitter, Amazon, BookBub, and Goodreads. You can also sign up for her newsletter:

Happy reading, everyone!

Other Books by Jennifer Estep

THE ELEMENTAL ASSASSIN SERIES
FEATURING GIN BLANCO

BOOKS
Spider's Bite
Web of Lies
Venom
Tangled Threads
Spider's Revenge
By a Thread
Widow's Web
Deadly Sting
Heart of Venom
The Spider
Poison Promise
Black Widow
Spider's Trap
Bitter Bite
Unraveled
Snared
Venom in the Veins
Sharpest Sting
Last Strand
Stings and Stones (short story collection)

E-NOVELLAS
Haints and Hobwebs
Thread of Death

Parlor Tricks
Kiss of Venom
Unwanted
Nice Guys Bite
Winter's Web
Heart Stings
Spider and Frost (crossover novella)

THE GALACTIC BONDS SERIES
Only Bad Options
Only Good Enemies
Only Hard Problems (Zane Zimmer novella)

THE SECTION 47 SERIES
A Sense of Danger
Sugar Plum Spies (holiday book)

THE CROWN OF SHARDS SERIES
Kill the Queen
Protect the Prince
Crush the King

THE GARGOYLE QUEEN SERIES
Capture the Crown
Tear Down the Throne
Conquer the Kingdom

THE BLACK BLADE SERIES
Cold Burn of Magic
Dark Heart of Magic
Bright Blaze of Magic

THE BIGTIME SERIES
Karma Girl
Hot Mama

Jinx
A Karma Girl Christmas (holiday story)
Nightingale
Fandemic

THE MYTHOS ACADEMY SPINOFF SERIES
FEATURING RORY FORSETI

Spartan Heart
Spartan Promise
Spartan Destiny

THE MYTHOS ACADEMY SERIES
FEATURING GWEN FROST

BOOKS
Touch of Frost
Kiss of Frost
Dark Frost
Crimson Frost
Midnight Frost
Killer Frost

E-NOVELLAS AND SHORT STORIES
First Frost
Halloween Frost
Spartan Frost
Spider and Frost (crossover novella)

OTHER WORKS
The Beauty of Being a Beast (fairy tale)
Write Your Own Cake (worldbuilding essay)

9 781950 076215